Acclaim for

The Stories of Mary Gordon

"Carefully drawn and gracefully written, [Gordon's] stories combine the intimacy of memoir with the shape and narrative energy of fiction. . . . Vivid and richly imagined." —*Chicago Sun-Times*

"Imagine fiction as a place—a small, close wooden room with a kneeler and a screen. Imagine the writer entering that room and telling her stories to a man behind the screen. . . . *The Stories of Mary Gordon* exists somewhere in this middle territory between truth and invention, fiction and sin." —*The Miami Herald*

"Incisive, intelligent. . . . Unerring wonders of sensibility and atmosphere." —*Elle*

"This one's a keeper." —*Santa Cruz Sentinel*

"It is the strength and dynamism of [Gordon's] characters that imbue each story with a distinctive radiance." —*The Free-Lance Star* (Fredericksburg, VA)

"Remarkable. . . . Gordon is a writer of profound imagination and empathy." —*The Boston Globe*

"*The Stories of Mary Gordon* is the finely tuned work of a craftswoman who molds her subjects with unblinking empathy, and sets their lives into motion with the utmost care." —*San Antonio Express-News*

"These forty-one pieces . . . masterfully capture the nuances of modern life." —*Ploughshares*

"[Gordon] is capable of rendering one story in dense, informative, workmanlike prose, and the next in airy, fragmentary, impressionistic lines." —*The Threepenny Review*

"These people are real and many of these people, Gordon forces us to see, ARE us." —*The Buffalo News*

"Gordon's work is marked by an old-fashioned interest in emotional narrative and a steady disregard for literary trends." —*Time Out New York*

"These stories . . . highlight a talented writer's ability to pick apart the emotional fragility of her characters." —*USA Today*

Mary Gordon

THE STORIES OF
MARY GORDON

Mary Gordon is the author of six novels, including *Final Payments* and *Pearl*; two memoirs, *The Shadow Man* and *Circling My Mother*; and an earlier collection of stories, *Temporary Shelter*. She has received a Lila Wallace-Reader's Digest Writer's Award, a Guggenheim Fellowship, the 1997 O. Henry Award for Best Story, and an Academy Award for Literature from the American Academy of Arts and Letters, of which she is a member. She teaches at Barnard College and lives in New York City.

ALSO BY MARY GORDON

FICTION

Pearl

Final Payments

The Company of Women

Men and Angels

Temporary Shelter

The Other Side

The Rest of Life

Spending

NONFICTION

Circling My Mother

Good Boys and Dead Girls

The Shadow Man

Seeing Through Places

Joan of Arc

The Stories of Mary Gordon

The Stories of

MARY GORDON

Anchor Books
A Division of Random House, Inc.
New York

FIRST ANCHOR BOOKS EDITION, NOVEMBER 2007

Copyright © 2006 by Mary Gordon

All rights reserved. Published in the United States by Anchor Books,
a division of Random House, Inc., New York, and in Canada by Random House of
Canada Limited, Toronto. Originally published in hardcover in the United States
by Pantheon Books, a division of Random House, Inc., New York, in 2006.

Anchor Books and colophon are registered trademarks of Random House, Inc.

Previous publication information for the stories that appear in this work
appears at the back of the book.

The Library of Congress has cataloged the Pantheon edition as follows:
Gordon, Mary, [date]
[Short stories. Selections]
The stories of Mary Gordon / Mary Gordon.
p. cm.
1. Irish Americans—Fiction. I. Title.
PS3557.O669S47 2006
813'.54—dc22
2006044275

Anchor ISBN: 978-1-4000-7808-0

Book design by Soonyoung Kwon

www.anchorbooks.com

Printed in the United States of America
10 9 8 7 6 5 4 3 2 1

For Peter Matson,

protector and companion on the journey

Contents

Contents

from TEMPORARY SHELTER

NEW AND UNCOLLECTED

City Life

Peter had always been more than thoughtful in not pressing her about her past, and Beatrice was sure it was a reason for her choice of him. Most men, coming of age in a time that extolled openness and disclosure, would have thought themselves remiss in questioning her so little. Perhaps because he was a New Englander—one of four sons in a family that had been stable for generations—perhaps because he was a mathematician, perhaps because both the sight of her and her way of living had pleased him from the first and continued to please him, he had been satisfied with what she was willing to tell. "My parents are dead. We lived in western New York State, near Rochester. I am an only child. I have no family left."

She preferred saying "I have no family left"—creating with her words an absence, a darkness, rather than to say what had been there, what she had ruthlessly left, with a ruthlessness that would have shocked anyone who knew her later. She had left them so thoroughly that she really didn't know if they were still living. When she tried to locate them, with her marriage and her children and the warm weight of her domestic safety at her back, there was no trace of them. It had shocked and frightened her how completely they had failed to leave a trace. This was the sort of thing most people didn't think of: how possible it was for people like her parents to impress themselves so little on the surface, the many surfaces of the world, that they would leave it or inhabit it with the same lack of a mark.

They were horrors, her parents, the sort people wanted to avert their eyes from, that people felt it was healthful to avert their eyes from. They had let their lives slip very far, further than anyone Beatrice now knew could even begin to imagine. But it had always been like that: a slippage so continuous that there was simultaneously a sense of slippage and of already having slipped.

It was terribly clear to her. She was brought up in filth. Most people, Beatrice knew, believed that filth was temporary, one of those things, unlike disease or insanity or social hatred—that didn't root itself in but was an affair of surfaces, therefore dislodgeable by effort, will, and the meagerest brand of intelligence. That was, Beatrice knew, because people didn't understand filth. They mistook its historical ordinariness for simplicity. They didn't understand the way it could invade and settle, take over, dominate, and for good, until it became, inevitably, the only true thing about a place and the only lives that could be lived there. Dust, grime, the grease of foods, the residues of bodies, the smells that lived in the air, palpable, malign, unidentifiable, impossible to differentiate: an ugly population of refugees from an unknowable location, permanent, stubborn, knife-faced settlers who had right of occupancy—the place was theirs now—and would never leave.

Beatrice's parents had money for food, and the rent must have been paid to someone. They had always lived in the one house: her mother, her father, and herself. Who could have owned it? Who would have put money down for such a place? One-story, nearly windowless, the outside walls made of soft shingle in the semblance of pinkish gray brick. It must have been built from the first entirely without love, with the most cynical understanding, Beatrice had always thought, of the human need for shelter and the dollar value that it could bring. Everything was cheap and thin, done with the minimum of expense and of attention. No thought was given to ornament or amplitude, or even to the long, practical run: what wouldn't age horribly or crumble, splinter, quickly fade.

As she grew older, she believed the house had been built to hide some sort of criminality. It was in the middle of the woods, down a dirt road half a mile down Highway 117, which led nowhere she knew, or maybe south, she somehow thought, to Pennsylvania. Her parents said it had once been a hunting lodge, but she didn't believe it. When she was old enough to have learned about bootlegging, and knew that whiskey had been smuggled in from Canada, she was convinced that the house had had something to do with that. She could always imagine petty gangsters, local thugs in mean felt hats and thin-soled shoes trading liquor for money, throwing their cigarette butts down on the hard, infertile ground, then driving away from the house, not giving it a thought until it was time for their next deal.

Sometimes she thought it was the long periods of uninhabitedness that gave the house its closed, and vengeful, character. But when she began to think like that, it wasn't long before she understood that kind of thought to be fantastical. It wasn't the house, houses had no will or nature. Her parents had natures, and it was their lives and the way they lived that made their dwelling a monstrosity.

She had awakened each day in dread, afraid to open her eyes, knowing the first thing they fell on would be ugly. She didn't even know where she could get something for herself that might be beautiful. The word couldn't have formed itself in her mind in any way that could attach to an object that was familiar to her, or that she could even imagine having access to. She heard, as if from a great distance, people using the word "beautiful" in relation to things like trees or sunsets, but her faculty for understanding things like this had been so crippled that the attempt to comprehend what people were saying when they spoke like this filled her with a kind of panic. She couldn't call up even the first step that would allow her, even in the far future, to come close to what they meant. They were talking about things out of doors when they talked about trees and sunsets. And what was the good of that? You could go out of doors. The blueness of the sky, the brightness of the sun, the freshness of a tree would greet you, but in the end you would only have to go back somewhere to sleep. And that would not be beautiful; it would be where you lived. So beauty seemed a dangerous, foreign, and irrelevant idea. She turned for solace, not to it, but to the nature of enclosure. Everything in her life strained toward the ideal of separations: how to keep the horror of her parents' life from everything that could be called her life.

She learned what it was she wanted from watching her grade school teachers cutting simple shapes—squares, triangles—and writing numbers in straight columns on the blackboard or on paper with crisp, straight blue lines. The whiteness of pages, the unmuddled black of print, struck her as desirable; the dry rasping of the scissors, the click of a stapler, the riffling of a rubber band around a set of children's tests. She understood all these things as prosperity, and knew that her family was not prosperous; they were poor. But she knew as well that their real affliction wasn't poverty but something different—you might, perhaps, say worse—but not connected to money. If she could have pointed to that—a simple lack of money—it would have been more hopeful for her. But she knew it wasn't poverty that was the problem. It was the way her parents were. It was what they did.

They drank. That was what they did. It was, properly speaking, the only thing they did. But no, she always told herself when she began to think that way, it wasn't the only thing. Her father, after all, had gone out to work. He was a gravedigger in a Catholic cemetery. Each morning he woke in the dark house. Massive, nearly toothless, and still in his underwear, he drank black coffee with a shot in it for breakfast, and then put on his dark olive work pants and shirts, his heavy boots—in winter a fleece-lined coat and cap—and started the reluctant car driving down the dirt road. He came home at night, with a clutch of bottles in a paper bag, to begin drinking. He wasn't violent or abusive; he was interested only in the stupor he could enter and inhabit. This, Beatrice knew early on, was his true home.

Her mother woke late, her hair in pin curls wrapped in a kerchief, which she rarely bothered to undo. She was skeletally thin; her skin was always in a state of dull eruptions; red spidery veins on her legs always seemed to Beatrice to be the tracks of a slow disease. Just out of bed, she poured herself a drink, not bothering to hide it in coffee, and drank it from a glass that had held cheese spread mixed with pimentos, which her parents ate on crackers when they drank, and which was often Beatrice's supper. Beatrice's mother would sit for a while on the plaid couch, watch television, then go back to bed. The house was nearly always silent; there were as few words in the house as there were ornaments. It was another reason Peter liked her. She had a gift, he said, for silence, a gift he respected, that he said too few people had. She wondered if he would have prized this treasure if he'd known its provenance.

Beatrice saw everything her parents did because she slept in the large room. When she was born, her parents had put a crib for her in the corner of the room nearest their bedroom, opposite the wall where the sink, the stove, and the refrigerator were. It didn't occur to them that she might want privacy; when she grew taller, they replaced her crib with a bed, but they never imagined she had any more rights or desires than an infant. The torpor, the disorder of their lives, spread into her quarters. For years, it anguished her to see their slippers, their half-read newspapers, broken bobby pins, half-empty glasses, butt-filled ashtrays traveling like bacilli into the area she thought of as hers. When she was ten, she bought some clothesline and some tacks. She bought an Indian bedspread from a hippie store in town; rose-colored, with a print of tigers; the only vivid thing in the place. She made a barrier between herself and them. Her father said something unkind about it, but she took no notice.

For the six years after that, she came home as little as she could, staying in the school library until it closed, walking home miles in the darkness. She sat on her bed, did what was left of her homework, and, as early as possible, lay down to sleep. At sunrise, she would leave the house, walking the roads till something opened in the town—the library, the five-and-ten, the luncheonette—then walking for more hours till sunset. She didn't love the woods; she didn't think of them as nature, with all the implications she had read about. But they were someplace she could be until she had no choice but to be *there* again, but not quite *there,* not in the place that was *theirs,* but her place, behind her curtain, where she needn't see the way they lived.

She moved out of her parents' house two days after she graduated from high school. She packed her few things and moved to Buffalo, where she got a job in a tool and die factory, took night courses at the community college. She did this for five years, then took all her savings and enrolled in the elementary education program at the University of Buffalo full-time. She'd planned it all out carefully, in her tiny room, living on yogurt she made from powdered milk, allowing it to ferment in a series of thermoses she'd bought at garage sales, eating the good parts of half-rotten fruit and vegetables she'd bought for pennies, the fresh middle parts of loaves of day-old bread. Never, in those years, did she buy a new blouse or skirt or pair of jeans. She got her clothes from the Salvation Army; it was only later, after she married, that she learned to sew.

In her second semester, she met Peter in a very large class: European History 1789–1945. He said he'd fallen in love with several things about her almost at once: the look of her notebooks, the brilliant white of the collar of her shirt as it peeked over the top of her pastel blue Shetland sweater, the sheer pink curves of her fingernails. He said he'd been particularly taken by her thumb. Most women's thumbs were ugly and betrayed the incompleteness of their femininity, the essential coarseness of it. The fineness of her thumb, the way the nail curved and was placed within the flesh, showed there wasn't a trace of coarseness in her: everything connected with her was, and would always be, fine. He didn't find out until they'd dated a few times that she was older, more than three years older than he was. He accepted that she'd had to work those years because her parents had—tragically—died.

Beatrice knew what Peter saw when he looked at her: clarity and simplicity and thrift, an almost holy sign of order, a plain creature without hidden parts or edges, who would sail through life before him making a path through murky seas, leaving to him plain sailing: nothing in the world to obstruct him or the free play of his mind. She knew that he didn't realize that he had picked her in part for the emptiness of her past, imagining a beautiful blankness, blameless, unpopulated, clear. His pity for her increased her value for him: she was an exile in the ordinary world he was born into, lacking the encumbrances that could make for problems in his life. He believed that life could be simple, that he would leave from a cloudless day and drop into the teeming fog of mathematics, which for him was peopled, creatured, a tumultuous society he had to colonize and civilize and rule.

She knew he felt he could leave all the rest to her, turning to her at night with the anomaly of his ardor, another equation she could elegantly solve. His curiosity about the shape of her desire was as tenderly blunted as his curiosity about her past, and she was as glad of the one as of the other. Making love to him, an occurrence she found surprisingly frequent, she could pretend she was sitting through a violent and fascinating storm that certainly would pass. Having got through it, she could be covered over in grateful tenderness for the life that he made possible: a life of clean linen and bright rooms, of matched dishes and a variety of special-ized kitchen items: each unique, for one use only, and not, as everything in her mother's house was, interchangeable.

So the children came, three boys, and then the farmhouse, bought as a wreck, transformed by Beatrice Talbot into a treasure, something acquaintances came to see as much (more, she thought, if they were hon-est) as they did the family itself. Then Peter's tenure, and additions on the house: a sewing room, a greenhouse, then uncovering the old wood-work, searching out antique stores, auctions, flea markets for the right furniture—all this researched in the university library and in the local library—and the children growing and needing care so that by the time Peter came home with the news that was the first breakup of the smooth plane that had been their life together, the children had become, some-how, twelve, ten, and eight.

He had won a really spectacular fellowship at Columbia, three years being paid twice what he made at Cornell and no teaching, and a chance to work beside the man who was tops in his field. Peter asked Beatrice what she thought, but only formally. They both knew. They would be going to New York.

Nights in the house ten miles above Ithaca—it was summer and in her panic she could hear the crickets and, toward dawn, smell the fresh-ness of the wet grass—she lay awake in terror of the packing job ahead of her. Everything, each thing she owned, would have to be wrapped and collected. She lived in dread of losing something, breaking something, for each carefully selected, carefully tended object that she owned was a proof of faith against the dark clutching power of the past. She typed on an index card a brief but wholly accurate description of the house, and the housing office presented her with a couple from Berlin—particle physi-cists, the both of them, and without children, she was grateful to hear. They seemed clean and thorough; they wanted to live in the country, they were the type who would know enough to act in time if a problem was occurring, who wouldn't let things get too far.

Peter and Beatrice were assured by everyone they talked to in New York that their apartment was a jewel. Sally Rodier, the wife of Peter's col-laborator, who also helped Beatrice place the children in private schools, kept telling her how incredibly lucky they were, to have been given an apartment in one of the buildings on Riverside Drive. The view could be better, but they had a glimpse of the river. Really, they were almost disgustingly lucky, she said, laughing. Did they know what people would do to get what they had?

But Beatrice's heart sank at the grayness of the grout between the small octagonal bathroom floor tiles, the uneven job of polyurethaning on the living room floor, the small hole in the floor by the radiator base, the stiff door on one of the kitchen cabinets, the frosted glass on the window near the shower that she couldn't, whatever she did, make look clean.

For nearly a month she worked, making the small repairs herself, unheard-of behavior, Sally Rodier said, in a Columbia tenant. She poured a lake of bleach on the bathroom floor, left it for six hours, then, sopping it up, found she had created a field of dazzling whiteness. She made curtains; she scraped the edges of the window frames. Then she began to venture out. She had been so few places, had done so little, that the city streets, although they frightened her, began to seem a place of quite exciting possibilities. Because she did her errands, for the first time in her life, on foot, she could have human contact with no fear of revelation. She could be among her kind without fear every second that they would find out about her: where and what she'd come from, who she really was. Each day the super left mail on her threshold; they would exchange a pleasant word or two. He was a compact and competent man who had left his family in Peru. She could imagine that he and the Bangladeshi doormen, and the people on the streets, all possessed a dark and complicated past, things they'd prefer to have hidden as she did. In Buffalo, in Ithaca, people had seemed to be expressing everything they were. Even their reserve seemed legible and therefore relatively simple. But, riding on the bus and walking out on Broadway, she felt for the first time part of the web of concealment, of lives constructed like a house with rooms that gave access only to each other, rooms far from the initial entrance, with no source of natural light.

By Thanksgiving, she was able to tell Peter, who feared that she would suffer separation from her beloved house, that she was enjoying herself very much. The boys, whose lives, apart from their aspects of animal survival, never seemed to have much to do with her, were absorbed in the thick worlds of their schools—activities till five or six most nights, homework, and supper and more homework. Weekends, she could leave them to Peter, who was happy to take them to the park for football, or to the university pool, or the indoor track. She would often go to the Metropolitan Museum, to look at the collection of American furniture or, accompanied by a guidebook, on an architectural tour.

One Thursday night, Peter was working in the library and the boys were playing basketball in the room the two younger ones shared, throwing a ball made of foam through the hoop Peter had nailed against the door. Beatrice was surprised to hear the bell ring; people rarely came without telephoning first. She opened the door to a stranger, but catching a glimpse of her neighbor across the hall, a history professor, opening her door, she didn't feel afraid.

The man at the doorway was unlike anyone she had spoken to in New York, anyone she'd spoken to since she'd left home. But in an instant she recognized him. She thought he was there to tell her the story of her life, and to tell Peter and everyone she knew. She'd never met him, as himself, before. But he could have lived in the house she'd been born in. He had an unrushed look, as if he had all the time in the world. He took a moment to meet her eyes, but when he did, finally, she understood the scope of everything he knew.

She kept the door mostly closed, leaving only enough space for her body. She would allow him to hurt her, if that was what he came for, but she wouldn't let him in the house.

"I'm your downstairs neighbor," he said.

She opened the door wider. He was wearing a greasy-looking ski jacket which had once been royal blue; a shiny layer of black grime covered the surface like soot on old snow. The laces on his black sneakers had no tips. His pants were olive green; his hands were in his pockets. It was impossible to guess how old he was. He was missing several top teeth, which made him look not young, but his hair fell over his eyes in a way that bestowed youth. She stepped back a pace further into the hall.

"What can I do for you?"

"You've got kids?"

For a moment, she thought he meant to take the children. She could hear them in the back of the apartment, running, laughing, innocent of what she was sure would befall them. A sense of heavy torpor took her up. She felt that whatever this man wanted, she would have to let him take. A half-enjoyable lassitude came over her. She knew she couldn't move.

He was waiting for her answer. "I have three boys," she said.

"Well, what you can do for me is to tell them to stop their racket. All day, all night, night and day, bouncing the ball. The plaster is coming down off the ceiling. It's hitting me in my bed. That's not too much to ask, is it? You can see that's not too much to ask."

"No, of course not. No," she said. "I'll see to it right away."

She closed the door very quickly. Walking to the back part of the apartment, she had to dig her nails into the palms of her hands so that she wouldn't scream the words to her children. "They didn't know, they didn't know," she kept saying to herself. It wasn't their fault. They weren't used to living in an apartment. It wasn't anybody's fault. But she was longing to scream at them, for having made this happen. For doing something so she would have to see that man, would have to think about him. An immense distaste for her children came over her. They seemed loud and gross and spoiled and careless. They knew nothing of the world. They were passing the ball back and forth to one another, their blond hair gleaming in the light that shone down from the fixture overhead.

She forced herself to speak calmly. "I'm afraid you can't play basketball here," she said. "The man downstairs complained."

"What'd you say to him?" asked Jeff, the oldest.

"I said I'd make you stop."

"What'd you say that for? We have just as much right as he does."

She looked at her son coldly. "I'm afraid you don't."

The three of them looked back at her, as if they'd never seen her.

"I'll make supper now," she said. "But I have a terrible headache. After I put dinner on the table, I'm going to lie down."

While she was cooking, the phone rang. It was her neighbor across the hall. "Terribly sorry to intrude," she said. "I hope I'm not being a busybody, but I couldn't help overhear the rather unpleasant exchange you had with our neighbor. I just thought you should understand a few things."

I understand everything, Beatrice wanted to say. There's nothing I don't understand.

"He's a pathetic case. Used to be a big shot in the chemistry department. Boy genius. Then he blew it. Just stopped going to classes, stopped showing up in the department. But some bigwigs in the administration were on his side, and he's been on disability and allowed to keep the apartment. We're all stuck with him. If he ever opens the door and you're near, you get a whiff of the place. Unbelievable. It's unbelievable how people live. What I'm trying to tell you is, don't let him get you bent out of shape. Occasionally he crawls out of his cave and growls something, but he's quite harmless."

"Thank you," said Beatrice. "Thank you for calling. Thank you very much."

She put down the phone, walked into her bedroom, turned out all the lights, and lay down on her bed.

Lying in the dark, she knew it was impossible that he was underneath her. If his room was below the children's, it was near the other side of the apartment, far from where she was.

But she imagined she could hear his breathing. It matched her own: in-out-in-out. Just like hers.

She breathed with him. In and out, and in and out. Frightened, afraid to leave the bed, she lay under a quilt she'd made herself. She forced herself to think of the silver scissors, her gold thimble, the spools and spools of pale thread. Tried and tried to call them back, a pastel shimmering cloud, a thickness glowing softly in this darkness. It would come, then fade, swallowed up in darkness. Soon the darkness was all there was. It was everything. It was everything she wanted and her only terror was that she would have to leave it and go back. Outside the closed door, she could hear the voices of her husband and her sons. She put her fingers in her ears so she couldn't hear them. She prayed, she didn't know to whom, to someone who inhabited the same darkness. This was the only thing about the one she prayed to that she knew. She prayed that her family would forget about her, leave her. She dreaded the door's cracking, the intrusion of the light. If she could just be here, in darkness, breathing in and out, with him as he breathed in and out. Then she didn't know. But it would be something that she feared.

"How about you tone it down and let your mother sleep?"

She closed her eyes as tightly as a child in nightmare. Then she knew that she had been, in fact, asleep because when Peter came in, sank his weight onto the bed, she understood she had to start pretending to be sleeping.

After that night, she began staying in bed all day long. She had so rarely been sick, had met the occasional cold or bout of flu with so much stoicism that Peter couldn't help but believe her when she complained of a debilitating headache. And it would have been impossible for him to connect her behavior with the man downstairs. He hadn't even seen him. No one had seen him except her and the woman across the hall who told her what she didn't need to know, what she already knew, what she couldn't help knowing.

She wondered how long it would be before Peter suggested calling a doctor. That was what worried her as she lay in the darkness: what would happen, what would be the thing she wouldn't be able to resist, the thing that would force her to get up.

She cut herself off fully from the life of the family. She had no idea what kind of life was going on outside her door. Peter was coping very well, without a question or murmur of complaint. Cynically, she thought it was easier for him not to question: he might learn something he didn't want to know. He had joined up with her so they could create a world free from disturbance, from disturbances. Now the disturbance rumbled beneath them, and it only stood to reason that he wouldn't know of it and wouldn't want to know.

Each morning, she heard the door close as Peter left with the children for school. Then she got up, bathed, fixed herself a breakfast, and, exhausted, fell back into a heavy sleep. She would sleep through the afternoon. In the evening, Peter brought her supper on a tray. The weak light from the lamp on the bed table hurt her eyes; the taste and textures of the food hurt her palate, grown fragile from so much silence, so much sleep.

She didn't ask what the children were doing and they didn't come in to see her. Peter assumed she was in excruciating pain. She said nothing to give him that idea, and nothing to relieve him of it.

After her fourth day in the dark, she heard the doorbell ring. It was early evening, the beginning of December. Night had completely fallen and the radiators hissed and cooed. She tried not to hear what was going on outside, so at first she heard only isolated words that Peter was shouting. "Children." "Natural." "Ordinary." "Play." "Rights." "No right."

Alarm, a spot of electric blue spreading beneath one of her ribs, made her understand that Peter was shouting at the man downstairs. She jumped out of bed and stood at the door of the bedroom. She could see Peter's back, tensed as she had, in fourteen years of marriage, never seen it. His fists were clenched at his sides.

"You come here, bothering my wife, disturbing my family. I don't know where the hell . . . what makes you think . . . but you've got the wrong number, mister. My sons are going to play ball occasionally at a reasonable hour. It's five-ten in the afternoon. Don't tell me you're trying to sleep."

"All right, buddy. All right. We'll just see about sleeping. Some night come midnight when everyone in your house is fast asleep, you want to hear about disturbing. Believe me, buddy, I know how to make a disturbance."

Peter shut the door in the man's face. He turned around, pale, his fists not yet unclenched.

"Why didn't you tell me about that guy?" he said, standing so close to her that his voice hurt her ears, which had heard very little in the last four days.

"I wasn't feeling well," she said.

He nodded. She knew he hadn't heard her.

"Better get back into bed."

The doorbell rang again. Peter ran to it, his fists clenched once again. But it wasn't the man downstairs, it was the woman across the hall. Beatrice could hear her telling Peter the same story she'd told her, but with more details. "The apartment is full of broken machines, he takes them apart for some experiment he says he's doing. He says he's going to be able to create enough energy to power the whole world. He brags that he can live on five dollars a week."

"Low overhead," said Peter, and the two of them laughed.

She was back in the darkness. Her heart was a swollen muscle; she spread her hands over her chest to slow it down. She heard Peter calling Al Rodier.

"Do you believe it . . . university building . . . speak to someone in real estate first thing . . . right to the top if necessary . . . will not put up with it . . . hard to evict, but not impossible. Despoiling the environment . . . polluting the air we breathe."

The word "pollution" spun in her brain like one of those headlines in old movies: one word finally comprehensible after the turning blur: Strike. War.

Pollution. It suggested a defilement so complete, so permanent, that nothing could reverse it. Clear streams turned black and tarlike, verdant forests transformed to soot-covered stumps, the air full of black flakes that settled on the skin and couldn't be washed off.

Was that what the man downstairs was doing? He was living the way he wanted to, perhaps the only way he could. Before this incident, he hadn't disturbed them. They were the first to disturb him. People had a right not to hear thumping over their heads. Suppose he was trying to read, listening to music, working out a scientific formula. Suppose, when the children were making that noise, he was on the phone making an important call, the call that could change his life.

It wasn't likely. What was more likely was that he was lying in the dark, as she was. But not as she was. He wasn't lying in an empty bed. He bedded down in garbage. And the sound of thumping over his head was the sound of all his fear: that he would be named the names that he knew fit him, but could bear if they weren't said. "Disreputable." "Illegitimate."

They would send him out into the world. If only he could be left alone. If only he could be left to himself. And her children with their loud feet, the shouts of their unknowingness told him what he most feared, what he was right to fear, but what he only wanted to forget. At any minute they would tell him he was nothing, he was worse than nothing. Everything was theirs and they could take it rightfully, at any moment. Not because they were unjust or cruel. They were not unjust. Justice was entirely on their side. He couldn't possibly, in justice, speak a word in his own defense. Stone-faced, empty-handed, he would have to follow them into the open air.

She heard Peter on the phone calling the people they knew in the building who'd invited them for coffee or for brunch. She kept hearing him say his name—Peter Talbot—and his department—Mathematics, and the number of their apartment—4A. He was urging them to band together in his living room, the next night, to come up with a plan of action before, he kept saying, over and over, "things get more out of hand. And when you think," he kept saying, "of the qualified people who'd give their eyeteeth for what he's got, what he's destroying for everyone who comes after him. I'll bet every one of you knows someone who deserves that apartment more than him."

She saw them filing into her house, their crisp short hair, their well-tended shoes, the smiles cutting across their faces like a rifle shot. They would march in, certain of their right to be there, their duty to keep order. Not questioning the essential rightness of clearing out the swamp, the place where disease bred, and necessarily, of course, removing the breeders and the spreaders who, if left to themselves, would contaminate the world.

And Beatrice knew that they were right, that was the terrible thing about them, their unquestionable rightness. Right to clear out, break in, burn, tear, demolish, so that the health of the world might be preserved.

She sank down deeper. She was there with those who wallowed, burrowed, hoarded, their weak eyes half-closed, their sour voices, not really sour but hopeless at the prospect of trying to raise some objection, of offering some resistance. They knew there could be no negotiation, since they had no rights. So their petition turned into a growl, a growl that only stiffened the righteousness of their purpose. "Leave me alone" is all the ones who hid were saying. They would have liked to beseech but they were afraid to. Also full of hate. "Leave me alone."

Of course they wouldn't be left alone. They couldn't be. Beatrice understood that.

The skin around her eyes felt flayed, her limbs were heavy, her spine too weak to hold her up. "Leave me alone." The sweetness of the warm darkness, like a poultice, was all that could protect her from the brutality of open air on her raw skin.

She and the man downstairs breathed. In and out. She heard their joined breath and, underneath that sound, the opening of doors, the rush of violent armies, of flame, of tidal wave, lightning cleaving a moss-covered tree in two. And then something else below that: "Cannot. Cannot. Leave me alone." Unheeded.

She turned the light on in the bedroom. She put on a pair of turquoise sweatpants and a matching sweatshirt. On her feet she wore immaculate white socks and the white sneakers she'd varnished to brilliance with a product called Sneaker White she'd bought especially. She put on earrings, perfume, but no lipstick and no blush. She walked out of the apartment. She knew that Peter, in the back with the children, wouldn't hear the door close.

She walked down the dank, faintly ill-smelling stairs to the apartment situated exactly as hers was—3A—and rang the bell.

He opened the door a crack. The stench of rotting food and

unwashed clothes ought to have made her sick, but she knew she was beyond that sort of thing.

She looked him in the eye. "I need to talk to you," she said.

He shrugged, then smiled. Most of his top teeth were gone and the ones that were left were yellowed and streaked. He pushed the lock of his blondish hair that fell into his forehead back, away from his eyes. Then he took a comb out of his pocket and pulled it through his hair.

"Make yourself at home," he said, laughing morosely.

There was hardly a place to stand. The floor space was taken up by broken radios, blenders, ancient portable TVs revealing blown tubes, disconnected wires, a double-size mattress. Beside the mattress were paper plates with hardened sandwiches, glimpses of pink ham, tomatoes turned to felt between stone-colored slices of bread, magazines with wrinkled pages, unopened envelopes (yellow, white, mustard-colored), sloping hills of clean underwear mixed up with balled socks, and opened cans of Coke. There were no sheets on the mattress; sheets, she could tell, had been given up long ago. Loosely spread over the blue ticking was a pinkish blanket, its trim a trap, a bracelet for the foot to catch itself in during the uneasy night.

A few feet from the mattress was a Barcalounger whose upholstery must once have been mustard-colored. The headrest was a darker shade, almost brown; she understood that the discoloration was from the grease of his hair when he leaned back. She moved some copies of *Popular Mechanics* and some Styrofoam containers, hamburger-sized, to make room for herself to sit. She tried to imagine what she looked like, in her turquoise sweatsuit, sitting in this chair.

"I came to warn you," she said. "They're having a meeting. Right now in my apartment. They want to have you evicted."

He laughed, and she could see that his top teeth looked striated, lines of brownish yellow striping the enamel in a way she didn't remember seeing on anyone else.

"Relax," he said. "It'll never happen. They keep trying, but it'll never happen. This is New York. I'm a disabled person. I'm on disability. You understand what that means? Nobody like me gets evicted in New York. Don't worry about it. I'll be here forever."

She looked at her neighbor and gave him a smile so radiant that it seemed to partake of prayer. And then a torpor that was not somnolent, but full of joy, took hold of her. Her eyes were closing themselves with happiness. She needed rest. Why hadn't she ever known before that rest was the one thing she had always needed?

She saw her white bathroom floor, gleaming from the lake of bleach she had poured on it. Just thinking of it hurt her eyes. Here, there was nothing that would hurt her. She wanted to tell him it was beautiful here, it was wonderful, it was just like home. But she was too tired to speak. And that was fine, she knew he understood. Here, where they both were, there was no need to say a word.

But he was saying something. She could hear it through her sleep, and she had to swim up to get it, like a fish surfacing for crumbs. She couldn't seem, quite, to open her eyes and she fell back down to the dark water. Then she felt him shaking her by the shoulders.

"What are you doing? What are you doing? You can't do that here."

She looked at his eyes. They weren't looking at her kindly. She had thought he would be kind. She blinked several times, then closed her eyes again. When she opened them, he was still standing above her, his hands on her shoulders, shaking them, his eyes unkind.

"You can't do that here. You can't just come down here and go to sleep like that. This is my place. Now get out."

He was telling her she had to leave. She supposed she understood that. She couldn't stay here if he didn't want her. She had thought he'd understand that what she needed was a place to rest, just that, she wouldn't be taking anything from him. But he was treating her like a thief. He was making her leave as if she were a criminal. There was no choice now but to leave, shamefully, like a criminal.

He closed the door behind her. Although her back was to the door, she felt he was closing it in her face and she felt the force of it exactly on her face as if his hand had struck it. She stood completely still, her back nearly touching the brown door.

She couldn't move. She couldn't move because she could think of no direction that seemed sensible. But the shame of his having thrown her out propelled her toward the stairs. She wondered if she could simply walk out of the building as she was. With no coat, no money, nothing to identify her. But she knew that wasn't possible. It was winter, and it was New York.

She walked up the stairs. She stood on the straw mat in front of her own door. She'd have to ring the bell; she hadn't brought her keys. Peter would wonder where she had gone. She didn't know what she'd tell him. There was nothing to say.

She didn't know what would happen now. She knew only that she must ring the bell and see her husband's face and then walk into the apartment. It was the place she lived and she had nowhere else to go.

My Podiatrist Tells Me a Story
About a Boy and a Dog

He says things to me like "There's no reason why you should feel any pain," and "I'll take care of everything." Why wouldn't I like seeing him?

I first went when I had something called a plantar wart beneath my left big toe. I thought it was called a planter's wart. "A lot of people think that and they're wrong," he said. "But you're a writer, you're interested in words, so you should know the truth." He draws me a diagram of the part of the foot called the planta. "I don't want you to imagine people walking around with shovels in their hands, putting plants into the soil," he said. "Because it's not the truth." I was glad to learn what he had to tell me; now I correct other people, for his sake and in his name.

His daughter plays the French horn in a symphony orchestra. But she's decided she wants to be a vet. To get into veterinary school, "which is already, you understand, very difficult in itself," she has to take more science courses. She lives in Boston. She told him she would take the courses in the local community college.

" 'Darling,' I said to her, 'veterinary school is very hard to get into, true or not true?'

"She said what she had to say: 'True.'

" 'So what's the best, and I mean the very best place in Boston to take courses?'

"She said what she had to say: 'Harvard.'

"So I said to her, 'You're my daughter and I want the very best for you. And I can give you the best. So: Harvard.' She thanked me profusely. I can't tell you how profusely she thanked me. She's enjoying her courses very much. Though, of course, they're a challenge."

On the bus home, I try to imagine what it would have been like to have a father who said, "I want the very best for you and I can give you the best." My life would have been wholly different.

It's not well known that the subspecialist most consulted by women over forty is the podiatrist. Over the years, many of us have been doing terrible things to our feet. High heels. Pointy toes. Damaging ourselves for vanity. For sex? From fear or from desire? A desire to please whom?

When I went to see him because of the plantar wart, he shaved my calluses, which, he said, were painful in places because of my gait. "Now everybody has a gait," he said. "Everybody's gait means something. In your case, problems. I can take care of them."

He shaved the bad calluses with a very sharp knife, a knife that looked as if it would have to hurt. I stiffened, thinking of my feet, those tender loaves. I've always liked my feet. Sometimes I think of them as my best feature. My second toe is longer than my first; for the Greeks, this is a sign of beauty. Also my toes make, on the top, a fanlike shape that I never look at without pleasure. So I didn't want anything happening to my nice feet. But he said, "You can trust me, I won't hurt you." I didn't believe him: I was looking at that knife. I waited for the shock of pain, which did not come. More than that: over the next days, I noticed that I was free from, if not pain, then a discomfort that had been so habitual I had assumed it was a part of life.

So of course I agreed to come back every three months, to keep myself in the state to which he'd brought me. Besides, he told me stories.

It began when I asked him how he became a podiatrist.

"Long story," he said. "Interesting story, or at least I think it's interesting. Since you're a writer, maybe you'll think it's interesting too."

As he began to speak, his eyebrows, which always had a tendency toward verticality, stood upright like two fuzzy letter *l*s. His small mouth, which I had seen in two positions—cheerfully amused in conversation, or concerned while holding an afflicted foot—became neutral: a vessel of information only.

"It goes back to when I was a child. You'll be surprised to hear it. But it goes back to an accident.

"So I can give you a background, so you can understand, you have to know something about my family.

"My father was a successful doctor. We were what you might call wealthy. Definitely wealthy. We lived in New York. It's not like it is now. One day, I was in my father's office with him, playing. By accident, a beaker of acid tipped over and burned my leg, right through to the bone. I became a cripple. And I'd been quite an athletic boy.

"As you can imagine, I grew downhearted. And my father was very guilty because he'd failed to cover the beaker of acid. So he devoted himself to me. He did everything. Built a gym in the basement—we had a brownstone, as I told you we were wealthy—and hired all kinds of teachers for me. Physical education. It was a struggle, but I persevered. And he was with me, urging me on. The thing about him, he was firm but kind. He took me to a podiatrist, who took excellent care of me. So I became interested in the subject, starting, of course, with my own case. The rest of my family became doctors, but studies were hard for me. If I were young now, I'd be called dyslexic.

"But I found the work I love. So you see how everything works out."

I think of his quizzical, cheerful face, but a boy's version. The shock of burning acid. And his poor father. Of all fates, one of the worst: to be implicated in the pain of your own child. I think of the phys ed teachers, with slicked-back hair, mustaches, sleeveless T-shirts, tights, lace-up shoes. I think of the tutors. And the cheerful, quizzical boy, struggling to keep up.

I think of the brownstone, its shining floors, the hanging chandeliers, the smell of coal and laundry in the basement, turned into a gym.

On one of my visits, the patient before me has come with a standard poodle. I try to understand what's behind the decision to bring your dog with you to the podiatrist. The dog, unleashed, walks around the waiting room, nosing the magazine rack. I hear his master's voice: the voice of Yankee privilege, but suggesting the Maine woods: summers with no running water, bilberries for breakfast, a view from the porch of Daddy's "camp" of half the state. The owner of the dog is a foot taller than the doctor. He tells her he hopes she'll be comfortable, and she says she will be, of course thanks to "your very good work, my friend."

I'm sure they aren't friends. Not like he and I are. I'm sure he doesn't tell her stories.

"Nice animal," he says when I sit in the chair. "Very nice animal. I don't do surgery anymore, so I'm glad to have dogs around, as long as they're well behaved. And that one is a real prize. I didn't even know he was there."

He says that everything I'm doing for my feet is exactly right and that the orthotics he made to be inserted into my shoes are working perfectly.

"Funny story about a dog. You want to hear a funny story about a dog?"

I say yes I would, very much.

"Every summer my family went and stayed in a hotel in the Catskills. My father was in New York, except for the weekends, and the rest of the family stayed there all the time. It was an excellent arrangement, suited everyone very well. Of course all meals included and the kitchen was top drawer. Every day, the chef would pack a lunch for me. Always the same thing, a chicken sandwich. He had a way of preparing chicken that I happened to like very much. I would take my lunch and my fishing pole and go down to the dock and fish for hours. Well, one day, I'm sitting on the dock and suddenly at the other end of the dock there's this very big dog. I mean she was big. I saw her looking at me and I looked at her and she didn't look dangerous, although she was so big. I wasn't afraid. I broke off a piece of my sandwich and left it on the dock a certain ways away from where I was sitting. After a while she took it, then she went back into the woods. Next day, same thing, she appears, I leave the piece of sandwich, she takes it and goes away. After a week of this, one day after she takes the piece of sandwich, she lies down next to me on the dock. Then she starts walking me back to the hotel every day. One day, we run into the owner's dog, a German shepherd, not a nice animal, a vicious animal. She takes one look at Brownie, puts her tail between her legs, and runs into the kitchen. I called the dog Brownie because she was brown. Even at that time I had a terrific imagination.

"Well, the end of the summer came and I begged my father to take Brownie home. But he said no, she was a country dog, a woods dog, she'd be miserable in the city, she'd pine away. Well, I was miserable, but what can I do? I get in the car and put my head against the seat and cry my heart out.

"Now, in those days, they didn't have the superhighways of today, so the fastest my father could go was forty-five miles an hour. After we'd been traveling about an hour and a half, my father yells out, "'Oh, my God.'" We didn't know what happened. "'Look out the back,'" he says. And there's Brownie, running along the side of the road keeping up with the car.

"So of course my father opened the door. The dog got in. She was so big she had to lie full length on the floor and still there wasn't room for her. She threw up, then she slept all the way home.

"Fortunately, we had a townhouse with a backyard, so she could sleep outside. We just left the back window open and she came and went as she pleased. It wasn't like now, with the crime, which is why I live in Westchester.

"My mother used to worry about me with my lame leg, but she knew she had to give me independence. You have to do that with a boy, and she knew it. So she let me walk to school if Brownie was with me. It was only two blocks away, and she watched me out the window. One day, she's looking out the window and she sees me walking into the street, not paying attention, and the next thing she sees a truck careening around the corner and she sees Brownie grab me by the waist and pull me to safety. I still have scars from the teeth marks, but I wouldn't be here to tell you about those scars if it weren't for that dog.

"She saved my life another time. I was back at the hotel, fishing, but not on the dock, by a creek this time. I was wearing waders and again not paying attention, because, let's face it, that was the kind of kid I was. I walk into the water to get the fish. I walk in too deep and the mud is very soft on the bottom and I don't have the strength in my lame leg to lift myself up because the boots are full of water. I start to be pulled under. The dog comes in and pulls me out. So that was two times my life was saved by that dog.

"Now I'm going to tell you something you didn't know. Until the 1930s, dogs were not licensed in the city of New York. So one day, the notice comes, and my father, who always did things very properly, makes an appointment with our vet, who's a patient of his, to have the dog examined for a license. Well, we go into the office and the vet takes one look at Brownie and gets a strange look on his face. He calls my father into a private office. He says, 'Who does the dog respond to most?' My father says it's me. The vet says, 'We have to put a muzzle on the dog. I have to take some blood.'"

I don't want to hear any more of this story. I can tell what's coming next: rabies, and this miraculous dog will have to be put down. I think of the little boy with his lame leg in his too-big room in the townhouse where everyone's heels clatter too loudly on the wooden floors.

"So I put the muzzle on the dog, she doesn't give any trouble, she'd do anything for me, but she gives me this terrible look when the doctor sticks the needle into her. My father and I sit in the waiting room, we don't know what's happening, our hearts are in our mouths. Then the doctor comes in and calls my father into his private room.

"'Doctor,' he says to my father, 'I don't know how to tell you this, but this animal you have isn't a dog, it's a wolf. A gray wolf.'"

Immediately, I hear howls, see wild eyes, enormous teeth, huge paws prowling in the moonlight on hard-packed snow that glistens blue and silver. Wolf: danger and magic, poverty and chaos too: the wolf at the door, wolf in sheep's clothing, crying wolf. Life lived at night, remotely, inexplicably.

"My father asks if he's sure. The vet says yes. My father says it's the best dog he's ever had, he tells him how she's saved my life twice.

"The vet says, 'The problem is, Doctor, it's illegal to have a wolf in the city of New York. You'll have to take her back to where she came from or give her to a zoo.'

"My father says, 'Doctor, you have been my patient for twenty years. If you want to go on being my patient, listen to me. This dog is a member of the family. I will not get rid of her. I will not separate her from the people she loves or put her in a cage.'

"The vet says, 'Let me make one call.'

"He finds out that he can get a wildlife license for us. Which he does. And this is how we got to keep Brownie.

"Well, we kept her for another three years. We'd take her up to the Catskills in the summer. She'd sleep in the woods at night and be waiting for us at the hotel in the mornings. One morning she wasn't there. We never saw her again. But I knew it was all right. I knew she'd returned to her pack."

"You don't think she just went into the woods to die?" I ask.

"She was too young for that," he says.

"Perhaps she was killed by another animal."

"I believe she went back to join her pack. I'll tell you why. I've made a study of wolves, for reasons I'm sure you find obvious. You see, in a pack, only one female, the alpha female, the dominant one, is allowed to mate. If a beta female wants to mate, she has to leave the pack."

"You think that's what Brownie did?"

"Most definitely, yes, I think so."

"So she left when she was young because she wanted to mate, and then when she got older she wanted to go back to the family."

"I would say so."

"It's sort of a story about female desire, then," I say. "And what happens when that ends, and it's replaced by an urge for conformity."

His eyebrows are almost up to his hairline now. "Maybe it's a story about that for you. For me, it's a wonderful story about a wonderful dog. And I have many more stories about this dog that I could tell you. But I won't be seeing you for quite a while because everything you're doing, from my perspective, is perfect. Just keep doing everything you're doing. One hundred percent."

Separation

The social worker said: "I think he needs a group experience."

Not looking at JoAnn, handing a piece of paper with a black design JoAnn saw later was the steeple of a church. Ascension Play School.

"It's no trip for you," the social worker said to JoAnn. "See that building there, behind the Episcopal church. They wrote to us, saying they're offering a scholarship to any child of ours who might benefit from a group experience."

Child of *ours*?
Of *yours*?
No one's but mine.

She put her hand over her mouth, to keep back something. Sickness? Bad words that would cause trouble later on? Words that would be put down in the file. She knew their ways. This Mrs. Pratt was not the first of them, she'd had a lot of them in towns over the years.

The game was shut your mouth.

The game was shut your mouth and keep it shut.

The game was shut your mouth and give them what they wanted.

Town after town. Arriving. Making your way to the county seat, the hall, the metal desks, the forms to be filled out, the bad lights with their buzzing noises, and the questions.

Name?

Her husband's. Not an out-of-wedlock child. Her son. Hers, but everything all right before the law. The husband, not abandoning, but driven off. Pushed out. No room for him, he knew it, and was sorry, but he knew. One day: "Well, I'll be shoving off."

"All right."

A night she stayed up, when the baby had the croup. Her husband saw her happiness. He saw how happy she was, after the steaming shower and the rush outside to the cold air, after all this, the easy, even breathing. And her humming. Song after song.

"Well, I'll be shoving off."

"All right."

Rubbing the boy's wet head with a dry towel. Wet from the steam she'd set up in the bathroom. His hair that smelled like bread. She put her lips to it, and breathed it in. His easy breath, the wet smell of his hair. And looked up at the father, at the husband, sorry for him, but it was nothing, he was right to leave, there wasn't any place for him.

Humming, his damp head and his easy breathing. Happy, happy. All I want.

He needs a group experience.

All I have ever wanted.

Her childhood: blocks of muteness. Of silence because what was there to say. Neglect, they called it. She was kept alive. Fed. Clothed. She saw now that could not have been so easy. The flow of meals, sweaters, jackets, in the summer short-sleeved shirts and shorts, a bathing suit, washed hair, injections that were law. She felt sorry for her mother, whom she could barely remember now. She had trouble calling up the faces of the past.

Her memory: the outline of a head, a black line surrounding nothing. The faces blank. Unharmful ghosts, but nothing, nothing to her. And of course no help.

It was why she didn't like the television. All the filled-in faces. She wanted, sometimes, to ask people about their memories. Do you remember people when you are away from them? The faces? At what point do they come alive?

Even her husband's face grown ghostly.

But she never said these things. She kept to herself. Smiling, quiet, clean. She and her son.

Never causing trouble.

Keeping things up.

Arriving on time for the social worker.

The clinic.

The dentist, who said it was all right if she sat on the chair and he sat on her lap to be examined. Otherwise he'll scream.

Fine, then, Mrs. Verbeck. Just keep it up. Keep him away from sugar snacks. Fresh fruit. Apples or carrot sticks. Water rather than soda or other sweetened drinks.

Yes, thank you. Yes.

You've done a good job. Not one cavity. You floss his teeth?

I will.

We'll show you how. Miss Havenick, the hygienist, will show you.

"Let's open our mouth, Billy."

Not yours. His.

And mine.

She wanted to phone the call-in radio and ask one of the doctors.

Are the faces of people empty to other people as they are to me?

Except his face. The one face I have always known.

At night while he slept she sat on a stool beside him just to learn his face. So that she never would forget.

* * *

An angry baby. Happy only in her arms.

He doesn't take to strangers. Thanks, no, I can manage. Thanks.

Did anyone look at her face? In the shadowy childhood, family of shadow, furniture the part of it that she remembered most. The green couch. The red chair.

Did anyone look at my face?

He needs a group experience.

But we are happiest alone.

But never say it. She knew what people thought. Children need other children. They believe that, everyone believes it.

Only I do not believe it.

Only he and I.

Happy, happy in the studio apartment, in the trailer, in the basement rented in the rotting house. Happy in the supermarket, laundromat, bank where we stand on line to cash the check from welfare. Singing, eating meals we love, the walks we take, bringing back leaves, pinecones. Puzzles we do in silence, cartoon shows we watch.

She wanted to say to them: "We're very happy."

She never said these things. She moved.

Five towns. Five different states.

He needs a group experience.

This time she thinks they may be right. Now he is four years old. Next year, no hope.

No hope. No hope.

All I have ever wanted.

On the first day of school, she dresses him. She didn't dare to buy new clothes for school. She puts on him the clothes that he has worn all summer. Black jeans with an elastic waist. An orange short-sleeved shirt with a design of a bear on the left breast pocket. White socks, his old red sneakers he is proud of. Velcro. He can do them himself.

The teacher says: "He's never had a group experience?"

"No, just with me."

"Maybe, then, for the first few days you can stay with him. For a little while. Until he adjusts to the group situation."

She sees the other mothers bought their boys and girls new clothes. And for themselves. She parks the car behind the church and waits till they have all gone in the little building, like a hut, built for the children. All the other mothers know each other. Like each other. And the children.

There is no one that we know.

The teacher is standing at the door. "Good morning Jessica, Kate, Michael, Daniel, Jason, Alison."

"And here comes Billy."

Children are playing on the swings and slides.

Children are playing in the sandbox.

Girls are pretending to cook at the toy stove, using toy pots and spoons and dishes.

Boys are in the corner making a house of large blocks, then shoving it down, building it, knocking it down, fighting, building.

Billy hides his face in her shoulder.

"I won't leave you."

"Maybe tomorrow," says the teacher. "After he gets more used to the group, you'll feel that you can leave after a while."

The teacher's pants are elastic-waisted, like the children's pants. She wears blue eye shadow, her fingernails are pink as shells. She is wearing sandals with thin straps. She is wearing stockings underneath the sandals. JoAnn wonders: Maybe they are socks that only look like stockings. Maybe they stop.

. . .

At night he says: "Don't take me back there."

"All right," she says. Later she says: "I made a mistake. We have to go."

The second day of school he will not look at anybody. When the teacher puts her hand on his shoulder to ask if he sees anything he might like to play with, he pushes her hand away and looks at her with rage. "No one said you could touch me." He hides his eyes. He grinds his eyes into his mother's shoulder blade.

She's proud that he can speak up for himself. But she is frightened. Now what will they do?

In the playground, he lets her push him on a swing. She lights a cigarette. The other mothers don't approve, although they try to smile. They tell her about their children, who had problems getting used to school.

"My oldest was like that. Till Christmas."

No one is like us. No one is like he is.

One morning he says he's tired. She tells him he doesn't have to go to school. She keeps him home for three days. Both of them are happy.

But the next day it's worse in school. Only one of the mothers smiles at her. She says: "You know, maybe Billy's finding the group too large. Maybe he could just come over to our house. Daniel's used to the group. If they made friends, maybe that would help Billy in the group."

"Thank you," JoAnn says. "But we're so busy."

The social worker says: "You're not working on this separation."

Everything has been reported. The social worker takes it as a bad sign that JoAnn refused the other mother's invitation. Which she knows about.

"If I were you," she says, ". . . or maybe some counseling. For both your sakes."

JoAnn is terrified. She tells the other mother she would like to come. The other mother writes her name and address down on a piece of paper torn from a pad in the shape of an apple with a bite out of it. It says "Debi—35 Ranch Road." And in parentheses, "Dan's mom."

For this, she buys her son new clothes.

He never cries anymore. Nobody can make him do anything he doesn't want to. His eyes are bright green stones. No one can make him do anything. This makes her feel she has done right.

The morning that they are going to the house they take a bath together. They laugh, they soap each other's backs. Lately she sees him looking at her sex a second longer than he ought to, and his eyes get hard and angry when he sees she sees. She knows they will not bathe together much longer after this year. But this year. Yes.

Debi, the mother, has to look several places for an ashtray. JoAnn hasn't realized there are no ashtrays until she has already lit up. They are both embarrassed. Debi says, "Somehow most of the people I know quit." She goes through her cabinets and then finds one from a hotel in Canada. "We stole it on our honeymoon," she says, and laughs.

Billy knows his mother doesn't want him to play with Danny. She knows he knows. But she can feel his bones grow lively on her lap; she feels his body straining toward the other children. Danny and his sisters, Gillian and Lisa. And the toys. The house is full of toys. Trucks, cars, blocks, toy dinosaurs are scattered all over the wooden floors. But the house is so big it still looks neat with all the toys all over. The house is too big, too light. The house frightens JoAnn. She holds Billy tighter on her lap. He doesn't move, although she knows he wants to. And she knows he must.

"Look at the truck," she says. "Should we go over and look at that truck?"

Debi jumps out of her chair, runs over to the children.

"Let's show Billy the truck. See Danny's truck, Billy?" She gets down on her knees. "Look how the back goes down like this."

JoAnn doesn't know whether or not to go down on her knees with Debi and the other children. She stands back. Billy looks up at her. His fingers itch to touch the truck. She sees it. She gives him a little push on the shoulders. "Go play," she says. She lights another cigarette and puts the match in the heart-shaped ashtray she has carried with her.

Billy isn't playing with the other children. He is playing alongside them. Danny and his sisters are pretending to make dinner out of clay. They don't talk to Billy; they don't invite him to play with them; they leave him alone, and he seems happy with the truck. She sees he has forgotten her. For him she is nowhere in the room.

Debi says, "Let's go into the kitchen and relax. They're fine without us."

JoAnn feels the house will spread out and the floor disappear. She will be standing alone in air. The house has no edges; the walls are not real walls. Who could be safe here?

In the kitchen in a row below the ceiling there are darker-painted leaves. She tells Debi she likes them.

"I did them myself. I'm kind of a crafts freak. Are you into crafts?" JoAnn says she always wanted to do ceramics.

"I do ceramics Thursday nights," says Debi. She brings a cookie jar shaped like a bear to the table. "I made this last month," she says. "And while you're at it, have one." She offers JoAnn the open jar. "I made them for the kids, but if you won't tell I won't."

The cookies frighten JoAnn. The raisins, and the walnuts and the oatmeal that will not dissolve against her tongue.

"If you want, there's room in our ceramics class on Thursdays. I think it's important to have your own interests, at least for me. Get away, do something that's not connected to the kids. Get away from them and let them get away from you."

JoAnn begins to cough. She feels she cannot breathe. The walls of the big room are thinning. She is alone in freezing air. Her ribs press against her thin lungs. Debi says: "You okay, JoAnn?"

"I smoke too much. This year, I'm really going to quit. I've said it before, but now, this year I'm really going to do it."

They hear a child scream. They run into the living room. Danny is crying.

"He hit me with the truck."

"Did you hit him with the truck?" JoAnn says. "Tell Danny you're sorry."

Billy looks at them all with his bright eyes. Except at her. He does not look at his mother. He knows she doesn't want him to apologize. He knows that she is glad he did it. He did it for her. She knows this.

"We've got to be going," says JoAnn, picking Billy up. He presses the truck to him. "Put the truck down," she says.

He doesn't look at anyone.

"Don't go," says Debi. "Really, they were doing great. All kids get into things like that. They were doing great for a long time."

"We've got to go," JoAnn says, looking in the pocket of her plaid wool jacket for the keys. "Billy, give Danny back his truck."

"Danny, can Billy borrow the truck till school tomorrow?" Debi asks. JoAnn pulls the truck from her son's grip.

"Thanks, but he doesn't need it," she says, smiling, handing back the truck. "It isn't his."

The truck falls from her hand. It makes a hard sound on the wooden floor. Hearing the sound, Danny begins to cry again.

"Let's try it again," says Debi. "They were really doing great there for a while."

JoAnn smiles, holding Billy more tightly. "Sure thing," she says.

At night, while he sleeps and she sits on the stool beside his bed to watch, she thinks of him in the room with the other children. Him forgetting. She thinks of him pushing the truck back and forth on the floor beside the other children, thinks of the walls thinning out, and her thin lungs that cannot enclose the breath she needs to live.

Alone. Alone.

All I have ever wanted.

In the morning he says: "You should have let me take that truck."

She says: "Do you want to go back to that house?"

"I want the truck."

"Danny's a nice boy, isn't he?"

He says: "Are you going to leave me alone today?"

"I don't know," she says. "I'll see."

When they arrive, the teacher says: "I think Billy's ready for a regular day today. I think the time's come definitely."

She doesn't look at JoAnn when she says this. She takes Billy's jacket off and hangs it on his hook below his name. She does not let go of his hand. "Billy, I heard you played with Danny yesterday. That's so terrific. He brought in the truck today, for you to play with while you're here."

The teacher leads him into the class, closing the door behind her so JoAnn can't see them. So that he cannot look back.

She stands in the hall. Her hands are freezing. She pulls the fake fleece collar of her plaid coat around her ears. Her heart is solid and will not pump blood. She walks into the parking lot. She gets into her car and starts it. She does not know where she will get her air, how she will breathe. The engine stalls. She pumps the gas pedal and starts the car again.

And then she hears him. He is calling. He is running toward the car. She sees that he has put his coat on by himself. She sees him standing at the car door, opening it, getting in beside her.

She can breathe, the air is warm and helpful for her breathing. They are driving, singing. They are happy.

She says to him: "Let's pack up all our things. Let's find another place, a better place to live in."

Happy, singing.

He will leave me soon enough.

Death in Naples

It was wonderful of Jonathan to have invited her. How many sons, her friends kept asking, would include their mother on a vacation with their wives? You could see it, her friends had said, if there were children: invite granny—a built-in babysitter. But there was nothing in it for Jonathan and Melanie but pure goodness of heart. How fortunate she was, her friends all told her, to have a daughter-in-law she was fond of.

And she was fond of Melanie, really she was, although she wasn't a person Lorna felt she could relax with. Certainly she was admirable, the way she dealt with everything: her job as a stockbroker, keeping their apartment beautiful, regularly making delicious meals. And she always looked splendid; she kept her hair long, done up in some complicated way that Lorna knew must take time in the morning. Braids or curls or a series of barrettes or clips. And beautifully cut suits and beautifully made high-heeled pumps. Lorna remembered when she had worn heels that high, and remembered how she'd loved them. But she remembered, too, how uncomfortable they had been and what a blessed relief, a consolation even, it had been to kick them off at the door. To give them up for something softer, slippers or loafers or tennis shoes. But Melanie didn't kick her heels off at the door. She kept them on even to cook her careful dinners. It occurred to Lorna that she'd never seen her daughter-in-law in slippers. She assumed that she must have a pair, but Lorna couldn't imagine what they might look like.

Lorna could be of use to them on their holiday in that she had some Italian and they had none. Don't overestimate my ability, she warned them: I'm not very good and I'm easily flustered. And when I'm flustered I lose the little proficiency I've had. Possibly, had she started younger, or lived in Italy for extended periods, her Italian would have been quite good.

That was what Richard kept telling her. They traveled to Italy every year the six years before his death. His death that was brief, composed, a line that completed itself effortlessly. He'd slipped into his death as a letter slips into an envelope, and is sent off, or as a diver, seen from a distance, enters the dark water, and swims into a cove from which he can't be seen again. Like the letter or the swimmer Richard had, she was sure, reached some proper destination. Only she could not name it or locate it. But she was sure there was such a place.

When they were in Italy, he was terribly proud when she could talk to waiters, and said it was nothing, nothing, when failures of comprehension occurred on either side. When a fruit vendor would say *"come,"* scrunching his face up when she had said perfectly clearly, she had thought, *uove* or *pere*, when she would have to say *"mi dispiace, no ho capito"* after someone had told her the directions to a museum, or when an Italian, losing patience, would lapse into English, Richard would say, "Relax, you're doing great." She knew she wasn't doing great, and even though Richard was right to tell her that no one in their conversation group could do half so well, she wasn't comforted. She knew that when real situations arose, she often failed.

The Italian conversation class was one of the things she and Richard did together after Richard's retirement. They'd hired an Italian student from the university to teach a group of them, four retired couples, or rather four retired men and their wives, because none of the women had ever worked. They'd planned to study all year and then travel, four couples, to Italy in the spring. The study had continued; the travel happened only once. For in reality the other couples hadn't really enjoyed themselves in Italy, had behaved dutifully rather than joyously, and were unable to conceal their real joy at returning home to Cincinnati. To their own bathrooms, their own beds.

But Richard and Lorna had gone back every spring for six springs. They had not been able to wean themselves from Tuscany, landing in Florence, spending a week there in the same hotel, where, after the fourth year, and because they were never there in high season, they were given a room with a view of Piazza San Marco. She was grateful that Richard didn't mind driving in Italy; she could never have; the speeds on the *autostrade* terrified her. So they visited Siena, Civietalla, Pisa, Lucca. Gentle weeks during which they could digest the beauty they had seen in Florence, avoiding what she had read in a guidebook was called Stendhal syndrome. The novelist had suffered a nervous breakdown, overwhelmed by the pressure of having to assimilate so much greatness, so much human achievement in so short a time.

During the long wet winters in Cincinnati, she would regularly place a postcard of something they'd loved next to Richard's breakfast plate: Donatello's saucy *David* in his feathered hat, Michelangelo's *Evening* languidly waiting for something to be played out.

And then Richard had died, and she hadn't been back to Italy since. Six years, could it have been? She was seventy-four now, unarguably an old lady. Some women she knew, but no one she knew well, traveled alone at her age. A friend of a friend had made, at seventy-five, a trip to Thailand on her own. She envied such women, wished she could be like them, but she was not. She kept her life full; she wouldn't sell the house or get help with the garden, she was a docent at the museum; she kept up with her Italian and her women friends—widows and divorcées. The couples had, somehow, stopped including her. But she met with her friends, regularly, to cook elaborate meals. They swam together at the health club. Three times a year, she traveled to Chicago to see Jonathan and Melanie, staying only a few days at a time, going to the Art Institute, to the symphony, to see some experimental theater, priding herself on keeping out of their way and not staying too long. She believed them when they said they were sorry to see her go; she believed their friends when they told Jonathan how lucky he was to have a mother who was so "low maintenance." Low maintenance. It amused her how many phrases had become common that hadn't existed when she was young—or even ten years later.

That was the world, that was language: it was a product of change. Change was a good thing; when you stopped believing that, you'd got old, you might as well chuck the whole business.

After a deprivation of six years, the prospect of seeing Italy with Jonathan and Melanie was particularly delightful. They were young and vigorous and full of curiosity. How strange that neither of them had been to Italy. Melanie had never been abroad. But Melanie's life, before she'd met Jonathan, had been difficult. Her parents had been killed in a car crash just after she started college; they'd seemed to leave her nothing. Lorna respected Melanie's reticence about her late parents; she saw her unwillingness to talk about them as an attractive fastidiousness—she was always uneasy at the modern tendency to reveal too much. She'd been surprised when, just before the wedding, Jonathan had said to her and Richard: "Melanie wants me to talk to you about what she's going to call you. She just doesn't feel comfortable calling you Mom and Dad; she says that's what she calls her own parents in her mind. Is it OK if she just calls you Richard and Lorna?" Lorna had never expected that Melanie would do anything else; she wondered what that suggested about Melanie's background, but as she thought there was no way of knowing, and as she was moved by Melanie's protectiveness of her parents' memory, she warmly agreed that Melanie should go on just as she had, calling them by their first names.

So it wasn't surprising that Melanie had never been to Europe; she had no indulgent parents to treat her; she'd had to augment her scholarship with a series of menial jobs. She'd gone to work at a bank a week after graduation. And Lorna and Richard had often remarked to each other that going to Europe, the whole idea of Europe, didn't mean to Jonathan's generation what it had to theirs. She and Richard had gone to Paris on their honeymoon, saving up a year for it, feeling that on the rumpled sheets of their Left Bank hotel, scene of so much illicit, such artistic lovemaking, they could legitimate their sexual union without its losing its allure. Jonathan and Melanie had gone to St. Bart's for their honeymoon. They both worked so very hard. Eighty-hour weeks sometimes. Who could blame them for wanting to lie on a beach, rest up in the sunshine.

Jonathan hadn't been to Europe since college; she and Richard had taken him to the South of France for a pregraduation gift. It hadn't been a success; Jonathan didn't seem to enjoy it as they did; Lorna thought he missed his friends. But now he'd be with Melanie; they were so perfectly matched; she knew that when Jonathan was with his wife, he felt no need for other company. She only hoped she wouldn't be in the way.

"We want to take you back to the old haunts, your old haunts with Dad, they're new for me and Mel. But we thought it would be fun for us to see something new to all of us. I've booked us into Naples, and from there, we'll tool around the Amalfi coast."

"Marvelous," said Lorna. "And maybe we can take a side trip to Pompeii."

"Archaeology's not Mel's thing," said Jonathan.

Lorna told herself it didn't matter that she'd miss Pompeii; they'd have more than enough to see.

For three months, she read and reread guidebooks, trying to select a few things that would spark for Jonathan and Melanie the love that she and Richard had felt. Not too much, not too much, she kept saying to herself, cutting back her plans as she would prune a vine or a bush that could choke out fragile life with its overeffulgence. One beautiful thing a day, we'll see what we see, they're young, they'll come back. She would leave them to themselves in the afternoon; she remembered the sweet sleepy afternoons of lovemaking with Richard in Italian hotels, in beds that weren't really double beds at all but twin beds pushed together, a sheet stretched tight over the top. And of course, they worked so hard, they'd need their afternoon siesta. One beautiful thing a day, she said, pleased at her own modesty—they'll have love, and rest, and delicious food as well.

She'd never traveled business class before; the luxury quietly delighted her. She knew Jonathan was uncomfortable about being thanked for upgrading her fare; he seemed impatient that she should think it was anything to mention. "Mom, for heaven's sake, everyone flies business class. It's no big deal. Mel and I have so many miles we don't know what to do with them. She's the queen of the upgrade, my wife, aren't you, babe."

"Jesus, yes," said Melanie. She reached into the tapestry bag at her feet and shyly handed Lorna a box wrapped in violet paper with a teal ribbon. "This is your survival kit for the airplane," she said. Lorna opened the box; there was an inflatable neck pillow, a set of earplugs, a lavender sachet that went over your eyes like a mask-sized pillow—it was supposed to induce a gentle sleep. There were Victorian tins of pastilles: one black currant, one lemon, with pictures of little girls holding parasols. Tears came to Lorna's eyes at Melanie's thoughtfulness—all the more touching because she seemed so uncomfortable at being thanked. She put her lavender sachet—hers was a paisley print of dark blue and magenta—over her beautiful gray eyes. She'd taken a sleeping pill.

"She's also the queen of the sleepers. Just watch, five minutes, she'll be dead to the world."

Dead to the world, Lorna thought, what a terrible expression. If you were dead to the world, what, then, were you alive to? She opened her map of Florence. She'd left map reading to Richard and she was afraid she'd forgotten everything, and Jonathan and Melanie were depending on her to lead them around.

She watched the young people sleeping. Beautiful, she thought, their health, their wholeness. They shared a kind of sleep that she and Richard had never shared, because she had never worked as hard as Richard. Melanie and Jonathan were together in feeling they had earned their rest, that it was equally hard-won, equally precious, because rare, to both of them. She thought of Jonathan's sleeping body when he'd been a little boy, how nothing had given her the pure peace and joy of holding her child's sleeping body. He was hers then. And now he was—what? The world's? Melanie's?

Melanie woke cranky; everything made her impatient. Their room in the hotel wasn't ready. Gingerly, Lorna suggested a coffee at a café in Piazza San Marco.

"What options do I have?" she asked.

"Chill out, babe," said Jonathan.

"Jonathan, I'm wondering what could possibly make you think that was a helpful comment," she said, snapping shut the lid on her blusher.

Jonathan and Melanie drank their coffee silently. Melanie kept looking at her watch. The girl at the hotel desk had said the room would be ready in half an hour. Melanie crossed and uncrossed her legs. Lorna noticed that her brown boots were very beautiful. She supposed Melanie would want to shop for shoes.

She took a sip of cappuccino. Her eyes closed with pleasure. "Isn't it wonderful, isn't it wonderful," she wanted to say, "isn't the coffee delicious, aren't the waitresses' uniforms charming, isn't the chandelier elegant." But Melanie was elaborately, ostentatiously making fanning gestures in front of her face.

"Haven't they ever heard of a nonsmoking section," she said.

"I'll bet there's no Italian word for secondhand smoke," said Jonathan.

"Unbelievable," said Melanie, and they moved closer together, united, a couple once again.

The bellman showed them to their rooms. Melanie didn't even open the shutters. "Don't wake me for lunch," she said.

"I think it might be better if you just took a short nap, and tried to get on Italian time," Lorna said.

"Look," said Melanie, in a way that Lorna knew was more polite than her impulse. "I'm just not up to it."

"I'm with you, Mom. I'll just snooze for an hour, then we'll meet for lunch and do some sightseeing."

"Whatever suits you, dear," Lorna said.

"One o'clock then, it's a date," Jonathan said, cocking his hand like a gun.

It was February, off-season. They had said it to each other time and time again, congratulating themselves for their cleverness—warning themselves in advance about disappointing weather and doors seasonally closed. But Lorna's heart was entirely light when she said the words to herself—off-season—approaching Cappella San Marco, home of the Fra Angelico frescoes. She dreamed that she and Jonathan would have the place to themselves. The silvery disc of sun that fell onto the flat leaves of the plane trees did not have to pass through throngs of tourists or buses; the square wasn't empty, but the traffic seemed normal, native, workaday. There were no lines at the ticket window and no one was ahead of her on the dark staircase that culminated in the famous fresco of the Annunciation.

She hadn't said anything to Jonathan about it; she wanted him to be taken entirely by surprise as she had been—could it have been half a century ago?—when she'd seen it for the first time. Nothing had prepared her for it; no one she'd known had spoken to her of it, perhaps because no one she knew well had ever seen it. The sweetness of the virgin's face, the serious blue of her skirt, the vibrant expectant lunge of an angel, as if he'd only just landed, as if he hadn't given over yet, completely, the idea of flight. And those miraculous wings: solid, sculptural, wings the colors of fruits or jewels, peach, emerald, rust red, the shade of blood but with no hint of blood's liquidity. Tears came to her eyes, as they always did when she saw the fresco. She was not a religious woman, nor a tearful one, but always when she saw it, she wanted to thank someone, she did not know whom. When she and Richard were together they would squeeze each other's hands.

But Jonathan was yawning when she looked back at him with what she hoped was not too expectant a smile.

"Great colors, Mom," he said. "You don't see something like this every day."

Now she must try not to make her smile disappointed. What had she wanted him to say? She wondered if it would have been better if he'd said nothing. And the guards chattered so that it was noisy: the place might as well have been full of tourists. She remembered the Italian word for chatter, which had pleased her for its onomatopoeia. *Chiacchiera*. But now the word didn't seem pleasing; it suggested restless, pointless busyness—not the atmosphere she wanted for Fra Angelico. Jonathan was walking down the corridors, stopping only seconds at each cell, each of which had its own fresco. At the opposite end of the corridor from her, she could see him stretching, doing exercises to loosen the tension in his neck.

Melanie complained that the room was noisy, that the beds were hard and the towels were thin. And Lorna told herself that all Melanie's complaints were justified and wondered why she hadn't noticed. It wasn't that she hadn't noticed, of course she'd noticed, but it hadn't mattered. Be honest with yourself, she said, it's not that you don't understand why it didn't matter to you, you can't understand why it would matter to anyone when there was so much out there, so much of beauty, of greatness. Why would it matter that the beds were hard, the towels thin. She simply couldn't understand.

Melanie would eat only grilled fish and salad. She said the vegetables were drenched in oil. "I wouldn't touch them with a ten-foot pole." Lorna tried not to be irritated as she ate her *farro*, the thick Tuscan soup she and Richard always enjoyed. She wanted to hold the bottle of olive oil to the light and ask Jonathan and Melanie to share her pleasure in its greenness. She wanted to have wine with lunch, but she felt she couldn't because she didn't want to appear a drunkard or a glutton to her daughter-in-law, so slender, so chic, with her long legs and complicated braid.

"Florence is supposed to be a great place for leather. Where's the best place to look for bags?" Melanie said.

Lorna felt that, in confessing that she didn't know where to shop for bags, she was letting Jonathan down, revealing herself as provincial, dowdy, and out of touch. But she didn't remember having shopped when she and Richard were in Florence.

And she didn't remember that, at this time of year, the Piazza del Duomo was so crowded with tourists. In summer, yes, at Christmas or at Easter, but they had purposely avoided those times; it was February now. Why was the square so full of buses? And wasn't this a new kind of tourist, a new kind of American, people in their sixties, abashed couples dressed in matching leisure suits in various shades of blue, new white sneakers dragging themselves across the cobblestones. Were there always so many of the nearly elderly? she wondered. She had read that people were retiring earlier now. Were they traveling because they had too much time and too much money and didn't know what to do with either? Had they always been here and she just hadn't noticed them? Or was it that they were younger than she was now, but seemed older? Herded through the Duomo, the Uffizi, they looked stunned, like oxen that had been struck with a mallet. They weren't seeing anything, they looked miserable; they made stupid jokes to each other. Melanie was right; they did spoil Botticelli's *Venus*, Michelangelo's *David*.

"Jesus, Americans are unbelievable," Melanie said. "The obesity is epidemic. Look at them, men and women, they all look like they're in their third trimester of pregnancy."

Lorna wondered if Jonathan and Melanie would have a child. She rather thought they wouldn't.

On the morning of the third day, Jonathan knocked on Lorna's door.

"Mom, we've had some bad news. One of Melanie's clients is losing his shirt. You know how all the dot coms are tanking. Mel's got to leave immediately and see what can be salvaged."

"Of course," Lorna said.

"Sweetheart, can you manage here alone? She wigs out when she's stressed. I need to be with her."

"Of course," Lorna said.

Dot coms are tanking, wigs out when she's stressed. The words made pictures her mind had to ingest; there were entities, ideas she'd never had to know about that she now had to try to understand. Talking to her son made her feel old. And crotchety. I am becoming a crotchety old lady, she told herself. So she was extra careful to make it clear to Jonathan and Melanie that she'd be just fine on her own, that they mustn't think about her.

"Mom, you're a great sport," Jonathan said.

Go with God, she wanted to say, which she thought odd. It was a thing she never before would have thought of saying.

She told herself it was a blessing in disguise that Jonathan and Melanie had to leave. It was the kind of push that did a person good, particularly a person of her age. What kept a person young was doing new things; what aged a person was giving in to the fear of the unaccustomed. Now she would be traveling alone, like the women she'd admired but had feared to be. Now she would be going, entirely on her own, to places she hadn't been with her husband. And how generous Jonathan and Melanie had been. Jonathan had put an envelope on her bed, full of lire. Fifteen hundred dollars it would come to. And the hotel bill had been taken care of.

It was not the kind of hotel she and Richard would have chosen: the art deco grandeur would have made them feel, as a couple, fearful and at sea. Her room was larger than any she'd ever stayed in with Richard; it was larger than their bedroom in Cincinnati. She looked over all the roofs of Naples. Vesuvius crouched in the distance, and if she stood by the window, the blue slice reminded her that she was near the sea. No, not the sea, she told herself, the bay. The Bay of Naples.

It would have been Richard who had read the history of the place they were visiting, but she had done that part too. He would have learned about the dynasties, the wars, the politics. Now it was her responsibility; she hoped she hadn't skimped. But if she had, what difference would it make now? Who would know? And if something was missed, there was no one to judge her. The loss was only hers.

From her bed she could push a button that opened and closed the blinds. Another turned the lights on and off, a third started the television. She kept mixing them up, and she tried to laugh when, attempting to close the blind, she brought into her room the Simpsons in Italian. She supposed she could learn something from watching it, but she didn't want to. She wanted the darkness. The bed was overlarge; she had not been sleeping well.

On the Neapolitan streets, she had to work very hard not to lose her way. Every few seconds she would look down at her map, then look up at the street signs, saying to herself if Via Chiara is to my left, if left is west, then I am all right, I am not lost. But it was very tiring, this kind of concentration, and she felt as if the part of her brain that had the words for things was being taken up with trying to find her way. She felt she could either get lost or remember the words for things, and she was more afraid of being lost than of being speechless. But it alarmed her that the simplest sentence seemed beyond her now; what she would once have found easy now seemed to her impossible.

She kept telling herself that she wasn't disappointed in Naples, not really, that the weather was really bad luck, that was it, that was what was keeping her heart from its Italian soaring. She very much admired what she saw in the great Baroque churches; she was charmed by the majolica cloister of Santa Chiara, there was a fresco in San Domenico Maggiore that came near to the Giottos in Santa Croce for the freshness of its blues. And beside it was a Magdalene, her gold hair covering her rosy flesh—it was miraculous, really miraculous. She was more tired than she remembered being anywhere else in Italy, and there seemed to be fewer cafés to rest in. She liked that it was a real city, a working city, not some hopped-up showcase for tourists. She remembered a poster in Florence protesting the banning of cars in the city center: "This is our home, not your museum," the poster said. And she had understood. But Naples wasn't Florence; it was a place where people went about their business, and their business was not tourism.

It was wonderful that she hadn't seen a single American in the streets, hadn't heard a word of English spoken. It made her feel proud of herself that she was negotiating this really foreign territory. She ordered her meals competently. On the street of the *presepii*, where figures for elaborate nativity scenes were sold, she had no trouble getting the sellers to show her the pieces that she wanted. Her trouble came in choosing; she was attracted to the elegantly costumed bisque angels hanging on wires from the ceiling—but what difference did it make whether she chose the peach one or the teal, the one in the coral robe with the serene expression, the one with the striped wings and impish grin? And did she really need a fancy Christmas ornament? Who would see it? They weren't expensive; they were lovely, every one of them had its own appeal. Leaning her head back to look up at them had made her dizzy. All the angels seemed to swim into each other, and blur into a wave of indistinguishable colors, features. She left the street of the *presepii* having bought nothing.

One waiter in a restaurant had been kind to her, telling her with a gruff paternalism that she had to have dessert, it was customary, and she needed her strength. She had probably overtipped him, but when she went back the following night she was glad she had. He took her arm and escorted her to her table and told her she must leave the ordering to him. She enjoyed his kindness as she enjoyed the pasta with mussels and clams, but by the time she was back in bed the pleasure of both had worn off, and she felt her body rigid, a supplicant for sleep, which did not come. Was she becoming one of those people she and Richard had secretly condemned: people like Jane and Harry, or Albert and Jean, who could only sleep in their own beds? She must get over this. She was in one of the places history had marked as great; she would get the good of it, she would expend herself, test her limits. For once, she was doing what no one she knew had ever done. No one she knew well had been to Naples. She realized that for her whole life, she had walked in the footsteps of others. Now she would be breaking her own trail.

At 3 a.m. there was a terrifying clap of thunder. You are perfectly safe, she told herself. Nothing can happen to you here. Yet the sight of Vesuvius, which she had only to prop herself on her elbows to see, suggested that the idea of safety was the most fragile of illusions. Flashes of silver lit the heavy mountain with what she thought was a capricious show of force. Then the mountain would hide itself behind gray and become invisible. It was easy to see its malevolence, its carelessness. She thought of the Pompeii mummies, turned to stone embracing, or foolishly trying to run. But was that so bad? What would be lost if she met her end in this way rather than some other? Why not be crushed by a huge, indifferent fist, squashing her insignificance? The idea of her insignificance didn't bother her; she found it comforting—the notion that she would not be very much missed. Richard had gone before her, and Jonathan—well, Jonathan had Melanie. He would grieve her passage, but his grief would not leave much of a mark.

The next day it was cold and rainy; she decided on a visit to the Archaeological Museum; she didn't need good weather for that. She rented a taped guide to the museum, a thing she ordinarily would not have done, but her guidebook had warned her that the museum might be overwhelming, and she felt that, as she was alone, she didn't want to be overwhelmed. But the machine confused her; she seemed unable to find what the voice told her was in the rooms; the spoken descriptions seemed to match nothing before her eyes. Reliefs, vases, tiles: what people had lived with and amongst before their lives were extinguished in a blink— none of it seemed connected to any human experience she could under- stand. After a while she realized that for half an hour she'd been walking up and down the same corridor, in and out of the same rooms. She sat down on a stone bench in front of a showcase displaying drinking vessels and she wept. There is nothing I understand, nothing I understand, noth- ing I understand, nothing I will ever comprehend, she heard her own voice saying. She put on her sunglasses, hailed a taxi in the freezing rain, went back to the hotel, and went to bed. She kept pressing buttons trying to close the blinds; she didn't want to see Vesuvius through the rain. But every button that she pressed was wrong; the lights went on and off; the television blared. She got out of bed and tried to pull the blinds shut, but only a button could effect a change, and she couldn't make the buttons work. She got back into bed, covered her head with blankets, and listened to the outlandish beating of her heart.

She had two days left in Naples. There were many enjoyable things to do. But if she was honest with herself, they didn't seem enjoyable enough to justify the effort. Everything seemed too difficult. Life itself was too dif- ficult, not just life but what life had become. Buttons and audio guides and dot coms tanking. And travel so comparatively cheap and easy, and people with too much money and too much time. Things that used to be simple seemed too taxing now. Taxing. Tax. What was the tax that was paid, what was the rate, and what the currency? And to whom was the payment made? Was it flesh or blood or spirit that was demanded? She thought of Caravaggio's *St. Matthew* in the church of San Luigi dei

Francesi in Rome. The last time she and Richard were there, even seven years ago, they had had to worm their way into a knot of tourists, all of whom looked bored and oppressed to be there. St. Matthew was a tax collector. He gave it all up to follow Jesus. What was it he was giving up, and what was it he was following? She remembered the mysterious light coming through the window, and Matthew's expression of shocked surprise at being called. She remembered her own joy at the painting, a joy that made her heart beat hard, perhaps dangerously so for someone of her age. There were many Caravaggios in Naples. Tomorrow she would begin in earnest to seek them out.

But the next day was Monday. The Caravaggio *Flagellation* was in the Museo di Capidomonte, and it was closed on Mondays. Well, she would look elsewhere. The guidebook said that the *Seven Mercies* of Caravaggio was in a still active charitable institution, the Pio Monte della Misericordia. The sun seemed weakly, tentatively, to be coming out. She would take a taxi to Piazza Jesu and walk down the Via Tribunali. She hadn't been getting enough exercise; at home she swam three times a week. Perhaps that was the reason for her low spirits.

She walked down the Via Tribunali, her money pouch tucked inside her coat, her collapsible umbrella in her pocket. It was a shopping street; it could have been in any minor city in the world. But not a great city; there was no place that lifted her heart with displays of unattainable beauty. She passed a section that specialized in bridal gowns. But all the lace on the dresses had an unfresh look, as if it had been worn before, but in the recent, ungenerous past, by an unsavory groom and unfortunate bride. Everything seemed made of cheap-looking synthetic material, surely not the right thing for a girl's great day. The mannequins seemed squat and fat and middle-aged. She could only imagine that shopping in such stores would be a lowering experience for the girl herself, and surely for her mother. And there was something about store after store of bridal gowns that made the possibility of uniqueness seem out of the question. People got married, as they were born and died; the species must be propagated and the ceremony ensuring the propagation must be marked by something that was meant to be special but, by virtue of its very frequency, could not be. She remembered her own wedding; she'd worn a navy blue suit; it had been a morning in November, a small wedding, but the day had been very happy. Jonathan and Melanie's wedding had been lavish; they'd taken over the Spanish consulate in Chicago; they had paid for everything themselves; it had cost, they told her later, fifty thousand dollars. No synthetic lace for Melanie. It had been, she remembered, quite a happy day. Except that Melanie had lost her temper at the photographer, and had burst, quite publicly, into tears. Richard had settled things somehow, and Melanie had collapsed into Lorna's arms. She'd been touched by the glimpse of the child in Melanie; the orphan child, gamely coping on her own for much too long. For the first time, she wished the young people were with her. She would spend time looking for a postcard that would please them both.

She came to the Pio Monte della Misericordia. The heavy oak door with its embossed studs was fastened shut. *Chiuso,* a sign said, unnecessarily. The guidebook had said it was a functioning charitable institution. But the place seemed so tightly, so permanently shut, it was impossible to imagine anything functioning inside there in the locatable past.

She walked back up the street, as quickly as she could, not wanting to look at the bridal dresses. She wasn't hungry, but she made herself have an early lunch.

The day was warmish now, with a weak sun. A few people were eating at outdoor tables. This seemed such a good idea, here in the land of sun, the *mezzogiorno.* She ordered an *insalata caprese.* The cheese was good, but the tomatoes were unremarkable. She wondered why she thought it would be good to order fresh tomatoes in March. Over coffee she caught the eye of a woman near her age at another table. The woman's formal dress pleased her. She was wearing a royal blue woolen suit, a white blouse that tied in a bow at the neck, plain black pumps, gold earrings. Her hair was pulled back in a French twist. Lorna didn't think that the new informality—dressing down it was called—had been successful. She wondered why everyone liked it so much. Didn't this woman look lovely? Wasn't it better that people should take this kind of trouble than that everyone wear sneakers? She thought with pleasure of her own outfit; her charcoal pants suit, pink silk shirt, black Ferragamo oxfords. She hoped that her appearance pleased the woman as the woman's had pleased her.

"Enjoying Naples?" the woman said, in an English accent.

"Oh, yes, very much," said Lorna. When she told the woman what she had actually seen, it seemed so scant that she felt ashamed. Yet she wouldn't make excuses for herself, for in doing that she'd have to express her disappointment in Naples, her annoyance that so many things had been closed. And she didn't want to do that.

"You must see the monastery of San Marco. Splendid cloisters, spectacular views, a great collection of eighteenth-century *presepii*. A glimpse of that particular Neapolitan mix of elegance and tenderness. And you must take the funicular to get there. You'll see the Neapolitans at their most natural. And you'll think of it whenever you hear the song 'Funiculi, Funicula,' which is written about it." Lorna wondered if the woman would begin singing, which she did not. She was a little sad that the woman, who had seemed to be taking her under her wing, did not invite her home for a cup of tea. She could imagine her apartment. It would be large and dark; there would be a cavernous sitting room with shabbily elegant, uncomfortable sofas and chairs; the light would be dim; on the walls would be etchings of nineteenth-century Neapolitan street scenes, darkish oils depicting the *campagna*. A small, silent servant would bring them coffee in small, gold-rimmed cups. If she was honest, she was more than a little sad that the woman had left without her. She wondered what would happen if she ran after her, caught up with her, started a conversation as they walked. You mustn't do that, she said to herself. The woman would think you were very peculiar if you did that. She ordered another coffee so that she would be sure not to get up, follow the woman, pretend to bump into her by accident. But the loss of the apartment she had conjured in her mind made her feel outlandishly bereft.

The sun disappeared again; she felt drowsy as she walked to the funicular. Had she ever, she wondered as she walked, visited another city where it was so difficult to cross a street? She felt it was entirely possible that the cars would not, in the end, stop for her. The scooters put their brakes on inches from her feet. She waited for the light to turn, hyperalert, as if she were waiting for the shotgun blast to signal the beginning of the race. She thought the light was very long. As she stood waiting for it, a boy on a scooter passed in front of her, carrying a sheet of glass over his head. His hands held the glass; he balanced on the scooter without holding on. Cars veered around him; annoyed at having to slow down, even a little, they honked their horns. His hair was dark and curly and he showed his beautiful white teeth in his smile of defiance and pleasure at this risky task. Delivering a pane of glass through the city of Naples on a motor scooter.

Suddenly she saw how it would happen: a car would not stop for him or would stop too fast, the glass would break and then, as if a line had been drawn across his neck, he would be beheaded. His beautiful head, the curls bloodstained, would lie in the street and cars would drive around it. She would have to pick it up, cradle it in her arms. And then put it where? What would she do with this treasure of a beautiful severed head?

She was trembling as she waited for the funicular. The boy was far away now, she would never know if he'd made his destination safely. Don't think of it, she said, or think of him delivering the glass, think of him sitting with his girl, having a *caffè*. But she could not stop thinking of herself holding the beautiful head.

The funicular started up with a frightening grind. Her eye fell on a mother and a child. The child was lively, unusually fair, she thought, for this part of the world. The mother was much darker. Her frizzy hair looked unclean; her skin was marred by blackheads; she wore rings on each finger, several with large stones; her nails were bitten and her cuticles were raw.

It seemed to Lorna that she talked to the child strangely, as if she didn't know her very well. No, Lorna thought, as if she were pretending to know her well, as if she wanted everyone on the funicular to believe she knew the child well. She could not be the child's mother. She had kidnapped the child, but the child didn't know it yet. She thought she was being brought back to her real mother. But Lorna knew that she would not be brought back. She imagined the dark room where the child would be taken; a bucket would be given to her so that she wouldn't have to go to the toilet; she would be given crackers, warm soda in cans, stale candy bars to eat. How could Lorna tell someone what she knew to be the case? The woman and the child got off. Lorna knew she had left the child to her fate, as she had left the boy on the scooter to his. She had left them to their fate because she had no other choice.

She thought of the beautiful child, the beautiful boy. Left to their fate, left to their fate, kept going through her head. And she could do nothing but get off the funicular, walk to the museum.

It had been a wealthy monastery, closed in the eighteenth century, a museum for thirty years. She bought her ticket, asking for the directions to the *presepii*, excited at the memory of the Englishwoman's words.

"Chiuso," said the guide, a somber blonde, clicking her silver finger-nails, as if Lorna's request had been ridiculous.

"Chiuso perche?" Lorna asked.

"Non so," said the girl. *"Forse in ristauro."*

It would be ridiculous to go back to the hotel, although that was what she wanted to do, go back to her room, close all the blinds, lie in her overlarge bed with the lights turned out. Sleep for a while, then read her book on the Bourbons and order dinner from room service. But this was her last day in Naples, her last day in Italy for who could tell how long. Perhaps the rest of her life. The Englishwoman had said the cloisters were extraor-dinary, the views spectacular. She had obviously been a person of taste.

She walked around the cloisters saying to herself, "I am an old woman now. I will never come back to this place."

The Englishwoman was right, it was a beautiful cloister, but it was beautiful in a way that seemed to Lorna wrong for a cloister. A cloister should be in relation to something growing at the center, grass, or roses, or something lively, natural: the water splashing in the central fountain. But this was a cloister whose referents were classical. The walls were gray, the borders white, the statues were not fragmented saints but white ivory reliefs of heroes. It reminded her of the Place des Vosges in Paris, which she had loved, because it seemed a tribute to geometry, to lines, angles, and planes. But a cloister shouldn't feel like that; a cloister should be a place of prayer. She felt as if she'd put her lips to a child's forehead and had felt cold stone. She pulled her coat closer around her, but she knew that she hadn't dressed warmly enough for the weather, and that nothing she could do right now would make her warm enough.

The guidebook said the chapel was a triumph of the Baroque, that there were paintings by Ribera and Pontormo. But she couldn't find them. The paintings were too high up, too far from their labels. She couldn't tell which painting went with which label, and none of the paintings seemed distinguished enough to be immediately identifiable as a masterpiece. She knew it was the genius of the Baroque to suggest movement, sweep, but she wasn't swept up, she was overwhelmed. Now her coat was too hot; the colors on the wall—mostly reds—were too hot and her head pounded. She nearly ran out to the courtyard, to the open air. She would go and sit on the terrace, where there was the spectacular view of the bay.

But she couldn't find the door that led to the terrace. She kept walking through rooms of maps, none of which had any meaning for her. None of the doors seemed to lead to the open air. Finally, not knowing how she did it, she was back in the cloister. One of the doors of the cloister led to the terrace, the guidebook had said.

She took door after door. None of them led anywhere but to dark rooms. Rooms of maps, of antique silver, of eighteenth-century carriages. She asked the guards for the terrace, and they answered politely, but she had lost all the Italian she once had and their words meant nothing to her. She knew they kept watching her walk into the wrong doorways, come back to the central passage, and take another wrong doorway. She couldn't imagine what they thought. Finally one guard took her by the hand and led her to the terrace.

She thanked him, she tried to laugh, to pass herself off as a silly old woman who couldn't tell her right from her left. But it was true, she seemed unable to tell her right from her left. She was grateful for the white marble bench, where she could sit, where she need choose nothing, make no decision. She looked out over the marble balustrade. Nothing was visible. There was no bay, no city, only a sheet of mild dove gray.

The rain fell softly on her tired face, on her abraded eyelids, her sore lips. It was cool; the coolness was entirely desirable. This gray was what she wanted: this offering of blankness, requiring no discernment. Nothing demanding to be understood. She leaned over the railing. A moist breeze wrapped itself around her like a cloak. She leaned further into it. It was so simple and so comforting, and as she fell she knew that it was what she'd wanted for so long, this free and easy flight into the arms of something she would find familiar. A quiet place, a place of rest, where she would always know exactly what to do.

Intertextuality

My grandmother was serious, hardworking, stiff-backed in her convictions, charitable, capable, thrifty, and severe. I admired rather than liked her, though I always felt it was my failure that I couldn't do both. I was named for her, but I believed that I did not take after her. Now, when I trace something in myself to her, it is always a quality I dislike. Most frequently the righteousness that does not shrink from condemnation, and that feasts on blame.

And so you can imagine how surprised I was that she came into my mind when I was reading Proust. A passage describing a restaurant in the town of Balbec, modeled on Trouville, a town that existed to arrange seaside holidays for the prosperous and leisurely citizens of the Belle Epoque.

What could be further from my grandmother, who never had a holiday until, perhaps, she was too old to enjoy it? Her last, her only holiday, happened in the year of her eightieth birthday. One of her sons and his wife invited her to join them in Florida. They would spend two weeks there, she would spend another two with her sister, who lived in Hialeah.

Just mentioning her sister makes me think of the effective and unsentimental nature of my grandmother's charity. Her sister was eighteen years younger than she, only a year old when my grandmother left her Irish town and crossed the ocean by herself. Twelve years after my grandmother's arrival in New York, having unshackled herself from work as a domestic by making herself a master seamstress, having married a Sicilian against everyone's advice, having borne a child by him and become pregnant with another, my grandmother paid for her mother, four sisters, and two brothers to come across to New York.

When the ship docked my grandmother was in labor, so she couldn't meet it. This meant she couldn't vouch for the new immigrants. So she sent her sister-in-law whose name was identical to hers. My grandmother was a strapping woman, nearly six feet, with large, fair features. My Sicilian great-aunt was a small dark beauty of five-two with the hands and feet of a doll. When my great-grandmother saw my great-aunt pretending to be my grandmother she refused, the story goes, to set foot off the ship. "If that's what happens to you in America, I'm not putting a foot near the place," she said.

Of course this story must be exaggerated, if not completely untrue. My great-grandmother wouldn't still have been on the ship, she would have had to go through the horrifying ignominy of the many examinations at Ellis Island. But the sense of ignominy was not the kind of thing any of my family would include in their stories. I am used to saying it was because they hadn't the imagination for it. I am used to saying they were a hardheaded, hard-hearted, unimaginative lot. But the story of my grandmother that came to me when I was reading Proust makes me think that I have never understood her. Who knows what follows from that failure to understand. What closing off. What punishing exclusions.

My family liked stories that were funny. If a story wasn't funny, there didn't seem to them much point in telling it: life was too hard and there was too much that was required of them all to do. They would never, for example, have told the story of my grandmother's sister and her children, and my grandmother's part in keeping that family intact.

Unlike my grandmother, all of her sisters seemed to have some taste for the feckless. One married a drunk; two married Protestants. My youngest great-aunt had more children than she could afford, although there was nothing to complain of in her husband. He was a good Catholic and had a steady job with the Sanitation. Nevertheless, they couldn't seem to make ends meet. My great-aunt told my grandmother she had no choice but to send her three youngest to an orphanage until things turned around. My grandmother told her sister she'd do nothing of the sort. The children would come to her house to live.

Her sister allowed this to happen, and my grandmother added her sister's three youngest children to her nine. The arrangement went on for two years, until it seemed the time (I don't know what made this clear) for the children to go home.

This wasn't a story told in the family, it was something my mother whispered to me, and it had to be dragged out of her. She had no joy in the telling of it. It was the kind of thing she was ashamed to be taking from where it belonged, that is to say under wraps.

And they would never have told the story of my grandmother's vacation to Hialeah.

The year was 1959. My father had died two years before and my mother and I were living with my grandmother in the house the family had been in since 1920. They had come to Long Island from New Jersey, a move made, I can only imagine, in crisis, although the story when it was told never mentioned crisis, or anxiety, or the alarm of forced change.

The family moved from Hoboken to a small town in the southern part of the state called Mount Bethel because there were nine children and my grandfather, a jeweler, couldn't support them in a city. My grandmother had been raised on a farm in Ireland, or that was the story. But I've seen the house she lived in. You couldn't say the family owned a farm, possibly a few acres, possibly a cow, some chickens, possibly a pig. This was the situation she replicated in Mount Bethel, and this situation was the source of the stories about that time. They were stories about animals, the pigs Pat and Patricia, the goats Daisy and Blanche, the chickens, the endless dogs. All these animals seemed to be in a constant state of adventure or turmoil: they were getting sick or getting lost, or getting hurt, or giving birth, and my grandmother presided over everything, and everything always turned out well.

Then one day the landlord decided he didn't want them there anymore. It was never clear to me exactly how this came about: was it a capricious decision, a vengeful one, had he come to dislike my grandparents, or had they failed to pay the rent? This part of the story was never told. The part they liked to tell (perhaps their favorite story of all because it contained one of the elements they loved to live by, Punishment) was the story of what happened to the house after the family left. After they'd been gone three months, the house burned down. And they were better off, much better. They'd moved to Long Island, which was farm country then, and very anti-Catholic. A cross had been burned on the rectory lawn. But they were able to buy a house there with just enough land to keep chickens. What happened, they liked to say, proved that God's will was in everything, and everything happened for the best.

In 1959, the year that my grandmother took her vacation to Florida, she'd been living in the house for nearly forty years. The house had gone from sheltering nine children to only one, my unmarried aunt, who'd grown to middle age there. Then my mother and I moved in, and there was once again a child for my grandmother to care for: me. I never felt that the house was a good place for a child or that my grandmother was a good person to be taking care of me. I was used to my father, who was playful and imaginative and adoring. My grandmother was busy, and she was a peasant: she didn't believe in childhood as a separate estate requiring special attention, special occupations, to say nothing of diversions. A child did as best she could, living alongside adults, taking what was there, above all doing what she could to be of help because there was always too much work for everyone.

My grandmother's mark was everywhere in the house. She'd sewed slipcovers for the furniture and crocheted endless afghans and doilies. She'd knitted trivets and braided rugs. She'd laid the linoleum on the kitchen floor and patched the kitchen roof in a bad storm. Every decoration was hers: the pictures of the saints, the pious poems, the planters in the shape of the Madonna's head, the dark iron Celtic cross. Inexplicably: the lamps with scenes that might have come from Watteau or Fragonard, the glass ladies' slipper, the tapestry sewing box with the girl in yellow reading by her window in the sun.

The house was my grandmother's and everything in it was hers. Then, one day, my aunt came up with an idea. The children, all nine of them, would chip in to renovate the house. To modernize it. Walls would be knocked down to create a feeling of space and openness. The back porch, which nobody really used, would be collapsed. The front porch would be added to the living room to make a large room, the side porch would become a downstairs bathroom with room for a washing machine. My grandmother would no longer need to go upstairs to the bathroom or down to the cellar to wash the clothes in the machine with its antiquated wringer. She was getting older, my aunt said: it was time she took things easy for a change.

They planned to do the renovations while my grandmother was in Florida, so that when she came back she would be greeted with this wonderful surprise. They hired a contractor who agreed to do all the work in a month. The house was full of busyness and disarray. And full, for once, of men. We teased my aunt that the electrician was in love with her, the contractor's unmarried brother, the man who installed the washing machine.

Miraculously, everything was done on time. One of my uncles picked my grandmother up at the airport. This had been her first airplane flight. The family—nine brothers and sisters, twenty-one cousins—gathered to celebrate her safe landing and the wonderful surprise that would greet her when she opened the door.

It was a new door that she opened, in a new place. She walked into the house and looked around her in shock and pain. Her kitchen, a lean-to that had been lightly attached to the back of the house, had simply been chopped off, carried away. All the appliances were new and all the kitchen cabinets. Her dining room was gone, and her carved table, replaced by what was called an "eat-in kitchen," and a "dinette." She walked around the rooms looking dazed. Then she began to cry. She excused herself and walked into her bedroom, which had been left untouched. We all pretended she was tired, and went on with the party as if she hadn't yet arrived. After a while she came out to join us, but she said nothing of what had been done to the house.

What were they all, any of them, feeling? This was the sort of question no one in my family would ask. Feelings were for others: the weak, the idle. We were people who got on with things.

But the new house weakened my grandmother. It turned her old.

Why could none of her children have foreseen this?

Why was I the only one who noticed that she didn't like the new house, that it had not been a good thing for her, it had done her harm?

But perhaps I wasn't the only one who noticed. Perhaps other people noticed as well. I'll never know, because it's not the sort of thing any of us would have talked about.

· · ·

The memory that was brought to life by my reading of Proust happened the summer after the renovation of the house. It must have been a Saturday because my mother and my aunt, who both worked all week, were home.

My grandmother called us all out to the side steps. She had leaned six green-painted wood-framed screens against the concrete stoop.

"I'm going to make a summer house with them," she said, pointing to me. "It will be yours. It will be for you and your friends."

My alarm was great, and there were, simultaneously, two causes for it. The first and most serious was that I had no idea what was meant by a summer house. I understood that my grandmother, who usually took no time for nor attached any importance to indulgence or endearment, was trying to do something wonderful for me. But I couldn't make a picture of the thing she wanted to do. I saw the six green-painted screens leaning against the concrete, and I couldn't imagine how anything approaching a dwelling could be made of them. And why another house? And where would it be placed?

The second reason for alarm was that I had no friends, and I didn't know whether my grandmother hadn't noticed that. Or whether she had noticed but believed this new thing she would build, this "summer house," would instantly draw people to me, people who once thought of me as having nothing to offer, but now would know they had misthought.

In the midst of my alarm, I heard an unthinkable sound. My aunt was laughing at her mother. That low, closemouthed, entirely mirthless noise that sounded like the slow winter starting of a reluctant car.

"What are you talking about, Ma?" she said. "You can't do that. You're not up to it. And where do you think you'd put it?"

"In the backyard," said my grandmother, with her accustomed force.

"There's no room for it there, we hardly have room for a barbecue. You must be crazy. I never heard you say anything so crazy in your life."

"The boys would help me," my grandmother said. I didn't know whether she meant her sons, her grandsons, or the neighbor children whom she barely recognized.

"Forget it, Ma," my aunt said. "It's not in the cards."

There was a moment of brittle silence, like a sheet of gray glass that stretched between them. My mother and I looked at each other. We were part of the silence, but we knew we were of no importance in it. We knew that something would happen, and whatever it was would be important. And we knew that there was nothing we could do. They'd taken us into the house out of charity. We were only there because they'd said we could be, and we had no right to anything.

My grandmother turned her back to all of us. She tucked three screens under each arm and walked away from us, into the garage, her back straight, her step unfaltering. She closed the garage door, passed silently before the three of us, and went into the kitchen to wash her hands.

The words "summer house" were not mentioned again.

And it's been thirty-five years since I've thought of them. Only Proust's words brought them back to me, his description of the dinner in Trouville:

"A few hours later, during dinner, which naturally was served in the dining room, the lights would be turned on, even when it was still quite light out of doors so that one saw before one's eyes, in the garden, among summer houses glimmering in the twilight like pale spectres of evening, arbours whose glaucous verdure was pierced by the last rays of the setting sun."

I am finishing dinner, alone at my table in the restaurant in Trouville among women in pink-tinted gauzy dresses languidly lifting ices to their lips, or grapes. Their men are in frock coats, indolently lighting cigarettes. The champagne is returned, pronounced "undrinkable." The young waiter reddens, scurries backward, produces the crestfallen maître d'. Outside the sea laps in the distance, the shore is phosphorescent, glow-worms flicker in the arbor, night flowers open, scent the air, retreat. Women rise slowly, men take their arms. No need to hurry, no need, really to do anything but make one's way to bed. A dream perhaps of the sun on the ocean, or a white sail against blue.

And then my grandmother enters in her stern shoes, old lady shoes, black low-heeled oxfords, a version of which she wears in all seasons and for all occasions. Her legs are thick in their elastic stockings, the color of milky coffee; she wears them for her varicose veins. Her housedress has a pattern of faded primroses; an apron is pinned to the bodice. Her ring sinks into the fourth finger of her square, mannish hands.

My grandmother doesn't know where to place herself in this company. For them she has only contempt. She is calculating, with a professional's knowledgeable eye, the cost of the gowns, the wastage of good food implied in every half-emptied dish on the exhausted table. She knows that she is saved and they are lost, that she is right and they are wrong, that she is wise and they are foolish.

Or does she? Is she, perhaps, not judging but yearning? Is she adoring those light, slow-moving people, with their empty hands? Their lovely skins, their high, impractical limbs. Their shoes that could take them nowhere. Perhaps she is not my grandmother, that is to say not an old woman, but a young girl. Her bones are delicate and long. The skin of her hands is bluish white, transparent. She is hoping that one of them will say: "What a pretty child. Perhaps she'd join us for an ice."

And she will sit with them in a summer house, eating an ice, pistachio, lemon, perhaps in the shape of something, a flower or a bird. They will ask her about herself.

And she will say nothing, because she knows that would spoil everything. She will shake her head, refusing words, lifting the spoon from her dish to her lips, silent. Happy, very happy, thinking perhaps of the word "glaucous," with nothing asked of her and nothing that she needs to do.

The Deacon

No romance had been attached to Joan Fitzgerald's entering the convent. She wasn't that sort of person, and she hadn't expected it. A sense of rightness had filled her with well-being, allowed her lungs to work easily and her limbs to move quickly, removed her from the part of life that had no interest for her, and opened her to a way of being in the world that connected her to what she believed was essential. Her faith, too, was unromantic; the Jesus of the Gospels, who was with the poor and the sick, who dealt with their needs and urged people to leave father and mother to follow him—this was her inspiration. Yet when she thought of the word "inspiration," it seemed too airy, too silvery, for her experience. What she had felt was something more like a hand at her back, a light pressure between her shoulder blades. The images she had felt herself drawn toward had struck her in childhood and had not left the forefront of her mind: the black children integrating the school in Little Rock, the nuns in the Maryknoll magazine who inoculated Asian children against malaria.

The source of their power was a God whose love she believed in as she believed in the love of her parents; she felt it as she had felt her parents' love; she believed that she was watched over, cared about, cared for as her parents had cared for her. She had never in her memory felt alone.

Her decision to become a nun, her image of herself as one, wasn't fed by fantasies of Ingrid Bergman or Audrey Hepburn. By the time she entered the Sisters of the Visitation, the number of candidates was dwindling and almost no one was wearing the habit except the very oldest sisters in the order; she'd been advised to get her college education first, and by the time she entered the order, in 1973, only two others were in her class. After twenty-five years she was a school principal in New York City and the only member of her class still in the order.

They joked about it, she and the other sisters, about how they'd missed the glamour days, and now they were just the workhorses, the unglamorous moms, without power and without the aura of silent sanctity that fed the faithful's dreams. "Thank God Philida's good-looking, or they'd think we were a hundred percent rejects," Rocky said, referring to the one sister living with them who was slender and graceful, with large turquoise eyes and white hands that people seemed to focus on—which she must have known, because she wore a large turquoise-and-silver ring she had gotten when she worked on an Indian reservation in New Mexico. Rocky and the fourth sister had grown roly-poly in middle age. They didn't color their hair, they had no interest in clothes, and they knew they looked like caricatures of nuns. "Try, as a penance, not to buy navy blue," Rocky had said. They seemed drawn to navy and neutral colors. They weren't very interested in how they looked. They had all passed through that phase of young womanhood, and sometimes, watching her Hispanic students, and the energy they put into their beauty (misplaced, she believed: it would bring them harm), Joan nevertheless understood their joy and their absorption, because she had been joyous and absorbed herself—though she had wanted to make things happen, to change the way the world worked.

All the sisters she lived with had the same sense of absorption. Rocky, who had been called Sister Rosanna, ran a halfway house for schizophrenics and was now involved in fighting the neighborhood in Queens where the house was located. "They want us out," she said, always referring to herself and the psychotics as "us"—believing, Joan understood, that they were virtually indistinguishable. Four days a week Rocky lived in the halfway house; the remaining three days she joined Joan and two other sisters—Marlene, who directed a homeless shelter, and Philida, who was the pastoral counselor at a nursing home. They shared a large apartment—owned by the order—on Fiftieth Street and Eighth Avenue. They had easy relations with the neighborhood prostitutes and drug dealers, who were thrilled to find that these people, whom they called "sister," seemed to have no interest in making them change their ways.

They could have been almost any group of middle-aged, unmarried women who made their living at idealistic but low-paying jobs and had to share lodgings if they wanted to live in Manhattan, housing costs being what they were. But at the center of each of their days was a half hour of prayer and meditation, led in turn by one of the four of them. They read the Gospel of the day and the Old Testament Scriptures; they spoke of their responses, although they didn't speak of either the texts or their thoughts about them once they had left the room they reserved for meditation. This time was for Joan a source of refreshment and a way of making sense of the world. If anyone had asked her (which they wouldn't have; she wasn't the type people came to for spiritual guidance), she would have said that this was why she loved that time and those words: they were the most satisfying consolation she could imagine for a world that was random and violent and endlessly inventive in its cruelty toward the weak.

Unlike the other sisters, including Philida, Joan had always been too thin. When she thought about it, she thought she had probably become stringy, and her skin, which had tanned easily, was probably leathery now. Perhaps her thinness and the coarse texture of her skin were traceable to her anomalous bad habit. Joan was a heavy smoker. She'd begun smoking in graduate school, the education program at the University of Rochester. Her study partners had all smoked, and she had drifted into the habit. She had wanted to persuade them—and herself, perhaps—that they didn't know everything about her just because she was a nun. Nuns didn't smoke; everyone knew that. But Joan did, though she had tried to quit. The women she lived with didn't allow her to smoke in the apartment; they had put a bumper sticker up on the refrigerator that said SMOKE-FREE ZONE. And of course she didn't smoke in school. She went over to the rectory to smoke.

She was the principal of St. Timothy's School, at Forty-eighth Street and Tenth Avenue. Once all Irish, it was now filled with black and Hispanic children. Joan was proud of what St. Timothy's provided. She knew that she suffered from what one of her spiritual advisers called "the vanity of accomplishment." She knew she had a tendency to believe that she could do anything if people would just go along with her programs, and she made jokes about it, jokes on herself, jokes she didn't really believe. When she made her last retreat, which was run by a Benedictine sister, the nun urged her to contemplate the areas of life that were unsusceptible to human action, the mysterious silences of God, the opportunities for holiness provided by failure. She tried, for a while, to center her meditations the way the Benedictine had suggested, but then concluded that this was a contemplative's self-indulgence; she was in the world, she was doing God's work in the world. There was work to be done, and (was this what she had grown up hearing described as "the sin of pride"?) she could do it. She had long ago given up heroic plans and dreams, but she could make her school run well, and she could give to children—who often didn't have it elsewhere—a place where they were made to feel important, where things were demanded of them, but where they were valued and praised.

Though Joan was frustrated and vexed by the poor quality of many of her teachers, she believed that the children got from her and her staff a quality of schooling they could never have gotten in the public schools. She came to understand that many of the teachers were at St. Timothy's because they wouldn't have been tolerated anyplace else. She put up with most of them, because at least they created zones of energy and discipline. She drew the line, though, at Gerard Mahoney. Gerard had been teaching seventh grade at St. Timothy's since he left his seminary studies, in 1956. Joan was sure he'd been thrown out, not for bad behavior or any spiritual failure but simply because he couldn't make the grade—not then, not in the years when the seminaries were full to overflowing. God knows, she said to herself, nowadays he would probably be ordained. But they'd sent him home, to his mother, who had been the housekeeper at St. Timothy's since, Joan once speculated to Rocky, Barry Fitzgerald was a curate. Mrs. Mahoney had been there when Steve Costelloe arrived, fresh from the seminary, thirty years earlier. Steve had been the pastor at St. Timothy's for the past fifteen years. Gerard's mother had died twelve years ago, after a long illness, when Gerard was fifty-two.

Joan and Steve got along, which was more, she thought, than a lot of women in her position could have said. Essentially, Steve was lazy; his saving grace was that he understood it. He was a pale redhead, with freckles under the gold hair that grew on his hands; he was going bald; he had broad shoulders, but then his body dwindled radically—he was hipless, and his legs (she'd seen them when he wore shorts) were hairless and broomstick-thin. He had a little pot—whimsical, like something he carried tucked in his belt, a crystal ball he tapped his fingers on occasionally, as if he were waiting for messages. He was incapable of saying no to people, which was one reason he was universally beloved. St. Timothy's was a magnet for people who had nowhere else to go; Steve was constantly cooking up vats of chili (his recipe said: "feeds 50–65"), and some unfortunate was always in the kitchen.

Often someone who had no real business being there was found to have moved into one of the spare bedrooms; the rectory, built for the priests, was nearly empty. It housed only Steve and Father Adrian, from the Philippines, who giggled all the time; when faced with the desperate situations of junkies and abused wives, he would say, "Pray and have hope," and giggle. Sometimes Joan and Steve said to each other—thinking of the hours they spent counseling people in trouble—that Adrian's approach might be approximately as successful as theirs, considering their rate of recidivism. In the Filipino parade he'd been on a float, playing a martyred Jesuit. His brother, who had contributed to the construction of the float, blamed Father Adrian for their failure to win the prize for best float. "You were laughing when they hanged you," he shouted at his brother. "That's why we didn't win." "I couldn't help it," Father Adrian said, giggling. "The children made me laugh." Steve was happy to have Father Adrian, because he was willing to take the seven o'clock Mass, and Steve liked to sleep late. Joan suspected that Steve was often hungover. He was in good form by noon, for the larger Mass that served the midtown workers, who came to him on their lunch hour and usually, she guessed, went back to work refreshed.

Problems arose when Steve felt that one of the people in the rectory rooms ought to be moving on; then he would come to Joan desperate for help. She would summon the person in question to the office (not in the rectory, of course, but in the school, next door) and speak firmly about getting a hold on life and going forward. Some of them just ignored her, and stayed on until some mysterious impulse sent them elsewhere. But a few of them listened, and that was bad: it encouraged Steve to ask for her help again, and she couldn't say no to his unhappiness; he was as hopeless as a hopeless child. She often said that the one temptation she could not resist was to try to fix something when it seemed broken and she believed she had the right tools. More often than not she felt she did.

Steve was dreadful with money, and a terrible administrator. He was saved by his connections; people he'd met when he played minor-league baseball, or when he sat in the Sky Box at the Meadowlands because someone had given him a Giants ticket, or people whose confessions he had heard on an ocean liner while he was a chaplain on a Caribbean cruise. Once a year St. Timothy's would have a fund-raiser, and somehow he'd be bailed out. He left the administration of the school to Joan, allowing that she was much better at it than he, and saying, "Just don't get our name in the papers, unless it's for something good." He had no stake in proving himself the boss, and she was grateful for that; when her friends ran into trouble with their pastors, it was because those pastors resented a loss of power. Steve wasn't interested in power; but Joan believed he was genuinely interested in the welfare of his flock. When she was angry at him, because he had foiled her or screwed something up, she thought he was interested only in being universally liked, and that he'd become a priest because it gave him a good excuse for not being deeply engaged with human beings.

In the end he'd backed her up about Gerard, whose shortcomings were impossible to ignore. When she walked down the hall past his classroom, the sounds of chaos came over the frosted-glass pane above the door. She had taken to making random visits; the sight of her in the doorway quieted the kids. Pretending she was in full habit, pretending she was one of the nuns she'd been taught by, she could stand in a doorway and strike what her mother would have called the fear of God into any class. Even the rowdy seventh-graders—the boys who could have felled her with a punch, the girls who were contemptuous of her failure to get the knack of feminine allure—even they could be silenced and frozen in place by the sight of "Sister" staring down at them, as if from a great, sacral height. It couldn't go on.

She talked to Gerard first. Gerard smoked too, and she saw to it that their cigarette breaks in the rectory coincided. She asked him—gently, she hoped (though she'd been told that she wasn't tactful and lacked subtlety)—if things were going all right in his class. He said, "As well as can be expected." She had to hold her temper. Expected by whom? she wanted to say. She said that keeping order among adolescents was difficult, and if he wanted to brainstorm with her and some of the other teachers, she'd be glad to set something up. Then she looked into his dull black eyes, eyes that seemed to have been emptied of color and life and movement, and thought that if there was a brain behind them, it, too, would be inert and dull. No storming was possible in or from that particular brain.

She wasn't someone who thought much about people's looks (whether people were good-looking wasn't a judgment she made about them), but Gerard's looks annoyed her. It was as if he had sat passively by and allowed someone to push his face in; the area from his cheekbones to his lower teeth was a dent, a declivity, a ditch; his lower teeth jutted above his upper ones like a bulldog's. Something about the way his teeth fit made it difficult for him to breathe quietly; he often snorted, and he blew his nose with what Joan thought of as excessive, and therefore irritating, frequency. His ears were two-dimensional and flat, like the plastic ears that came with Mr. Potato Head kits. His clothes were so loose on him that she could not envision the shape of his body. He wore orthopedic shoes, and she imagined that he had a condition no one talked about anymore, something people didn't need to have, which he just held on to out of weakness or inertia. Gerard had flat feet.

He said he was doing just what he'd been doing for forty years, and it seemed to work out all right. He mentioned that one of his earliest pupils was already a grandfather.

She wanted to say to him, What the hell does that have to do with anything? But she was trying to keep in mind what would be best for the children. She suggested breaking up the class into focus groups; she suggested films and filmstrips; she offered him more time in the computer lab. They didn't actually have a computer lab; it was a room with one computer. But Joan thought that by calling it "the computer lab" she would encourage everyone to take it seriously. Gerard, remarkably, was more skilled with computers than most. She imagined him honing his skills alone in his apartment, the one he'd lived in with his mother, playing game after game of computer solitaire, or computer chess, or some other equally solipsistic and wasteful pastime. To whatever she suggested, he responded, "I guess I'll just go on doing what I've been doing. It seems to work out all right."

She was slightly ashamed of her glee when Sonia Martinez, the mother of Tiffany, one of the smartest girls in the seventh grade, came in to complain about Gerard. Sonia Martinez said that the children were learning nothing; that she wanted Tiffany to do well on her exams and get a scholarship to one of the good high schools, Sacred Heart or Marymount; and that Tiffany was going to be behind if she stayed in Gerard's class. She mentioned her tuition payments. You've got to be kidding, Joan wanted to say. Parents paid St. Timothy's a tenth of what was charged at private schools—less if they were parishioners, which Tiffany's parents were. She didn't like Sonia Martinez, who was finishing a business degree at Hunter College and worked for the telephone company, whose children were immaculately turned out, who was obviously overworked and naturally impatient. But she admired her tenacity, and she knew that Mrs. Martinez was right. Sonia Martinez threatened a petition by the class parents.

"Just wait on that," Joan said. "Give me a little time."

Sonia Martinez trusted her; she said all right, but the semester was ticking on, and the placement exams came early in the fall of the eighth-grade year.

As Joan walked over to the rectory, she felt the liveliness in her bones. A salty, exciting taste was in her mouth, as if she'd eaten olives or a salad of arugula. She thought that if she tried to run now, she could run easily, and very, very fast. She felt no concern for Gerard; she told herself that his job was no good for him, either, the way things were, and anyway he was sixty-four; the time had come for him to retire. If Catholic schools were going to have credibility, they would have to have standards as high as those of other private schools. They had to get over the habit of thinking of themselves as refuges for people who couldn't make it elsewhere. Anyway, she told herself, I'm doing it for the students. They're my responsibility. My vocation is to serve them.

This is what she said to Steve, who, of course, said she was overreacting, that Sonia Martinez was overly ambitious, that they had, in charity, to think of their responsibility to Gerard, who had been with the parish all his life.

"So we have to forget our responsibility to the children we are pledged to serve?" she said.

"It's one year of their lives," Steve said. "This school is his whole life. It's all he has."

When she talked it over with her friends, Rocky—who because she dealt with schizophrenics was in an excellent position, she said, to deal with the clergy—suggested that she tell Steve that Gerard probably wasn't happy: dealing with chaotic, aggressive adolescents couldn't be pleasant. Joan should think of something else for him to do.

"What, what can he do?" asked Joan, who was wishing more than ever that their apartment wasn't a smoke-free zone. "He's a complete loser."

"He must be good at something."

"He can't even read the Gospel properly," Joan said. "Didn't you hear him last week—'When Jesus rode on his donkey into Brittany'? You were the one who had to dive under the seat and pretend you were looking for a Kleenex."

"Everybody's good at something. What's he interested in?"

"Smoking."

"Didn't you say he did computers?"

She understood at that moment why people believed so literally in the Holy Ghost, in the purges of fire. A heat came over her head; her own wisdom was visible to her. She would put him in charge of the computer lab. That they had no computer lab was a minor problem. She had been reading about how obsolete computers sat around in offices. She would get Steve to schmooze up his executive friends for donations: Steve would get free lunches, the gift would probably be a tax deduction for them, and they'd think they were buying a few years out of purgatory.

Steve, as she told her friends afterward, fell for the scheme like a ton of bricks. Within a month they had six computers, none of them new but all of them workable. Gerard was more adept at the technology than any other teacher in the school, but so were most of the students. After he'd given the teachers some minor instruction, he had little to do but sit in the corner, watch the teachers and the students work, make sure the switches were turned off at the end of the day, and occasionally dust the keyboards. Everyone was happy—especially Sonia Martinez, who was doing a paper on computer literacy and minority advancement. One of Joan's friends, who taught education at the college run by their order in Brooklyn, was able to pump up one of her students for a stint teaching seventh grade. Joan knew this wouldn't last: the good young teachers left because they could earn more elsewhere, or they got married and then pregnant. But for now things were much better. She hardly saw Gerard except when their cigarette breaks coincided. When she did, she congratulated him on his new job. He said, "We are all in the hands of the Lord."

She wanted to smack him.

Steve told her that the parish was going to celebrate Gerard's twenty-fifth anniversary as a deacon.

"What the hell does he do as a deacon anyway?" she said. "Besides mangle the Gospel?"

"He brings communion to the sick, though sometimes he gets lost and wanders around midtown with the Blessed Sacrament. To tell the truth, he doesn't do much. But it means a lot to him. His mother was heartbroken when he was sent down from the seminary. I think the old pastor really pushed for his deaconate. It's a good thing. Or, as my grandmother would have said, 'It does no harm.' And sometimes that's the best you can hope for."

She wanted to say to Steve, It's the best *you* can hope for, but she held her tongue.

"We're going to have a little party. We'll have Mass, and then wine and beer and pretzels and chips in the basement. Can you organize the children?"

"To do what?"

"Have them sing something?"

"What do you think this is, *The Sound of Music?*"

"Come on, Joanie, give me a break. I'm stuck with this."

"So I provide the entertainment?"

"Entertainment—you? Do you think I'm crazy? Just the organization. That's more in your line."

Joan was surprised at how much what Steve said hurt her. But she determined to forget it. She asked him who was going to be in charge of the food and the decorations. "Marek," he said. Marek was from Poland; he had been an accountant there, but now he wanted to be an artist. He was living in one of the spare rooms at the rectory. He was supposed to be the sexton, and to do odd repairs, but he was as bad at that as Gerard was at reading the Gospel. She wasn't hopeful about the food and the decorations, but one of the things she had learned was that if she tried to do everything, nothing would get done well. It's not my problem, she said to herself; she would forget about the food, the decorations, what Steve had said to her, and concentrate on the children and their song.

She chose the littlest children, who still loved any excuse to perform. She herself had no musical talent; she had hired Josie Myerson, a niece of one of the sisters, who was getting a Ph.D. in music, to come to the school once a week to do music with the children. The girl was energetic and talented, and what she did, if inadequate in its extent, was at least first-rate in its quality. Josie, who was plain and misunderstood by her mother, looked at Joan with a hopefulness that made Joan uneasy. Soon, she expected, Josie would talk about wanting to enter the convent. Joan would discourage her; Josie was too neurotic, and the last thing the order needed was someone who joined because she couldn't make it in the larger world. But Joan knew how to use her power over Josie when she needed to, and she needed to now. Josie taught six of the girls and six of the boys the song "Memories," from *Cats*, which she thought would be appropriate for a twenty-fifth anniversary. Then they would break into a Latin medley, including dancing, which would make them all happy and lighten the tone.

Steve announced at the beginning of the Mass that it was to be said in thanksgiving for Gerard's ministry. Most people, he said, didn't understand the role of the deacon. He could do all the things a priest did except consecrate the Host. His ministry was in the community, and he was of the community; Gerard certainly was, having lived here, on the same block, all his life. Joan was sure that almost none of the parishioners had any idea who Gerard was, other than that he was funny-looking and often made mistakes in the reading. Nevertheless, they applauded him when Steve called for applause, and because it was a Sunday, enough people were there to make the applause sound genuine and ample.

Just after communion Joan went downstairs to determine where the children should stand; she didn't know where Marek would have put the tables, and how she would accommodate the arrangement. When she turned on the light, her heart sank. Marek had done nothing to make the place festive. On one long table were two boxes of Ritz crackers; a slab of cheddar cheese on a plate; some unseparated slices of Swiss, the paper still between the slices; a plate of dill-pickle spears; a bowl of green olives; two bags of potato chips; and a bag of Cheetos. There were two half-gallon jugs of red wine, a bottle of club soda, and a bottle of ginger ale. Two dozen paper cups, still in their plastic. A packet of napkins, also wrapped. On the four pillars that supported the ceiling were taped white paper plates with the number 25 written on them in blue ballpoint.

Desperate, Joan ran upstairs to the rectory kitchen for bowls to put the crackers and the chips in. Frantically she unwrapped the paper cups and unwrapped and spread out the napkins. She ran upstairs again for some ice and looked for an ice bucket; unable to find one, she emptied the ice trays into a large yellow bowl. When the children came downstairs, she told them to stand in front of the food table; somehow, she thought, they made the whole thing less dispiriting.

She'd been worried that there wasn't enough food, but only three adults came downstairs from the church: Father Adrian; Lucinda, the Peruvian housekeeper; and Mrs. Frantzen, who had taught in the school until her retirement, fifteen years earlier. Then Steve came downstairs—he was always surrounded after Mass, and had a hard time getting away—but said he could stay only a minute. He had a baptism in Westchester—one of the assistant coaches of the Knicks had had a baby, and no one but Steve could baptize her. He told Gerard he'd take him to Gallagher's for dinner—that he'd be back at five. "You, too, Joan," he said, running out the doorway. "You'll join us too." He didn't wait for a reply.

She told the children they could eat what they wanted, and they dived for the potato chips. Their activity was a welcome spot of color, because no one had anything to say. They kept congratulating Gerard, and saying what a wonderful thing the deaconate was, and how wonderful it was that he had served the parish all these years, in all these ways. No one said what the ways were exactly. Mrs. Frantzen said how proud his dear mother would be. Father Adrian offered a prayer for the repose of Gerard's mother's soul. The children sang their song but skipped the Latin medley. Father Adrian and Lucinda drifted upstairs. Mrs. Frantzen said she'd have to be going.

Gerard lingered while Joan collected the food to take upstairs. She supposed that eventually Marek would get around to it, but she much preferred being busy over trying to think of something to say to Gerard.

"Well, Gerard, it's quite a day for you," she said, with a false brightness that turned her stomach.

"I count my blessings," he said. She could think of nothing else to say. He helped her carry the leftovers up the stairs. She thought of the upcoming dinner at Gallagher's. She thought that Steve had selected the restaurant because the management knew them, and because they could smoke there. She rarely thought about drinking, but she planned that as soon as she sat down, she'd order a Scotch and soda.

When she got to the apartment, the other sisters were watching a video of W. C. Fields's *My Little Chickadee*. She was glad to take her shoes off, settle on the couch, and join the laughter—much too raucous, they said happily, for a bunch of nuns. It was three o'clock. At four she'd have to get ready for dinner, and at four thirty she'd leave. But she had time to watch the movie. Marlene had made chocolate-chip cookies, and Philida was putting coffee Häagen-Dazs into their blue-and-white ice-cream bowls.

"Now, this is heaven," Rocky said. "Forget eternal light and visions of unending bliss. This is it."

"Ten years in purgatory for blasphemy," Marlene said.

"If only this weren't a smoke-free zone," Joan said.

"If only you weren't trying to kill yourself," Rocky said.

"All right, all right, I'm sorry I brought it up," Joan said. She thought about how Fields's cruelty was delightful, and wondered what it had to do with Gospel generosity, and decided that it had everything and nothing to do with it and she should just relax. She wondered what W. C. Fields would do with Gerard. He certainly wouldn't be going to Gallagher's with him. Or maybe he would. For the steak and the Scotch.

At four thirty the phone rang. It was Steve, from his car, or from the highway beside his car. He was waiting for a tow truck. He wasn't going to be able to get to the city by five. They'd have to go on without him; he'd be there as soon as he could.

"Don't do this to me, Steve," Joan said.

"I'm not doing it. It's in the hands of God, Sister."

"God has nothing to do with it. Just get here. Can't one of your rich friends lend you a car?"

1ary Gordon

"I'm in the middle of the highway. I have to deal with this first."

"Just hurry. Just go as fast as you can."

"Aye, aye, sir," he said, and clicked off.

When she told the other nuns what had happened, Philida was suspicious. "I'll bet he's sitting in someone's rumpus room and just said his car broke down."

"Steve wouldn't lie."

"Steve takes care of Steve."

"And a lot of other people, too. You can't say he's not generous, Philida."

"When it's easy for him."

"I'm just not going to think about it," Joan said, angry at Philida for making things more difficult. "It's impossible enough as it is. Will one of you come with me? Steve'll pay for it. Or probably no one will pay. The people who run Gallagher's are in the parish; Steve probably baptized all their kids."

"Joan, if you had a choice between dinner with Gerard and watching *The African Queen* and ordering in Thai food, which would you choose?" Marlene asked.

"In solidarity with a sister, I'd go to Gallagher's."

"Solidarity is one thing; being out of your mind is another. Offer it up, for the poor souls," Rocky said.

"This is community life? This is my support network?"

"We'll keep the movie out for an extra day, so you can see it tomorrow. The community will pay the late fee."

"That's Christian charity at its most heroic."

"We gave up the virgin-martyr thing years ago, Joan. Hadn't you heard?"

She had what she thought was a brilliant idea. She phoned Gerard and explained what had happened to Steve, and asked if he'd like to put off the dinner until another day, when Steve could join them.

"But then it wouldn't be my anniversary," he said.

"Well, it could still be a celebration."

"This is the day of my anniversary," he said. "No other day will be that."

She gave up. People's wanting something so much often wore her down. She very rarely wanted anything for herself enough to try to force someone into giving it to her. Gerard wanted this, and like a lot of people who had very little else in or on their minds, he had plenty of room for a stubborn will to grow in.

"Great, then I'll meet you at Gallagher's," she said. She couldn't remember when the prospect of anything had made her so sick at heart.

Slabs of beef hung from hooks in the restaurant window. On the pine-paneled walls, behind the red-leather booths, were pictures of New York sporting, political, religious, and show-business figures from the 1890s to the 1950s. Diamond Jim Brady, Fiorello La Guardia, Jack Dempsey, Yogi Berra. Stiff-looking monsignors beside men in fedoras and coats with collars made of beaver or perhaps mink. An age of easy, thoughtless prosperity, a slightly outlaw age, of patronage and conquest and last-minute saves from on high. She thought how odd it was that she liked this place so much, since it had nothing to do with the way she had always lived her life—was the opposite of the way she had lived her life. Yet she didn't feel out of place here; she felt welcomed, as if they had made an exception for her, and she liked the feeling, as she liked the large hunks of bloody meat and the home-fried potatoes and the creamed spinach, more than the Thai food the sisters would be eating, more than the cookies they would devour while they watched the film.

"So, Gerard, it's a great day for you," she said with what she hoped he wouldn't notice was a desperate overbrightness, masking her terror at the fact that after she said this, she would have nothing to say.

"I thank God every day of my life. I count my blessings. Except I have to say I was a little disappointed. None of the old students came. I thought they'd come. The celebration was mentioned in the parish bulletin."

"Oh, Gerard, most of the old students don't live in the parish anymore. And besides, you know how busy people are."

"Still, you'd think at least one of them."

"I'm sure they were at the Mass. You know how shy people are to come to anything after Mass. Catholics simply weren't brought up to do it."

"I was surprised, though."

He wouldn't let it go. She felt, at the same time, hideously sorry for him and angry that he wouldn't accept the ways out she offered him. Did he have any idea how horribly he had failed as a teacher? Was today the first news of it for him? If it was, her mixture of pity and dislike was even stronger, though equal in its blend.

"I'm surprised Father Steve went off to the baptism. You'd think he could have found a substitute."

"I think it was a very good friend."

"He's known me for years."

"Well, you know Steve, he always thinks he can do everything. I'm sure he'll show up. You know his way of pulling things off in the end."

"It's a very important day to me."

"Of course it is, Gerard, of course."

"It was a great blessing, my being called to the deaconate."

Yes, she wanted to say, a job with so little to it that you couldn't screw it up.

"My mother was very upset when I was sent home from the sem. I just couldn't cut it. The pressure was very tough. I think these days they'd say I had a nervous breakdown."

Suddenly she wondered if she had to think of him in a new way, as someone with an illness rather than with a series of bad habits. She didn't know which she preferred, which was more hopeless, which less difficult to bear.

"My mother wanted a son as a priest more than anything. All those years being a housekeeper in the rectory. I really disappointed her. I just couldn't cut it."

"I'm sure you were a great comfort to her in her last days."

His dull eyes brightened. "Do you think that's it? Do you think it's the will of God? That I couldn't cut it at the sem because if I had been a priest, she would have been alone in her last illness?"

"I've heard you were very devoted to her."

"I took care of her for fifteen years. It was a privilege. It was a very special grace."

"Well, then, you see," Joan said, not knowing what she meant at all.

"Still, I was a big disappointment to her. There was no getting around that. And I was disappointed today, that so few people came. Next to my investiture, it was the most important day of my life."

Gerard began to cry. The waiter hovered behind them and then disappeared. Joan wondered what on earth people in the restaurant imagined was going on between them, who people thought they might be to each other—this unfortunate-looking old man and the underdressed old maid across from him.

She tried to give her attention to him, not to think of the waiter or the other diners, not to be mortified at the sight of this man—he was an old man, really—crying, trying to light a cigarette.

"Sometimes I just don't know what it all means."

A wave of anger rose up in her. Anger toward Gerard and toward the institution of the Catholic Church. What was it all worth, the piety, the devotion, if it left him crying, struggling helplessly over an ashtray? Seeing life as meaningless. At least it should have provided him with sustenance. He had missed the whole point; he had taken only the stale, unnourishing broken crusts and missed the banquet. She was angry at him for having missed the whole point of Jesus and the Gospels, when he had been surrounded by them every day of his life, and angry at the Church for having done nothing to move him.

"Surely, Gerard, you know that you are greatly beloved."

He stopped crying and shook his head like a dog who had been fighting and had had a bucket of cold water thrown on him.

"I appreciate that, Sister. I appreciate that very much. That's why even Father's not showing up is the will of God, I think. I always thought that of all of them, you were the one who really cared about me."

She felt sick and helpless. How could she say to him, I wasn't talking about me, I was talking about God. He was looking down at the tablecloth; his shoulders were relaxed, not hunched and knotted as usual. He lifted his head and gave her a truly happy smile.

"You see, you were the only one who cared enough to notice what I was going through. Everybody just let me go on teaching, doing a terrible job, giving me class after class to screw up. Do you think I liked it in there? I was just afraid of losing my job. It's all I have, coming to the school."

"There's the deaconate—you could make something of that."

"I'm not very good with people," he said. "But you figured out what I was good at. You looked at what I was really like. You saw that I had a talent for computers. You paid attention. That's what caring really means. You were the only one since my mother who cared enough to tell me I had to improve. Everybody else thought I was hopeless. They didn't want to look at me, just kept me around so I wouldn't be on their conscience. You really looked, and you found my gift."

Turning computer switches on and off? she wanted to say. Dusting keyboards? Turning out the lights and locking the door?

"Now I know I have a real place, a place where I'm needed, and it's all thanks to you. That's the kind of thing Jesus was talking about."

Oh, no, Gerard, she wanted to say, oh, no, you're as wrong as you can be. Jesus was talking about love, an active love that fills the soul and lightens it, that draws people to each other with the warmth of the spirit, that makes them able to be with each other as a brother is with a sister or a mother with her child. Oh, no, Gerard, I do not love you. You are a person I could never love. Never, never, will I feel anything for you when I see you but a wish to flee from your presence. She prayed: Let me stay at the table. Let me feel happy that I made Gerard happy. Let me not hate him for his foolishness, his misunderstanding, his grotesque misinterpretation of me and the whole world. She prayed to be able to master the impulse to flee.

But she could not.

"Excuse me," she said, and ran into the ladies' room. In the mirror her eyes looked dead and cold to her. She believed what she had said to Gerard, that all human beings were, by virtue of their being human, greatly beloved. But the face she saw in the mirror did not look as if it had ever been beloved, or could ever love.

She looked in the mirror and prayed for strength—not to make herself love Gerard but to sit at the table with him. Only that.

He believed that she loved him. He believed that she had his interest at heart, when all she cared about was keeping him from doing damage to her children, whom she did, truly, love. Only Steve had prevented her from throwing him out on the street. Steve, who, she was more sure than ever now, was relaxing in Westchester.

The poor you always have with you. She heard the words of Jesus in her head. And she knew that she would always have Gerard. He was poorer than Estrelita Dominguez, thirteen years old and three months pregnant, or LaTrobe Sandford, who might be in jail this time next year.

The poor you always have with you. She thought of Magdalene and her tears, of the richness of the jar's surface and the overwhelming scent of the ointment—*nard,* she remembered its being called—and the ripples of the flowing hair. She saw her own dry countenance in the greenish bathroom mirror. She combed her hair and smoothed her skirt down over her narrow hips. She returned to Gerard, who had been brought a Scotch and soda by the waiter.

"On the house," Gerard said. "I told him we were celebrating my anniversary."

"And you, Sister," the waiter said. "What can we give you? A ginger ale?"

"Just water, please," she said. "A lot of ice."

The waiter was an Irishman; he'd be scandalized by a nun's ordering Scotch. She didn't want to disappoint him.

Bishop's House

The Morriseys bought their house in County Clare in the early sixties, before the crush of others—Germans mostly—had considered Irish property. It had been a bishop's residence, a bishop of the Church of Ireland, a Protestant, but it had fallen into decay. Repairs had to be done piecemeal. The Morriseys were both editors at a scholarly press, and they had three children who needed to be educated; it was twenty years before the house was really comfortable for guests.

The house looked out over a valley whose expanse could only be understood as therapeutic. So it was natural, given the enormous number of bedrooms and the green prospect, like a finger on the bruised or wounded heart, that the Morriseys' friends who were in trouble, or getting over trouble, ended up in the house. Sometimes these visits were more indefinite than Helen would have liked. But she and Richard must have known, buying such a house, that this outcome was inevitable. And it soon began to seem inevitable that friends from three continents—

North America, Australia, where their son had lived, and Europe, where they had numerous connections—were always showing up, particularly now that the Morriseys had retired and were spending May to October of every year at Bishop's House.

Lavinia Willis ran into Rachel, Helen and Richard's daughter, on the Seventy-second Street subway platform. Lavinia was crying, or rather she was sitting on a bench trying not to cry, but tears kept appearing under the lenses of her sunglasses. She was crying because she'd just broken up a fifteen-year-old love affair, and although she hadn't seen Rachel in three years, Rachel was the perfect person to run into if you were crying behind your sunglasses. You'd be able to believe she hadn't noticed since it was perfectly possible that she hadn't. Rachel was an oboist and she often seemed not to have too much truck with the ordinary world.

She and Lavinia had been roommates at Berkeley during the troubled sixties, but had both avoided politics. Not that they were reactionary or opposed to what the demonstrations stood for. In Lavinia's case, it was that she had a horror of anything that she might understand as performance. In Rachel's case, it was simply that her devotion to her instrument, a mixture of passion and ambition, cut her off from quite a lot.

Lavinia's parents had divorced and remarried, both unsuccessfully, and had divorced and remarried again. When Lavinia was at Berkeley, they were on their third partners. This made the decision of where to go on holidays a nightmare; even Rachel could see this. For all her musicianly abstraction, she had inherited something of her mother's thin skin for people in distress. She invited Lavinia to come home with her for Christmas of their freshman year.

Lavinia slept on a cot in the living room of the Morriseys' lightless, book-encrusted railroad apartment on the corner of 119th Street and Amsterdam Avenue. But she only did it once; in her sophomore year she left Berkeley to get married. Everyone understood why she'd done it, or at least they understood that it had something to do with the extreme disorder of her parents' lives. Those who thought the marriage was a good thing were happy that Lavinia would have a comfortable and stable home, for clearly Bradford Willis was the essence of stability. Those who thought Lavinia was rushing into something feared she had inherited her parents' heedlessness, a shaky understanding of marriage learned at her parents' joined or separated knees.

But it surprised everyone when, two years into the marriage, when Lavinia was only twenty-one and not finished with her degree at N.Y.U., she became pregnant. Before that, her professors hadn't known quite what to do with her. She was studying history, focusing on the Dutch renaissance; a period she liked because of its subtlety and attention to detail. They could see she was an outstanding student but, since she was married, they were reluctant to suggest graduate school. So it was something of a relief to them when she got pregnant; they no longer had to consider her.

Brad was in a management program at Chase Manhattan, and his parents were happy to help them with their rent. They lived on Eighty-first Street between Lexington and Third, but moved three blocks north a year and a half later when, surprising everyone again, Lavinia became pregnant a second time.

In those years, Helen Morrisey was more help to Lavinia than she would have guessed. She'd drop by once a month with a pot of jam and a book for Lavinia to read, something Lavinia in her fatigue had to work hard to concentrate on. But the mental effort reassured her, and she was strengthened by Helen's belief that she was still capable of abstract thought.

Helen would come on a Friday morning—she worked a four-day week—and talk to Lavinia about politics. She was a draft counselor and encouraged Lavinia to get involved but Lavinia said she was in an awkward position generationally; she'd feel uneasy advising men not much younger than herself. She was sure they'd see her as an East Side matron with two children, and it would make her feel finished, done-up. Helen absolutely understood. She left Lavinia the address of congressmen and senators to write to, and Lavinia did, regularly, following Helen's instructions, changing the text of her letters slightly each time in case that might mean something.

She loved Helen because Helen had a way of asking you for things that were a bit difficult for you, but not impossible. You felt enlarged doing the thing she asked you for, and never hopeless. She would do things for you, but she always made you believe they were things she wanted to do, and if she found them too onerous, she'd stop doing them. She made you feel that her life was full but not overcrowded. She and

Richard always seemed to have room for people, partly because they worked as a tag team. More than Richard, Helen would suddenly need to be alone, and would wander off sometimes when someone was in the middle of a sentence, leaving Richard to say, to the bewildered speaker, "Yes, yes, I know exactly what you mean." They seemed to swim through people, lifting their heads occasionally to offer a meal, a blanket, a magazine. If you were in trouble, they conveyed their belief that your situation was only temporary. They knew you had it in you to overcome whatever was, at that moment, in your way.

They managed to convey that to their own children because the three of them prospered quietly, unspectacularly. Rachel moved back to New York where she taught at the Manhattan School of Music and played in various chamber orchestras. Neal was working in ecological waste management in Melbourne. Clara was the only one who had made money. She and her girlfriend ran a catering business in San Francisco that had, for some reason they didn't understand, become fashionable. When Helen talked about her children she said she felt they all worked too hard. Only Neal had children, two sets, by his two marriages (his first wife had died in a train wreck), but they were in Australia. So Helen had room, in her grandmotherly imagination, for Lavinia's boys. She liked boys increasingly as she aged and grew more boyishly valorous herself, more romantic about the untrammeled, the ramshackle, the hand-to-mouth.

When the boys were ten and eleven, Lavinia went to Teachers College at Columbia for a master's. She got a job teaching history at the Watson School, the best girls' school in New York. She was considered a thrilling teacher, demanding and imperious, although everyone understood this was a mask thrown up by shyness, and that her heart rejoiced and bled at the triumphs and failures of her girls. They adored her; they fell in love with her. She grew, with middle age, into a surprising voluptuousness: her field hockey player's body somehow suddenly understood itself. Men looked at her, as she left her thirties, in the dangerous way they'd looked at her mother, a way that, before this time, she'd tried to forestall.

But as she approached forty, it began to seem ridiculous to forestall it any longer. She had a series of enjoyable but otherwise pointless affairs. One day she was in the back of a cab, changing under her coat from a silk blouse to a cotton shirt. She'd left the house in the cotton, to keep Brad from suspecting, and had changed into the silk in the cab on the way to the hotel. Now she had to change back, and wipe the perfume from her neck with a Handi-Wipe. She caught a glimpse of herself in the driver's mirror and felt grotesque. She was only thirty-eight; she'd been married eighteen years, she'd done all right with her marriage. The apartment was elegant, they had a nice house for the weekends in Dutchess County. But here she was, changing her blouse in a cab. Her youthfulness seemed like a gift and a challenge it would be not only foolish but ungrateful to ignore. She knew Brad would be hurt, but she imagined it would take him about a year to remarry. He was shocked, at first, mainly by his failure to foresee the breakup. He was more hurt than she knew, but she was right that, within a year and a half, he'd married again, a Swiss woman who sometimes wore little hats to dinner parties, and who ruled his social calendar with an iron hand.

For several years, again to everyone's surprise, Lavinia didn't settle down. Then she met Joe Walsh, who was so clearly *the wrong type* that everyone knew it couldn't last, not long anyway.

But it went on for fifteen years. He was a "player" in the Koch administration, nobody was exactly sure what he did, only that it was something that had something to do with City Hall. When Koch lost, he kept doing whatever it was he did for Dinkins, which was unusual, people thought, and must mean that he really knew what he was doing, whatever that was. As all Lavinia's friends began drinking less in the late eighties, Joe didn't. For a while, people thought it was just that he was drinking as he always had and they noticed it more because they'd stopped. But then they had to admit to themselves—they wondered if Lavinia had admitted it—that Joe was, if not an alcoholic, then a problem drinker. He also kept smoking when everyone else had quit, and even took up cigars. One night, after a dinner at the Morriseys' on 119th Street, he earned Richard's enmity forever by putting his cigar out in the water of a glass bowl Helen had filled with nasturtiums. Richard had grown used to the transgressions of his friends, his children, and his children's friends, but he adored his wife as if they were new lovers, and seeing her face when the cigar sizzled in the nasturtium water, he knew that she felt violated, and this he could not forgive.

It was soon after that night that Lavinia decided she'd had enough of Joe. Fifteen years of feverish arguments followed by feverish lovemaking, sour-mouthed morning accusations, resolutions, and recriminations seemed suddenly to settle in her spine like the aftermath of a debilitating fever. She realized that this feeling of bruised exhaustion had become so habitual that she hadn't noticed it. But she noticed it now. And so the next time Joe did something mortifying—he insulted one of their guests on the new color of her hair, asking her who, for God's sake, she thought she was kidding—Lavinia simply said, "I've had enough." It was her apartment they were living in. She gave him a month to find a place to live.

Of course, she would have to go somewhere while he was still in the apartment, and she didn't have time to make plans. But plans had to be made. That was why she was crying when she ran into Rachel on the subway platform. "My parents would love to have you, I know they would," Rachel said. "I'll phone them tonight. You're still at the same number?"

Lavinia said yes she was, that was what was ghastly about it. She was sleeping in her son's room, in the bottom bunk of his childhood bed.

The next morning, Helen phoned as if she knew exactly the right moment to call; it was eleven in the morning but Joe had just left for work. She said that of course Lavinia must come to them, only she'd have to get herself to Bishop's House from Shannon. It was only forty-five minutes, but anyway, Helen said, she'd be happier with her own car, she'd want to see the countryside and not be dependent on the Morriseys to shepherd her.

Lavinia left two days after she spoke to Helen. She slept five hours of the six-hour flight, so she hadn't a lot of time for speculating about what her stay at Bishop's House would be like. She knew it would leave her feeling quiet and without malice—"all passion spent" was the phrase that kept going through her head. She reminded herself that Helen and Richard were eighty and eighty-two, and was prepared to do a lot of the cooking.

The drive from Shannon was as easy as Helen had said it would be. Lavinia had never been to Ireland before, and kept trying to resist making clichéd remarks to herself about the quality of the greenness. But she couldn't help it; it was so purely green, so without blue or yellow, or purple even, that she wanted it in her mouth, which felt scalded from recriminations, or against her eyelids, which had been abraded by hot tears.

She'd brought a dozen bagels and two pounds of hazelnut coffee, which she knew Helen especially liked. They'd be pleased by the gift, its cheapness, its knowledge of their habits. The coffee smell seeped through the shiny fabric of her suitcase and made her anxious for arrival, anxious to feel at home.

The front of Bishop's House was white stucco; it was surrounded by old trees, elms and chestnuts, at once domestic and venerable. The kind, Lavinia thought, you just don't get in America. There were two cars parked in front of the house, a small white Ford and a black convertible sports car. It was a 1965 Karmann Ghia, Lavinia knew, because Brad's parents had bought them one as a wedding present. It was in perfect condition and Lavinia wondered if restoring old cars was a hobby Richard had taken up. It seemed unlikely.

How wonderful they looked, Lavinia thought, both of them opening their arms to embrace her. They were so American, the best of America, forthright and reserved and generous. They became more themselves as they grew older, softer and more tolerant. Tears of love came to her eyes and she buried them in the wool of Richard's shoulder.

"I'll take you to your room," Helen said. The huge black front door opened to a hallway, tiled black and white. Almost directly behind the door was a wide mahogany staircase with a red stair carpet that had faded in places from the sun. Lavinia's room was the second door from the staircase; she knew from Rachel that Bishop's House had six bedrooms.

"You look done in," Helen said. "You probably want a sleep, but I'd resist it. Try to stay awake till nine or so, get yourself on Irish time. I'll make coffee and we'll have a walk."

"Look what I've brought you," Lavinia said, flourishing her Zabar's bags.

"Hazelnut," said Helen. "You're a perfect angel, as always. I'm afraid I'm not, neither perfect nor an angel. I'm afraid I'm a bit of an old fool, I've allowed something stupid to happen."

Lavinia's heart sank; she was afraid Helen was going to tell her that she was ill, or that Richard was, and that she'd have to leave because one of them was going to the hospital. She couldn't bear the thought; she could have taken the illness or death of one of her own parents more lightly than Helen's or Richard's. It was absolutely essential to the well-being of the world that they be in it.

Helen sat down on the bed and patted it so that Lavinia would sit beside her.

"Do you remember our friend Nigel Henderson?"

"I'm afraid I don't," Lavinia said.

"You must have met him one time or another. He and his wife Liz lived next door to us for three years. He was on lend-lease to Columbia back in the seventies. They're English. Perhaps you were too busy with the children."

"I'm not young enough for you to be erasing whole decades," Lavinia said.

"Nonsense, you're a baby. It's just that you're getting over a love affair. It makes everyone feel ancient," Helen said, making Lavinia wonder, for the first time, if she'd been unfaithful to Richard.

"Poor old Nigel," Helen said. "He's sort of a mess. Liz left him for a woman, and he stopped taking an interest in teaching. He shacked up with one of his students and took early retirement. They were going to live in Bali or something but it never came off. She took off instead. Anyway, here he is, no job, no girlfriend, and I'm afraid he's just been told he has terminal cancer."

"How terrible," Lavinia said. "How old is he?"

"Fifty-six."

"My age," Lavinia said.

"So you see when he phoned two days ago, really sounding desperate, asking if he could come over on the car ferry, we didn't feel we could say no."

"Of course not," Lavinia said.

"He's always been a bit pathetic, one of those overgrown boys, but this is really dreadful."

"Dreadful," said Lavinia.

"And dreadful for you. You come here to be petted and recover your spirits and we turn you into an angel of mercy."

"Maybe it'll be good for me," Lavinia said. "Put my own trouble in perspective."

"And there's always the Irish countryside. Nothing can spoil that."

The kitchen was in the basement and was dark, but Helen had made it cheerful with flowering plants and brightly colored pottery. Richard was at the stone sink, filling an electric kettle.

"Angelic Lavinia brought us some hazelnut coffee," Helen said.

"Good God," a voice said from the other darker end of the kitchen. "You Americans can never leave well enough alone."

"This is Nigel," Helen said. "We make him go to that dark corner if he has to smoke."

There are some bodies that belong to a particular time period, Lavinia thought. Medieval bodies, eighteenth century bodies. Nigel Henderson's was the sixties model. He was long-legged and narrow-chested; his jeans were tight and he wore sandals with a leather ring for his big toe. His hair was gray and wavy and he wore it to his shoulders.

He walked toward her. "Somehow in all my ghastly years in New York we managed not to meet, which made them even ghastlier."

His eyes traveled from Lavinia's breasts to her thighs in a way that made her feel the time difference. It was four in the morning in New York and she wanted to be asleep.

"I'll just help Helen with the coffee," she said. "We all know Richard's useless."

"Unfair, unfair," Richard said.

"Perfectly true," Helen said. "I only put up with him for his conversation."

Helen walked with Lavinia through what she called "our field." Nothing grew there but grass, and Helen apologized for that. It made her feel like a tourist, she said, wasting the country's riches, but she really wasn't up to raising cattle or even keeping goats.

"I think it's all right, Helen. The country's lucky to have you."

Helen frowned and said something that Lavinia couldn't hear though it sounded like "humbug." She hated being complimented, and Lavinia knew that and felt slapped, or slapped down.

"I wouldn't be surprised if Nigel tried his charms out on you. I suppose it's understandable, given what he's facing right now, but it might be a bore for you. On the other hand, it might be amusing for you. I can never tell."

"Tell what?"

"What, or who, young women find attractive. Or anyone, for that matter. Of course he's attracted to you. I suppose it's unfair of us, offering him a bed down the hall from such a sexy girl."

"Hardly a girl, Helen," she said.

"That's how I think of you and I'm sure Nigel does, too."

For a moment, Lavinia liked thinking of herself as a young girl, walking down a street, her step bouncy with the knowledge that all eyes that fell on her desired her. But only for a moment. Then she realized her body was tired, worn out, dried up, and what she wanted was not sex but replenishment and rest.

"Oh, God, Lavinia, I'm afraid we've put you in an awful spot. I hope at least he'll leave you alone to read and walk. And the lake just down the road here is lovely for swimming, if you can bear the cold, which I know you can because of your summers in Maine. I know he can't stand it. He's always complaining about the cold. And he's a late riser. So get up early with me, we'll have breakfast together. I'll make a lunch for you and you can pack it on your back with a book and be on your own. And thank God you have your car."

It sounded like a good plan, a refreshing plan, and Lavinia knew that was what Helen meant. But it made her feel a little sick, both fearful and ashamed, her childhood feeling when she was being packed off somewhere, sent off for someone else's idea of her pleasure.

Richard and Helen didn't modify their policy of leaving their guests to themselves because Nigel had terminal cancer, or because when he was left alone he seemed to do nothing but take over the sofa in the pretty sitting room, empty Richard's whiskey bottles into his Waterford glasses, and fill the clear air with the smoke of his cigarettes. He left the packets— Silk Cuts—in the grate of the fireplace. They collected there until someone—Helen probably—removed them. It was summer, no one was lighting fires. Did he think, Lavinia wondered, that his packets just disappeared? She wanted to say that to him and she wanted to ask him if he thought it was good for someone with terminal cancer to go on smoking, or didn't he feel that all that smoking had brought him to this pass. But she didn't say anything because she didn't want to upset Helen and Richard, who could only go on as they did if they believed their guests were getting on just fine.

Nigel wanted attention—from the Morriseys, from Lavinia—but he went about getting it exactly the wrong way, as wrongheadedly as a child who will never win his parents' love and whose every gesture leaches what little sense of duty they might have. Helen walked in the mornings. Lavinia sometimes joined her but only sometimes, on the days that Helen specially asked her to. She knew if Helen didn't ask her it was because she wanted to be alone. In the afternoons, if it was warm, she swam in the little lake and she did want Lavinia's companionship. Richard didn't swim, but she made him come with her if no one else was swimming, in case "I got a heart attack and disappeared."

She said it matter-of-factly, as she might have said "In case there are no bananas in the market today." This was the way the Morriseys dealt with their age. Nothing was blinked, but nothing was dwelt on longer than it should be. They always made you feel, Lavinia thought, that they knew how to live. That was why it was good to be around them, and that was why Lavinia said nothing to Nigel, even at his most unpalatable.

She said nothing when she opened the door after her bath and found him leaning on the wall right across from the bathroom, slouched against it like a juvenile delinquent, smoking one of his endless cigarettes. And she said nothing when, one night, he'd had too much wine to drink and went on a tirade about what he called today's woman. "Wombman. They have a womb but they want to be men.

"I mean, for God's sake," he said. "Anatomical differences count for something. Men have more strength. Women can bear and nurse children. I mean, shouldn't that tell us all something? Or am I quite mad? Perhaps I am quite mad. That's what Liz thought. No, I'm wrong. That's not what she thought at all. She just thought I was stupid. Plain stupid. 'You think with your cock,' she said. That was her greatest insult. And precisely that dyke's greatest asset. Made her brain clean: no cock to cock it up."

"I'll just make coffee for everyone," Helen said.

Richard suggested that perhaps one day soon, if the weather was good, they might all drive up to Coole Park, where Lady Gregory had lived, and see the tree where Yeats and Synge had carved their names.

"I mean really that's what it was all about with Liz. She couldn't stand that I had a penis and she didn't. That's what it all came down to. She rejected my penis out of her own bloody envy at not having one."

"I think that's been considered, and rejected as a theory," Lavinia said. She looked at Richard's disappointed eyes, and wished that she'd kept her resolve of saying nothing.

"Wall, wot wuz yer problem," Nigel said in what he thought was an American accent. "Was your husband's cock too big or not big enough?"

"Nigel, you must go to bed now," said Helen. "You seem overtired."

He covered his face with his hands. Lavinia thought that his hands were his best feature; he should have covered his face with them all the time. Then she could see that he was weeping. His shoulders shook and he began sobbing loudly, with no impulse to silence himself or to stop.

"I'm not overtired, Helen. As you perfectly well know. I'm drunk, and I'm dying."

It would have helped if there were some background noise: the ticking of a clock, the rumble of a dishwasher. Even the chirping of a cricket. But there was no sound in the room at all; it was a mark of how simply the Morriseys lived. And simply, they had to sit in the tumult of noise Nigel was making and endure it, unadulterated. Then Nigel stood and shook himself like a wet dog. He walked up the stairs, saying good night to no one.

"Oh, God," Helen said after she'd heard his door close. "I behaved like a fool. The poor, poor desperate creature. He's dying and he has not one real human connection. And I made it worse."

"No, Helen," Richard said.

"Well, I didn't make it better."

"That's as may be," he said. "But you didn't make it worse and there's a difference."

"And you did make it better, both of you," Lavinia said. "He feels less alone here. Less as though life were ridiculous, or hopeless or absurd. You make everyone feel that."

"Well, we could all use a rest," Richard said, pointing the way up the staircase, which Nigel had climbed in the dark.

Lavinia couldn't sleep. There was a full moon and the muslin curtains didn't keep it out. It made a pool of not quite light—but illumination—on the oak floorboards. She thought of all the people who'd slept in this room before. Most of them long dead. And Nigel was facing death alone. What was it like for him? Was he looking down a long, dark corridor? A tunnel? Or into an endless sky or into an endless well? She wondered if he was terrified or numbed. She wondered what it would be like for her.

It would be different. She would have her children, her friends, students whose lives she'd touched. It wouldn't be what it was for Nigel: that horrible aloneness, that sense that you'd been given a life, that it was being taken from you and you'd done nothing with it but make a mess.

She was thinking of him so intensely that she wasn't surprised when she saw the knob turn, and the door open. He stood in the doorway, framed by the light from the hall.

"Do you mind?" he said.

"No, not at all."

He walked directly to the bed and sat down on it. She propped herself up on her elbow. He kissed her; his mouth was rough from cigarettes and wine. His hair was a little unclean and she could smell his armpits, not dirty, exactly, but unfresh. None of that mattered. He was alone and he was dying. She could give him this, if this was what he wanted. They both knew that it could be his last time.

He nuzzled her breasts halfheartedly, he knew what he was after. He didn't make much attempt to arouse her, they both knew it wasn't about that. He finished, and lay on top of her a few moments. Then he said, "At moments like these, I need a cigarette. Do you mind if I turn on the light?"

She put on her nightgown and looked around for an ashtray, but of course there wasn't one.

"It's all right, I'll flick it out the window."

"Careful," she said. "We don't want to wake Richard and Helen."

"What's the matter? You don't want them to know what you've been up to?"

"No, I don't want to disturb their sleep."

"What do you think they'd say? That you were a nasty girl, or an angel of mercy? Jezebel or Florence Nightingale?"

"There's no need to be unpleasant."

"I don't do it out of need. I just seem to be rather good at it. Which is why I find myself alone most of the time."

He was challenging her to meet his eye, but she wouldn't.

"It's remarkable how many friends a death sentence brings you. For instance, yourself. You'd never have let me have you if you didn't think I was on my way to never-never land."

"That's not true."

He snorted. "Oh, get off it. You're not going to tell me you're fond of me, or that you found me strangely irresistible. You fucked me because you think I'm going to die."

"Nigel, there's no need for this."

"You're feeling quite good about the whole thing," he said. "You feel generous and mature, and womanly. You gave of yourself. The supreme sacrifice. Like wartime. Give him a little of what he fancies before the cannonball gets him. But suppose I told you it was all bullshit? Suppose I told you the biopsy report came back and I was given a clean bill of health?"

"I don't believe you," she said.

"Oh, my dear, it's quite true. I did have a tumor. You see here." He took her hand and made her feel an indentation in his thigh. "The quacks said it was quite possibly malignant. Well, I was scared at that, and I fell apart, rather. And I told people, I thought, why the hell not. And people were wonderful. I mean, fucking heroic. Better to me than they'd ever been. And of course whose parental bosom did I want to rest my head on but good old Helen and Dick? Normally, I wouldn't have had the nerve to invite myself. But I called up, told them the news calmly, like a good soldier. So they said, of course, dear, come right over on the fucking car ferry. Only just before I left, the doctor called. Quite thrilled. Benign, old chap, he said. Apparently I'll live forever.

"Well, I couldn't tell Helen and Richard that. Think how disappointed they'd be. Dying, I had a certain tragic interest. Healthy, I'm just a pathetic pain in the ass. And think how they've always loved being the still clear pond for the world's lame ducks. Why, they wouldn't know what to do with themselves if everyone's lives were shipshape. They must know it. Certainly you know it. Still, they are a couple of old dears. And not as young as they once were. Which is why I know you'll keep our dirty little secret. Won't you, love?"

He reached over to kiss her.

"You're disgusting," she said.

"That's as may be, but I've just fucked you, haven't I?"

"Get out," she said.

"Right you are. And I'll clear out in the morning. Everyone will understand that I'm abashed after my little weeping fit last night. And I'll let them know you were a real help. A great comfort."

She wanted to go to the bathroom to brush her teeth. Her mouth felt foul from his foulness. But she didn't want him to hear her doing it.

She wondered if it were possible to make him believe that the whole thing meant nothing to her. That she went to bed with anyone, absolutely everyone, because it was easier than saying no. But she had no idea how she would do that.

He wasn't stupid. He seemed to understand things very well. He'd even made her see the Morriseys in a way she must always have known was possible, but had always avoided. Were they parasites, feeding off the misery of others for their own prosperity? Was the misfortune of those they called their friends the elixir that kept them safe? That kept them from the kinds of risks that could distort or wreck a life? The kinds of risks she'd taken, and her parents had, and Nigel and his wife and his wife's girlfriend? But not the Morriseys. And not their children.

She'd have to stay a couple more days so it wouldn't appear that her leaving had to do with Nigel's. Perhaps the day after tomorrow they'd all go to Coole Park. She'd take them out to a good restaurant. They'd talk about Nigel, the pity of it, the waste. They would say she must come back to Bishop's House again soon. Perhaps next summer.

But she wouldn't. She couldn't now. And when the Morriseys came back to New York, what would happen then? They were getting older. They'd be needing help. But there would be hundreds of people who'd want to help them, grateful, eager people. They wouldn't need her.

After a while they might say, "We haven't heard much of Lavinia lately." They'd assume it was because she was happy.

The Translator's Husband

I never told Barbara about being married before. It didn't occur to me that there was any point. It had happened long before I met her, it was very brief, and I couldn't imagine they'd cross paths.

Brenda was very young when we married. So was I, of course. We were both students. She was over on a year's exchange from Birmingham. She wasn't too serious about her studies. She had an ear for languages, but that didn't mean she was a real student. A kind of giggly girl, and there was a market for that kind of giggly English girl then, in the late sixties. The Beatles and all. You know that kind of blonde girl with milky skin and chunky calves, the kind that her own kind would have called "a thoroughly good sort." The kind who wouldn't mind a friendly slap on the rump from a stranger who'd had an extra beer or two. The kind who wouldn't take things the wrong way. She was really good-natured, Brenda.

She left me for someone else. A ski instructor. I was the one who'd hired him. I was the one who thought I needed help, she thought the whole thing was a big joke. She could have easily broken her leg and spent the entire time in the hospital. She was completely unprepared. Hans, his name was. He was Austrian. They spoke German to each other. I was completely in the dark.

I suppose I was always too serious for her. "You're so serious, Dickie," she used to say. No one but Brenda called me Dickie. I used to be called Dick, but now everyone calls me Richard. She said she liked it, that I was so serious, but I think she got tired of it pretty soon. My mother'd warned me; she said Brenda was flighty. I was working hard; it wasn't easy getting accepted in comp lit at Indiana in those days. I had to pass proficiencies in French and Spanish, which is how I met her: she was offering Spanish tutoring. I mean, I couldn't be out on the town every night with the kind of exams I had to take. I don't blame her, but it's impossible not to connect my failing the prelims with her leaving me for Hans. Well, they were very competitive, a lot of people didn't make it. I'm not the only one in the world with a terminal master's. Barbara says that sounds like some kind of mortal disease, when I mention it. But it qualified me well for what became my job. I teach French and Spanish in a very fine prep school. One of New York's very very best, and that means among the best in the English-speaking world.

That's how I met Barbara: her son was failing Spanish. I really pulled him through. She was very grateful. A lot more grateful than Nathan was. He was never much of a student. Which is surprising in the child of two such accomplished parents. Barbara's former husband is a neurologist and anyone who has the sense of literary fiction knows her name.

I hadn't heard from Brenda in fifteen years when I met Barbara. We've been married for twelve years now, and we dated for three years before we tied the knot. "Tied the knot." That's the sort of expression Barbara laughs at me for. She says I'm the only person she knows of who qualifies for the description "quaint." Sometimes she calls me her old-fashioned beau.

She teases me a lot, and I don't mind it really. It's all in good fun. All her friends join in, sometimes it might seem a bit rough, but I never let on when they've cut a bit close to the bone. I think her friends consider me a babe in the woods. They'd be surprised if they knew what a lively time Barbara and I have between the sheets, and they'd be shocked at the number of students' mothers who made their way into the foldout bed in the studio where I lived before I moved into Barbara's duplex on Park and Eighty-ninth.

Barbara's novels are translated into several languages. I used to keep track of the French and Spanish. You'd be appalled if you knew how many mistakes are let through the net. I used to make a list and send it to the translators, but Barbara told me to forget it, they wouldn't change anything and it just made her look "compulsive." Is there a line between compulsion and accuracy, I asked. She said I should just relax, that she had better things in mind for my energy. And she pulled me into bed.

So I never even looked at the Spanish translation of her latest book, which is why it wasn't till we were actually in Madrid that Brenda's name jumped at me from the page. Or rather, hit me like a ton of bricks.

What were the chances of it happening? That my first wife should turn out to be the translator of my second? I mean, really. I couldn't have anticipated it. If I could I certainly would have told Barbara about Brenda. But it wouldn't have occurred to me that Brenda would turn out to be that intellectual. Translating someone on Barbara's level. I mean, she left me for a ski bum. And Barbara is of the very first water. It only just dawned on me that both my wives have two-syllable names beginning with *b* and ending with *a*. I don't suppose it means anything really.

I guess it's a good sign that Brenda didn't write to Barbara first crack out of the box to tell her what they had in common. But then it's possible she didn't know. Likely even. My name isn't mentioned on the book jackets. Only "Barbara Hanover lives in New York." She thinks more information is vulgar.

It isn't such a big thing really, except for that one little sentence. I mean, if Brenda had translated any of her other novels it wouldn't have been a major event at all. And it's only that one sentence. Just a very small detail really. It's very likely Brenda didn't even notice.

Barbara likes me telling her things about the sexual behavior of the women in my past. It isn't that it turns her on. "Material" is what she calls it. I mean she is a novelist. Human behavior is her bailiwick. It would be like keeping the details of a disease to myself if I were married to a doctor. I simply wouldn't feel I had the right to do it.

Brenda did have this odd little tic. She liked to be on top, that was the only way she liked it. There's nothing so unusual in that. But when she climbed on she'd start saying this nursery rhyme. Quite a silly thing, really. "Ride a cock horse to Banbury Cross / To see a fine lady upon a white horse." She would get more and more excited as she said, "Rings on her fingers and bells on her toes." And when she got to the word "ever" in

"She shall have music wherever she goes," well, that was her point of climax. You have to admit it was noteworthy.

Barbara used it in this novel. The one Brenda translated. It's not spoken by a major character or anything. Just a little fling of the protagonist. The whole episode between them is over in two pages. It's hardly even there at all. And I was married to her less than a year.

I told Barbara's Spanish publisher he didn't have to have the translator come to Barbara's interviews. My Spanish was flawless, I told him. I made a point of saying that Barbara and I were very much on a wavelength. He kept saying. "No, no, my dear sir. You must rest. Or see our beautiful city." I'd already told him I'd never been to Madrid before. There wasn't any way I could unsay that. Water over the dam.

The day we were supposed to meet Brenda, I told Barbara I was feeling sick. She's used to my having a jumpy stomach, particularly when we travel, so she didn't bat an eye.

I'm sitting on the couch in our suite in the Ritz on the Place Cybele. Right down from the Prado. God knows how many thousands of pesos it's costing a night. I've now finished the fourth little bottle of Glenfiddich in the minibar. I'm starting on the fifth.

I've been sitting by the window for an hour waiting to snap to attention the minute I see Barbara walking up the plaza, approaching the entrance to the hotel. It's been a very long lunch. But I guess that's a Spanish custom.

Oh, dear, Barbara doesn't seem to be alone. She's with another woman. It seems to be Brenda. I can see them walking up the plaza now, between the rows of plane trees. Their arms are linked. They are swinging their free arms, the ones that are holding their black purses, which are very similar.

That's a relief. I'm sure now everything will be all right. I hadn't remembered they're exactly the same height. Barbara colors her hair platinum. For all I know Brenda might still be a natural blonde. I mean, it has been thirty years.

They don't look a bit angry.

They're both laughing.

Now they're under the awning. Now I can't see them. They must be waiting for the elevator. They'll be here any minute.

I am casually but quite correctly dressed. Brooks Brothers khakis, yellow Lacoste shirt, Bally loafers with tassels. Brenda will be quite impressed. Last time she saw me I got my clothes in the Salvation Army. And I was thin as a scarecrow. I work out three times a week with Barbara at the gym. We're both fit as fiddles.

I'll be very casual when they'll come in. I think I'll say, "Of all the gin joints in the world, you have to come into this one." I'll say it in a Humphrey Bogart voice. I'm sure she'll laugh.

Now Barbara's key opens the door.

I close my eyes. I hear them both still laughing.

"Richard, darling," Barbara croons.

"Dickie, love," cries Brenda.

I must say they're both being marvelous about it. They both keep saying "what a hoot."

We all go out to supper. They say it has to be my treat. Which is a little hard, since the publisher was prepared to pick up the tab for all Barbara's expenses. Under the circumstances, though, I suppose I have to go along with the gag.

Brenda introduces me to the waiter as "our husband." He looks puzzled, but he nods and smiles. I think they've both had a bit too much champagne. Dom Perignon. Of course, I don't begrudge them. I really should be celebrating too when I think of what the situation could be.

Every now and then one of them breaks into "ride a cock horse," and they both fall over laughing. They seem to get along like a house on fire. I've hardly got a word in edgewise the whole evening.

Not that I have that much to say.

The Epiphany Branch

Florence Melnick went to the library every day. Well, not every day: the library was closed on Sundays and legal holidays. Christmas was considered a legal holiday although in her opinion there was nothing legal about it, it was religious, and Florence was Jewish and Christmas was nothing but another day to her. So she resented it that everything was closed up on that day. She thought it violated the principle of separation of church and state, which had been so important to the Founding Fathers.

The branch of the New York Public Library that was, unfortunately in her opinion, closest to where she lived was called the Epiphany Branch. It was on Twenty-third Street between Third and Lexington Avenue, or, as everyone who didn't have something wrong with them said, Third and Lex. That was one thing she took comfort from when she moved there from Brooklyn: it seemed friendly that she'd be living on a street that had a nickname.

But she'd never been happy in the neighborhood, never. She'd never felt that she belonged. In the old days in Flatbush, she'd known every-body, but everybody had moved out when they had the chance. Including her, when her nephew Howard had presented her with the opportunity. Her sister Ethel had had a stroke. Ethel was a widow and Florence never married. Why exactly she never knew. She would have been willing with the right kind of man. But not a fool, not someone with nothing in his head except what was between his legs, not someone with no ideals who only thought about food and money. Florence loved to read, she always hoped to meet someone who loved to read, but it hadn't happened. Not with any of the men she'd met in the forty-five years she'd worked as a saleswoman at Lerner Shops on King's Highway. Of course, you could say, in her line of work, retail clothing for women, it wasn't that likely that you'd meet so many men. Salesmen you'd meet, but rarely of the right type.

So she'd retired after forty-five years. They gave her a lovely party and a silver tray with her name engraved. Everyone said, "Keep in touch, Flor-ence," but when she tried to think who she really wanted to keep in touch with, no one came to mind. Her parents had died. Ethel was in Manhat-tan, but she had a life of her own, they didn't share too many interests. But when she had the stroke and Howard made the suggestion—tactfully try-ing to point out that Flatbush wasn't what it had been, and that his mother had a two-bedroom apartment that he was paying the mainte-nance on, not chicken feed but nothing compared to what a nursing home would be, to say nothing that his mother would rather die first—well, it all seemed to make a great deal of sense.

And really there was nothing she really missed about Brooklyn except the Main Library at Grand Army Plaza. That was a library: marble and carpets and big ceilings and mahogany. They knew how to use materials in those days. They spared no expense. The library was right on the park, and the other side was a square with a statue of a soldier. When she walked into the door, the word "cavernous" came to her mind: empty space, dark air. Even the air was scholarly. You could take a book off the stacks, walk up the stairs, and read it in the reading room. Real wood pan-eling. The Epiphany Branch was one big room, materials skimped every-where. But what could she do; it was where she lived, she was seventy-eight, she wasn't up to much traveling. Not in Manhattan.

Ethel only lived two months after Florence moved in. And there she was, in the middle of Manhattan, but no, not in the middle, it wasn't really midtown. It was the middle in the worst sense. It was in the middle of a lot of things, downtown from the theater district and the museums, uptown from the village, which she'd always wanted to explore. She had come too old to Manhattan; the streets overwhelmed her and she never ventured uptown to the Forty-second Street Library or to the Metropolitan Museum, which she'd thought she'd visit quite often when she'd imagined herself a Manhattanite. She didn't move far beyond a five-block radius. Even so, she didn't really know anybody in the neighborhood. Nobody seemed to speak English, or at least no English she understood.

Once she went into one of those coffee places, she thought maybe she'd meet people there. But they were very young and asking for things she'd never heard of—skim lattes, macchiatios. And they charged what she considered an arm and a leg. And the conversations were ridiculous, people talking about horoscopes: "Are you a Capricorn, that means you're a warrior, but there must be something rising, because I not only see aggressiveness, I feel gentleness as well. You're a person in conflict. Like, I see that you're really a people person but sometimes you need to be alone." "I can't believe you see that," the girl said. The man in his fifties with a ponytail and the girl no more than twenty-five, a lovely blonde girl. Scandinavian-looking, though she didn't have an accent. She sounded well-educated, although Florence didn't understand how a well-educated person could believe in something like astrology. "I see it completely," the guy said. Well, girlie, I hope you see he's not interested in horoscopes, just hanky-panky, Florence wanted to say. She left the place disgusted. She would never go back.

The only good thing she could say about the Epiphany Branch was that it was convenient to her apartment. Other than that, it had nothing to recommend it. Although she thought the name was interesting. She thought it had some kind of other meaning, so she looked it up in the dictionary. It meant "manifestation," a sudden understanding or revelation. She loved dictionaries; she wondered if people would be surprised if they knew she personally owned four different dictionaries: a Webster, a Random House, the *American Heritage,* the *New Collegiate.* If she'd had a lot of money she would have bought herself a copy of the *O.E.D.* But that would be ridiculous. She wasn't that kind of person. But she very much liked looking things up in it in the library. Although she sometimes worried who'd touched the magnifying glass before her. There were all kinds in that library, all kinds.

People you wouldn't think belonged in libraries. People who didn't even know how to be quiet. In her day, librarians were strict about enforcing quiet. And people respected them for it. They respected libraries as places of quiet. Now, people seemed to her to be making all kinds of noises left and right. When she complained about it once, the librarian said, "We think of a library as not just a place where people come to read, but a community resource center." What the hell does that have to do with people keeping their voices down, she wanted to say. But she didn't want the librarian to turn against her. She was very good at getting things from interlibrary loan.

But there really were all kinds. The boy who always wore one of those undershirts with the straps, winter and summer, with a kerchief on his head. Very well-built, like a lot of black fellows. Studying some kind of mathematics. But he'd say the problems out loud, and not quietly. She supposed he deserved credit for trying to better himself, but he disturbed her, and he frightened her a little, so she didn't want to move, in case he took it the wrong way.

Some of the people in the library didn't seem completely clean to her. A couple of the men never seemed to shave, and some of the older ones gave off that smell of old men who never wash their hair. She hoped she didn't give off some kind of old-lady smell, but she showered every day, and also used deodorant and talcum power, which she was sure these types had never heard of. Or if they'd heard, they'd long ago forgotten. Some of the Chinese people looked very respectable, but she didn't know if they spoke English. Some younger people came in to use the computers, and sometimes they'd curse so loud everyone in the place could hear them. Because of having trouble with the machines. And some people just seemed crazy. They made big fusses about nothing. There was one man, a young man too, he never wore socks, whatever the weather, and he was always calling the librarians morons and idiots and saying, "Do you have to be an imbecile to work here, is it a requirement or does it just help?" She thought the librarians were very patient with him. In their shoes, she would have been tempted to kick him out for good. Forbid him entry forever. She wished they would, for her own sake. And she knew there were other people who agreed with her, but everyone pretended not to notice him, whenever he started up.

Some people, and mostly they were older, came in, went to the bathroom, sat down with a pile of books, and fell asleep on top of them. She was very careful about never falling asleep. At her age, she thought it made a bad impression.

No, it wasn't the best, the Epiphany Branch, but still there was a lot to learn in this world if you applied yourself. She felt she was giving herself the education she'd never had a chance for when she was younger. Now everyone went to college; there was no doubt she'd be considered college material nowadays. But then it was a big deal, especially for a girl. She was determined to make up for what she hadn't been given; sometimes she had a daydream that a very distinguished woman, someone about her age, would engage her in conversation about a book, and, after a few cups of tea, maybe a few lunches in the diner, she'd say, "Florence, even though you have no formal education, you have much more learning than many with a college degree." She could imagine the woman very clearly. She had fine white hair that she clipped to the back of her head with a silver barrette. She had eyeglasses with silver frames that hung around her neck on a silver chain. She always wore gray sweaters or gray silk blouses that had a touch of lavender in them. Very well-made.

Florence would assign herself a subject and then read a lot of books on it until she felt she'd really got it under her belt. By which she meant ten books on the subject; she wouldn't quit unless she'd read ten books, cover to cover, even if she was feeling a little bored. She'd make notes; write down words she didn't understand, look them up in the dictionary and copy down all the various meanings. Now it was the Civil War. Before that, it was Ancient Greece. The cradle of democracy. She certainly would have rather lived in Athens than Sparta, she had no doubts about that.

She never talked to anyone at the library, but there were people that she recognized, people she thought of a better type. They kept to themselves and she kept to herself; they all seemed to like it that way. The last thing she wanted was to strike up a friendship with someone in the neighborhood who she'd never be able to get off her back. Sometimes someone looked possible at first, but she was always disappointed. Like the woman she thought looked so refined, but not stuck-up, wearing a very nice sweater set, Fair Isle, they called it. She wondered where Fair Isle was. She wondered where she could look that information up. The words "Fair Isle" kept going through her mind; she imagined it was an island somewhere in Scandinavia, but it was always green, in spite of the cold, and the ground was always covered with a light green moss and deer ate berries off the bushes there. Fair Isle. She thought she might get herself a Fair Isle sweater. Although maybe it was too late, she was too old for that. She considered asking the woman where she'd got her sweater set. That would be a good way of striking up a conversation.

But when the woman got up and put her coat on, Florence was glad she'd never spoken up. On her lapel was a very large button that said "Lose weight now, ask me how." Florence knew that was ridiculous. She'd never had a weight problem, but she knew that if she did she would never just walk up to somebody, some stranger with a button, tap her on the shoulder and say, "Excuse me, how do I lose weight now?" Any fool would know that wasn't the way to go about it. And if the woman didn't know that, she was a fool. Or money-hungry.

That morning she thought the older man in the plaid shirt and the tweed cap might be worth talking to. She thought he looked like a cultured gentleman; he wore tortoiseshell glasses and his nails were nicely kept. Was coming to the Epiphany Branch lowering her standards? Did she now think anyone who looked like he bathed regularly was a gentleman? Because she was wondering why this man didn't take off his cap. A gentleman wouldn't wear a hat indoors. But maybe it was doctor's orders. Maybe he had to keep his head warm at all times. Or he might have been some kind of intellectual. European. The plaid shirt and the tweed jacket, and then that tie in the abstract expressionist pattern. She had recently learned the term "abstract expressionism." Before, she would just have called it modern art. She learned it when she read that book on art by that nun. A very intelligent woman. Florence thought it was a shame she hadn't done anything about her teeth. But maybe it was against her religion. Florence was glad that in Judaism there was nothing against looking your best.

She herself would never have mixed prints and plaids. But then she thought maybe that was the style in Europe and she shouldn't judge. She wondered if he had a college degree from Europe, maybe a Ph.D. She wondered what he had done for a living. Probably not a doctor or a lawyer, not with that kind of mixing of plaids and prints. She thought he probably was some kind of college professor. Maybe some kind of scientist. Maybe he had worn one of those white coats to work every day so he wasn't used to making choices about fashion. Maybe he was a widower, and his wife used to make sure his shirts went with his ties.

She sat across from him when she arrived that morning; she was pretty sure he'd know how to be quiet, that she wouldn't be disturbed. As always, she was curious about what people were reading. Often she'd try to get a look, although sometimes she was sorry she did, like the time the week before when she saw the young blonde woman reading the "Alternate Therapies" section of *Dr. Susan Love's Breast Book*. And then she had to think about the girl having breast cancer. A man came up and stood behind her, put his hand on her shoulder, and started reading along with her. Florence wondered if it would ruin their sex life if the woman lost her breast. She kept thinking of what the breast would look like on the operating table after the doctor had cut it off. What did they do with cut-off breasts? Florence had made herself go back to her book on the Battle of Antietam. It did no good to dwell on unpleasant things. That had always been her motto, and she believed that it had served her well.

The European gentleman was reading a book called *The Nothing That Is: A Natural History of Zero*. So perhaps he had been a mathematician. But after fifteen minutes, he put that book down and walked around the room. She followed him with her eyes, trying not to. She saw that he went to another table, picked up a book that had been left there by someone else, and brought it back to the place where his coat and hat were, where he'd settled himself originally. This book was called *Radical Walking Tours of New York*. He sat down with a smile and a satisfied sigh, as if he were about to tuck into a good meal. But in about ten minutes, he got up again, walked around the room as he had before, and picked up another book that someone had left on another table. Again, he brought it back to his original place. This one was called *How I Play Golf* by Tiger Woods.

Florence could not concentrate on her own book, a history of women in the Civil War. She'd been very absorbed in it before she started paying attention to the European gentleman. But maybe he wasn't a gentleman. A gentleman would not put a book down so quickly, having read so little in it, just leaving it aside for something else. She felt the disrespect in it. The way she figured it, an author had worked very hard on a book. Whatever you thought of it, it probably had a lot of information in it that someone had spent a lot of time putting together, and you had no right to put it down until you'd finished it to the very end.

It drove her crazy to see him flitting around like that. Every time someone left a book on one of the tables he picked it up and read it. And there were a lot of books on the tables; the librarians preferred it that you leave the books on the table rather than putting them back. Too much mis-shelving, one of them, a Puerto Rican girl, had told her. There was no rhyme or reason to what he did. Sitting down, picking up one book, putting it down. It drove her crazy.

Florence was trying to read her book on women in the Civil War. And not just nurses, either. Then she felt a call of nature. She never liked using the bathroom in the library; sometimes men didn't put the seat down and she'd have to touch the seat herself when who knows who had been there before her. She didn't know why some men didn't have the consideration. It was beyond her, that kind of mind.

When she came back to the room, he was sitting in the chair next to hers, where her coat was, a place that was obviously still hers. He had taken the book off the top of her pile—underneath it was a dictionary of American history and one of American biography, and a book with maps of the Confederate states. He was reading her book on women in the Civil War. As far as she was concerned, this constituted a bald-faced theft.

She was a lady, though; she had no intention of stooping to his level.

"Excuse me," she said, "you seem to be inadvertently reading my book."

He gave her a very warm smile, she thought, considering the circumstances. "It's not inadvertently, not inadvertently at all. I'm reading it precisely because it is yours. I spent a lifetime as a scholar, devoting myself to one specialty: Romance philology. Now, I'm picking up knowledge in a different way. I like to wander after people, like a kind of gleaner in the fields of knowing: I pick up what someone else has put down. I think of it as a kind of quilt made up in a community of learning. I just pick up a scrap of what someone else has taken in, and with that scrap I connect with that person. It seems much friendlier to me."

Florence didn't know when she had ever been so angry. Romance philology. She didn't even know what it was, but the man must have had to study for a long time to even be involved in something like that. So he had had all the advantages. Languages, probably. All those hours studying, with people who respected him, took him seriously. The greatest gift a person could be given in this world. And what did he do with it? Did he sit down and put his mind to something, his mind that had been trained like a professional's? What did he do? He picked up and put down, as if it were nothing, as if books were toys, as if learning was just a game. He was nothing but a spoiled brat. Learning was sacred, and he was treating it like a game. You didn't treat sacred things like a game, you just didn't do it in this world. Not for her money. Or he could do it if he wanted to, but he wasn't going to get away with it.

She tried to put on her most judgmental face. So he would know she had authority. Where her authority came from she wasn't sure for a minute. Then she figured it out: she had authority because she knew what was important and what wasn't. Because she knew what was what.

"You're nothing but a butterfly," she said. Even though it was a library, she was thinking of the movies. She was trying to sound like Bette Davis, when she talked to a man who wasn't worthy to lick her boots.

But in the movies, the men always seemed to be crushed; they backed out of the room, or hung their heads. That didn't happen with the gentleman from Europe. He did two things. Three things. He took his cap off. You could say he tipped his hat, or cap. And then he laughed. And then he put his cap back on.

"And if I am a butterfly, then pray, dear madame, tell me, what are you?"

He was trying to insult her. She knew what he was implying. Because what was the opposite of a butterfly? She tried to think. A caterpillar, no, that was a stage in the butterfly's development, it would suggest that one day she could become a butterfly, one day she could become him. And that was impossible. No, the opposite of a butterfly was something heavy, slow, and dull. That was what he was trying to suggest. That was always what people tried to suggest when they were lazy and careless and your hard work made them look bad. Well, what about the story about the grasshopper and the ant? But she wasn't buying into that one either. Whatever he had in his storehouse, the ant was still dull, still nobody you wanted to be around. She wasn't going to fall into that. Because what she had stored up wasn't just pieces of grain, it was treasure. Knowledge, learning, wasn't just something you put in your mouth to keep alive, it was gold. Shining, precious, valuable. People like the European gentleman didn't realize how valuable it was. They took it lightly; they felt they could take it or leave it. Or throw it away. Or flit around it.

No, she knew the real value of things. Knowledge was a treasure, and it had to be guarded, fiercely guarded. Thinking about it, she felt fierce. And it came to her then: that was who she was. If he was a butterfly, she was a tiger, standing at the gates, guarding the treasure. Maybe one of those tigers with the turquoise eyes that come from Asia, that she'd studied when she'd studied Asia. She was a fierce tiger with turquoise eyes standing at the gates of knowledge, guarding. Guarding against who, against what? She didn't know exactly. But that wasn't important. What was important was that she was on guard.

The gentleman from Europe had got up from his seat and settled himself at another table. He was reading some book, she wasn't even going to give him the satisfaction of trying to find out what it was. He thought he was smart, but he wasn't going to make a fool out of her. She was the white tiger, standing at the gates of knowledge, keeping guard.

And then it came to her, the words that she would say to him, the answer to his question. It wasn't just ordinary words, it was poetry. A poem she'd learned when she'd studied the poets of the romantic era. William Blake. That poem about a tiger. She'd wished she'd been able to ask somebody why tiger was spelled with a *y* and if you pronounced the last syllable of *symmetry* "try" or "tree." Probably that was something the European gentleman knew. She shot him a look of pure contempt across the room and spat the words of the poem straight at him: "Tyger, tyger, burning bright," she muttered, "In the forests of the night / What immortal hand or eye / Dare frame thy fearful symmetry?"

But he did not look up, because of course he didn't hear her. It was a library, after all, and she didn't want to disturb anyone, so she had said it low, under her breath.

Cleaning Up

When the first man walked on the moon, Loretta's mother, as the town said, "snapped." And it was almost like that, as if you could hear a sound and then see something fly up into the air, not like a bird but like a rubber strap that had broken from too much strain.

"Her life was just too hard for her," Martine Lavin said to Loretta, sympathetically, without a hint of judgment. Loretta understood that Martine was being kind and that she ought to be grateful. So many people avoided talking to her, so they gave her meals and washed her clothes and tried to find a place for her in their homes beside their own children. She wasn't uncared for, the parish saw to that. But as they packed her bologna sandwiches, identical to their own children's, as they poured milk or juice, careful to distribute identical amounts, they rigorously avoided mentioning her mother or what had happened in St. Rita's church on the day of the moon walk.

Martine Lavin never went so far as to bring that up, but she did at least refer to Loretta's mother, didn't erase her from the pages of life, not as if she'd been dead but as if she'd never lived. And Loretta was grateful to her, but only partly, because what she could see in everyone's eyes was how much they loved themselves for doing what they did, how much they loved themselves for their knowledge of their own humility: "Well, I didn't do much. I did what anyone would do."

If one of them, just one, had been without that shadow of self-love, so visible to Loretta, perhaps she would have felt free to relinquish the hard stone she carried beneath the flesh of the palms of her hands. The thin flesh, the pointed stone that had penetrated beneath the skin, causing a new skin to grow up around her hate. She hated Martine Lavin most of all because of her belief that she was different from the others. And she wasn't different, or only in ways that carried the kind of tiny risk that allowed her to think of herself as an adventurer, when really, she had never been in any danger and would never be. She was only different enough to be a problem, because she created the temptation in Loretta to let down her guard. And that was dangerous.

Loretta knew about danger. It was the element her mother lived in and carried with her. The women in the Altar Society (Martine was one of them) had seen it, and they wanted to turn their eyes away from it, but they couldn't entirely, because Loretta was a child, thirteen years old.

Her mother had smashed through the barriers of decency that day in church. Why had she chosen a time when the Altar Society was there? The decent women of the parish, polishing, arranging flowers, genuflecting with dustcloths in their hands each time they passed the tabernacle.

Loretta had seen it all, she had to, she had to follow her mother out into the street. Her mother was raving, tearing at her clothes, shouting out words of the most unbelievable filth, some unrecognizable to Loretta, some recognizable to her as the names of body parts she associated with the bathroom.

"Mama, please, Mama come home, be quiet, you're disturbing people, Mama come home with me, we'll eat something, you can lie down, we can lie down together, we can take a nap."

But she didn't listen and Loretta knew she couldn't, knew, really, that her mother couldn't hear her, no matter how loudly she spoke. But she couldn't speak too loudly. She was trying to encourage her mother to be quiet so she tried to keep as quiet as she could herself. It didn't matter. Whatever she said the words were wrong. Her mother's words didn't make sense to her, either. They were speaking to each other in languages the other didn't understand. Loretta recognized the foreignness although up to that time she had never heard a foreign language spoken, except the Latin of the Mass, and that she knew there was no need to understand.

She had hoped that her mother would be calmed and silenced by being in the church, but she wasn't. Being in the church made her wilder. Or maybe that wasn't it, maybe she was acting the same way she had on the street and it just seemed worse in church.

Loretta's mother took her blouse off at the church door. She began raving about the men walking on the moon and saying it was an abomination, an abomination of desolation because the moon was desolate and the astronauts were abominable. She said that God should not allow it and she was here to punish God for his abomination and filthy, filthy, filthy shit and filthy piss and filthy filthy she was going to punish God.

The Altar Society ladies got scared, thinking she meant to do something to the Host. One of them went next door to the rectory to get Father Rafferty. He was watching the television, watching like everyone else the sight of the men walking on the moon.

Father Rafferty came in with his red face and red dome of a bald head and said, "Now Margaret, now Margaret," and all she said was filthy filthy and that he was as filthy as the rest of them, particularly the astronauts, they were the filthiest of all, the moon had always been a clean place, she'd relied on that, but now they were going to make it filthy just like they were and how could the Blessed Mother look on and let it be, she was going to tear the Blessed Mother's eyes out to punish her, no not to punish her just so that she couldn't see. She was walking toward Our Lady's altar, she was starting to climb onto it, when Father Rafferty came behind her and pinned back her arms. And then the police came and took her away, and Father Rafferty told the Altar Society ladies not to say anything of what they'd seen and he told Martine Lavin to take Loretta home with her and her family for the night.

She had never before that night slept in a strange bed, since she and her mother didn't know anybody. Certainly not well enough to sleep in one of their guest beds. In all her life Loretta had never slept in any bed but her own. She and her mother had never taken a vacation, and so she had never so much as brushed her teeth in a sink other than the one where she saw her face each morning in front of the accustomed mirror, really the door to the medicine chest. She felt at a complete loss as to how to behave in the Lavins' house. Martine Lavin had driven her home and tried to straighten up the devastated kitchen. Her mother had pulled everything off the shelves, emptied bags of sugar and flour into the sink, saying they were filthy, she knew they had bugs in them, but the stuff didn't go down the drain, it stuck in an igloo shape in the sink, solidifying, to a texture like cement.

Her mother had left the water on and run to the church. Of course Loretta had followed her, horrified at her mother's exposure. Going outside, she went beyond her rights. Loretta felt that whatever her mother did or said in their house was her right, really, she had paid for the house. "My hard-earned money" were the words she always used when Loretta failed to turn the light off in the bathroom or filled the bath too full. She earned her money as a saleswoman in a children's clothing store on Madison Avenue. Her job fed her bitterness. She hated her customers and their children, hated the effort she had to make at tailored suits and coiffure and manicure to be acceptable to them, hated their money and their carelessness and the easiness of their lives.

Loretta confused the term "hard-earned" with "hard labor," words that she'd heard in a movie that had frightened her. It was on *The Late Show* one Saturday night and her mother had fallen asleep watching it, not noticing Loretta, rapt and horrified, looking through the banister rails. The movie was called *I Was a Fugitive from a Chain Gang*, and it made visible one of her greatest fears, that someone could be punished, punished terribly, for something he hadn't done. But she understood why people thought he had, why they wanted to punish him. He had that look, that dark look around his eyes that made people feel in themselves the wish to punish. "That hangdog look," her mother said about her, ordering her out of the room sometimes just for having it. And she understood why her mother did it, why her mother said, "You make me feel hunted with that look." She saw the look in the mirror, saw it again in the Lavins' mirror, a mirror surrounded not by chrome but by white-painted wood with a light on the top that was softer than the one in her own bathroom, but not soft enough to hide the look that she knew would always make people, as it had her mother, want to be in a place away from her.

"Your father was always sickly," her mother would say resentfully whenever Loretta would get a cold or the flu. Only once she was nicer, when Loretta got the croup. Her mother seemed to like the flight from the steamy bathroom to the cold outside, she sang as she ran through the house, her coat open, holding Loretta as she ran, as if the shock of the cold was a delight to her, a particularly pleasant and imaginative game they were playing, not a desperate effort to restore a child's breath.

Loretta couldn't sleep in the sewing room in Martine Lavin's house. She lay much of the night wakeful on the cot beside the headless figure that Loretta supposed represented Martine's body. What was it called? A form? As the hours passed, Loretta grew more and more anxious about not sleeping, not about the wakefulness itself but about her fatigue the next morning. Because however tired she was she would have to go to school and school was in the world and the world required alertness. Particularly now when she knew all the children knew about her mother. They had heard it from their mothers, who had either seen it for themselves or heard it from their own friends. She had to keep alert to clarify the smudgy look around her eyes so that she would seem not like one of their potential victims, but a potential danger to them.

In the mornings, wakened by her own alarm clock, she would try to lie alert in her bed until Martine's husband Richard had gotten out of the bathroom. And then Martine would use it herself; she'd stay in there until she heard the baby cry. Then she would leave it and only then Loretta knew it was all right for her to use the bathroom.

The house where she'd lived with her mother hadn't had a shower, only a tub, she'd never taken a shower. She knew, somehow, that the Lavins would have thought it strange if they'd heard her taking a bath in the morning. Or even a bath at night. Their children took baths; it was a playful, time-consuming ritual, only in a minor way having to do with cleansing. Loretta felt that, in taking a bath, she was putting herself in the camp of the Lavins' children, suggesting she required the same brand or quality of care as they, suggesting she thought herself entitled to it.

But she didn't know how to use the shower. She didn't understand what was to be done with the curtain, whether it was to be put inside the tub or outside. And she knew she couldn't ask. She couldn't say the words, "How do you take a shower?" They sounded too pathetic, too deprived, simply too odd. And she knew it was crucial for her not to sound any of those ways. So in the six weeks she lived with the Lavins, she washed only at the sink. She didn't know what they thought of that. But she could be sure that they had not assumed she was claiming any kind of false position as a child of the house.

Martine wanted Loretta to share her joy in her young children. Four of them, four sons, four blond boys, four perfect angels. John was five, Matthew four, Mark three, and Luke, the baby, seven months. Richard said maybe they'd quit when they'd gone through all the books of the Bible. "Of course Hebbukah might feel a little badly done by." "Or who knows, darling," Martine said, with a reminder, sunny, irrepressible, that all those babies had to do with something bodily between her husband and herself, "we might, one day, between us, actually produce a girl."

Loretta did not like children. She wished she could have been in a house without them, or at least without ones so near babyhood, so full of incessant hungers and incessantly expressed demands.

Of all of them she preferred John, because he was the oldest and the most self-sufficient. Martine remarked over and over what an independent child he was, but Loretta was so disgusted by the endless circle of need and response to need that made up the relations between Martine and her children that she couldn't muster anything like admiration for John's behavior. It seemed the only slightly less reprehensible behavior of someone who understood he had only to express the slightest wish to have it granted by his mother. A wish having nothing to do with whether or not he was capable of accomplishing what he wanted for himself. She judged those children for their weakness, and Martine for fostering this quality, which, she was sure, would serve them badly later on. She was sure that her mother was right in what she said, in what became, later, one of the few things Loretta could remember her saying, "You've got to look out for yourself in this world, there's no one looking out for you."

No one making you another beautiful breakfast if you didn't like your scrambled eggs, no one making you a placemat out of one of your laminated drawings, no one finding you a wooden napkin ring in the shape of your favorite animal, no one taking you on their lap to hear your side of the story when clearly your behavior had been abominable, no one singing you songs in Spanish or in French or teaching you the words of the Mass in Latin, which no one used anymore but which you would know because you were special children, and you must remember that, it must be marked.

The Lavin family life made her feel choked and suffocated and disoriented, as if she were in a tepid whirlpool where distasteful objects were constantly being thrown up against her, in her way, then out of her grasp: placemats, napkin rings, foreign picture books. In the vortex she attached herself to one thing which of all the unbearable things seemed least unbearable to her: the five-year-old John.

For she knew she was expected to attach herself to something. People did. Or at least, they had to appear to be doing so. She understood perfectly well the currency of the transaction in which she was involved. She paid her board by seeming to be aware of the superiority of her new situation to her native one, by suggesting tender yearning and a poignant sense of loss, and always always everything backlit by a constant sense of gratitude. It sickened her, but she had no choice. She had to have a place to live. Her house was empty. She was a child; she could not live in an empty house.

So she did a few things, as few, she calculated, as she could do and still pay her rent. She made clay animals with John. She rather enjoyed it. Not very much, but she didn't enjoy anything very much, and at least, shaping the clay with John she could be silent, or nearly. She enjoyed silence. And she almost allowed herself to admire the little boy's ability to be silent for quite a long time. Much more than most people. More than most adults. She almost liked him for it, but she saw the trap of that. She was an employee, a tenant, and it was another thing her mother had taught her: the boss is the boss and whatever he says, at the end of the day he gives you your money or he doesn't, whatever he likes, it's up to him. Loretta kept in her mind that she was a wage earner. And, like her mother, she considered herself overworked.

Martine could be said, Loretta knew, to work very hard. Yet there was nothing in her that conveyed the strained, burdened sense that had been so much a part of Loretta's mother's posture. Martine sang while she worked; she played the record player while she cooked; she told Loretta it was a way of keeping up with the music. She'd majored in music in college, had played the piano, although she knew that because of the children these were not her years for "the instrument." At Christmastime, or teaching the children, yes. "But those days," she told Loretta, "of hours upon hours of practice, hours lost in, given up to music, those are in my past. Maybe in my future. My family is my present tense," she said, with a smile that Loretta turned against, feeling herself excluded from what the smile suggested, and glad to be.

After six weeks with the Lavins, Loretta was sent to her uncle and his wife in Hartford. They didn't want her and they made it clear that they had money and would send her to boarding school at the Madames of the Sacred Heart when she graduated from eighth grade the next year. She could spend her holidays with them. Christmas and Easter. Other arrangements would be made for summers, as their summers were for traveling. Loretta's uncle was eighteen years older than her mother; he'd just retired from Hartford Accident and Indemnity; they'd had no children, they'd saved for years for their new freedom, and they weren't going to let Loretta get in their way. Brother and sister had not been close; Loretta hardly knew her uncle, and she understood his position.

Her years in the Convent of the Sacred Heart were better than any that had gone before. She excelled in foreign languages, particularly Latin. The Latin teacher, Mother Perpetua, arranged for her to attend summer programs at the Sacred Heart Convent in Rome the first three years of high school. The last year, she was sent to a summer program at Harvard to learn Greek. "My smattering's not good enough for you," Mother Perpetua said. "You can do better than me."

She liked Mother Perpetua, although the other girls were afraid of her. She liked her white hands, and the unhealthy pallor of her face beneath her wimple, liked the fact that she didn't change out of her old habit when the younger sisters modified or discarded theirs. She admired Mother Perpetua's deliberate and unwavering impersonality. Unlike the other nuns, she didn't lapse into jokes or slip in some details of mothers, sisters, mischievous younger brothers, schoolgirl episodes, lovable teenage pranks. Loretta and Mother Perpetua met only in the high, unfinished rooms of a language which, being spoken by none of the living, being not at all part of the mess of daily life, was high and calm and beautifully inhuman.

Mother Perpetua sent her to Bryn Mawr for college. She graduated with highest honors in classics. From there she went to Berkeley, where her thesis on Horatian odes was given highest honors as well. Jobs in Latin were scarce, the young had little interest in this language of the imperial-minded dead, so she was lucky, very lucky to be hired at Peabody College, so near Boston, so near New York, arguably the most prestigious small college in America, where the tradition of the classics was honored even if the classes were nearly empty.

She had had no training in what might be called personal life, and so friendships with her colleagues were difficult for her. Friendship didn't tempt her; she mistrusted most people, and they bored her. She was fond of Mother Perpetua and she knew it would have pleased the nun if she'd joined the order. Loretta guessed that Mother Perpetua's thinking of her being part of the community was the one fantasy, the one indulgence she'd allowed herself in a life made up of strict self-discipline. But Loretta knew the convent, living in a circle of women, even, as the life was consti-tuted now, living in apartments in university towns or in the poorer parts of cities, was impossible for her.

She learned that there was one connection that was possible. She craved the bodies of men. Not their love or even their attention, or not the kind of attention that could go on over time. What she wanted was an unclean place she had to travel to, treasured, a place of truth, the other side of the light, high truthfulness of the Latin language, of the surgical precision of the Horatian line. This low, dark place pleased her, made her smile, secretly, because it itself was secret and a home to her in a way no home had ever been. It pleased her because it was such a transgression to invest in this place the word "home." She knew what she thought of when she thought of the word "home," and she compared it with what came to other people's minds: dining tables covered with rich foods, soft furni-ture, a predictable cast of characters—mom, pop, brother, sis, grandma, gramps. Her idea of home was silent and anonymous, populated only by furtive creatures taken up only with their own drives, frozen in the pos-tures of their striving toward each other, toward satiation and the obliv-ion to which it would inevitably lead.

The darkness that she knew was in and around her eyes, the darkness that her mother saw and hated, that made her mother drive her from the room, was the sign of her true homeland, and the sign by which she could be recognized by other inhabitants. She was small and dressed, as befit the academic fashion beginning with the midseventies, almost entirely in black: close-fitting but unrevealing knits, overlarge shoes or boots that made a joke, a parody of her smallness.

In the déclassé bars where she liked to go, no one had college degrees and Horace was the name of somebody's cracked uncle. They played

Kenny Loggins and Kenny Rogers on the jukebox, and she stood out among the women because of her short hair and boyish clothing. She gave the signal to these men, who at first could not understand her, that she might be easily approached. She might have been in danger, but she had known danger once, with her mother, and she knew its smell. Nothing bad had ever happened to her at the hands of one of these men, or in their beds, the motel beds where they met for what it was they both knew they wanted, leaving an hour, two hours later, not meeting again. Thirty years earlier this kind of behavior might, if it were found out, cause a kind of nontenurable scandal, but by the eighties such activities were commonplace in the academy, the ordinary fare of faculty dining-table talk, and she risked nothing. Most of the people who would judge her fitness to be among them were men, and although she was careful not to approach them physically or allow herself to be approached, she knew that she suggested to them an allure far from their comfortable wives, women of large amber beads and madrigal groups and Birkenstock sandals. And so, craving what they only guessed at, they would want to keep her close to them. So that, if ever, or in case ... Meanwhile she attended their dinner parties, and gave a couple a year of her own, and produced work that earned their respect, that they couldn't ignore (for fear of lawsuit). She had, she believed, everything she wanted. She had chosen what she wanted in a life.

She had seen his name first on the roster. It had jumped out at her: "John Lavin." An intrusion, an eruption, a penetration into the matte backdrop of her life, of the thunderous, and violent, unmanageable past. In three days, the days between the first sight of his name on the roster and the first meeting of the class, she allowed the form of the intrusion, the propulsion, to recede. John Lavin was, after all, not an uncommon name, it was unlikely that it would be he.

She knew everything when she saw him seated at the seminar table—one of only six students in a course on Horace in the original Latin—the only stranger in class, the rest having been brought to this rare level of proficiency by Loretta herself. It was not his face she saw but a boyish version of Martine, the same thin, light gold curls, the skin, milky white with an undertone of bluing, transformed only a little by a residual, not yet manly beard. When she saw the slope of his shoulders as he bent over his notebook, the combination he had learned from his mother of uprightness yet devotion to a task, the shoulders of a supplicant who would never fully abandon himself to his petition, when she saw the shape of his hands, the thumbnail, more recessive than the ordinary, heard the hesitation when she asked them for a sight translation and he paused after what she understood was a false semblance of puzzlement or frustration, when he put his hands on his head, a girlish gesture, that she had seen his mother perform, especially if she knew herself to be in the range of her husband's appreciation—she knew there was no doubt.

For a brief while she wondered if he knew her connection to his life. But her name—Moran—was no more unusual than his. And she had disappeared entirely from the life, not only of his family, but of the parish. Martine had for several years sent copies of a Christmas letter to her at her uncle's address. "John has made us all proud playing Bach solos at his school recital. Mark, our athlete, continues to astound us all as the perfect shortstop. Luke began by playing with his Daddy's movie camera and did what we think of as the Lavin version of *A Child's Christmas in Wales*—it had us all in stitches. Matt loves to garden, and seems able to make anything grow."

But she had last seen them thirteen years ago, and after many years of nonresponsiveness, Martine had stopped writing. Loretta wondered if Martine had ever talked to the children about her time with them. Which would have meant, of course, that she had talked to them about Loretta's mother, the "scandal," the "performance." It was then that her bitter protective heart contracted to a point under the thin bones of her chest. "How dare they?" were the only words that came into her mind. "How dare they speak of her?" Her mother had made a performance of it, insisted on an audience, insisted upon being watched, and, then, of course, spoken of. It was then that she was steeped in her dark pool of unforgiveness that spilled over onto everyone. Her mother should have kept herself hidden. And she, herself, Loretta, thirteen years old, what should she have done? The torrent of her mother's madness was too strong for her, a hurricane of disorder and discrete force. And yet, in the thousand times when she replayed the scene, focusing on her non-silence, then her timid, pitiful, half whimpers of suggestions, "Mama, go in the house, Mama lie down, Mama don't go outside," it was herself she hated, for her weakness, and her failure to think boldly or at all.

She began to realize that he didn't know that she had a connection to his past. And with that understanding grew the struggle in her mind. Should she deal with him justly, a gifted first-year student with a passion for the Latin language, and attend to him as his gifts deserved, as she would any other gifted young man in his place. Or should she reveal their connection and say that she was unable to work with him, he should find someone else. But there was nothing to justify that; the connection would seem too weak, too tentative, too far in the past, and then she would have to bring her mother and her mother's fate to light. Her mother, whom she went months without thinking of, still in the hospital in Central Islip where she'd been brought fifteen years before, whom she had not seen after that, not even once, her mother whom the doctors agreed was too far gone, even, for de-institutionalization. And that had been a blessing, if not for her mother, Loretta knew, then for herself; it allowed her to think she was right not to think of seeing her mother again. There was no real mercy for her mother but the mercy of death.

She tried to behave justly or at least professionally, but the darkness underneath the thin bones of her breast sharpened, then hardened to a solid point. John Lavin would be punished. She would punish him. She would punish him in his place as representative of the people of the parish. And in her mother's name.

He made it easy for her, he made it easy by being completely himself, blond, quiet, with a series of identical Bic pens clipped to the pocket of his short-sleeved shirt, always some variety of blue (to match his eyes?), some plain, some with a white stripe, or a yellow. His translations were always on time and always nearly perfect, yet not so perfect as to render them unlovable: there were one or two words crossed out, never an infelicity, but occasionally a slight swerving away from the most desirable nuance, the word's best, truest sense.

And he helped by the way he looked at her, adoring, and yet with a calmness none of the others, particularly the young men, could muster. It was only the young men she gave her attention to; the young women, reminding her too sickeningly or too pathetically of herself, were never candidates for her full regard, with their implied dreams of palhood, confidences exchanged, cuddle-ups under quilts with the inevitable redolence of domestication.

Sometimes he came carrying an instrument in a small black case.

She had heard a classmate ask which instrument it was and he said, simply, "Oboe" with the confident person's lack of need for further explanation.

And yet, because, after all she was his teacher and possessed of a knowledge and accomplishment he clearly valued, because she was female and young and small of stature, with a hint of the fashionable in her close-to-the-skull hair, the multiple silver studs in each of her earlobes, she knew she could, if she chose, exercise what all this had given her: the power to intrigue him, John Lavin, a young heterosexual man.

At first, she was undecided as to what her path might be. Would she keep him at arm's length, be hypercritical, hyperdemanding, and in the end order sex from him as her due, as a privilege he ought to think of himself as fortunate in having been asked to exercise? Or should she start this way and gradually soften, suggesting that everyone who had preceded him had been a disappointment and that he, only he, had fulfilled the promise which made her feel less futile, less alone.

She had no desire for him. He was all transparency, there was no place that was fecund or capable of the dense growth that was the only environment in which desire and then satisfaction could, for her, take root. His lightness was repulsive to her. But taking the place of a darkness emanating from him was the sense of stain she would impose from her own body onto his, his blondness, his fairness, his quiet sense of his own worth, his embodiment of the notion of right doing, of having got things straight once and for all and living that way, with no sense of any future need of emendation fueled her purpose. A purpose not sexual in its flavor but which, she knew, could only be worked out on the unused, pure body of this boy. She would approach him and leave him unfresh; his sweet skin would nevermore be lovable in quite the same way. The vessel of dreams would be not only scratched and flawed, but its surface invaded with a growth.

She knew it would be easy, but circumstances made it easier still. He told her that the next year he was going to Rome, taking a year off to study with his oboe teacher, who had relocated there.

"Well, then," she said, handing him his final paper, on the shape of the Horatian line, which she had graded A+, "Your grade's in, I have no more power over you, I'd like you to join me for dinner, so I can wish you bon voyage, and congratulate you for your first-rate work."

John Lavin blushed. The boy is blushing, she said to herself, seeing his heart, the red tight muscle in the center of his chest, overflowing with blood from the presence of—what, she wondered—astonishment, embarrassment, desire, shamed desire, gratitude, the apprehension of a pleasure?

At dinner, in the town's best restaurant, which offered oversmall portions of pasta or fish, she insisted that he talk about his family. He was glad to, she could see the pleasure, greater than the one with which he approached his meal, at the prospect of opening up his family's life to her.

"I guess I'm proudest of my mother," he said. "She was trained as a musician, but she really gave it up for us. She went back and got a social work degree, she's working in the hospice movement. I mean, she does what I think of as the hardest thing in the world. She's with dying children and their families.

"My father works in insurance, but I don't think that's really where his heart is. But he had all of us to support, and he was great about it."

Loretta realized she never knew what Richard Lavin had done, she had never cared; he was hardly present, only as Martine's husband, or the children's father; for himself, he was nothing.

"His real love is woodworking, that's what makes him happy. He's set up an amazing workshop in the basement. And my mom's even got him to learn the recorder. I have three younger brothers, and we have a family recorder group. My mother really has to lean on the younger ones to practice. I'm the only one she didn't have to force, but everyone's glad she did it, because we always have our music. I'm the most grateful to her, she gave me my music, what an incredible gift. But we're really a happy family, I think it's because my mother's so incredible. All my brothers feel good about themselves. My brother Luke's into acting, Matt's a great organic gardener, I sometimes think Mark thinks of nothing but soccer, but my mother says I should get off his case. He's the least musical of us all.

"Sometimes I feel bad about my mother's music. She has a lot of talent as a pianist, but it's been so long since she's practiced. Sometime I'd try to get her out of the kitchen to practice, but she'd just laugh at me, and say she'd made her choices, and she knew they were right."

Loretta saw the kitchen. She would have liked to ask him if the kitchen had changed, but of course she knew she couldn't. She saw the shower that she was afraid to use, and the cot she slept in in the sewing room, and the form in the shape of Martine's body.

Then she saw her mother in the church, and what she imagined was the look on Martine's face, although she'd allowed herself to see nothing when her mother was doing what she did. But it was Martine who came over afterward, when her mother was taken away, came to where she was standing near Our Lady's altar, which her mother had attempted to destroy. She leaned down toward Loretta, putting her arms around her shoulders. And, meeting Martine's eyes, Loretta didn't know what she needed to find there but she knew it had to be exactly the right thing.

What she saw was relief. She saw that Martine was relieved that it was Loretta's mother who had done this thing and not Martine and not any-one connected to her. And Loretta knew that Martine believed that because she'd seen it up close, but not so close that it had touched her, that she'd been spared.

But she had not been. Loretta would see to that now.

He accepted her invitation to come back to the apartment. She told him to sit on the couch while she made coffee.

In the kitchen, she put the coffee into the espresso pot and lit the flame. Then she walked into the living room. He was sitting with his eyes closed, his hands folded at the top of his head. She ran the top of her thumb around the outline of his lips. She allowed him to initiate the kiss, then she took over.

He was overwhelmed by his own ardor, and for a moment the sim-plicity of what he was so visibly experiencing made her want to send him home. But she thought of his mother's face, and of her mother's—wild, defeated—her mother whom she had not seen again after that day. Because of this she did not give in to her impulse to end the whole thing right there. She made herself go on.

She took his hand and led him, like a child, into the bedroom. He seemed willing to leave everything up to her. She unbuckled his black belt and pulled his jeans down but did not take them off completely. She left his shoes on but kicked off her own. She took off her skirt and panty hose and underpants. She unhooked her bra but did not take it off and she kept her shirt on. She climbed on top of him. It was important to her that she felt she was doing something to him, that nothing was being done to her. It was she who was planting the seed, a seed which, without her, might never have taken root in the pure soil that could have been his understanding of the world. He would know now that it was not a sure thing, not a guarantee that he would remain spared. That the darkness that invaded Loretta's mother and taken her over and made her do shameful things, a darkness stronger than anything that could be fought against, was not something to which he was impervious. And if he knew this was true of himself, he would know it was true of the people connected to him. Perhaps he might think there were people in the world who were impervious, who were safe. But he would understand that they were people very unlike himself, so unlike himself as to be unrecognizable.

As she expected, it was over quickly. So quickly that she ought not have been surprised at the speed and completeness of his transition from abandonment to shamed regret. She put on her skirt, leaving her panty hose in a coiled lump at the side of the bed. He didn't know what to do about covering himself.

"I haven't done this before," he said.

"Well, you have now," she said, stepping into her underpants.

She could smell the coffee, which had boiled over; she imagined the mess that had been made. She had stopped thinking of him. She was thinking of how angry it would make her to clean up the coffee which would have spattered all over the white surface of the stove, maybe onto the walls and floor, that the pot would be ruined, that the kitchen would be full of the dark, bitter, ruined smell of burnt coffee for days, perhaps.

"It's time you left," she said, and he obeyed her.

She was glad of his obedience. It made her feel that she had done her job and done it well.

As she wiped the brown spots from the stove, the walls, the floor, imagining all the time what he might be doing as she scrubbed, she knew that she was feeling something like what others might call happiness.

She thought it was unlikely that he would say anything of what had happened to his mother, and too bad she could say nothing to hers.

I Need to Tell Three Stories
and to Speak of Love and Death

I want to tell someone these stories that have come together as one story in my mind. There is no reason to connect these stories. Only one of them happened to me, not in the sense that it was done to me, but I was there when it happened. The other two were told to me by a friend who was dying at the time we spoke, but neither of us knew that he was dying.

The person who told me the stories has been, for forty years, the lover of one of my closest friends. I will call the lover of my friend N. You should know that both of them are men.

We were sitting at the dining table, a long refectory table, in my friend and N.'s London flat. The flat is very beautiful; a place of elegance and order. N. and my friend are close to many artists; on the walls of the living room, or sitting room as they would call it, are paintings and drawings and some sculptures by the artists who are their friends.

N. is famously fastidious. Guests are warned: There are twelve rules for the bathroom alone. The toilet paper must unroll upward and not downwards. The towels must be two inches apart. The showerhead must be replaced exactly. There are more rules, but I do not remember them. I would like you to remember this, this fastidiousness, the lapse from which you will witness when you hear the third of the stories. I believe that there is an ideal of fastidiousness in the world. An ideal of impossible purity in a world that is, in its very essence, impure.

I don't remember why N. was telling me these stories, why he began telling me the story of his friend and her father. We must have been talking about fathers. I don't remember why or what we said. I am very often thinking about my father, but I work hard on not talking about him as much as I would like. In part, I think I can't talk about him because I have written about him so much that I'm afraid all talk about him is not real talk but literature. I do not want to turn my father into literature. So I talk about him rarely, when I'm sure that what I'm saying is something simple, something I have not gone over and over in my mind.

My father died when I was seven.

My father, whose love for me shines always on the horizon of who I am: pure, glowing, unblemished. The moon of my father's love over the lake surface of my life. Like a romantic painting: the black or purple sky, the black or dark green sea, the wide moon slinging spears of light across the darkness.

It is possible, of course, that I didn't mention my father at all, perhaps N. only mentioned the woman, only told her story because he was about to meet her for supper that night. I don't remember, I really don't. The story is so powerful that it obliterates the lead-up, like a wave that would obliterate a path to the shore. This was the story as he told it:

"My friend loved her father very much. He was a scholar and she herself became a scholar in the very field where he had achieved his eminence. Her father was very handsome and very charming and her mother was beautiful but cold. She did not love her mother and she believed her father did not love her mother. She believed, although they never spoke of it, that her father loved her more than he loved her mother. She was actually quite sure of that.

"Her father died when she was twenty-four. Some months after he died, her mother said she had something that the daughter must see. She took her daughter up to the attic of their house and opened an old trunk. In the trunk there were many notebooks.

"'I found these after your father died,' the mother said. 'I think that you should see them.'

"When my friend opened the journals and began reading she discovered that they were the record of explicit pornographic fantasies that her father had had about her from the time that she was a very little child. My friend had a nervous breakdown. She has never recovered."

When N. tells me this, I try to make a heading under which to file this story in my mind. I have several from which to choose:

1. Moments that are never recovered from
2. Causes of rage and hate
3. Unspeakable desires
4. Ugliness that should be hidden or destroyed

She thought she had what I have with my father: pure, unblemished love. Safety, clarity, a place as clean and sheltering as my friend's flat. Fastidious.

She was wrong. How could she recover from this? And the mother? How could she have shown her daughter such a thing? How could she act with, from, such rage and hate? Why didn't she destroy the evidence?

I ask N.: "What would make a mother show her daughter such a thing?"

He says, "She had to show it because it was unbearable to her. Because it must have been that the father and the daughter's love was always unbearable to her."

I wonder what my mother would have done.

No, I don't: I know she would have shown me. She would have said, "I want to rub your nose in this. The stink."

Because, although we never spoke about it, she must have known that my father loved me more than he loved her. And how could this not have enraged her?

But my mother didn't seem to be enraged by it: it was simply something that we, as a family, always understood. I think she was rather proud of it, that she had such an unusual husband, that she had married a man who would turn into such a praiseworthy father. It was not said that she loved me more than she loved him, but that was also understood. But of course, it must have been enraging for her. Something I have always accepted: the truth of my mother's rage.

Having told me the story about his friend and her father, N. tells me a story about his own father.

"This incident that I am about to describe happened just before my father's death. I was eight years old. My aunts had dressed me up for a costume party. They dressed me as a girl. They curled my hair and put ribbons in it. They put me in a dress and girl's shoes. They put lipstick and rouge on me. They took me to see my father, who was on his deathbed. He was in pain and very weak. They thought seeing me dressed up like that would amuse him.

"At first, I knew he didn't recognize me. Then a look of horror passed over his face. He didn't say anything. He turned his face to the wall. It was the last time I ever saw him. He died that night."

As N. speaks, I think of something that happened to my father and me. I was six years old. It was the night of my dance recital. I had a solo. Two solos. I danced to "Easter Parade." I wore a blue and yellow flower-printed dress, which I liked very much, and a straw hat with ribbons. "In your Easter bonnet with all the frills upon it, *pas de bourrée, pas de bourrée.*" I can hear my dance teacher's voice singing these words. I had another number: tap. I was dressed in navy blue satin with silver stripes and a red border at the neck. I tapped to "You're a Grand Old Flag." I was very proud of myself; I thought the whole thing very fine.

The night of the recital, my father came down with stomach flu. I was heartbroken that he wouldn't be able to see me dance. But he said nothing would keep him from watching me dance. He said he couldn't sit down because he might have to keep jumping up to go to the bathroom, but he would stand in the back.

When he sees me on the stage, my father runs up the length of the aisle and stands at the edge of the stage. I can see his smiling face. I can hear him saying, "That's my little girl." I am dancing for him. I sometimes wonder if there is anything in my life I am not doing for him.

No one has ever looked at me again like that: as if everything I did was miraculous.

My father's adoring gaze.

N.'s father, turning his face away from him. A father: turning his face to the wall.

N. is dying. Of all the people I know, N. and my friend have loved each other the most purely.

My friend cannot bring himself to tell N. that he is dying. When N. asks the doctor what is happening to him the doctor says: You're waiting. N. does not ask: For what.

My friend does not want to face his lover's death. He does not want his lover to face it. He does not want it faced. He wants to turn his face away. And with loving fingers, to turn his lover's face. From the thing that cannot be faced. The face of death.

When N. told me these stories, his death was in him. Of course, all our deaths are always in all of us, but this death, this particular death, was sickening in him, growing in him, consuming him. He was being consumed by something inside himself.

Now I need your help. Now, as I am about to tell you the third story. Because I don't understand why, to the two stories that N. told me, both of us sitting at his table on a September afternoon, I connect the third.

I hope you understand that I know that the place where the third story happened is a strange place to be writing about. A place that I would not have imagined myself writing about when I was young and thought of myself as writing, thought of what I might be writing as a woman in her fifties. When I was young, I might have imagined myself a woman alone in a sunny room with a dog asleep on a blue rug at her feet. But I did not imagine that I would be writing about something that took place in a gym. I wouldn't have been able to imagine myself using the phrase "I belong to a gym." *Belong* and *gym*? I would not have put the two words together in connection to myself. Who knows what sentences I will be speaking as an eighty-year-old woman that I cannot imagine now? It is possible that I will never be an old woman, that I will die before I am old. Before I am eighty. When I was thirty, I did not believe I would be fifty-five. I may have pretended to believe, but I didn't, not really. No.

It isn't difficult to imagine that I will be dead before I reach eighty. So many around me have died. N. will die in his sixties. He will die quite soon. He does not know it. Or does he? He does not speak of it, he does not speak of knowing that he knows.

Gym. Gymnasium. We only use the nickname. We never say, "I'm going to the gymnasium. What gymnasium do you belong to?" And when we say the word *gymnasium*, we do not think of the European, the German word *gymnasium,* pronounced with a hard *g.* Kafka attended a gymnasium. It is difficult to connect Kafka with the kind of gym I am about to describe. Ridiculous to connect the two words: *Kafka* and *fitness.* Kafka is all that is not health.

But perhaps you find it ridiculous that I intend to describe my gym to you. *My gym. Mine.* In the sense that I belong to it. In the sense that I am a member. In the sense that I have paid what some people whom I respect would believe is a shocking amount for this membership.

For two reasons. Because it is a place that I can dance to Broadway show tunes and disco with other women. Fantasizing ourselves in the chorus. Chorines. A word that has disappeared from the language: *chorine.* Impossible to imagine what words we now commonly use that in the future will have disappeared.

I have also paid the money for this gym because of the terror of becoming fat. Perhaps this is why most of the women are here, except for the few athletes in training, or the semi-invalids here for therapy. In the locker room, women are naked in a pretty unself-conscious way, although, being women, we all know, we must know that we are looking at each other. I think that most of the women in my gym have better bodies than mine. I tell myself that many of them are younger, but some are not, and I know that, I acknowledge that, I take that in. There is, however, not unmixed with judgment and self-hate, some sort of sisterhood in this room. We are safe here, except from the eyes of each other, and even the sharpest eyes do not linger, do not dwell.

Always clothed, always completely clothed, are the women, Latina and quite young, who clean up after us.

One day when I'm getting dressed in the locker room, there is a terrible smell. I think it must be me: I must have stepped in dog shit and not noticed it. Perhaps my dog vomited on my coat and I (how could this have happened) didn't see. Furtively I examine the bottom of my shoes, all my clothes. Pretending I am searching for something in the locker, I sniff my armpits. I squat down so that my nose is nearer to my crotch and sniff. Nothing. It is not coming from me. The relief! But where is it coming from?

I haven't told you that most of the time the locker room is exceptionally clean. Snowy towels, as many as you need, rest on counters in immaculate piles. In the air: the scents of different shampoos, conditioners, moisturizers, perfume, and over all the eucalyptus that is sprayed in the steam room.

So where is this smell coming from? From which of these clean-seeming naked women?

I am ashamed to suspect the Latina women, but I do. They are the only ones in clothes. Clothes: sign of the dirty outside world.

The Latina women begin shouting angrily. One of them comes by with a hose. The floor is sluiced with water. Others run in with buckets, mops, rags.

None of the naked women has said anything, but for a moment we all love each other in our innocence.

Then a very old woman walks from the lavatory into the locker room. She looks like an Indian: long white skirt, black shawl, another black shawl covering her head, her hair hanging down her back, incomprehensibly dark and glossy. She glides out, like a ship progressing through calm water.

A woman I know says: "Somebody had an accident on the bathroom floor."

An accident? At first I think she means a collision of automobiles. Crash! Metal upon metal, flashing lights.

But then I realize: what she means by *accident* is shit.

We know, all of us, the naked women, the women with hoses, the women with mops and buckets, the women with rags, that it was the old Indian woman who sailed by us a moment before. She was the one that did it. We know that it was she and what she did but we do not know why. Could it have been some kind of colonial revenge, that she hated us as a group, for our cleanliness, our prosperity? Is she the mother, the grandmother of one of the cleaning girls, enraged that her beautiful daughter, her beautiful granddaughter has to clean up after these fat white bitches? Is that why we are all ashamed?

We know that we are all ashamed. But we do not know why.

Breaking the silence, one of the naked women says, "I thought it was me."

"Oh, God," says another. "I thought it was me."

"Me too."

"So did I."

What can it mean: that all of us, clean, naked, believe that we are carrying, only temporarily, only inadequately hidden, something that stinks. That being female, the corruption we are carrying is more than the seed of our own death, it is noxious, poisonous, to ourselves and to others, that the task of our life is to seal it up.

You must believe me: it is only now I begin to understand why I connected the three stories. Only after I have told them all. Told them to you. It is only now that I see: that the woman whose father thought about her with unspeakable desire, that N.'s father, who saw the female in his son, that all of us clean naked women believe that we have somewhere in us the dangerous, the foul thing that will make everyone turn away.

Is that what we believe?

If we do not it would not be surprising if we believed it.

But why do I believe it? What about my love for my father and his love for me?

That pure love. Fastidious.

And who was that woman? And why was she there?

You can see why I need you to hear me.

Why I would not want to be considering these things alone.

My friend's lover is dying.

It is difficult not to be ashamed.

The Baby

When people asked Kathleen if she was homesick in America, she said she wasn't, and it was the truth. She'd come over with Kevin from Ennis, County Clare, a week after their wedding; they had a honeymoon at Niagara Falls. People teased her about it afterward, and she pretended to know why. She laughed along with them, and made a face to show she got it, but she never did.

At first it was like a big holiday. There was the wedding, and the airplane ride, the food on the little trays. There was her trip to Niagara Falls on the train, Kevin telling her she was great not to be feeling the jet lag. And her first night ever in a hotel. Her first night really alone with Kevin. The week after the wedding they'd spent in her parents' house; her brothers had cleared out of their room and were sleeping on the sitting room floor. It made her and Kevin self-conscious, trying to sleep together in her brother James's bed, too narrow for them, only they couldn't give up what seemed like the treat of sleeping in the same bed. The times they'd been together before in the back of someone's car or in a field she'd felt a little bad about it, but she hadn't wanted to say anything for fear of spoiling Kevin's time. Maybe he'd felt bad about it too, it seemed to mean so much to him, sleeping in her brother's cramped bed, with the pictures of footballers looking down on them. "It's great not to have to sneak around, not to have to skulk home afterward, to look your mam in the eye, not feeling lonely for you in the bed, thinking of you while my brothers were snoring," he said.

Kevin had no sisters; he'd come from a family of seven, all boys. And in her family, she'd been the only girl. Everyone was thrilled when she and Kevin had the baby and it was a girl. They named it Margaret after Kevin's aunt, who'd died young, but they called her Maggie and not Peg, as the aunt had been called, to break the bad luck. So that was another part of the holiday, having Maggie fifteen months after she'd set foot in the States, decorating the nursery and buying baby clothes. Kevin was doing well so they could afford to splurge, and she'd banked her whole salary while she'd been pregnant.

Her life had been wonderful the last five years, everything was better than it had been at home. She even looked better a bit older. She always knew she'd been good-looking, but there were little things that had tormented her that seemed to have gone away after the baby. Her face used to break out, and that had stopped. And there were secret deformities that possibly no one had noticed but were a torture to Kathleen. Before the baby her palms and fingertips had always been damp, so that she'd dreaded shaking hands with anyone for fear she might disgust them. And her fingernails had had little ridges cut into them, so that she felt she never could wear nail varnish, because it would draw attention. But now her hands were perfectly fine; she didn't think of them at all now.

After the baby, after she got her figure back, she'd looked at herself naked in the full-length mirror. She'd never done that before in her life. She was surprised at how pleased she was at the sight of herself, surprised and a bit ashamed. She understood what Kevin meant now, that her breasts were round and lovely. She liked that she had a waist, some women didn't even if they were thin, and if she wished her thighs were a bit smaller, she knew it wasn't really serious. She'd always known she had nice eyes, green like the sea, Kevin said, and she began wearing a bit of makeup, blue eye shadow and black mascara, and she was pleased with the way it made her eyes look bigger and brought out the color.

She'd got used to feeling good about things; it had seemed strange at first, a different way from the people at home she'd known most of her life. When they walked into church on Sundays or when they went dancing sometimes on Saturday nights, if they could get a sitter for Maggie, she knew that people looked at her and Kevin and admired them and she didn't feel she had to pretend anymore that it wasn't happening. She liked the way Lawrence at the Hair Emporium cut her hair. She knew he was queer, and she wondered what they'd think of that at home, but she liked him and he liked her too. He told her about his boyfriend and that they were saving up for a house. He was very complimentary about her hair. He said very few had the red highlights without being brassy. He said not to worry about it being a little oily. He recommended a special shampoo. The price shocked her, but she went for it, although she kept it from Kevin. That was the good thing about having her own job, she didn't have to be asking her husband for every blessed penny.

She wasn't even afraid anymore that Kevin had quit his job as an air conditioner repair man, the one he'd got his green card on, and was selling mobile phones and home systems. Rockland County was a boom location, he said, and the brogue never hurt. She even liked the name of the town they lived in: New City. She didn't tell anyone that she liked the name because it sounded new. She knew they'd think she was simple for having an idea like that.

She was very proud of their house, she didn't worry that one day they wouldn't be able to make the mortgage; she planted petunias and zinnias and she thought it was great that because the house was sided with aluminum they'd never have to paint it. At first she wasn't sure she liked that shade of yellow, but she'd come to see that it was fine, it always cheered you up, no matter what the weather.

Maggie was three now, and she'd gone back to work two afternoons a week in the cafeteria of the elementary school while Maggie went to preschool. She didn't like the net she had to wear around her hair, and she hated the feel of the plastic gloves, but it was worth it because the hours were perfect. Maggie went to school from eleven to three and she worked from eleven thirty to two thirty. With Kevin making his own hours, he could pick Maggie up sometimes and she had an hour or so on her own.

But the best thing about her job was the girls she worked with. She couldn't believe her luck. The four of them that worked together were like sisters. They called her the baby. They all had some Irish blood, but

Joanne was half Italian, and Marty's father was Polish and Italian. Lois had the least Irish in her, only a great-grandmother, but she was the one Kathleen was closest to. She had a bit of a weight problem and Kathleen was sympathetic. She never got impatient with Lois like the others did, she never teased her about it, even when she went on the popcorn and grapefruit diet. She knew Lois needed encouragement.

Joanne was married to a man who sold TVs and other appliances; he didn't do too well. She liked suggesting that he was good in bed. She'd gone into debt to have what she called "a boob job" but Kathleen didn't like to think about that, having plastic bags put in you so you'd look bigger. Marty's husband drank, but she was loyal. She was very thin, maybe a bit too thin, and this was hard for Lois, the way she always made a point of having to eat more to keep her weight up. But Marty was right, when she lost a pound or two it really showed on her face, it aged her. Marty's and Joanne's children were all grown up, so they loved making a pet of Maggie. On Kevin and Kathleen's fifth anniversary they chipped in to send them to the Marriott in Bear Mountain for a special weekend, and they all stayed at the house to watch Maggie. They put a gift-wrapped package in the back of the car. It was a sexy nightgown. Kevin was thrilled with it, but Kathleen thought it made her look too pale. When they got home, she saw that Maggie didn't seem to miss them at all. She was very attached to Lois. Lois was the one who spoiled her most. It made Kathleen sad, knowing how much she would have loved a baby. She kept asking Kevin wouldn't he try to fix Lois up with one of his friends. Kevin said Lois was great but his friends weren't her type.

Every Friday after work the four of them went to Harrigan's Pub for happy hour. The whole thing was pretending to be an Irish pub, but Kevin and Kathleen laughed because they hadn't a clue. The brothers who ran it, Joe and Jeff Harrigan, loved it when Kathleen came in; they loved to hear Kathleen order for everyone. "That brogue just knocks me out, just knocks me out," Jeff would say. They never let her pay for her drinks. When he put in the karaoke, the four girls began singing together, and they were up there every happy hour. They taught Kathleen to sing songs that were around when they were young, songs she hadn't sung before. They liked one by the Carpenters called "Close to You." Apparently the girl who sang it originally died because she'd taken too many laxatives. "Could you credit that," Kathleen said, and they laughed at her for the expression. She didn't think a thing like that could happen in Ireland, people weren't so appearance-conscious there. But she didn't tell them that because she didn't want them to think she was criticizing America. She thought America was great, she didn't even know if she'd move back home if she had the chance. Kevin said they would when they'd saved enough, but they didn't seem to put very much away.

Jeff Harrigan got Irish songs for the karaoke. He made Kathleen sing them. She told herself she didn't have to, it was her choice, but she didn't like the way they looked at her when she was up there. He asked her to learn "H-A-double-R-I, G-A-N spells Harrigan," and they split their sides laughing because she pronounced it "Haitch," beginning with a breath, instead of "Aitch." When somebody got drunk, they always asked her to sing "When Irish Eyes Are Smiling." She didn't know how to tell them she'd only just learned it; they never sang it at home.

She and the girls started practicing routines and their big hit was "My Boyfriend's Back." They'd all wag their fingers at the guys in the audience, and everyone cracked up. Their finale was "Lean on Me." She thought the words were really great. "Lean on me, when you're not strong, I'll be your strength, I'll help you carry on." When they sang that, they all leaned into each other, and everyone always clapped. She liked singing with the girls, it was just when they made her sing the Irish songs by herself it made her feel self-conscious. But singing in the group was a great gas. When she said "great gas," they fell over themselves laughing.

It must have been at Harrigan's that they came up with the plan of the four of them going to Ireland. She'd gone back every year. If you didn't go in high season (she went during the spring vacation), the fare was dirt cheap really and once she got home there were no expenses. Her father picked her and Maggie up at Shannon and they were right home in her own bedroom in forty-five minutes. It was great living that near the airport. When people asked her where she came from she'd said, "Ennis, County Clare," and that didn't mean anything to them until she said, "Forty-five minutes from Shannon." They all relaxed; they could place it in their minds. But all the time she was growing up she never thought a thing of being near the airport.

Her mother spoiled her and Maggie when they were there. Her sisters-in-law noticed it. All her brothers had married and settled near the town, and she knew how the wives felt, never getting a holiday for themselves, never being waited on like Kathleen was by her mother. One of her brothers' wives was particularly spiteful about it. Kathleen had known Brid Callahan all her life; they'd been in the same class and Brid had always disliked her. Brid was clever, but the nuns didn't take to her, not like they did Kathleen and some of the other girls who didn't do so well at academics. Kathleen never understood why of all the ones he could have had—and he could have had any girl in town, he was that kind of boy— her brother Jimmy chose Brid. Jimmy was the sweetest boy in the world, the next youngest of them, just before Kathleen. He had Kathleen's eyes, only bigger, and beautiful teeth as white as milk. And his skin was so white the freckles made it look like you could see through it. His skin and his teeth made him seem very light, and he moved lightly, but the lightness also came from something about him that made it seem he never cared if he got his way or not.

Jimmy was the brother Kathleen was closest to and it was a blow for her when he married Brid. She was the brains of the outfit, everyone said, and that was good for Jimmy, he didn't seem too cut out for the rough and tumble of making a living. He was good at carpentry, and what with the building boom they'd done well with Brid managing the accounts. She'd taken the money and invested it in a gas station and convenience store. The year before she'd had Jimmy build on to it and was starting a bed and breakfast. She certainly had go, Kathleen had to say that, accomplishing all this with two-year-old twins. But she'd never like Brid. She made it hard for Kathleen to have a minute to herself with Jimmy and she was always passing remarks about people being waited on hand and foot.

Kathleen always kept hoping that in time things would get easier with her and Brid, and the day at Harrigan's when the idea came up about all of the girls going with her to Ireland she thought it was perfect because they could all stay at Brid's new B & B. Not her, of course, but the other three. She didn't know whether Brid would give them a cut rate, but she thought there was at least a chance of it.

They were all over the moon about the trip and Kevin loved teasing her about them. "The witches' coven come to Ennis. I'll be ringing my mates to tell them to look out for their lives." The girls were pretending to hit at him, and teasing back. "They'll be grateful to their dying day. We'll show them what the real thing is." Kathleen understood that they prized Kevin because, among the four of them, she had the only husband who could be recognized as a real man.

"Would you want to leave Maggie and me for a week?" he asked Kathleen. "Just go off by yourself with your girlfriends. Really let your hair down. Then I could join you."

At first the thought made her sick. She'd never been separated from Maggie for more than a night. And then she knew her mother would be terribly disappointed.

"It's just a week, Kath," he said. "Then I'll be there and we'll make it up to her. We'll go home for Christmas too this year."

"Oh, she'll take it out on me anyway," Kathleen said.

"You're your own person, Kath. You've lived in America, you're different. It would do them a bit of good over there to see a woman with some freedom. Your mother has to understand you're not the same girl she put on the plane five years ago."

Kathleen didn't like to hear that. She hoped it wasn't true. But Kevin was right: they'd come to America for freedom and opportunity. And they'd found it.

The girls booked their flight for August 15, the Feast of the Assumption, Marty said and laughed, they all knew they'd been thinking it, all of them had gone to Catholic school.

"What'll the weather be like?" Lois asked.

"Well, I can't promise. It can be unpredictable."

"It won't be like the New York steambath," Lois said. They all understood that she felt the heat because of her weight.

The drinks were free on the flight, and they each had several. Except for Kathleen. She'd read an article that said that alcohol could be dehydrating, and made the jet lag worse. She'd found she did better just drinking lots of water. The girls seemed loud on the plane, and she wondered why she hadn't noticed it before, if she was just being oversensitive, worrying that the Irish on the plane would think badly of them. It was one of the things the Irish said about Americans: that they were loud.

They'd been hoping to get some sleep on the plane, but none of them could get comfortable. Joanne said she was sure that when she'd flown to California the seats had been wider. "That was American Airlines though," she said, and Kathleen felt chastised.

They were exhausted after the flight, and Kathleen was worried they might be a bit hungover. They weren't looking their best, and she regretted that. Marty and Joanne were sharp dressers; their hair was dyed— Marty was red-haired and Joanne streaky blonde, they all went to

Lawrence the same as her and she'd always admired the way they used makeup. But now they looked different. She thought for the first time that they were older than her. That she was young, but perhaps they weren't young. She wished they looked better for her family's first sight of them. She didn't know who'd pick her up, but she hoped it was her father because the look of people wasn't something he noticed.

It was Jimmy who picked them up. That was fine, she was proud of him, she was convinced that just seeing him would perk her friends right up. But they were only just polite to him, they said hello but barely; they seemed to expect him to carry their luggage and she thought they talked to him as they would to a porter. She was afraid she was being oversensitive. She was always afraid people would take advantage of Jimmy. His good nature. Even though he was older, she'd always felt she had to look out for him.

The weather didn't help. "Jesus, it's pissing down with rain," Kathleen said.

"I never heard you use that kind of language in America," Marty said, and Kathleen couldn't tell if she was kidding.

"You should have been here yesterday," Jimmy said, "the sun would have blinded you."

"It's always my luck. I always have bad weather on vacation," Lois said. Kathleen thought she should be careful; people didn't like to hear overweight people complain.

"It might break," Jimmy said, but Kathleen could tell he wasn't hopeful.

The rain had never bothered her. Especially when she came home from America, it seemed comforting and right, she felt cleansed, but gently, rinsed, as if she were undergoing some treatment particularly good for the complexion. The kind of thing very rich women might arrange for when they got what were called facials. The girls had talked about it to her: facials were steam cleaning and all sorts of lotions. But when the rain fell on Kathleen's face at home she felt as if she hadn't realized how all the makeup and grime of America had clogged her pores, dried the skin around her lips. She felt she got her baby skin back after walking in the rain. She thought now of the girls calling her "the baby," and that she was the baby of her family. She knew there was something in her that made people want to protect her. She didn't know what that was.

Her mother had laid out an enormous breakfast for them. Eggs and bacon and sausage, fried tomatoes, mushrooms, fried bread.

"This is going right to my arteries," Joanne said. "Fried bread. Grease and carbohydrates. I've died and gone to heaven."

Kathleen could tell her mother wasn't sure whether or not she was being praised.

Lois asked for fresh fruit. She was on Weight Watchers. Kathleen's mother blushed; she said she'd look around for some. Kathleen said she'd do some shopping after they'd had a rest. Lois said she'd need to go with her; there were things she needed "for her program," or the whole thing would go up in smoke.

"Brid will have the rooms ready for you now," Jimmy said.

"I'll get down on my knees to anyone who will show me to my bed," Marty said. Jimmy laughed, and Kathleen could see that pleased Marty. She relaxed; everything would be all right.

Jimmy drove them to the B & B. "We're staying in a gas station?" Joanne said.

"No," Kathleen said. "It's just attached."

But she could see they were disappointed. They'd probably dreamed of a thatched cottage, of their eyes falling on green fields. Whereas what they could see outside their window was a twenty-foot-high sign saying Esso.

The way Brid was acting made Kathleen sick. She was acting like a nervous dog, anxious to please, saying how great it was to have them with her. That she felt she must have built the whole B & B with them in mind. They'd be her first guests. It was a blessing, she said. Bull, Kathleen wanted to say, you had the idea for this two years before you knew we were coming. And as for blessing, Brid never darkened the door of a church.

The girls thought Brid was wonderful. She offered them tea in their rooms. "You must be dead, longing for bed," she said.

Kathleen suggested they'd be better off trying to stay awake, trying to get on Irish time.

"I've never heard of that," Brid said. "And it's that damp, you might want to put on your electric blanket. It's under your sheets; the switch is just at the side of the bed."

"Lead me to it," Marty said. "Sandman here I come."

The way Brid laughed at that was really phony, Kathleen thought. As if she knew what they meant. Kathleen couldn't remember whether Irish people had the Sandman the way they did in America, but she was pretty sure they didn't, and Brid was faking so they'd think she was something great.

Jimmy brought their bags into their rooms and they settled down to sleep. Kathleen was annoyed that they hadn't taken her advice about trying to get on Irish time, and she was worried. If they didn't get on Irish time, they'd feel wretched for days. And the whole holiday was only meant to last a week.

"Your friends are much older than you, except the stout one," Kathleen's mother said. "Haven't you friends your own age, pet?"

She'd made lots of plans for things that they could see; she'd take them to Blarney Castle, to the ruined Abbey, to the Cliffs of Moher, to the Burren.

She asked her mother if she could borrow the car to get what Lois needed for her diet from the store in Ennis.

"You can, of course," her mother said. "We'll try and make a great time for them."

She tried to think what Lois would want to eat. She bought celery and carrots and yogurt. She bought large bottles of diet Coke. But she'd never had to watch her weight herself, so she was guessing.

"I need nonfat yogurt. Don't they have nonfat?" Lois said.

"This was all they had."

"Four percent fat. Sugar, the works. I might as well forget about it," Lois said and began to cry. Kathleen was mortified in front of her mother, but her mother was running the water loud rinsing the carrots and celery and cutting them up small, as if she were going to put them in a soup. That was the wrong way, Kathleen knew, but she didn't know how to tell her mother.

Her mother had made them ham sandwiches for lunch, with raspberries and vanilla ice cream for dessert. When she offered second helpings, Lois took one. Kathleen felt like a fool, making a special trip to buy food for her diet.

It was hard to get them to go on the outings Kathleen had planned with the rain coming down in sheets. They got into the car, trying to be cheerful, but they were all asleep every time Kathleen tried to point something out.

"Is there any way you could remind your friends breakfast's over at nine thirty, Kathleen," Brid said. "It's clearly posted in the rooms. After all they're paying guests, like anyone else."

"You have no others, Brid," Kathleen said. "Maybe you'd accommodate them. They're having a rough time with the jet lag."

"I have my schedule, the B & B's not the only thing. I have the petrol pump and the counter at the convenience store, I'm not on holiday like you. No one's waiting on me hand and foot."

Kathleen said she'd mention it to them, but she never did.

She didn't know what else to do with them except take them around in the car and pretend they weren't sleeping. She'd tried to find a nice place for lunch every day, but she forgot that Irish pubs had a certain limited menu, which repeated itself from place to place.

"You'd make a fortune with a good old Greek diner here," Joanne said. "God what I wouldn't give for a bacon cheeseburger. I don't know what they call bacon here but it's nothing I'd call by the name."

"It's more like what we call Canadian bacon," Marty said, and Kathleen knew she was trying to be nice.

"Crisp is a foreign concept to them here," Joanne said.

"Crisps is their name for potato chips," Lois said, and they all laughed.

After the drive and the lunch, they'd all go back to bed. They were better in the evenings, and Kathleen was proud of them as they sat around her mother's table. Her father was silent. He'd never heard women talk like this. Her mother seemed to be having a good time, and when Jimmy drove by he seemed to have a good laugh with them, and that made everyone feel good.

He took them to the pub every night and Kathleen was glad to see how much they enjoyed it. They were generous buying people drinks, and Kathleen wished that the people in the town were equally generous. She tried not to be counting, but she couldn't help noticing that after a while her friends weren't being treated as much as they treated the men. It made her nervous and it made her even more nervous to see Lois deep in conversation with Kieran Donnelly, who was known for nothing good. She felt sick at Lois's excitement when she talked about him.

"I was asking Kieran about how they thatched the roofs and he invited me out to his place so he could show me," she said.

Kathleen knew Kieran's house; it was an old whitewashed house he lived in with his father. But his father was dead now, so he must live alone. The house was in a dark patch of trees a quarter mile from the Gort Road. She was quite sure it hadn't a thatched roof.

But she told herself that she hadn't been there for a long time, maybe she'd misremembered. Still she thought she should give Lois a warning about Kieran. He was a drinker and he was known to bring a not nice type of woman back to his house when he went to Limerick for the day. He was a good plumber but unreliable, everyone was always complaining that you couldn't trust him to show up.

"You just think anyone who's interested in me would have to have something wrong with him," Lois said, bursting into tears. Kathleen didn't remember that in America she'd cried so much.

"No, that's not it, Lois. Only I've known Kieran all my life."

"Well, I'm not planning on settling down with him. Don't worry about that. I'm not that bad off that I'd land myself in a place like this."

Kathleen didn't say anything, but she felt bad for what she wanted to say, "Find out yourself then what he's up to," to Lois, who was her best friend. She wouldn't have said anything like that to Lois before. Everything was topsy-turvy now.

Lois came back from Kieran's looking sullen and disappointed, but she didn't say a word about what had gone on. It was after that she started taking out her Weight Watchers' books and writing things down on the blue-and-white charts.

"I don't even want to think about the number of points I'm over," Lois said.

Kathleen and all the girls knew Weight Watchers was on a point system: you got a certain number of points for everything you ate, and you were supposed to lose weight if you didn't go over the weekly points.

"But I don't see what I could have done. There's nothing to eat here that I can eat. There isn't any way I could get to a supermarket and buy some of the things I need, is there?"

"You can, of course," said Kathleen, ashamed for her country and its famously poor cuisine. "We'll go to the big market outside of Limerick tomorrow."

The idea of going to a supermarket cheered the girls up; they invited Kathleen to do the Ouija board with them in their room, but Kathleen said she was tired. She was glad she was staying in her mother's house instead of the B & B. She was glad she had somewhere to go.

By the morning, the plan had grown and bloomed: the girls had decided they were going to make a meal for Kathleen's family to show their gratitude. A real Italian meal. Had Kathleen forgotten they all had Italian blood?

They were going to make it a surprise. So they didn't want Kathleen involved in it, not even the shopping. They'd worked it all out with Jimmy in the pub the night before. He'd drive them into Limerick to do their shopping. Kathleen would have the day to herself.

"The day to myself." She was ashamed at the joy that spread over the whole of her skin when she heard the words. It had been a long time since she'd had a day to herself. Years. But how many?

She saw the girls off waving from the parking area between the door-way to the B & B and the petrol pump. There was no car available to her, but she didn't mind the half-mile walk back to her parents' house, even though it was along the main road with nothing to look at but a few new houses, which looked as if they'd stolen the land from the trees and stood there glancing at the road, shamefully naked. As she walked on the side of the road, she was a bit worried at the cars whizzing by. She was sure there hadn't been that much traffic when she still lived here. And it was only five years ago she'd left. What would it be like five years from now? Crossing the road, she had to remind herself to look the opposite way from the way she looked in America. It always took her a few days to get that straight. She wondered which was the better way of doing it, driving on the right side or the left. She reckoned that each side probably thought their side was right, and each of them probably had good arguments.

She borrowed her mother's Wellies to walk through the fields to the stream she always liked. She enjoyed the squelch her rubbery feet made in the wet grass and the low bellow of the cattle and the foolish bleating of the sheep. She'd hoped the girls would take this walk with her, but they hadn't the footwear for it, their sneakers would be ruined, it was that wet. She wondered should she have told them to bring some sort of boots, but they would have been heavy in their luggage, and there was nothing like Wellies in America. Nothing that would really have served.

She felt that the light rain on her skin was doing her whole body good, her insides, not just her skin. She didn't know why people made such a thing about sunshine. If you just put your head in the right place gray skies and a soft rain and wet grass could be just as beautiful. It was just that sunshine had better PR.

She sat by the stream and threw stones in the water, enjoying the look of them sinking in the clear. Maybe I am young for my age, she thought. She imagined how nice it would be sitting there with Maggie throwing stones and twigs into the water. Then she worried that Maggie wouldn't like the wet weather, and would fuss about having to wear her raincoat all the time. She'd take her to Gort and get her a new raincoat. Your Irish raincoat, they'd call it. It would be something to show her friends back home. Kathleen wondered if she wore a raincoat when she was a child. She couldn't remember, but she couldn't remember having been wet. It would be great when Kevin and Maggie came here next week. In two days, the girls would be gone and she'd have three days with her parents. She looked forward to that.

She could hear the girls giggling when Jimmy stopped the car. The sun was shining, it was beginning to be warm; they'd driven with the windows open. Jimmy looked pleased with himself, and the girls looked more like themselves, laughing and teasing like she was used to.

Kathleen and her mother watched out the kitchen window.

"Mother of God, they've bought enough food to feed an army," Kathleen's mother said. "How many do they think they're feeding and what size do they think my kitchen is? Where am I going to put all the stuff?"

Kathleen felt worried about the size of the refrigerator. It hardly came to her waist; it was less than a quarter as big as her fridge in New York. There was no way the girls would understand that.

But they were in their best moods, and showed Kathleen and her mother out of the kitchen. "The Irish are banished. Italians rule," Marty said, holding two cans of tomatoes over her head. "Kathleen, would you believe, we had to go three places for parsley. Apparently they think it's a gourmet item here."

"Yes, they would so," Kathleen said, realizing she never used "so" at the end of the sentence like that when she was in New York.

She wanted to go for a walk with her mother, but her mother was jittery about strangers in her kitchen.

"They work in a kitchen, Mam," Kathleen said. "They're professionals."

"But they don't know our ways. I'm not fond of their saying the Irish are banished."

"It's their sense of humor."

"Funny kind of joke. More like an insult to me."

"They wouldn't have meant it that way, Mam. They'd be mortified if they thought they'd insulted you."

"Aren't there any nice Irish girls in New York for you to be friends with?"

"They are Irish, Mam. All of them have Irish blood."

"Funny they didn't mention it. You think Maggie's all right without you?"

"She's fine. Kevin's with her. They're having a ball, they'll be here in three days."

"I'd never have left you at three years old."

"Do you think I'd have done it if I thought it was bad for her?"

"Don't you be talking to me like that. D'ye think I'm one of those Americans? Getting tanned and playing tennis at my age? The sky's the limit with that lot."

Kathleen didn't know exactly what her mother was talking about. They walked along in silence. Kathleen asked her mother if she wanted to go to the movies.

"See a fill-um in the middle of the day with the sun cracking the pavestones?"

"Just for a change, Mam."

"All right then, for a change." Kathleen knew her mother agreed because she didn't want to fight and couldn't think of anything to say that wouldn't start a fight. They drove into Gort. It was an English movie. People said it was supposed to be funny. She didn't think her mother would like it, but she hoped it would take her mind off what was going on in her kitchen. But she didn't like it, and she said, "I guess you have a different sense of humor if you're from a different place."

She dropped her mother at Brid's and said she'd go home to set the table. She was walking in the grass at the back of the house; she could hear the girls through the kitchen window.

"I've been in trailers that had bigger kitchens than this," Joanne said.

"I knew it was simple, but this is depressing as hell. The poor baby. No wonder she couldn't wait to get out," Marty said. "I mean that shower. I think it was made of Styrofoam, and if that's their idea of hot water."

"They're very nice, though," Lois said.

"I like that Brid. She's got gumption. More than her husband with his big blue eyes," said Marty.

"We ought to get something for them, to thank her. Brid, I mean."

"Do you think there are really stores that we could go to that sell stuff that's tacky enough? That lamp made out of fake shells. And the fabric on the sofa. I thought I was going to die it was so itchy."

"I don't think we have the right to complain. We're staying there for free, so we have to be nice about things."

Kathleen felt terror in the middle of her chest, as if she'd been stung below one of her ribs. They thought Brid was letting them stay for free. Where had they gotten that idea? She was sure she'd never said that. Should she have told them right away what the cost would be? She'd hoped she'd be able to work that out with Brid, that Brid would give them a break. But she'd never dreamed of asking Brid not to charge them.

She'd have to make up the money. She couldn't imagine how she'd do it. She thought of telling them they'd have to pay. But their faces when she told them were a horrifying prospect. Anything would have to be better than that.

She'd have to call Kevin. She tried to make herself walk slowly to Brid's house and say calmly that she'd told Kevin she'd call at this time, but that she'd reverse the charges, like it was normal she was doing it from here instead of her parents'.

"Fine then," Brid said. She was standing behind the counter at the convenience store, being oh so pleasant to an American couple who were buying candy and soft drinks.

"Isn't it great for you the weather broke?" she said, smiling. Kathleen saw she'd spent a fortune at the dentist.

"Oh, we didn't come to Ireland for the weather, or the food. It's the spirit of the people," the woman said. She was wearing a turquoise running suit and her husband had an identical one in teal. They both wore immaculate white sneakers. Trainers, they were called in Ireland, Kathleen remembered.

When she heard Kevin's voice she burst into tears.

"I suppose I could tell them they have to pay for it, but, oh, Kevin, the thought of it kills me."

"No, no, I understand," he said.

"Only, how will I get the money?"

"Not a problem. Put it on the Visa. Tell Brid the girls gave you a certain sum of money and you deposited it in your bank in America."

"Brid would never believe me. She'd know something was up. I'd never hear the end of it. Isn't there anything else? Couldn't we borrow money off the Visa?"

"Go see Martin Cunningham in the Ennis bank. Tell him you need five hundred pounds off the Visa."

"What'll he think I need it for? He'll think I need to go to England for an abortion."

"He'll think no such thing, Kathleen. Besides, what do you care what he thinks?"

"He'd have it all over town."

"Of course he won't, he's a professional. Don't make it a problem, baby."

"Don't you call me baby. Ever ever again."

"Don't you be chewing out my guts because your friends let you down. I'm on your side, remember? I'll be with you in two days. I should have known better than to let you loose in the world on your own."

Her palms felt moist the way they used to all the time before she had the baby. She wondered if they'd feel like that all the time now. She kept walking up and down the sidewalk in front of the bank, then she realized she was looking conspicuous. She walked in and walked up to Martin Cunningham's desk.

"Well, Kathleen, aren't you a sight for sore eyes? How long are you home for?"

"Two weeks," she said, and she was blushing. "Only, you see, Mr. Cunningham, Kevin's coming next week and I'm afraid I've overspent what he gave me to tide me over. I'm just off the phone with him, he said I could get a cash advance on the Visa."

"You can, of course," he said. "Just hand it over, said the dodo."

She had no idea what he meant by that dodo bit. She was worried that the lie came to her so easily.

He took the card and came back with a slip for her to sign. Then he went away again and came back with five hundred pounds.

"Anything else we could be doing for you?"

"No, you're grand," she said. "Thanks."

She ran out the door before she could start worrying that he was looking at her funny.

As she drove home, she wondered how they'd make the money up. They just made it month to month, and they were careful. Maybe it meant they couldn't come over again at Christmas. Or maybe she'd get another job. Kevin was always saying she could make more money somewhere else. With her looks and her way with people. She was getting to be known in town; people knew her from church, and with the singing in Harrigan's.

She'd taken Jimmy's car and she left it in front of the B & B. Slowly, she walked the half mile to her parents' house. The nausea that began when she thought of the Visa bill grew when she smelt the heavy smell of the tomato sauce. She couldn't bear the thought of eating it. She knew what would happen. She'd walk into the kitchen and they'd give her a piece of bread dipped in the sauce. She'd cut it up into small pieces with a knife and fork and eat it slowly, piece by piece. When they asked her how it was, she'd tell them it was fantastic.

Rosecliff

We should begin with the house, or the story of the house. Or the facts that make up part of the story of the house.

The name of the house is Rosecliff. Its location is Newport, Rhode Island.

What am I doing in Newport, Rhode Island? What am I doing looking at the mansions of Newport, Rhode Island? I who pride myself on having no interest in the habits of the wealthy, or in architecture that's overembellished, self-proclaiming in its tone. The answer: I am meeting a friend who is at a conference there. An old friend, and like me, brought up in the working class. We will stay in a bed and breakfast, walk and talk, catch up.

I don't like the bed and breakfast because although my room has a four-poster bed, it doesn't have a bathtub. A working fireplace (although instead of logs, there's an artificial log wrapped in paper, ignitable at the touch of a match), but no bathtub. A stall shower. And worse: communal breakfasts, at a long mahogany table—Chippendale, I think, because of the ball and claw feet. Everyone, except for my friend and me, is part of a couple. On a pilgrimage to the unimaginable wealth of the past. They talk, without exception, about money. "CAN YOU IMAGINE WHAT THAT'D COST YOU TODAY?" They are fecund in their idioms having to do with money. "That'd set you back quite a lot." "They must have been rolling in it." "That was worth a pretty penny."

Furthermore, it's raining and we have to be out of the room at ten so that the place can be made up. It is in a spirit of anarchic churlishness that I approach the great houses, walk through the avenues of trees where water drips extravagantly from the costly leaves of horse chestnuts, copper beeches, elms.

Of the great houses, Rosecliff appeals to me most, because it's white: an asset in a blinding rainstorm. Also, I'm disposed to its original owner because she has a wonderful name: Theresa Fair. And she was arriviste and unlucky. Not completely unlucky: her father discovered the Comstock Lode, a vein of silver worth two hundred million dollars. "Know what that'd be in today's dollars?" my breakfast partners would say.

I don't know, but it sounds like quite a lot.

Theresa Fair married Herman Oelrichs, scion of a shipping fortune, turned her back on the crude society of her native San Francisco, and took up the business of New York society with an avidity that must have burned like lust. She hired Stanford White to build her Newport summer palace. Or cottage, as they were called. Stanford White: killed by a maniac for love of a floozy.

Already the substantiality of Newport is being undermined.

Theresa Fair Oelrichs and Stanford White argued about the details of the construction of Rosecliff. He'd meant it to be a copy of the Petit Trianon at Versailles, which was a pleasure palace, not a residence. Mrs. Oelrichs needed rooms for her guests. Reluctantly, White added a second story. But Mrs. Oelrichs needed rooms for her staff. White agreed to a third story, provided it would be narrow, short, and invisible. He built forty rooms, each of them only ten feet high. They must have been cubicles. They cannot be seen from the outside, because they are set back and hidden by a balustrade. The comfort of the servants was in no one's mind.

In the Grand Ballroom, where Stanford White had commissioned a painted sky in the middle of the ceiling, Tessie Fair Oelrichs had her famous *bal blanc* (she was obsessed with whiteness, with the color white) in imitation of the one given by Louis XIV. All the women were told to wear white, and if their hair wasn't white, to powder it or to wear white wigs. She herself wore a headdress made of ostrich feathers and diamonds. She tried to get her friend, who was secretary of the navy, to dock some navy ships outside her house. But he refused. So she had mock ships built by Newport craftsmen, outlining their sails in newly invented electric light.

She doesn't seem to have been happy. Her husband, it was said, traveled a lot on business and was rarely in the house. One day, in 1920, when she was supervising some construction, perhaps in the ballroom, a piece of plaster fell from the ceiling, blinding her in one eye. She suffered a nervous breakdown, and took to her bed in Rosecliff, entertaining imaginary guests. Of her son, not much is known. She died in 1926, so the house was his during the Depression, that time that was so hard on great houses. Fortunes were lost; servants could not be hired, since their wages could not be paid. During the thirties, says our tour guide (without whom you can't see the house), the great houses were "white elephants." You could buy them, the tour guide says, "for a song." Immediately I see houses, especially the white Rosecliff, lumbering, vulnerable, loyal as old elephants, and then I see sharpsters in checkered suits putting nooses around the melancholy pachyderms' noble necks, leading them off singing something like "ja-da-ja-da-jadajada jig, jig, jig."

I don't know what condition the house was in in 1941 when Anita Niesen bought it for her daughter Gertrude's twenty-first birthday. She paid only twenty-one thousand dollars. Perhaps a thousand dollars for each year of her daughter's life. Gertrude was a cabaret singer. A nightclub singer. They were from New York.

. . .

This purchase was not a good thing for the house. Anita and Gertrude lived in the house only one season: the summer of 1941. Having spent money on the house, they couldn't afford servants to maintain it. They had a summer there alone, mother and daughter, playing house. At the end of the season, they closed the house, but they neglected to drain the pipes. They didn't arrange for proper heating. So in the winter, the pipes burst and the house was ruined by water damage. The great heart-shaped staircase, copied by Stanford White from a French original, was encased with ice. The tour guide shows us pictures.

Suddenly, I am jolted from my torpor. The torpor I always feel when I hear the word "wealth," one syllable, top-heavy, though single, over-upholstered, a soft mountain, an avalanche, the dark pulpy apple with an unfathomable center. Something about the word "wealth" overtires me. Makes me long for sleep. Or death. I don't like these big houses because they're death houses. Built by people who, like the ancient Egyptians, are choking to death on the fat of the land.

But when I hear about Anita and Gertrude, and not having money for servants, and not knowing enough to drain the pipes, I am no longer breathing the thick air of wealth.

It is the air of carelessness. The air of ruin caused by carelessness. Stupidity or lack of knowledge. I can think of nothing but the staircase encased in ice, and the fact that you can't talk about it without repeating the syllable "case." It is the case that the staircase was encased in ice.

For two years I think about the nightclub singer and her mother and the staircase encased in ice. I go to the newspaper morgue and find everything I can about Gertrude Niesen.

But I'm not really interested in Gertrude or her mother. I'm interested in the damage to the house. The damaged house. I'm not really interested in the house before or after its damage.

The shame of a damaged house. I'm interested in the house's shame, and what I believe must have been the people's lack of shame.

I want to tell the story of a damaged house, but I don't know how. I don't want to make the story an anecdote.

Or a study in the clash of social forces.

I thought of inventing a third character and telling the story from her point of view. A poor relation. A female cousin. First censorious, then shy. In love with Gertrude's father. I had thought of having her explain the father's presence in Gertrude's career and Gertrude's plan to win her father away from this poor cousin, who gave him the attention his wife and daughter would not.

I didn't know how else to explain the father's presence in the articles about Gertrude. There, he's portrayed as being initially so reluctant for his daughter to have a career in show business that she's forced to run away from home: her respectable home in Brooklyn Heights. This is the hook, with Gertrude: she's well brought up, genteel even, she went to a finishing school, the Brooklyn Academy. Eventually, though, Mr. Niesen relents. He sees that talent will out, so in the later articles he's hovering, attentive, making sure the reporters get things straight. He's the detail man. Calling the coast. Making train reservations.

What I can't explain is why, since he was involved in real estate as a profession, he would have allowed his wife to buy a property she couldn't possibly maintain, why he wouldn't have told her that pipes had to be drained, that the house couldn't be left as I imagine they left it, closing the door behind them, taking a taxi to the train.

But I'm not really interested in the father. I'm interested in the damaged house. Because I think one of the things I fear most is that my carelessness or ignorance will cause a damage I could never have foreseen and can never repair.

You'd think I'd be interested in Gertrude. I always wanted to be a cabaret singer. A torch singer. Lounging like Gertrude, in smoky lounges. Gertrude's big song was "Light My Cigarette." Gertrude, the finishing school chanteuse. Gertrude, born, in the photos I xerox from the morgue, to embody the word "blowsy." Short, with a brassy pageboy, overfull lips and bosom. A beauty mark, which may or may not have been penciled in. Her Russian mother. Her Swedish father, the detail man.

But what I think about is the staircase encased in ice. The ruined fabrics. The woodwork a sponge, the plaster a chalky milk. The terrible, aggressive stupidity of being careless with something that took so much time to create and maintain. The dreadfulness of how easy it is to do damage. The shamed house, like a grand lady given the pox by her philandering husband, full of tremors, marks on her face like carbuncles, like the shells of snails.

Two years after I saw the house I talk to another friend about this story and what it means to me. She says: "There are some things you can't play with. They're too powerful, they always win in the end."

But, I say, it was the house that was hurt, not the people, really.

But, she responds, that kind of hurt humiliates whoever inflicted it. And besides, the house was rebuilt by another rich person.

But I don't think Gertrude and her mother suffered. I don't know why I believe that: perhaps because of Gertrude's smoky eyes, and the way she ordered her father around. And the fact that her mother sold the house at a profit. I would never have been able to sell the house. I would have been so ashamed that I would have had to live there forever, to bear witness to my carelessness, my dereliction. I wouldn't have been able to repair the house myself, or come up with the money, so I would have insisted upon my own continued presence at the center of the ruin. This is how I know that Gertrude and her mother were nothing like me. And why I'm jealous of them, and contemptuous. I believe they were incapable of suffering.

My friend and I both feel that, given damage that extensive, someone must have suffered.

But we don't know who.

If you know that there was suffering, but you don't know who suffered, how do you tell the story?

The Blind Spot

Tom was her blind spot. Everyone knew it, everyone else could see it, of course—that's what a blind spot is, after all, something everyone else can see that you can't see. I guess we all have one. At least one. Well, Tom was Sister Bertie's, that's for sure. Sister Roberta Conlon, O.S.N. The Order of St. Norbert. That's what those initials stand for. Once thriving, now nearly extinct. Once a community of several hundred souls, now dwindled to thirty-five. A median age of seventy-six. At sixty-eight, Bertie was among the youngest.

No, you would not say the Order of St. Norbert was thriving. You would have to say that it was dying on the vine. But Sister Bertie was thriving, and everything that she touched seemed to thrive. That is, if you don't count Tom.

I met her more than thirty years ago. I think it was 1971. No, 1970: the year we invaded Cambodia. I met her on a march protesting the invasion of Cambodia. I'd never met a nun before. I'm not a Catholic. My family was Congregationalist, but there was nothing serious about our churchgoing.

I couldn't quite place what was odd about her at first; a middle-aged woman, plainly dressed, a denim skirt, a madras blouse, a cross that looked like it was made of iron in the middle of her chest. She was friendly, but without allure. I was ashamed of myself for thinking in those terms when I realized she was a nun. That was before we were friends.

But before we were friends, we were colleagues. I'd come out to Rockford, Wisconsin, as dean of Fisher University, a small-sized private university with a surprisingly large endowment that had its roots in the production of beer; I didn't even know there was another institution of higher learning in the town: St. Norbert's College, a liberal arts college for women run by the Sisters of St. Norbert. Bertie was the president. She still is.

I don't think I'd moved most of the boxes out of my office when she called for an appointment. "Well, what can you do for me?" she asked. "I know that's been on your mind. Uppermost in your thoughts. That's why I'm here: to relieve you of the burden of the burning questions: what can I do for Sister Roberta? so that you can get on with your life."

It took me a while to realize that she was kidding. When she realized that, she began to laugh. "Oh, God, I'm always in trouble because people think I'm serious. My problem is that everyone takes me at my word. I'm Irish, Dr. Winthrop. You shouldn't always take me at my word."

I wanted to say, "But you're a nun."

But she beat me to the punch. "You think that's a strange thing for a nun to be saying. Don't think of me as a nun. Or, all right, I guess you have to. Think of me as an educator. Think of me as a poor relation. But there are things we can do for you over at St. Norbert's. We have things that we can provide; resources that we can share. We have, for example, a lot of land. Aren't you a little short on hockey space?"

She was wrong; it wasn't hockey; it was lacrosse, but we were short on playing fields, and in exchange for their playing fields, we allowed the St. Norbert's girls to take our film courses. To use the equipment. The equipment was the main point. In all the years I've been dean, not more than ten girls from St. N.'s used the equipment. One of them did a program about Bertie, and it was shown on local television and then nominated for an Emmy. I remember something Bertie said on that show, about her religious life. I always thought it explained a lot about her. She said the point of faith wasn't that it brought certainty, but that it allowed you a place of trust.

I don't quite know what the point was to my hiring Tom in the art department. Or what the point was supposed to be. I wasn't the one she convinced, though; it was Ray Ringswold, the chairman of the department. He was the one who came into my office to tell me Tom Conlon would be a great addition to the department; it would be a feather in our cap to have an M.F.A. from Yale, someone who'd shown in New York, not recently, of course, but no one on the art faculty had even come that close.

I don't know what Bertie had done to convince Ray Ringswold that it would be a good idea to hire Tom—she was very good at convincing people of things. It wasn't just her charm, which was considerable, or the force of her character, also considerable: she had vision. Now I know that's a word people use carelessly nowadays, but Bertie really had it. Take what she did with St. N.'s. In the forties and fifties, it was a kind of finishing school for future Catholic mothers; in the sixties, it had a brief hectic flush as a training ground for Catholics planning to work in the Third World; by the seventies, it was turning moribund. Bertie had thought it needed more than cosmetic surgery. Some people think she beheaded the institution they had loved and cared for and created a whole new animal. This was her vision: St. Norbert's was going to devote itself to the education of underclass urban women. She began with her education department, offering literacy classes in the projects; her psychology department organized a day-care center there for the mothers. Her dream was to move women (many of them were girls, although they'd had several children by the time they entered the program) from a G.E.D. right through to a B.A. On-site learning, at first, and then buses taking them to the campus. She thought it was important for working mothers to have green, and space, and quiet. Foundations loved the project; she was a whiz at getting major grants. The occasional middle-class white girl who still made her way to St. Norbert's, because of her mother's alumnae loyalty or because she couldn't get in anywhere else, either left soon or was transformed. And there were transformations among the inner-city women. "A miracle worker," people said about Bertie. They said it all the time. It made her laugh. But she couldn't work miracles on her brother Tom. Perhaps because she didn't think he needed any changing: not a bit.

I'd met him before, because there were periods when he'd live at the convent: the convent had many empty rooms; it had been built when the order was thriving; now it was like a hotel in a ghost town. Bertie had told me there were forty-five bedrooms; there were only eleven sisters living there. She wanted to bring some of the women and their children to live there, but the other sisters refused. They didn't refuse Tom, though; I guess they knew that would be going too far. Bertie could seem flexible, but when she wanted something, there was an implacability that could be a little frightening. She would say things with a laugh, but if you looked at them closely, her eyes were steel.

Bertie's explanations for Tom were extravagant, absurd: she compared him to the medieval troubadours; she compared him to St. Francis of Assisi. She kept saying, "My brother is a true original. He cares nothing about money. He lives for his art." I didn't know him well enough to question what she said about his relationship to money and his work. Certainly, he looked poor; his clothes were thrift-shop shabby; his car was a study in rust; it worked only in some favorable climatic conditions; its failures always seemed to surprise Tom, but I don't know how he could imagine that the car would be dependable. What would you have a car for if you couldn't depend on it? I suppose that's unfair; I suppose a dependable car is a luxury of the middle class. And Tom prided himself on not being a member of the middle class. And Bertie was proud of that part of him.

Although I didn't find myself in a position to doubt his unworldliness or his devotion to his work, I knew enough to know he wasn't what Bertie called "an original." Anyone who'd spent any time around a major city or a major university would have met someone like Tom. One of those people who hung around after graduation, who made themselves a fixture at coffeehouses and poetry readings, still driving a taxi or waiting tables in their forties. Calling themselves artists and despising others who had sold out. Maybe some of them were good artists; I'm not in a position to know. I don't trust my own taste in art—I've learned that as a dean, dealing with some of the more creative types. My degree was in economics. But I don't want you to get the wrong idea about that. Like all I care about is money. The Board of Trustees sometimes accuses me of not paying attention to the bottom line. My dissertation was on the Ujimah villages in Tanzania; I'd learned about them when I served in the Peace Corps there. *Ujimah* means brotherhood. The villages were meant to be based on ancient kinship networks. In the beginning of my research, I thought they were a viable option; by the time I published my book, I had to name them what they were: a noble, failed experiment. Maybe I should have known better than to try the experiment of hiring Tom. But Ray Ringswold convinced me. All that feather in our caps talk, I guess, went to my head. And I couldn't have borne disappointing Bertie.

Because, unlike the rest of us, she was a person of hope. A person of hope because a person of faith; I watched her once, at a wedding. It was a Catholic Mass, and I saw her face when she prayed after communion. I would never call Bertie beautiful, but her face was shining. Something happened to her when she prayed. Because she believed in it, and from it took hope. And she really loved people; she said, "Joe, I really love you," once when a project we'd worked on together came up trumps. And I believed she did.

She was something of a legend. There was the story of the woman who was going to kill her baby and herself rather than give the baby up to child welfare. She'd gone back on drugs; she was one of Bertie's failures. Bertie was in the projects one day; sometimes she taught classes there: she said she wanted to keep an eye on things, and she liked being back "on the ground." As if she were, most of her life, somewhere else. But no one would have said of Bertie that she was "up in the air."

The police were at the door, but they were stymied. None of them wanted to take the chance with a baby's life. Bertie came up and knocked on the door, as if she were in a first-class hotel and were stopping by to see if a friend was ready to go to luncheon.

"Janice," she said. "It's Sister Roberta. I'm here. I won't let anything happen."

"You'll let them take my baby."

"I'll take your baby," she said. "I'll keep him until you're better. Then you can get him back."

"They won't let you. They'll give him away to some foster people who'll treat him bad."

"Of course they'll let me," Bertie said. "You know me well enough by now. People always do as I say. Now just let me in and we'll talk."

The woman let her in. They talked. No one knows what they said, but Sister Roberta took the baby. She did get a family that she knew to take care of the baby. But it didn't turn out well. Janice was killed in prison. Knifed by her cellmate: a lover's quarrel. What did Bertie make of that? And whatever happened to the baby? I don't know; at least his mother didn't kill him, and at least she didn't kill herself. So that was something. "Something is better than nothing, Joe. You've got to believe that. Or you're paralyzed." Did she know how often I feel paralyzed? I never knew quite what Bertie knew.

But I know she didn't know some things about her brother. Maybe it was because he was so much younger than she; they really didn't grow up together; he was five when she left the house for the convent, and as she told me, in the years of her preparation for final vows, she wasn't allowed to see her family very much. Her parents both died while Tom was still a teenager; she was very protective of him, and very, very proud.

He got a scholarship to Yale. That was quite something for a family from Marion, Illinois; no one from the town had ever gone to the Ivy League. Then he stayed on for his master's in painting. He was still living in New Haven when I hired him; he worked as a janitor in an apartment building; he said it was good for his work. He said he didn't want to live in New York, didn't want to be part of the rat race. The gallery scene was a trap; it killed real art, he said. I don't know why he never showed after the first time; I suspect that his show wasn't successful, but I have no proof of that. No one keeps track of people who don't show after the first time; they just disappear. That's what I've been told by people who seem to know the business.

"My brother's a real beatnik," Bertie would say. At first I thought she was in a time warp, that she really meant hippie, but she was right—Tom's model wasn't minted in the sixties; it was a decade earlier. He carried copies of *Howl* in his pocket, and memorized Ferlinghetti. Kerouac was his god. He liked to hint that he'd done hard drugs, but he also liked to be vague about it. "Not just that mind candy Tim Leary was passing out, I mean the real hard stuff," he'd say, after a drink or two. With a certain kind of student, this had real appeal. Needless to say I didn't like it. I preferred seeing him with Bertie; he didn't talk about that kind of stuff in front of her.

I wasn't the one who told him to stop referring to our female students as "chicks." It was actually Andrea who did it, very kindly, very gently—Andrea had that way about her, but I think she made her point. Andrea was another of Bertie's transformations. Or miracles, depending on which word you liked to use. She, too, was something of a local legend. She'd worked as a secretary at St. N.'s; she'd started there just after high school and never worked anywhere else. She'd married her high school sweetheart, and they had three children. But everyone knew he was a drunk. Then one night—we've all heard the details quite often, everyone in town I mean—he went after her youngest daughter. Not sexually, but with a belt. And Andrea knocked him out with a frying pan. Then she sued for divorce. And he sued back, got the police to press charges against her for assault.

Bertie was the one who talked her into fighting it. She was the one who called in the press. I don't know where they came from, but there suddenly seemed to be hundreds of women who'd been abused, or felt they'd been abused by their husbands. Vince Crawford had to crawl with his tail between his legs for quite a long time. Then Andrea went back to school; first she got her B.A. from St. N.'s, then her M.A. in psychology. She worked for a while at a battered women's shelter. Then Bertie hired her as her assistant. That was when I met her—I mean really met her, not just knew her as a local cause célèbre. I always found her wonderful to work with. It wasn't just that she was efficient, although she was, very, and that's always a good thing. She was efficient without being contemptuous: that's not so common. And she liked to laugh. Things would strike her funny—often it was something Bertie said—and she had a way of putting her head back so her neck was exposed; it was a winning gesture. I enjoyed it when I would meet up with her at parties. I suggested to my wife that we have her over for dinner, but my wife was adamant. "Oh, Christ, Joe, not another of your wounded birds," was what she said. She hates what she calls "professional victims." She goes ballistic over the Oprah show. She says she doesn't know what happened to good old-fashioned reticence. I'd never say it to my wife, but I think she's a little jealous of Andrea's daughter: she's a Rhodes scholar now. Our two have done fine—they're still finding themselves, but neither of them has done anything with college that a parent could brag about.

I would have liked to get to know Andrea better, but I know it won't happen. I think she likes seeing me when the circumstances dictate. Work or parties, is what I mean.

Am I being unfair in my suspicions that Bertie made it happen? Tom and Andrea, I mean, as a couple. She didn't lift an eyebrow over their living together, although they're not married—I can't help thinking she'd like them to make it legal, but of course we've never talked about it. I'm not close to Bertie in that way. I don't know if anybody is.

I suppose a lot of women would find Tom attractive, although I must say I find it as difficult to figure out what women think is attractive in a man as I do to determine what's a good work of art. He had a boyish quality, Tom, and I guess that goes over well with a lot of women. Brings out the mother in them. I never found him much to look at. Tall, skinny, still has all his hair; it still fell into his eyes, and he had this gesture of pushing it out of his eyes that most men my age have given up. He is my age, Tom Conlon; we once discovered we were born two days apart.

He was popular with the undergraduates, male and female. I always thought it was that his work was so obvious that it was easy for them to relate to it. A couple are hanging in the college gallery: Tom's face on a female body: called *Self Portrait*. And one that's just the word "Why" written over and over, in different kinds of script. It's called *WHYWHYWHY-WHYWHY*. You should have seen Bertie's face the night of Tom's opening. She kept taking me by the elbow and bringing me over to the *WHYWHY-WHYWHYWHY* picture. "It's the *question*, isn't it? He's so courageous to put it so baldly. What we all wake up thinking. What we're most of us afraid to say." I told her I was enjoying the paintings very much. "Great, Joe, it's a great thing for the university. And for the world," she said.

Her eye fell on him, and his on her; smiled at each other; they walked toward each other. I didn't hear them say anything. They just stood next to each other; he had his arm around her and she—well, the only thing to be said about it was she was beaming. I'd never realized she was so short. Standing next to her brother, his arm around her, she looked smaller than I'd ever understood her to be. The both of them looked entirely happy. I stood next to Andrea. "They're quite a pair," she said. And she looked happy, too.

Bertie moved away from Tom when the students began buzzing around him. They were standing so close to him that when he moved his arms to gesticulate (he did that a lot when he spoke) he often knocked the wine out of the students' plastic glasses. He was certainly popular with the students. I suspected it was partly because he let students determine their own grades. He often went out with them for beers. I was tempted to tell him that was a dicey proposition, but I didn't want to appear to be an old fogy. In retrospect, that was probably a mistake.

For three years, everything went fine. Tom taught his classes; he painted his paintings; he and Andrea took a Chinese cooking course. When I saw them at parties, I thought he embarrassed her sometimes; he could be loud when he'd had a bit too much to drink. One time, I thought she was looking for me to quiet him down when he was spouting off about the poison of the marketplace for artists. But I didn't say anything: I couldn't think of anything to say. In any case they seemed happy enough, and when Bertie was with them (Tom never drank in front of Bertie) they seemed like the dream of a happy family. Enviable, really. I never found my situation enviable. Occasionally, I'd look in *The Chronicle of Higher Education,* but there were no jobs that seemed like the risk of moving might be worth it. Besides, my wife has a real place in the community. Real estate. She does very well.

Then there was the incident with Amber Wirthman. Amber wasn't the type you'd think of as trouble; she was a weedy-looking girl with reddish blonde hair and protruding teeth. A little too long-legged, so she reminded you sometimes of a stork. Or in winter, when she wore this gray fake fur hat that she seemed devoted to, an ostrich. She was a business major with a minor in accounting. But she liked to paint; she'd taken three of Tom's classes; she was one of his groupies, but to my mind, she didn't stand out among them.

I forgot to say that her father owns the company my wife works for. Wirthman Realtors, a division of Coldwell Banker. I always found the name confusing; as if they couldn't tell whether they were a real-estate company or a bank. I never liked Jim Wirthman, and I certainly didn't like his wife, Donna. She was active in our alumni association; the president had once called her "one of our jewels."

So she went to the president first, and then he came to me.

"It seems there's a problem with one of the faculty," he said.

This is never a sentence a dean likes to hear. But I'd been a dean long enough to know there was no sense in panicking. Students were easily disgruntled, and in the current climate—education as a consumer good—they felt entitled to complain.

"Tom Conlon," the president said.

What did I feel when I heard that name? I have to admit: at first I was glad that it wasn't a faculty member I was really fond of. Then I thought of Bertie, and I dreaded hearing the details.

"It's old-man sex, of course. But it's always sex or money, isn't it Joe?" The president liked adopting a men-of-the-world conspiratorial tone with me; he usually did it when he was going to pass me the buck. Or a particularly steamy, stinking mess.

"Donna Wirthman came in really upset. It seems Conlon stepped over barriers in all kinds of ways. He and Donna's daughter had an affair: she has letters to prove it. That's bad enough. But he gave Amber a sexually transmitted disease, and now it's possible she isn't going to be able to have children. The Wirthmans are talking lawsuits. Big-time, Joe."

I knew better than to ask the president what he thought we should do. That was why he'd come to me; if he'd had any good ideas, the matter wouldn't have gone any further than his office.

"Set up a meeting, Joe. You, me, and Conlon. And get Larry Casper. Don't say a thing without him being there."

Larry Casper was the university counsel. I'd be glad to have him in the room.

I don't know whether Tom Conlon suspected what was wrong, but if he did, he didn't dress for an occasion that might be serious. He was wearing jeans and a workshirt; his boots were spattered in paint. He didn't make eye contact with the president or Larry Casper; he looked to me as if he considered me the one ally in the room. I didn't know how I felt about that. Or no, that's wrong; I did know how I felt. I wanted to say to Tom, "Don't look to me for help. You got yourself into this mess, get yourself out of it." Then I thought of Bertie.

"Amber Wirthman's parents have been in to see me," the president said.

I had to give Tom credit; he blushed. "OK," he said. "That can't be good."

"It's unfortunate," Tom said. "But she's an adult. She was twenty-three last July. She works half-time for her father; that's why it's taken her so long to get her degree."

"Her age is neither here nor there, nor is her degree status," the president said.

"Well, actually, Mort, it's better that she's not a minor," Larry Casper said.

"You understand we'll have to ask for your resignation. You're not tenured, so we can do that. I'm sure you understand why we would want to. I'm hoping that will forestall a lawsuit, but I can't promise."

"You're saying I could be completely wiped out; I'm losing my job; and then they could sue me on top of it? Well, the good news is I haven't got a cent. What are they going to take, my car? I suppose they could put me in debtors' prison."

"I think you fail to understand the gravity of the situation," the president said. "You committed a very serious breach of student-teacher trust. You've betrayed your position; you've betrayed the values of this college."

"Save it," Tom said, getting up. "I'll pack up my gear, but I don't want any bullshit about students and teachers. She's an adult. I'm an adult. I didn't hurt her."

"She may be unable to have children," I said.

"That's a crock," he said. "Lots of people have chlamydia and do just fine."

"I wouldn't suggest taking that line with the Wirthmans," Larry Casper said. "I would have no contact with them without an attorney present."

"Are you my attorney?" Tom asked.

"No, I represent the college."

"How am I supposed to pay for a lawyer?"

"Maybe you should have thought of that before," Larry Casper said.

When I phoned Bertie to ask if I could take her out for coffee, I was hurt by the eagerness in her voice.

"To what do I owe this incredible pleasure, Joe?"

"A sticky issue, I'm afraid, Bertie," I said. "I can't talk about it on the phone."

She ordered a mocha frappuccino with whipped cream. I had a double espresso. After I left Bertie, I had to go to a faculty budget committee meeting. I needed straight caffeine.

"It's about Tom," I said.

"He's all right, isn't he," she asked, looking alarmed. "He's not sick or anything? He isn't hurt?"

I explained the situation to her.

"I don't believe it," she said. "The girl is trying to frame him. She was probably infected by some rich boy who can afford expensive lawyers and the parents know Tom's an innocent, a babe in the woods, an easy mark."

"Your brother hasn't denied anything," I said.

"Why would he do something like that with a student? He has Andrea to keep him on the straight and narrow. It doesn't make sense. He's too old for all of that; he's put all that behind him. Let me talk to the girl and her parents; I'll get to the bottom of this."

"I can't stop you, Bertie, but I don't think it will do any good. You have to consider the possibility that they might be telling the truth."

"I won't consider it for a moment, Joe. And I'm surprised that you would. I'm going to leave now." She walked out of Starbucks like she'd like to set the whole thing on fire, with me inside it.

I don't know what happened with Bertie and the Wirthmans, but they decided not to sue. Tom's gone back to New Haven. Andrea's stayed in the apartment. I don't know if she considered going east with him or not.

I really don't get to speak with Andrea anymore, because I don't have a lot of contact with Bertie. When Bertie has some business at the college, she makes a point of going over my head. Sometimes I think of talking to Andrea about the situation—offering my condolences, or something like that. But why would I say condolences? No one died. Anyway, what could I tell her? About a situation like the one with Tom and Bertie, I don't think there's much that can be said. And what could I ask her? I saw her once, in a parking lot—I think it was the supermarket, or it may have been the mall. It was late September; she was pushing a shopping cart, but it didn't look like it had much in it. The light was clear and it fell straight onto her; her hair looked golden; she was wearing a red jacket that looked quite wonderful that day. But I didn't say anything to her; I didn't even wave; I don't know if she even saw me.

What would I say to her? I would have liked to say, "I miss you and Bertie. I miss the two of you terribly." I would have liked to say the words accompanied by some gesture; I would have liked to put my hand on her shoulder; I would have liked to touch her hair. I would have liked to say, "How are you, the two of you? Are you all right? Tell me how you are, what has happened to Tom. How has Bertie taken it all?"

I understood very well that there really wasn't anything I had a right to know. I wasn't close to anyone involved. I hardly knew Andrea, and I would be the last person Bertie would want knowing the details of her life.

I sometimes wonder what Bertie said to Tom. I could imagine her saying something like "Forget it, Tom, it's over, go on with your life. No one appreciates you like I do. No one understands you but me."

And there'd be no one, no one at all, to tell her she was wrong.

Walt

I own a famous store. In the back of the store, we cook the food that people buy, the food we set out in the showcase. Our food is created as much to be looked at as tasted: it is a thing of the eye as much as the palate. More of the eye, perhaps, because it's food that's meant to be more representative than nourishing. People bring home my food so that in solitude or in their two-person families they can feel bountiful, part of the generous world.

Sometimes we cater parties, and I often wonder whether the hosts pretend to have cooked the food themselves. Now that my food is so famous and desirable (we couldn't possibly serve everyone who wants us) I'm more and more curious about whether or not people acknowledge that the food that they are serving came from me. It's questionable now whether people would receive more praise, would be seen as doing more for their guests, for having cooked the food themselves or having had what is required—luck? wit? discipline? connections?—to be among the ones I choose to serve.

From time to time I cook on television. I did today. This morning I woke up at four to be ready for the limo they were sending at five. It could have been dangerous, out on the street at that hour, but I didn't feel in danger. I'm often on the street at four, four thirty, on my way down to the market for what is to me the most pleasurable and most important part of my work. I love everything about the market: the hum and buzz of money changing hands, insults, praise, the sound of tearing paper, barrels scraping across pavement, snatches of song, curses, the glazed eyes of fish, the redness of radishes, whiteness of cauliflowers, dewy cabbages with the pallor of a damp summer moon.

This morning I wasn't dressed in jeans, workboots, and sweatshirt, my market garb, but in a long, wide skirt and a teal-colored silk shirt (for television it's important to have a well-defined neckline). Everything I was experiencing made me feel a rich and blameless joy. Innocently as a child, I reveled in it all: the deep breeze that lifted the hem of my skirt, exposed my legs to the damp air, then chilled them; the dark limo jetting through the half light; the new smell of the car's upholstery; the cavernous backseat where I could doze for the half-hour ride.

From the moment I got into the car, there was a while when everyone I saw was uniformed, beginning with my driver, proceeding to the guards of the television station: a series of underemployed young men directing me down corridors as if I were an astronaut and they were showing me the way to outer space. Even the receptionists wore blazers with the network's symbol on the breast. Among them, I always felt alone. I knew that I was neither one of them nor important enough to engage their imagination. Later in the morning, politicians, actors, sports figures would arrive. They would be important to the uniformed ones; they would receive their smiles, their engaged nods, their grateful gestures. Sometimes one of the young women would say: "My mother made that cheesecake you did on the show last month," or "One of these days I'm going to try that cabbage soup." That was the most I'd ever get.

After every TV appearance I make, two things happen. Business increases and somebody from my past reappears. This morning, after the TV show was done, I was in the back of the store going over the books. I do this now more than any other work. It's surprisingly pleasant, so different from the rushed, hot work done in the kitchen, the room of white tiles and stainless steel industrial-style appliances. Different, too, from the subtle, ingratiating work of selling that goes on in the front of the store: consisting as it does of the offering of samples, along with a word suggesting a paradisiacal outcome that can only be effected by the customers' giving up more money than they'd like. As I was working in the back, the young man from Argentina who was serving customers up front knocked on the office door. "An old friend of yours is here," he said to me.

At first I couldn't believe it was really Walt. I'd feared seeing him for so long that the reality of him was rather reassuring. Often, on the street I'd think I'd seen him, but I'd turn away, convincing myself that it was impossible for us to be living in the same place. Although we both were born here.

"I thought it was time I came to see you."

It sounded like a threat, but I knew he didn't mean it as one. He never meant to seem dangerous; he wouldn't have understood if I said he'd often frightened me. "I only did what you wanted. That's all I would ever do," he'd say if I told him he'd frightened me. But that's just the kind of idea that can set many horrors in motion. Certainly with somebody like Walt.

The way I've just been talking about Walt and me gives you the wrong sense of us. The wrong historical sense. And this story is very much of its time. The way I was starting to tell it is the way people told stories for only a few years: 1958–65. At that time there were a lot of stories about mysterious girls in sunglasses and sheath dresses, wearing very pointed shoes with very high heels, walking around Paris waiting to be killed. Pointlessly killed by strangers. They would walk into dark bars in Rome or Paris saying, "I only live for death." And some dark man in a cheap suit would kill them. Probably they would have sex first. These girls always had the right kinds of cars. The cars were very important. The ominous sound of an expensive car door slamming in the empty, monumental street.

In 1965, these stories stopped being told; these films stopped being made. People became expansive. Their mysteriousness was drug-induced, communal. No one dreamed of wearing chignons or sheath dresses or high heels, except parodically. What happened to all those mysterious girls? What did they become when it was chic to be happy with wild hair and loose but transparent clothing?

You had to be young then, in the sixties. There were older women who wore black velvet pants and boots and white peasant blouses with brocade vests, or red crushed-velvet shirts. We pitied them. They wore too much makeup. When they got stoned their mascara smeared, and it reminded us of middle age.

Not everyone enjoyed the sixties the way people think. You needed some money or flexible plans. Walt and I had neither. We were both the first in our families to go to college. My father repaired TVs; he had a little shop in the town in Queens where we lived, Maspeth. After the store was broken into several times, he decided to get a guard dog. A German shepherd whom he kept chained in the store basement, tying him to a post in the middle of the small plot of grass in the back lot of the store so the dog could pee and shit three times a day. The dog never walked free. It was the nearest thing to a pet we had.

My mother, who'd lived above the store the first years of her marriage, was in love with her house, and the idea that its surface might be marred by an animal was unthinkable to her. She was so afraid of dust and grime that there were no carpets in the house. A speckled linoleum covered every inch of floor space: bedrooms, kitchen, living room, bathroom. Wherever you were in the house, if you looked down at your feet, you saw the same thing. At three o'clock every day, my mother would begin cooking: stewed meats, recipes made from ground beef, overcooked vegetables, some form of potatoes, a dessert. All her cleaning was done by noon; she prided herself on that. The hours between noon and three were spent on errands, or on mending or ironing. I don't think she ever sat down to read the paper or to make a phone call or to have a cup of coffee with a friend. Sometimes I would come upon her standing in the middle of the room wringing her hands. She was both honored and overwhelmed by the task of keeping house.

Certainly, she cared for me, perhaps even with some tenderness in the years before my memory, but it was clear to me from early on that we would not have much to do with each other. She didn't seem to have the time, and anyway, we shared no interests. My father came home from work at five fifteen, exhausted, even less communicative than he had been in the morning. At five thirty we ate in silence. We were finished by five forty-five, glad to be away from the table. My mother and I washed up. My father sat in front of the television. After washing the dishes, I went to my room.

In fifth grade, an art teacher famished for appreciation discovered that I had a talent for drawing. A talent for anything made me alien to my parents and their world, but drawing—creating things that were of no use—made the breach even wider. When I was much too young for this, my parents began to feel inferior to me. They stood back, so as not to be in my way. Eagerly, yet full of shame, they accepted Miss Jackson's offers of free art lessons and working trips to the museum. One night, when I was in high school, she made a drunken phone call to my parents, telling them I was a rose among thorns, that they didn't deserve to have me, but that she did, she'd never had anything, why should they have something and she nothing at all? After that call she never spoke to me in school, and there were no more trips to the Metropolitan. But by that time, I knew how to find my own way. I bought the *New York Times* and the *New Yorker*. I would read "The Talk of the Town" as if it were in a foreign language and think that the day when I could understand its references, I would have arrived. I went to the Guggenheim and the Modern and the Frick; I walked around Washington Square; I found my way to the Thalia. Long before I started N.Y.U., I had left home.

That was my journey out. Walt got out by being good in math. During the Sputnik years, there were a lot of opportunities for boys like him; his teachers, Christian Brothers, saw to it that he took the opportunities. We both took what was offered us, which would inevitably remove us from our parents, who were abashed even at our high school graduations, hearing our names called out in the auditorium, watching us step up for medal after medal. On the first day of college, they helped us bring our things to the dorm then left as quickly as they could. They didn't even say: "Don't let us down." They didn't need to. We knew we never could. They had worked so hard. Whatever we did, we would never work as hard as they had.

Walt was in the Socialist Workers Party, and he said that to talk about your family was a bourgeois affectation. The only things he said about them—that they lived in the Bronx, that his father worked on the docks— were offered as evidence that his working-class roots were grittier than mine: the soil of struggle still clung to his; mine had been rinsed. We met in a class on Eastern religion. I think of him whenever I hear the word

Zoroastrianism. It was the beginning of the course, when we were studying Zoroastrianism, that he first asked me out.

He wasn't at all what I wanted. Even his name seemed wrong; it was impossible to do anything with it that would make it sound hip, or sharp, or new. It sounded like a limp, white, tasteless vegetable: watery cauliflower in a chipped bowl, peeled boiled potatoes without salt. But from the first time he spoke to me, I knew I was exactly what he had in mind. He wanted to go home.

I was angry that I was so legible to him; I was trying hard to hide the clues about my past. I'd jettisoned all my new clothes—Villager dresses, Pappagallo shoes (the working-class idea of what the middle class would wear, all wrong as it turned out). They'd cost a month's salary from my summer typing job, but I didn't care. I started to wear jeans and outlandishly colored shirts or short dresses. How did he recognize me in that costume? He always wore olive green work pants, desert boots, and a white shirt. The white shirt always seemed very clean, very well pressed. The boys I wanted were wearing work shirts and boots, heavy and dangerous looking; you felt that if they stepped on your foot your toes would be crushed, your arches flattened like flounders. You'd be happy to have them try it, just to let them know you didn't mind.

He kept wanting me to read what he thought were Marxist classics. Every time we went out he'd give me a new book: *The Master and Margarita,* a multivolume biography of Lenin by Rok. I took pleasure in refusing to read these books. I was reading *Siddhartha,* and Walt Whitman, and Rilke's *Letters to a Young Poet.* "Why don't you ever read anything real?" he'd ask. I'd shrug in a lazy way that he found sexually inflaming. "I just want to kiss you . . . I just want to kiss you," he would say. Firmly, I would shake my head no. "I don't want to give you the wrong idea," I'd say. But everything about my being with Walt was wrong. I kept telling him that, but I continued to go out with him.

Sometimes we'd go to demonstrations together, and, taken over by a wave of political fervor, I'd let him hold my hand. He would analyze, in class terms, our relation to the demonstrating crowd. We were further away from them, he kept trying to remind me, than from the cops who were trying to beat us on the head. "So what?" I'd say. "So everything," he'd reply. But he was always so anxious to touch my hair, to put his arm around me, that he couldn't keep his mind on his arguments, and they lost their force.

I wondered at the time whether it was to get more information about my class status that he showed up at my house, unannounced, one day during spring break. He called me from a phone booth in the candy store on the corner and said he happened to be in the neighborhood. Nobody ever just happened to be in my neighborhood: they either lived there or they were visiting someone. But it was an hour subway ride from the Bronx, and I felt I couldn't send him back.

My parents never had visitors, and even someone requiring so little impressing as Walt made my mother feel inadequate and unprepared. She went to a lot of trouble to serve us "a nice lunch": tuna salad sandwiches with sweet pickles mixed in. She wouldn't let me lift a finger. "You kids are tired from all that school," she said. I didn't try to change her mind. Afterward, when I walked Walt to the subway, he said, "Your mother is a worker, and you oppress her like any boss in any factory anywhere in the world." I was outraged by that. I felt like an exceptionally dutiful daughter since I visited my parents ten times more than any of my friends whose families lived in brownstones right in the Village or in large, cool apartments on the Upper East Side. I also felt a mixture of pride and resentment in not taking any money from them. "I don't take a cent from them," I said. He said that was nothing. He could see the real story. He wasn't like the rest of my fancy friends.

To these new friends I proffered my past as a sort of exotic plumage that would make me worth their interest. I would imitate the men on my block who shouted at war protesters: "Why don't you go back to Russia where you came from." I would make fun of the foods they ate (ambrosia: a mix of sour cream, canned mandarin oranges, coconut, and baby marshmallows), the pictures on their walls (waif-eyed little girls or toreadors), the TV shows they watched (*Wunnerfulla, wunnerfulla*, I would say, like Lawrence Welk). I prided myself on how far I'd come, and I knew I could never go back. Walt denied the distance. When he finished college, he was going to be a labor organizer. I pointed out how reactionary American labor was, how racist, how war-loving. He insisted that was not their essential nature but a perversion of capitalism, relatively shallow, easily changed. "Besides," he said, "it's easy for you not to be a racist, you never see any blacks. I bet there wasn't one black kid in your high school class. Your whole idea of race is a big bourgeois fantasy."

He snickered when I told him that I'd accused my cousin of committing a sin when he said he wouldn't "use a toilet a nigger had just used."

"Well, aren't you a real little liberal," he said. When I got mad and walked away from him, I saw the panic in his eyes. "I'm sorry," he said. "I just want you to be real."

It frightened me that he seemed to know so readily what was real, to be able to discern so easily when I was being unreal or not real, or whatever the opposite of real was. I wouldn't have dared to say to Walt what I only half believed, that what you hoped to be was as real as what you came from, maybe even what you were. He would have said that was bullshit, that what you were was what you were, everything else was a fake. I was always afraid when he talked like that, as if he were in danger of smashing and then stealing the ruins of what I was painfully trying to create and protect. I was always afraid that I would let on too much, give him the wrong clue, and he'd move in and defoliate the territory I was only tentatively exploring. I knew that at any moment I might let something drop and he'd pounce on it. So I had to be very careful of what I told him. If, for instance, I began to feel safe one night and told him my childhood fantasy of a black friend, he'd have made me feel like a fool.

But that story was one of the ways that, in my childhood room, I could know myself as heroic, different from those among whom I lived. Each night after the TV news of the desegregation of the Little Rock schools, I would make up stories of the children I had seen, brave little girls in stiff dresses and tight braids, walking like the saints past fat-bellied and brutal men who would have been quite glad to shoot them, to set their dogs on them, to blow them up. I pretended that one of these girls was sent to my class to get her away from danger. But I was the only one in the class who would befriend her. One day in the playground, someone pushed her off the swing. A deep cut formed, running from her elbow to her wrist. The teacher said that one of us would have to give her blood, would have to have his or her arm opened identically to hers so that the blood would flow from arm to arm. I stood up by my desk. "I will do it," I said without flinching. Awestruck, my classmates watched as I pressed my arm, vein to vein, against my friend's and saved her life. My blood mixed with hers. After this, we held hands every day in the playground. The other children wanted to play with us, but we had nothing to do with them.

Walt would have listened to that story with a knowing sneer on his face, mocking the idea of heroism, of mixed blood, of the danger of death.

He'd say, "But it never happened. You only made it up." He would know that I'd forgotten that. And that was what scared me: he knew.

He believed only in the visible. Like my parents, he was interested only in what was of use. One of my new friends loved to quote Baudelaire about the bourgeoisie: "Lovers of utensils, enemies of perfume." I smiled dreamily every time he said this, which was often. I hoped that, when the time came, I would choose the scent of gardenia over a carrot peeler, but I wasn't sure. I knew what side my parents were on. That was Walt's side. He had read even more books than I had and made choices that were like the ones I knew I had to flee.

His reasons for them were unassailable: he hungered and thirsted after justice, but he insisted he was interested only in practical measures, things that would "work." If he'd ever had heroic childish dreams, he would have denied them, and, anyway, at that time I would have been unable to believe that he'd experienced anything like me. Rather, it was important to me to believe that he had not. I said I was interested in beauty. But I knew that, when it came to it, you had to say the most important things were to feed the hungry, clothe the naked, give shelter to the shelterless, stop the war. I marched and marched for all these things. But when the time came, what I hoped was that the revolutionaries wouldn't take over the Metropolitan Museum and that they'd give me time to draw. Walt said, "You have to keep your eye on what's important." But I knew that whatever he said were the most important things to him—justice, a workers' state—he would have given anything up for me. Knowing this, I was able to dismiss his analysis of my new values and my friends. I could leave him and go back to them and to the work which they convinced me was of greater importance than anything else in my life. Or should be. You have the gift, they said. I only half believed them.

I thought I was a painter then. I was working in a style that imitated the medieval. Bestiaries. Illuminated letters. For my friends' birthdays, I would invent composite mythic animals that expressed the nature of the one to whom I gave the gift. Or I would ornately design their first initials, and within the letter I would place the friend's ideal city, containing all his or her pleasures. This required thorough studying of them, which was easy for me: I was studying them to learn from them. Their code, so easy for them, all the things they had seen and had, which were so far away from me I feared that when they came my way I wouldn't even recognize them. It was crucial that I attend closely to the details of their lives. Having done this I could easily render what I'd learned. So, for example, I would put in my friend Charlie's *C* a plump white cat, green grapes, a hint of Venice, and rowing the gondola a thickly muscled, barrel-chested boy. Daria had Paris, steaming bowls of café au lait, croissants, baguettes, a tiny Seurat, Belmondo and Seberg running in matching striped shirts. I was never sure whether my friends liked what I did because they admired the looks of it, or its technique, or because they so enjoyed having been so thoroughly attended to. Walt would watch me sometimes working on one of these drawings.

"Can I just sit and watch you draw?" he'd say. "I'm reading. I'll be quiet."

I'd shrug my shoulders, as if to refuse him was too much trouble. But I knew he wasn't reading—he was watching me. His foot would jiggle with the surplus energy of his frustration. He would run his hands back and forth over his mouth. I knew exactly what was going on, and it excited me to make it happen. I would cross my legs so that my skirt rode up to my thighs. Sometimes, pretending absorption, I would sit with my legs outspread. I would lean over, not wearing a bra, so that if he peeked he'd be able to see my breasts. Then, when I caught him peeking, I'd pull at the neck of my shirt impatiently.

"What the hell do you think you're looking at?" I'd say.

"Nothing," he'd say, abashed.

"Well, watch it."

A few minutes later I would languorously scratch the inside of my calf or stretch my arms above my head and leave them there an extra second. He would struggle like a guilty child not to look. But he would never win.

Once, he asked me if I'd make him one of those letters for his birthday. He told me it was coming up soon.

"I doubt it," I said.

"Why not? I'd really like one. I'd really like it."

"I don't think of it as your thing."

"You're wrong. You're wrong about me. I really want one."

"I guess I just really don't know you well enough," I said. "I have to know the person really well. I have to think a lot about them."

"Couldn't you try?" he asked.

"I don't think so."

Didn't he know that the more he seemed to want the drawing, the less likely I'd be to give it? How could he not know? He had to be able to see that what I liked was refusing him, and if he saw it why did he keep doing what he did? Didn't he see that the reason I made these elaborate gifts for my new friends was precisely because they would never yearn for them, might even leave them on their trays in the cafeteria or in their rooms at the end of term? They were so used to receiving gifts that one more (and from me) could never mean that much.

Nothing excited me so much in those days as refusing Walt. I was going to bed with a lot of boys, without much pleasure, because I felt I should. But every night after I came home from a date with Walt, when I was taking off my underwear, I had to face the evidence: I'd been turned on.

But I didn't think of going to bed with him until my friend Charlie said the words. I was mortified when I ran into Charlie while Walt and I were walking down the street. I barely said hello. "Well, I can understand why you wanted to keep that little dish to yourself," he said. "Personally, I wouldn't let him out of my sight. I'll bet he's one of those tough, scrappy types that just goes on and on for hours."

Charlie's talking to me in that way made me feel that he considered me more like him than like Walt. In on something that Walt wasn't. At that point, I decided it was safe to go to bed with him.

He'd never even hinted that we go to bed. I think he felt he didn't have the right to. We went out to movies and to dinner at a cheap Greek restaurant, and I always let him pay. When I went out with other boys, I always paid for myself, on the liberated understanding that if they paid for me it was because they were buying something, and since I was probably going to have sex with them anyway, I didn't want it to seem as if they'd bought me for the price of a movie or a meal. But I felt I didn't have to have that scruple with Walt since I wasn't going to go to bed with him. He was everything I was trying to get away from, and a large part of the point of going to bed with boys was to prove I'd got away from home. And it seemed to me he was lucky to be going out with me. I was giving him hints that could be helpful for his future escape. If he didn't seem to want to take them now, well, that was not my fault.

After Charlie had put the idea of going to bed with Walt into my head, I knew it would be very easy. I'd just have to ask him. The signs of his wanting me were pathetically visible: his jiggling right foot, his hand wiped over his mouth, his touching me whenever it seemed possible. The important thing would be to do it but to let him know that it wasn't important. Which was exactly what I said when I suggested sex. "Look," I told him, "our not fucking makes it seem like such a big deal. I know you're dying for it. I'm sort of into it. You're like the only guy I know that I'm not fucking. That's not gay, I mean."

He tried to seem casual, but he couldn't wait. When he took me in his arms, he was trembling. I couldn't help it; the pureness of his desire, its immaturity, its rawness, created ardor in me. I was in love with my own power to make someone want me. And he did want me, want *me* rather than wanting *it*, whatever *it* was: sex, my sex, the experience, the ability to recount it afterward. At that time, we were supposed to pretend it was an *it* we wanted. Girls like me had grown up listening to *South Pacific* in our bedrooms, but in a twinkling of an eye we were supposed to give that up for "I'm into fucking tonight if you're into it."

My experience of sex was mostly an extended pretense. I had to pretend to want sex without wanting attention. The reality was usually exactly the opposite. I had sex because it was the best way of getting attention from the boys I thought worthwhile. But when Walt's sweaty, trembling hands ran over my body, I realized that for the first time I really wanted sex. I wanted sex and he wanted me.

He would never have said he loved me or used any of the language of romance. All that was a bourgeois trick to sell unnecessary products to the workers. It was blinding dust flung into their eyes by cynical tyrants to keep them from the vision of revolution. He may have thought he had his eyes on revolution, but I was the only thing in his sight. He never wanted not to be looking at me. When he got his first glimpse of me, coming up a stairway or entering a room, he always looked delighted, as if his good fortune in seeing me was more than he could bear. I was always moved by that look, but I would never greet him pleasantly. I always pretended that I hadn't seen him at first, that I was looking for something else and he'd just happened to come into my line of vision.

He always kept his eyes closed when he touched me. I always watched him, and I always let him do all the work. I would never touch him voluntarily. He would have to take my hand and move it as if it were asleep, as if I'd fallen asleep from boredom. He'd hold my hand and place it on his body, then he would move underneath it. He was fair and freckled, and his penis seemed wrinkled and unfresh to me, like the white of a fried egg cooked in a too-hot fat. Finally, in a kind of stoic despair at my lack of response, he would let go of my hand, enter me, and satisfy himself. Before he satisfied himself, though, he would work hard at satisfying me. And he did. But I was never grateful to him, as I was to the boys who took only their own pleasure and then hurried out the door. After he separated himself from my body, he would lie next to me and hold my hand. We would be on our backs, looking at the ceiling as if we were shipwrecked, as if we were waiting quietly for help to come.

After a few months of sleeping with Walt, it became clear to me that it hadn't become a topic of conversation among my new friends. They hadn't even noticed. I was beginning to find my own behavior to Walt insupportable; all his wanting was exhausting me, making me feel inadequate and cruel. And I was cruel to him all the time; I couldn't stand any longer how easy he made it for me to be cruel. I told him we shouldn't see each other over the summer so that we could think things over, just cool off.

He came to my house on the Fourth of July. "A friend of yours is on the phone," my father said. I hadn't let my friends know I was staying in Queens for the summer, working for Con Edison in the billing department. When they'd asked what my plans were, I'd said vaguely, "Traveling, I guess." So I heard my father with an alarm, an alarm that turned to irritation when I heard that it was Walt.

"I'm in your neighborhood," he said. "I'm on your corner."

He tried to make it sound casual, as if it weren't an hour subway ride from his house to mine.

I said absolutely nothing because I couldn't think of what to say.

"Can I come over?" he asked. "I'm at the candy store on your corner."

"Well, if you're here, you have to come, don't you?" I said in the cruel voice I always used.

In ten seconds he was at the door. He was unshaven, his eyes were red, and his breath smelled as if he hadn't eaten or slept in days. He had a harmonica in his back pocket, and he kept whipping it out and playing snatches of melodies, then wiping his mouth with a handkerchief and putting the harmonica away. He didn't say anything. He kept walking around the kitchen table, around and around it like a dog trying to find a comfortable place to rest. My mother stood by the kitchen sink offering him various things to eat and drink which he refused. Finally she just stood in front of the refrigerator wringing her hands.

"I came out here to tell you something," he said, pacing around the table. "You, I mean," he said looking at me. "You two can stay and listen to it, you're her parents, I mean. I don't have anything to say that you can't hear."

I was terrified that he was going to tell them we'd had sex. I believed that my parents could deal with my being a college student, traveling in an orbit that would take me from them, once and for all, only if they could convince themselves that I was still a virgin.

"I mean, you're her parents, you're the people in the world that care the most about her. Even if she doesn't understand that, I understand it."

My parents thanked him for saying that. This gave him the signal to address his remarks only to them.

"This is why I'm here: because I figured something out. You know, I always thought she was better than I was. She treated me like she was better than me, and I believed her. I mean, she's so beautiful, and she knows everything, and everybody likes her. And she's a great artist. I mean, she's a really great artist. In a hundred years everyone will know her name. Everyone. So I always believed she was better than me. But now I know she isn't. Now I know I'm just as good as she is. Just as good. I always was and always will be. Just as good."

He sat down at the table, and he put his head in his hands. He began to weep. He wept in a way that told us he had forgotten we were there, as if he were in the room by himself. My parents and I looked at one another. None of us knew what to do. We just let him sit there, weeping, his whole body shaking with sobs. None of us went near him, or said anything to him, offered him anything: a handkerchief, a drink, a phone call, an embrace. Finally, my father stood up. He put his thumbs in his belt loops and walked over to the chair where Walt was sitting. He put his hand on Walt's shoulder. "I'm going to take you home now, son," he said.

Walt pulled himself together. He took his handkerchief out and blew his nose. He began playing his harmonica, some song like "Home on the Range." My father backed the car out of the driveway to the front of the house. My mother shook Walt's hand at the door. I don't remember what I did.

That was twenty-five years ago, and I hadn't seen him since then. He'd dropped out of school. I didn't know where he went, and since I didn't know anyone who knew him, I thought there was no way of my finding out. There might have been ways for me to find out about him—I could have called his parents' home—but I'd had no inclination to try.

I looked at him standing at the other side of the counter. He hadn't changed in twenty-five years. He was still boyish, amateurish in his body, as he had been then. I remembered what his body looked like without clothes, that it had been inside mine, had taken pleasure from my body and given pleasure to me. I remembered that I had not been kind to him. Not once.

I understood that if he'd come to the store to hurt me, it would have been, somehow, his right. I showed him into the office. I closed the door. I told the young man working in the front of the store that we were not to be disturbed.

Looking more closely, I could see that his hair had thinned, and it made the bones of his skull seem a feature as expressive as eyes or lips. I kept trying to decide if I liked his looks, if other people would consider him attractive, if his looks would appeal more to women or to men. But I couldn't bear to rest my eyes on him too long. He looked so unhappy; most people try to hide their unhappiness as if it were a wound that should be bandaged, covered up. Walt looked at me, freely exposing his unhappiness as if he thought it was something I had a right, or a duty, perhaps, to see.

"I know you're married," he said. "You said so once on television. Who'd you marry?"

"A man."

"What man?"

"A lawyer. We live near Battery Park. I like the view."

"Does your husband like your food?"

"Everyone asks me that. He's usually on a diet."

I looked down at the papers spread on the table. I shuffled them to indicate that I didn't have much time.

"That's nice that you live near the water. You always liked the water. You always wanted a view."

He mentioned the names of all my friends, and he sounded pleased when I said I still saw some of them.

"Keep that up," he said. "It's important to keep up old friendships."

I said I thought it was.

"Do you think I should get married?" he asked. "I never can get married. I would like to."

"Anyone can get married," I said. "It's the easiest thing in the world."

"I wanted to marry you," he said. "But I don't anymore."

"That's good," I said.

"You never wanted to marry me. Not for one minute."

He looked at me with great fixity, as if he were daring me to say yes or no. Then I began to feel again what I had always felt when I was with him. It was anger, anger that I could never feel only one thing with him, that it was always two, and always at the same time, and always exactly the opposite of each other. I knew perfectly well that he was right, that I hadn't ever wanted to marry him, but at the same time, I seemed to have some fleeting sense that I'd thought it would be comfortable to marry someone who could understand my parents so that I wouldn't have to tell funny stories about them, savage tales that would make them comprehensible. I could tell him that, that part of it. He would be happy, and I always partially wanted to make him happy. Then I remembered that he would always ask the kind of question that no one with good manners would ask and then not listen for the answer. While I was worrying about what to say, his attention had wandered to something else. So I just waited, looking down at the papers on my desk.

"I bet your parents are really glad about the way things turned out with you," he said. "That you have a good business, secure and everything."

"My parents are both dead," I said, hoping the words were brutal enough to banish their image, which I didn't want right then.

"Well, they'd really be impressed with this food if they were alive. That's some terrific food you have out there," he said, turning his back toward me, staring at the closed door.

I could tell by the way he'd looked at the food that he was really hungry, that hunger had perhaps been a problem for him, and might be once again. That he was hungry in a way that none of my customers was: a hunger that could lead to starvation. I didn't ask him what he'd been doing all those years; if I had seen the details of his life, the small disasters following one after the other, piling up, I'd have entered his life and allowed him to enter mine. As it was, I had to allow the possibility that someone who had entered my body actually needed my food to keep alive. He was clean, but except for that he might have been one of the people who ripped open the garbage bags and made such a mess on the street that the other storeowners were complaining. One of the people who went to the shelter where we gave our leftover food.

"It isn't my fault," I wanted to say. I escorted him out of my office. I was about to ask him what he might like to take home. Truffles? Eggplant terrine? Chicken with olives and artichoke hearts?

As I was imagining the combination of foods he might like, planning their arrangement in the dish, my eyes fell on his hands, freckled, hairless, dried out a little now with age. I began to wonder what they would feel like on my breasts, the rough surfaces twisting my nipples, teasing them into arousal. I thought of sitting on the floor, taking my shoes off first, and then my panty hose, then slowly, tantalizingly my bra, holding my breasts in my hands, proffering them to him like two floury potatoes. Then I thought of lying back, my arm underneath my head, opening my legs, gradually, deliberately, revealingly, watching him want me, listening to him say he'd do anything, anything, opening my legs a bit more, thrusting my hips up so he'd have to see, so he'd be able to see everything, so everything he wanted would be available to him, and he'd only have to approach and enter, that would be all he'd have to do. Abject, trembling with hunger for me, he would shudder soon inside me, and I would demand some satisfaction, indicating with an angry, imperious gesture (and no words) what I would have him do. I'd make him go on and on till I was finished, then I'd make him leave.

He was drumming his fingers on the counter, whistling noiselessly, then rubbing his hand over his mouth. I couldn't stand the sound of it; I just couldn't stand it one more minute. I was going to have to make him leave.

"Well, I hope you'll be able to try some of our stuff sometime. Maybe sometime if you're having a party, give me a call."

He looked at me in shock, almost in horror. "A party's not the kind of thing that I would have."

"Yeah, well, you never know," I said, looking down at my papers. "It's been great seeing you, but I'm up to my neck in work. Stop by again some time."

He turned his back and walked out of the store.

"Who the hell was that," asked Jasmine, six feet tall, from Madagascar.

"Honey," I said, "let that be a lesson to you. Be careful who you fuck in a moment of youthful carelessness. They can keep turning up for the rest of your life. I mean, like forever."

"Yeah, remember that T-shirt your friend Charlie had. Some guy with a beard and granny glasses and underneath it said 'Someone I slept with in the sixties.' "

"Please," I said, "spare me the story of my life."

I hated myself for the words I'd just said. I wanted to call Walt back, to tell him I was sorry, to give him a particularly extravagant package of food to take home with him, wherever it was he would go. But then my glance traveled out the window and I could see him, a little to the side of the glass door, peering in to get a glimpse of something of whose nature he was already far too well aware. I saw him watching Jasmine and Armando laughing with me, our heads thrown back too far, our mouths too wide, too open. I knew that he knew exactly what was being said, exactly what was being laughed at. There was no reason for him to be seeing it. If only he had left and gone home when I sent him, he wouldn't have had to know. He was always doing it to himself; it was always his fault; he was always seeing more than he needed to, more than would do him good. And that is why I never could forgive him. I could pity him, but I would always want to hurt him, and I would always find a way of doing it, and, however long it took—it could be thirty years next time, or fifty, or a hundred—he would come back. He would always come back.

I had to act as if I didn't see him and walk into the back office, pretend to pore over the numbers printed on the spreadsheets, seeing him in my mind's eye, alone on the sidewalk, watching the people coming into my store, carrying out in their full hands the things he couldn't have. He must have known what I was thinking. He was only standing there to make me think these things; it was why he did the things he did, to make me do things, to make me think things that were even worse than the things I'd done.

I couldn't help it. Nothing was my fault.

I let Jasmine and Armando close up, clean out the showcase, take home what couldn't be salvaged, put the rest into the refrigerator, swab the white enamel surfaces, mop the white-tiled floor, the occasional tile imprinted with a dark blue, pompous-looking fish. I pretended to be working on accounts; occasionally I would write down a false number, something with no connection to anything in the world. I waved to Jasmine and Armando when they said good night, not looking up, as if it would be fatal to remove my attention from what was spread before me even for the second that a civil farewell might require.

I must have sat there for two hours. The silvery twilight of a steamy June changed all at once, turned yellow blue, and then blue black. I called the car service. I stood for a while in the front part of the store, trying to breathe in what I could usually rely on: the satisfaction of knowing that all this was mine. I tried to revel in the calligraphy on the labels of the mustards and jams, the roseate and amber vinegars, the chocolates in the shapes of mermaids and shells. But my eye kept falling on the empty showcases, which looked as if they had been stolen from, as if an invading army had entered and, at gunpoint, cleared them out. Their emptiness seemed shameful to me, ruinous. I turned the lights on in the store, inhaling the sage, the cinnamon, the cardamom, the chaste hominess of the peach pies sleeping underneath their plastic sheets.

Outside the store, the driver was waiting for me in the car. He was reading a book; the light falling on him from the car ceiling illuminated him and the book as if they were onstage. I didn't know if he could see me. I was afraid to do one thing or another: leave the store or stay inside. Anything I would do seemed dangerous. Finally, the driver looked up, saw me, and waved. I knew what his hair oil would smell of: a fruity yet bracing smell, suggesting his determination to both cut a swathe and better himself and his family. I would be all right with him.

As I walked out to the sidewalk, the breeze lifted my skirt a bit and blew some papers past me, and a plastic bag. The driver opened the door for me, nodded a polite greeting, waited for me to settle myself, then closed the door with a civilized and plosive thud. I looked around to see if anyone was lingering. If Walt was.

The block seemed empty. But I knew better than to trust that. He might not seem to be there. He might have pretended to have gone. But he was there, even if I couldn't see him at that moment. He was there; he was waiting for me. He always would be.

Storytelling

I went to Florida to see my brother Ted because I was tired of reading and writing. I'd just finished the first draft of a novel—a labor of two years. I knew what was wrong with it—everything that was wrong with it—but I couldn't think of how to fix it, or even how to take the first step. It came upon me that I had misspent my life: all those years laboring over words, words, words, and for what? What difference did it make to anyone? Who cared what I had to say? I had lost the appetite for telling.

I wanted to visit Ted because, whatever else shifts in my life, one thing is constant: I have always loved my brother. Is this really so unusual or does it just seem so to me, that there should be a person you have loved and been loved by your whole life? What does this say, my finding it so unusual, about the age we live in, or the way I live?

Perhaps it isn't love I'm talking about, constant love, but rather constant enjoyment, which is even more rare. I guess there must have been times in childhood when Ted and I didn't get along, but I don't remember them. I remember always a sense of safety with him, a safety of a rather special kind, because although he was older than I, he wasn't the oldest child. Our parents had, in effect, had two families: three older children who were like aunts and uncles to us, whom we seemed hardly to know, who had moved out of the house and married before we started school, whose children were a bit of an embarrassment to us, and whom we embarrassed.

Our parents were worn-out by the time we came and it seemed to me later (though it's nothing I would have thought of as a child, or even while they were alive: they died when Ted and I were in our twenties, in a car accident) they were a little abashed by our existence, proof as it was of their untimely fecundity. They tended to us—we were physically well cared for—but they had no interest in our entertainments. Mostly, they left us alone. We had the orphan's luxury without the orphan's anxiety. We understood that our parents didn't think about us much, and so we couldn't go to them for understanding. Ted guessed, though I don't think it dawned on me, that our parents couldn't be looked to as a source of pleasure, either. We divided the world up, then, into kingdoms or protectorates of which he and I were in charge. His domain was pleasure; mine was understanding. That meant that the smooth movements of home life—that which made it more than bearable: decoration, desserts, no hurt feelings, no anger that lasted after sundown—were his charge. He made things happen and later I would suggest what they had meant.

He was popular in school, an astonishing social success, but his grades weren't good. I had no friends but was valedictorian. So he went to a poor state school and I to Radcliffe on a scholarship.

We were proud of each other in those years, but our orbits didn't touch. Happily, I watched him drive by in convertibles, picked up for tennis or for swimming by bronzed gods, their golden hair absorbing more than its fair share of light. Sweetly, every year he drove me to Cambridge in our sky blue Rambler, the only family car. Then after college he came back to New York and worked for an advertising agency, where he met Pete.

It would be wrong to say that Ted came out to me: there was no need. That he would have a man seemed to me unremarkable. That we could keep it from our parents the expected thing. Pete and I liked each other; we liked to laugh at the same things, and we both loved Ted. Ted was twenty-five when they moved to Fort Lauderdale and opened a wallpaper business. They've been there ever since. Twenty-five years.

They enjoy their comforts. And I travel to see them when I want comforting. Their house (which, as Ted says, is a living hymn to wallpaper) looks over a golf course. It has all the things I enjoy that I wouldn't think of having: a refrigerator with crushed ice that appears, magically, through the door, a swimming pool, a hot tub, a shower as big as my Upper West Side kitchen.

Ted picks me up at the airport. He takes my winter coat: "You still own one of these?" He carries my bag, complains about the weight of my laptop.

"We'll bury all this under a palm tree while you're here. But I'm not even going to give you the time to unpack. We'll lock everything in the trunk. We're having lunch by the water. I want to introduce you to Jean-Claude."

"So who's Jean-Claude?"

"Jean-Claude is an expert on bathroom lighting. Particularly boat bathroom lighting. He works on our upmarket jobs. That's where we met. He's from Grenoble. If he's not from outer space. I'm never quite sure. There's something a little extraterrestrial about him. But as our grandmother would have said, he's good for what ails you. At the very least, he's awfully pretty."

He pointed to a table where a man was sitting alone, a man of about our age, fifty or so. He was attractive, certainly, but I wouldn't have called him pretty; there was nothing fine or fresh about his looks, and nothing girlish. His hair was thick, dark brown with a few strands of gray. His eyes were bluish green and gave the simultaneous appearance of being hooded and alert, as if he couldn't decide whether to succumb to something or spring for its throat. His shirt was Polo, navy blue, tucked into khaki trousers. He wore loafers without socks.

"So," he said, before I had sat down. "You're wondering whether to start coloring your hair. Don't. I love the silver. It makes you look experienced. People aren't going to want to take advantage of you. But with that wonderful skin, those fabulous eyes, of course they'll be intrigued. And, you begin dyeing, it's nothing but enslavement."

"This is Jean-Claude," said Ted.

"I'll bet you want her to color her hair," he said. "So you look younger."

"I want her to start when I start."

"Edward, please. I can't begin to tell you the calamity of someone with your complexion embarking on such a course. So, you're depressed," he said to me. "What happened? Have you lost your lover?"

"I don't have a lover," I said. "I've been married for twenty years."

"And how old is your husband?"

"Fifty-eight."

"You need a lover."

"My problems aren't about love. They're about work. I'm tired of my work."

"I understand completely. Then you must travel. When I'm tired of my work, I go somewhere completely new. That's how I got to America."

The waiter came by and took our drink order. Jean-Claude ordered Beaujolais nouveau, which had just arrived that week.

"Tell me about your coming to America," I said. Recognizing that I was feeling curiosity, I realized how long I'd gone without.

"Yes, tell me," my brother said. "I've never known."

"First, we take a moment to appreciate the beautiful young waiter. If you're young, you don't have to do anything. Just your health and youth is beautiful. Look at the fresh color of his lips, even his gums are beautiful when he smiles. Because everything of him is healthy it says, 'Nothing will grow old and sick and dead.'"

"How's Ray?" my brother said.

"Terrible. Suffering. Dying."

"Jean-Claude volunteers with the AIDS crisis center. He takes people to their doctors' appointments, helps them with meals. This guy Ray that he helps is, what is he, Jean-Claude, twenty-three? You're very good to him."

"Well, what I am feeling is it's the least I can do. It's my way of saying 'Thank God,' when I am spared. I am not sick, and really I deserve to be sick, so much more than these other people. I mean, I was really promiscuous. Not only that, I made a living off it."

"Being sick isn't something anyone deserves," I said.

"I know what you mean. But I did all the things you are supposed to do to get it. And I'm spared. So I do this in gratitude."

"You were telling us how you came to America."

"Well, of course, it starts in Grenoble. I'm a bastard, I mean literally. Let's say that right away, because it isn't something that bothers me or something I try to hide. It's like the color of my eyes: just something that's there, that I was born with. So why try to hide it? My mother was very young when I was born and she left for Canada with a man when I was six. My grandparents were kind and good, but too old for a wild boy like I was.

"Probably now, I'd be called A.D.D. I couldn't stay still in school and all the teachers hated me. I was bored, so I made trouble to entertain myself. Doesn't everyone do that, do anything to entertain themselves when they're bored? I swear people do the most unbelievable things because they're bored. I never had any teacher who liked me. Not one. I wonder what would have happened if I did. That's why I never learned how to read very well. Do you know I've never read a whole book in my life? Not one. And here I am talking to you, a real writer, who's written so many books. But it doesn't matter, does it? Because we're just people, talking, enjoying each other. It would matter if we were bored, but we're not bored so it doesn't matter."

I thought how odd it was that he was right, that it didn't matter. And that I didn't know what I felt about his never reading a book, and what that meant about his life. I wondered whether or not I should be sad for him, and I didn't know why I was so insistent on introducing a note of sadness when Jean-Claude told the story of his life with so little self-pity, such an easy sense of "once upon a time," "and then this happened and then that," such a peaceful sense of proceeding without thoughts of "The End."

"Perhaps if some teacher had taken an interest in me I would have been different. Now I make up this story about this retired teacher who moves onto my street. One day I see her having trouble carrying a heavy package from her car, and I offer to help. She invites me for tea. She plays the piano for me. We become friends. I help her around the house. She gives me books to read and helps me with my reading. We go to the opera. In the summer we go on vacation, where we go to museums and read books in the hotel. But when I was young I never met anyone like that, or maybe I wouldn't have ended up on the streets of Paris at the age of fourteen. But if I hadn't gone to the streets of Paris, I wouldn't be here, having lunch with you in the sunshine by the pine trees and the beautiful green sea. Maybe I'd be a grandfather now, working for the telephone company in Grenoble, with a fat wife getting varicose veins. Your legs are great, by the way, you still have a girl's legs."

"Why do you think you'd have a wife?" I asked. "Haven't you always liked men?"

"I've had two wives already."

"Jean-Claude," said Ted, looking amazed. "You've never told any of us that."

"Well, all right, I haven't had two wives, only one, according to the law. But I lived with a woman I wasn't married to for six years."

"This is incredible," Ted said.

"She had great legs, too, but not like yours. Hers were very long, very strong, like trees. Like a man. And she gave great blow jobs, as good as the best man, which is very unusual, most women just don't get it. We had a restaurant together. Well, a café, more of a bar. When I met her she was already pregnant. I went to the hospital with her. Her son called me daddy. I was always the one who got up with him and then took him to school. She was a lousy mother. She started picking up men in the restaurant. Then she threw me out, so one of them could move in. He beat her up, he hit the kid. The kid came to me, trying to get away from them. I was living with a rich American then, and he wanted to take me to America. But I'd have given it up and stayed in Grenoble if she'd let me have the kid. She said if I ever came near the kid again she'd have me arrested as a pedophile. I saw him ten years after that, he was nineteen, a complete mess, greasy hair, missing teeth, sitting in a filthy hamburger place drinking wine, he already had a kid. We had nothing to say to each other."

"What happened with the rich American?" I asked.

"I went to America with him, but it didn't work out. So I made my way to Aspen. I'm a great skier, of course everyone in Grenoble is, and I got a fabulous job on the ski patrol. With a lot of good tips from lonely widows. That's where I met Penny. She was a waitress there and we got married for the green card. We were great friends, but the fucking was no good. I don't know why, because we really liked each other."

"How did you get here?"

"A Cuban guy brought me to Miami. I learned bathroom lighting. Then I met George. I went home with him because I thought he was rich, but even when I found out he doesn't have shit, I stayed with him. I guess we're in love. Maybe that means I'm getting old. I don't feel old, but I could never support myself by my cock anymore. That's over."

"Well, it's too dangerous nowadays," I said.

"What do you think about the waiter? Would he like to go home with you or me?"

"Probably with someone his own age," I said.

"Are all your books depressing?" asked Jean-Claude.

"I think I write about life as it is."

"Why would you do that when what everyone wants is to forget about it? Why don't you write something funny? Something romantic. Something about the waiter who meets his long-lost father, the oil sheik, who's dying and is going to leave him ten million dollars, so he buys a house for himself and this older guy who's the love of his life."

"That's not the kind of story I can do."

"Anyone can do any kind of story if they want to," he said.

My brother called for the check. He and I fought over it. Jean-Claude looked at the palm trees, or the waiter, or the boys, bare-chested, roller-blading down the middle of the street.

On our way to the car, my eye fell on a dress in a store window. Gray wool, sleeveless, a jacket trimmed in Persian lamb.

"Remember Grandma's Persian lamb coat?" I said to my brother.

"You must try it on," Jean-Claude said. "It will be very elegant for you."

He was right. I did feel elegant, although it seemed odd to be trying on gray wool when, fifteen yards away, people were dressed in almost nothing, in neon colors, their bare arms and legs absorbing the last of the October sun.

The dress was more than I could afford. But I'd been working hard, and no one else I knew was going to treat me to anything in the foreseeable future. I shook off the self-pity that was ready to drown my sense of well-being about how good I looked in the dress. I looked at myself carefully from all angles, partly hoping in one of them I wouldn't look good, so I wouldn't have to spend the money, or take the risk on so much pleasure, partly praying that when I turned I'd still look as good as I had a few seconds before.

"Magnificent," said Jean-Claude.

"Terrific, honey," said my brother.

Jean-Claude came by with a black velvet-and-silk scarf, velvet flowers embossed on the silk plainness. He wound it around my neck. The dress, already a success, was transformed into something entirely other; it turned from a success into a triumph. I looked at the price. The scarf was $300.

"That's higher than I can go," I said, handing the scarf back to Jean-Claude, trying to keep my spirits from being dashed.

I was happy with the dress, and Ted kept telling me I was doing the right thing, the dress was a luxury, but it was clearly worth it; the scarf might make me feel bad in the end. I know I'd be happy when I got back to New York, but at that moment all I could do was mourn the scarf.

"You two go on ahead," Jean-Claude said to me and my brother.

He caught up with us in half a block.

"So," he said. "You're happy with your dress."

"Oh, yes," I said.

"But you're sad about the scarf."

"Well, it doesn't really matter."

"Bullshit," he said, and threw a small bag at me.

I opened the bag. The scarf was wrapped in aqua-colored tissue.

"Jean-Claude," I said. "Don't be ridiculous. You can't afford this."

"Baby," Ted said. "It's a lovely gesture, but you can't afford it. You're up to your ass in debt as it is."

"Of course I am, you idiot. Of course I can't afford it. Do you think I'm an idiot like you? I didn't pay for it."

"You stole it?"

"What do you take me for? I've been many things, but not a thief. No, I didn't steal it. All I did was tell him that you and Ted were married but what you didn't know was that this would be the last shopping you'd do for some time because Ted was leaving you for me tomorrow. That I was terribly guilty, but we couldn't live without each other. So I told the guy who owned the store that he should give you the scarf because your life was about to be ruined, that I would buy it for you, but I had no money, the money was all Ted's, and he was a monster but I loved him and what could I do?"

"So he gave you the scarf?"

"Of course. For a while I was trying to decide whether to tell the story as I did or to say that you and I were running away, that you were leaving Ted for me because you loved me and what could I do. I had to figure out whether the guy was straight or not, and I had to do it quickly because the way I told the story depended on it. I have trouble telling which way these guys from the Islands go. But I liked his ass and I'm usually not into straight men. I decided he was one of us. Thank God I was right. I knew everything was riding on my telling the right story."

"Jean-Claude," I said. "You must bring the scarf right back."

"Of course I won't," he said. "Why should I? I earned it. And everyone gets something they want. You get the scarf. The guy from the Islands gets something to think about, and a warm feeling inside, like he's the Good Samaritan. I get to give you the gift I want for you and can't afford. Only Ted didn't make out so well. But, what's the difference, he's got love and money. Life is good for him. And one day, you'll write something and Ted will be the hero of the story and you'll let everybody know how wonderful he is. Then he'll be paid back for not looking so great in my story. And one day, you'll write something about me."

"Jean-Claude," I said. "No one would believe me."

"Of course they will, if you do your job."

When we got home, Ted put my bags and laptop into the spare room, the one that looked out on the golf course. I said I needed not to be disturbed. I put the scarf around my neck, sat at the desk, and wrote all night. I didn't move until the sun came up, a garish red over the flat, prosperous green where soon real humans would appear, to my astonishment, alive beyond the rim of my invention.

Sick in London

Paul collapsed.

She had heard of people collapsing but she had never seen it, and never before had a picture formed in her mind. Collapsed: like an umbrella or a beach chair. The end of uprightness. The end of use.

They had been walking in Hyde Park. It was late summer; August twenty-third. A perfect day. "It's a perfect day, isn't it?" everyone had said: the desk clerk in the hotel, the waiter who had served their breakfast. The blueness of the sky had delighted them. It wasn't like an American blue sky. Clarity was not everything; there was a hint of white underpainting, nothing metallic, a softness, and a sense of water. Wasn't sky vapor, really, she had thought, and wasn't vapor really water? That was the sort of thing she would say to Paul, and mostly he was amused but sometimes she suspected he was secretly appalled by the depths of her scientific ignorance.

In place of knowledge of the physical world she had language. He couldn't string a sentence together in anything but English. In college she had minored in Spanish and still had what could pass for fluency, and she could make her way in French and Italian. She'd never been to Portugal but she imagined that if they traveled there, she'd be able to get them through. But this trip was to England. A trip to look at famous gardens. A trip to a landscape that did not make heroic demands on her imagination.

They'd landed in London on a Thursday night, and moved into a small, pleasant hotel that had been recommended by a colleague of Andrea's. She had used their frequent-flier miles to upgrade to business class. She wanted to pamper Paul; he'd been working too hard, he had been told. Possibly a beach vacation was what he would have preferred, but he seemed pleased with the idea of touring English gardens. Two weeks, starting in Yorkshire, then proceeding to the Lake District and after that Dorset and then Kent.

Paul was thirty-four and Andrea was thirty-one. He was a chemical engineer; she worked in the human services department of the same company that employed him. She liked her job, or as she would have said, she liked it well enough, and she was good at it: fitting people to jobs, putting out small brushfires of interoffice conflict. She particularly liked the people she worked with: Jeff Mortimer, the head of the department, though he was sometimes disorganized and often promised things he could never hope to deliver on. And Anne, Anne Webster, ten years older than Andrea, her immediate supervisor. They worked together wonderfully. Hand in glove, Jeff said, and sometimes when they'd worked overtime filing a complicated report they'd go out together for a drink, high-five each other, and after they'd clinked glasses Anne would say, "Are we a fabulous team or are we a fabulous team?" And Andrea would answer: "We are a fabulous team."

There was no word for it, she reckoned, thinking of Jeff and Anne, this thing between good colleagues, people who worked well together. Was it wrong to call it love? If it was love, it wasn't like any of the other feelings she had thought of as love. She had loved her parents and her sisters; she had loved the friends she had kept since girlhood. Certainly she had loved Paul, whom she had met in sophomore year in college: not her first lover, but, she told herself, her only real one. What she felt for Anne and Jeff was not like any of that. And yet she found that when she was away from them, on weekends, or on vacation as she was now, she thought of them often and happily. And although she was happy, on weekends, on vacations, to sleep late, not to feel so rushed or pressed to accomplish things—both ordinary domestic tasks and more difficult professional ones—she always looked forward to opening the door of the office on Monday morning, knowing they would be there every time. When she and Paul talked about having a family, they agreed that Andrea wouldn't work while the children were small. And although she couldn't honestly say she was very attached to her work as work, she knew she would miss working beside Jeff and Anne. And she wondered: wasn't that a kind of love?

She and Paul planned to begin trying to get pregnant after they came home from vacation. Then they changed their mind: they'd begin on their holiday. It would be fun to say their baby had been conceived in England, on the holiday that they had spent looking at gardens. She wondered if they'd be able to pinpoint what garden they'd come from seeing, or been about to see, when the baby was conceived. Paul had told her it would be impossible to pinpoint the moment so precisely. "Not if we're having the kind of good time I plan," he'd said.

And then he had collapsed.

It had been a lovely morning, the proper beginning of their holiday. They had made love for the first time ever without protection. Thinking of it, the word seemed odd: protection. Protection from what? From life? But it was true, sometimes it wasn't life you wanted, sometimes you wanted life kept back. Or maybe it wasn't that there was just one kind of life, that it was a mistake to use the same word for the child they hoped to bring into the world and a bacterium that could wipe out a population.

She was unused to the feeling of Paul's semen inside her. She was afraid of washing, in case she might wash it out. She wanted it to work; next year at this time, she wanted to be a mother.

They both had a full English breakfast—eggs, sausage, what they called bacon but what seemed to her a greasy limp unsatisfying slice. Then they walked to Hyde Park, a five-minute walk from their hotel.

Soon after they'd gone through the gates, they passed fountains with statues of mythological figures whose identities she could not place. Nor did she know the name for the stone beasts pressed into the pavement, on top of which were raised letters proclaiming that this walk was a memorial to the dead princess Diana. She thought of all the things she didn't know the names for. She thought of Princess Di, who was considered not very bright. Andrea had had no interest in her while she was alive, but when she died, Andrea felt her loneliness; the little girl deserted by her mother, the young wife who thought her beauty would keep her safe. She wondered if Princess Diana's most frequent emotion had been disappointment. And she thought of what a common thing it was to be disappointed. It was a rare thing to reach middle age not disappointed. She was still young, thirty-one, and she could say, certainly, she had not been disappointed. Looking at Paul as they walked in the mild August air, she hoped that she would never be.

It was just as she was having these thoughts that Paul had collapsed.

He was carrying a tray with two cups of coffee on it and a packet of cookies called Bronte biscuits, which she'd asked him to buy because the name pleased her. And then, wordlessly, he was on the ground. The first thing she noticed was that the coffee had soaked into his trousers just above his knee; she was worried he would be burnt; she was worried that his trousers would be spoilt. And then, as if it were a gesture she'd been carrying around with her in a bag she'd forgotten she had, she put her hands to her face. "Somebody help me," she cried. Then people gathered. And then, in her memory, everything was a series of whirling intersecting circles.

Someone rolled up a sweater and put it under Paul's head, and then there was a siren and the police asking her questions and then the ambulance, which she wasn't allowed to ride in. He'd opened his eyes as he was being put in the ambulance and said, "Well, Andy, I've made a mess." She was most frightened then because he had never called her Andy.

The police drove her to the hospital in their car. She didn't even ask the name of the hospital and later, when she was with him in the emergency room, she tried to find signs on the wall that would let her know the name of the place where she was. But there was nothing and she was ashamed to ask the nurses, "Excuse me, could you tell me where I am?" Because the answer to that question, the answer she needed was so complicated, so extensive, that she had no faith that anyone could give her the answer she needed. "I don't know where I am," she kept hearing herself say.

When the doctor came, and she saw on his ID badge the words UNI-VERSITY COLLEGE HOSPITAL, she could have wept with relief. She could call his parents without sounding like a fool, without having to answer the ordinary question "Where are you?" with the ridiculous answer, "I don't know."

But the relief was temporary. Quite soon a new sentence was drumming through her brain: "I don't know what to do."

She knew that what she was experiencing must be called fear. She had experienced something like it, of course, a dimmer, milder version of it, when she had prepared for an exam or slammed the brakes on when a car veered toward her. But when she looked at Paul, his face so pale, his breathing so labored, when the nurse asked her to step outside the curtain and she came in later to see him attached to tubes, she knew that nothing she had felt before could properly be called fear. Her husband was near to death. What did that mean and what was he near to? She knew he was near to something that he had not been near to just that morning. I am very tired, she said to herself. Her fatigue was making her brain do strange things with language. Metaphors seemed literal to her now; when she said, "His breath is labored," she saw him carrying huge stones up a steep hill.

The doctor was young and handsome and Indian. He introduced himself by his first name: "I'm Sanji," he said, "I'm the attending physician. Your husband's had a mild heart attack. We'll have to keep him with us a few days. But I'm afraid we're rather short of beds at the moment, so he'll have to go to the geriatric ward until things open up."

They were in no position to argue. They'd been in the emergency ward seven hours; she was relieved to see him permanently placed.

"Why don't you go home now, Mrs. Jamison," Dr. Sanji said. "You've been through a lot and you'll be fresher in the morning. Your husband will be fine. He's a strong young man, he'll soon be back to normal, and he's in good hands."

"Do as he says, sweetheart," Paul said, his eyes half closed. "I'm fine."

But I don't want to leave you, she wanted to shout. I don't want to be alone in this strange city, in this foreign country. But Paul's eyes were closed and Dr. Sanji's did not seem as if they ever would be sympathetic to what he might think of as a hysterical display.

She took a cab back to the hotel. In the morning, she would have to make arrangements to stay on; they were meant to go to Yorkshire. But right then, she wanted to speak to no one. She ran a bath and fell, to her surprise, immediately to sleep.

At four a.m. she woke hungry. She remembered she'd had nothing to eat all day. She missed Paul terribly. She went to the bottom of the closet where Paul had put his soiled laundry the night before. She took his dirty

T-shirt and spread it out on the pillow beside her. She woke many times in the early morning hours. Every time she woke, she sniffed his shirt and she said to herself, "No one who made this shirt smell this way could die." This relieved her; it allowed her to fall back to sleep.

"But my dear, what a nightmare, what an utter nightmare," the hotel manager said when Andrea spoke to her about extending her stay. She was a large-bosomed woman, and the dress she wore was silky, belted at the waist, the color of ripe, bruised plums. "Of course you must think of this as your home from home."

Andrea did not want to cry, and yet she did at the same time very much want to put her head on Mrs. Romilly's overlarge bosom and say over and over, "I'm afraid, I'm terribly afraid, and I have no idea what to do." But she was in a foreign country, England, where she knew reserve was prized, and besides Mrs. Romilly was a stranger. There were ridges in her fingernails; her rings made a deep groove in her soft pink-fleshed hands, and Andrea couldn't tell whether what was on top of Mrs. Romilly's skull was her own hair or a wig, so stiff was it, so unnatural. And yet, Andrea thought, it was strange that she very much liked the look of her.

"Sit down, let me give you a cup of tea," Mrs. Romilly said.

Andrea felt she had already drunk too much tea with her boiled eggs and toast. She never drank tea at home unless she was sick, but the coffee at Mrs. Romilly's was Nescafe and she knew tea was a wiser choice. The tea settled then rocked at the bottom of her stomach like water needing to be bailed from the bottom of a boat. But if she didn't sit and drink tea with Mrs. Romilly she would have to go out on the street alone.

"Right there in the park, imagine," Mrs. Romilly said. "And what age did you say he was. Or is, I meant to say."

They both blushed at the suggestion of death, as if a man had entered the safe feminine room, opened his coat, and exposed, to the seated women, his rude private parts.

"Thirty-four," Andrea said. "My husband, Paul is his name, is thirty-four."

"Well, then, he'll soon be right as rain. Never you fear."

But I do fear, Mrs. Romilly, she wanted to say, that is all I do from the minute I wake up: I fear. But she said, "I'll be off to the hospital now. Thank you for your kindness."

She was unsure whether to say "to hospital" or "to *the* hospital." She thought it better to use the diction of her childhood. She did not, above all, wish to appear false.

Paul had been moved to a different building from the one he had been brought to in the ambulance. Andrea had trouble finding it; the sign in the tube station had been misleading and no one she met on the street could tell her where to go. What would happen, she wondered, if I were dying, or my child was dying and I had to get to the place. Finally, she asked a flower vendor. "The sign is a mistake," he said. "It points in the wrong direction." She wanted to complain to someone, but she had no idea to whom she would complain.

The hospital was a brick building that looked as if it had been built before the war, but not too long before. The thirties. When she entered the corridor, she came immediately face-to-face with a garish mural, strong doctors and nurses of mixed races treating patients who all seemed to be white.

She walked past the shop, past the chapel, which she looked into, surprised at its richness: marble pillars, gold mosaics on the ceiling like the ones in the churches in Ravenna she and Paul had seen last year. At the elevator, a bald man, with a tattoo of a dragon on his forearm, standing ordinarily, as if he were no different from Andrea or the other waiting people, was carrying a box that said ORGAN FOR TRANSPLANT. Andrea was alarmed by his nonchalance. Shouldn't he at least look as if he were hurrying? Shouldn't he be in a special elevator?

She passed through an area under construction, stepping gingerly around pieces of plaster, hard to see in the inadequate temporary light of the single bulb hanging from a wire. The elevator—or lift, as she reminded herself she must call it now—that should have taken her to Paul's floor was out of order. She followed the crude makeshift signs down several corridors.

She had to pass through two open rooms of old women before she got to the section of the ward where Paul's bed was. It was nine o'clock. The women were just eating breakfast. All of them seemed absorbed; none of them looked at her as she passed by. The light fell on the white hair of an old woman eating a banana she'd cut up into round slices; she was piercing each slice with a plastic fork. Her hair was beautiful in the light; it shone like something precious, and Andrea would have liked to touch it. But her eyes were drawn quickly to Paul, whom she could see lying on his back, his face three-quarters covered by a plastic cone that looped over his ears. Oxygen, she thought. My husband needs help to breathe. My love cannot breathe on his own.

His eyes were closed; she didn't want to wake him. His hands, which she loved, which had been, in her life, the source of such great pleasure, were folded over his breast as if (she was afraid to think of it) he were in rehearsal for the role of corpse. She made her eyes rest on his shoulders, which were strong and had not been diminished by what had happened to his heart. His feet, peeking out from the covers (his feet were always hot: that was a good sign, that had not changed), looked golden, as if at any minute their robust good health would propel him from the bed, from his sickness, from this false identity he seemed, somehow, to have taken on.

Paul's neighbor to the left was a fattish old man, bald except for a few strings of long greasy hair. His front teeth were missing. His hospital gown had slipped off his shoulder, like a toga worn by a dissolute Roman, revealing a disturbing slope of voluptuous wax-colored flesh.

"Catherine," he called out, in a voice that surprised her by its richness, its theatricality. "Catherine, my love, might I be an awful pest and trouble you for just a bit more sugar?"

"Hang on a tick, Reg," said the blonde nurse. "I'm taking Mr. Nelson's blood pressure."

"Oh, Lord," said the man called Reg, and let out a luxurious stage groan.

The man the nurse had referred to as Mr. Nelson closed his eyes as his blood pressure was taken, as if the procedure were somehow shameful. He was a beautiful old man, with a clean, fine skull; his blue flannel bathrobe was immaculate, and his slippers, a reddish brown leather, spoke of style. "Thank you so very much," he said, bowing slightly to the nurse when she removed his blood pressure cuff. His voice was low and Andrea could hear (although she told herself she was a stranger and might be wrong) the breeding in it.

Next to Mr. Nelson was a tan old man with a grizzled cap of hair. He sat slumped over in his chair, asleep. His posture looked precarious and Andrea wondered if she should warn the nurse that he might be in danger of falling out of his chair. On his bedside table was an opulent assortment of fruit: pineapples, grapes, oranges, apples, figs. The man's legs were swollen and mottled; dark blue spots punctuated the shiny stretched red flesh. Andrea looked away; she wanted to pull the curtains around Paul to protect him from contamination. From the others. Their sickness and their age.

"Where are you from in the States?" asked Reg in his plummy voice.

"A suburb of New York," she said. "A town in Westchester called Hastings."

"Ah, Hastings, 1066 and all that. The Battle of Hastings, you know. William the Conqueror."

You must think I'm an idiot to imagine that you would have to explain the Battle of Hastings, she wanted to say and then wondered if he was one of those Englishmen who thought all Americans were idiots. She felt affronted and then surprised, because she'd never thought of herself as patriotic; as a matter of fact, she thought, defending herself against some unknown accuser, some of her friends teased her about being downright Anglophilic.

"I studied history at university," she said, carefully and misleadingly adopting the English usage in a way that she knew probably called up a misunderstanding, an assumption of graduate education, whereas in fact she only had a B.A. from the University of Michigan.

"How fascinating. And what was your speciality?" he asked, giving his last word an extra British syllable.

"The Spanish Civil War," she said, calling up the subject of her long-forgotten senior thesis.

"Utterly fascinating, history," Reg said. "Shakespeare's histories are my favorite. There'll never be another Hal after Olivier. Lovely man, Olivier. Absolutely lovely. Charmed everyone, high or low, didn't matter a particle to him."

"Andrea, can you help me," Paul said, in a petulant tone she'd never heard him use before. "Pull the curtains, will you?"

He motioned her closer to the bed. "Don't talk to that old horror, he doesn't shut up when he's started."

"Catherine, oh Catherine, might I trouble you for the tiniest thing," Reg said.

Andrea hoped that when there was something really wrong, he wouldn't have used up all his nurse's goodwill.

. . . .

Paul slept a lot. They would be holding hands and talking about something inconsequential, their garden at home, the gardens they'd intended to visit but would not now, and suddenly he would drop her hand and his eyes would be closed. It wasn't as if he closed them; it was as if something or someone closed his eyes for him, not unpleasantly, not aggressively; it was a task done simply, among other tasks needing to be done. But by whom?

She didn't know what to do with herself while Paul was sleeping. What she wanted to do was, she knew, unthinkable. She wanted to lie down on the bed beside him, to place her body against him, to position herself against his body as they did every night, to rest her head on his shoulder, on his chest, impaired now, damaged—must she think of it in danger? But she couldn't do that, of course; she had to sit up and seem to be calm and alert, ready for something, but in no way alarmed.

She would walk up and down the corridor, passing the old women, stretching her fingers, bending them backward from the palm, an exercise she'd learned at work to prevent carpal tunnel syndrome. She picked up one of the magazines in the guests' waiting room. She read an article titled "My Boyfriend Made Me Fat." It was about a woman who realized that she could only lose weight if she dumped her boyfriend because he wanted to keep her fat so he could hold on to her without anxiety.

When Paul woke, she helped him select his lunch from the menu left by Catherine, and sat with him while he ate. "Would you mind if I went out for lunch?" she asked.

"Of course not," Paul said. "Take your time." But she could tell that he didn't really want her to take her time; he wanted her back as soon as she could. She understood that; he didn't want to be alone among the dying and the old. But he would never say something like that; they had always been careful not to let their marriage press too hard against their personal freedom. What would happen when they had a child? There was no sense, she told herself, in thinking of that now.

Outside the hospital, she was surprised at how the sun blazed, how blue and cloudless the sky seemed after the colorless air of the ward. The stones on the building took on luminosity, the leaves, still green but drying out with the approach of autumn, turned themselves over in the vigorous wind and showed their silver undersides.

She stopped at a restaurant called Trattoria Siciliana. *"Buona sera,"* said the waiter. He was a small man with very bad posture and a bad toupee. There was a mole the size of an English halfpenny under his left eye; his eyes were sad and doggy, a doggy reddish brown.

"*Buona sera*," she said to him. "*Un acqua minerale, per favore.*"

She hoped it wasn't an affectation, ordering in Italian. It was the second time in one day she'd had to suspect herself of intellectual fraudulence. Was it just being in England? Or was it that she felt so out of control that she needed to assert mastery in some realm?

"*Inglese?*" the waiter said.

"*No, Americana.*"

He asked why she was in England. She explained that her husband was in the hospital up the road. How kind his dark eyes were; how generous his sympathy seemed when he told her he hoped it wasn't serious. He sat down across from her. He told her to tell him all about her husband's illness. She began to cry when she told him about Paul's collapsing in the park. He said that she had gone through a very terrible time and that she must have a glass of red wine with her lunch, that *insalata capreses* was not enough for her to be eating, she must start with pasta, *pasta arrabiata* because chilies were good for the heart, and her coffee would be on him. He said that she must come to him for all her meals; it was terrible to be alone with illness in a foreign country. She enjoyed her lunch; he was right, the spicy pasta did seem to give her heart. But the wine made her head light; she rarely drank in the daytime. But in her lightheadedness everyone on the street seemed charming. She felt much older than the skinny boys and girls, pierced and tattooed, but she admired their playfulness, the quick tap of their boot heels on the street. She studied the haircuts of middle-aged women and felt that most had chosen well. Businessmen seemed exceptionally well tailored; businesswomen exceptionally well shod. She particularly admired the way one woman wound a scarf around her neck; it was a peach color that deepened, as it approached her throat, to a smoky rose.

She wanted to tell all this to Paul; she was disappointed to see him asleep again when she came by.

The dignified old man, whose name, she remembered, was Mr. Nelson, smiled at her as he walked to his bed from the bathroom.

"It must have taken quite a lot out of him, your husband I mean," he said to Andrea. "It's a very good thing for him to get his rest."

She wanted to say, "It has taken a lot out of me too. I am very lonely.

There is no one in this country who knows anything about me, who knows who I am."

But she said, "Yes, I'm glad to see him resting comfortably."

"I do hope you won't think I was eavesdropping, but I couldn't help hearing you tell Mr. Cox-Ralston that you'd studied the Spanish Civil War at university. I was a member of the International Brigade. The P.O.U.M."

"George Orwell's affiliation."

"Yes, we were wounded in Barcelona at the same time."

She felt shy; his silence made her think she ought say something, or ask some question; at the same time, she felt that, being English and reserved, he might experience any question as an intrusion.

"It was an experience I wouldn't have traded for anything, despite the bloodshed, despite the betrayals. All in all, I'd say it was a privilege to have gone through it. The young today have no political stamina, no sense of the long haul, the long struggle. I shan't be sorry to leave this world, you know. I'm ninety-three and I won't regret not being around to get the Queen's telegram."

Mr. Cox-Ralston had been listening in.

"What he means by the Queen's telegram, my dear, is that if you reach your hundredth birthday, you get a telegram from the Queen."

"Yes, quite," said Mr. Nelson with an authority that made Mr. Cox-Ralston tuck his head in like a turtle, whereas before he had, in his eagerness to overhear, waggled it at the end of his neck like a goose at the edge of a fence.

"I shouldn't talk in such dark terms to a lovely young woman like you," he said. "I don't mean to be depressing."

"She is lovely, isn't she, Dick?" said Mr. Cox-Ralston. "She could be a film star. Rather reminds me of a young Deborah Kerr."

"I rarely go to films," Mr. Nelson said.

"Cinema has been my life," said Mr. Cox-Ralston. He spent a long time on the last syllable of "cinema," pronouncing it as if the word ended in "ah" so that it finished in a drawn-out sigh.

"What was your work, Mr. Nelson?" Andrea asked, wanting to cut Mr. Cox-Ralston out of the conversation.

"I was a biologist. Plant genetics was my field. I worked trying to develop a new species of maize. Somehow I'd hoped I might be doing something to feed the hungry. None of it came to much, it seems."

"Tea, everyone?" said an Indian woman pulling a heavy cart.

"Will you have some tea, Mrs. Jamison?" asked Mr. Nelson, and Andrea bowed her head, touched by his gallantry.

She didn't wake Paul for tea; she sat next to Mr. Nelson's bed to have it, wondering if she were being disloyal. But she told herself that she was doing the right thing: Paul was young; Mr. Nelson was old; she was with Paul all day every day and Mr. Nelson had no visitors.

She wanted to know about Mr. Nelson but she didn't want to breach his reserve. She might, she thought, reasonably ask where he was from.

"Scotland, originally. Near Aberdeen. My people are there. I have relations; they'd like me to go back there but I don't think I could. It's been too long, too much between us. For years, they called me a communist. I never was, though, never a member of the Communist Party. I simply believed in justice, in equal distribution of wealth. I'm afraid they're too snooty for me, my relations."

Andrea was surprised at the personal quality of what he'd said. Perhaps she was wrong about the English; the famous reserve, perhaps, was only the stuff of myth.

"Ah, your husband seems to be awake," he said. She thought she heard relief that she might be moving away. So perhaps he felt he had been excessively revelatory; perhaps she had done something wrong, something to disturb him, but she didn't know what. Had it been a mistake to ask him where he was from? How would she have known that?

"You seem to be enjoying yourself," Paul said. "But be careful. I'm afraid your new best friend dips in and out of lucidity. Last night, in the middle of the night, he shook his cane at me, accusing me of sneaking into his house and stealing his things."

"I don't believe you."

"Andrea, why in God's name would I make something like that up?"

"Of course you wouldn't," she said, trying not to dislike her husband, who was still having trouble breathing even though he was wearing an oxygen cone. "It's just that he seems like such a fine person."

"He can be a fine person and go in and out of lucidity, Andrea, for God's sake, one has nothing to do with the other. After all he is ninety-three."

The man across from Mr. Cox-Ralston, sitting behind his bower of fruit, raised his teacup as if to toast them.

"I lof Ni York," he said.

"Another of your fans," Paul said, smiling and waving. "Why don't you go over and sign his autograph book?"

Had Paul been prone to this kind of pettiness before? She couldn't remember that he had. She told herself that he must be very frightened; the ground on which he had stood so firmly all his life, all the thirty-four years of it, had proved unstable. He could never really feel safe again. She saw how terrible it must be for him, and she understood why it would make him touchy. The best thing was to pretend that he had meant it as a harmless joke; she would laugh as if it were a good joke. She kissed the top of his head.

"Go on, Madonna, you belong to your public." He was trying, too, to make a joke of it, and that in honor of their marriage they must both engage in this pretense.

"I lof Ni York," the old man said. "I was there once, one time. 1952."

"Where is your home?" Andrea asked.

"Cyprus."

Andrea was trying to place the political situation of Cyprus; she knew it was a site of conflict but she couldn't call up the details, so she was afraid to say anything specific.

"It's a long way to New York from Cyprus," she said.

"I had lived in Germany. I was in German army. I was deserter. That was why I was in New York: I didn't want to fight for the Germans in Korea."

Andrea's mind spun. She couldn't get the pieces of the story to fit together. Why was he in the German army? And why would he have fled to America to avoid fighting in Korea when it was an American war?

"I'm glad you liked New York," she said, not knowing what else to say. "Many people find it difficult."

"I lofed the subways. Many different peoples."

"But you have that in London too."

"More there. Better."

She looked at the table beside his bed. On it were arranged, in descending order, a pineapple, a papaya, a bunch of purple grapes, an apple, and two green plums.

"I see that you like fruit," Andrea said.

"Fruit keeps me alive," he said.

She didn't want to ask: Are you sure you want to be alive? What do you live for? She had seen him sitting all day in his chair, tilting danger-ously when he slept. Was that life? Was that so precious?

"I must get back to my husband," she said.

"Lucky," he said. "Lucky." He lifted up the grapes and holding them up to the fluorescent light, he took a small bunch and put them, all of them at once, into his mouth.

When the dinner was brought around, Andrea left for her own meal. It was early; she was the only one in the Trattoria Siciliana, and her friend, the waiter whose name she didn't know and was too shy to ask, was delighted to see her.

She looked at his toupee, his sunken chest, the belly he made no attempt to suck in, and wondered about the details of his private life. He asked after her husband. He said that when her husband was well they should both come in. He said to be sure to come back tomorrow. Her meal cost less than five pounds; she waved the check gaily, as if it were a banner she was waving at a game.

"At these prices, how could I refuse?"

"Too many people thinking too many thoughts about too much money," he said. "Come back tomorrow, early, like this, where there are not too many people."

On the subway, she felt lonely and tired, yet proud of herself for having mastered a system that was not her own. Mrs. Romilly heard her come in and offered her a cup of tea. She sat on the wine-colored couch, looked at the dim watercolors and the stuffed birds, and cuddled the brindle-colored cat, Ivy, worried that she would not have the courage to leave when the time came and make her way up the dark stairs.

"Ivy was a stray," Mrs. Romilly said. "Strong she was. I found her in front of a church in the Dordogne, in France, where my sister retired. I don't think they care about animals in the southern countries. Not the way we do here."

Andrea was amused that Mrs. Romilly considered France a southern country, like Libya, or Sudan.

"A stray's more grateful, that's what I think. They don't take you for granted, like some of those snooty types."

Andrea wondered whether, when they had children, she and Paul would get a pet. She would prefer a dog, but perhaps it would be wiser to start with a cat, as neither of them had any experience with animals.

The next morning, when she got out of the tube station, Andrea saw a beautiful display of fruit on sidewalk tables. She was drawn to the figs, purple at the base, narrowing upward and lightening toward the top, ending in a dot of yellow green. She bought three figs for her Cypriot and six for Paul. She stopped at a newsagent and bought two bars of dark chocolate—she was sure Mr. Nelson would like dark rather than milk chocolate. She bought a magazine with Nicole Kidman on the cover for Mr. Cox-Ralston. She bought the *Economist* for Paul and a bunch of yellow chrysanthemums. She bought no flowers for the old men.

They were so happy with their gifts, she wished she had thought of them sooner. Paul seemed in better humor; his parents had finally gotten through on the phone. Andrea had asked them to sort out the details of their insurance; they had determined that their American company would cover Paul's hospital stay. This cheered him enormously. He had had a shower and shaved. He loved the chrysanthemums.

"Pull the curtain," he said, "and sit down beside me on the bed."

He unbuttoned her shirt.

"Paul," she said, "one of the doctors, one of the nurses could come in."

"They've just been," he said, and put his hand inside her bra.

"Is this all right for your health?"

"It's excellent for my health," he said, running his thumb over her nipple.

She was embarrassed when she pulled the curtain back a few minutes later. She didn't want to face Mr. Nelson's eye.

"Do you work here?" he asked. "At this hotel?"

"No, Mr. Nelson. I'm Paul's wife. Andrea. We've met before."

"I'm sorry, I don't remember. But I wonder if you could do me a favor. I'm expecting a visitor, an Indian sort of chap—he wears traditional clothing, and sometimes people who work in this sort of hotel are ill educated and can be quite rude. Would you make a point that Mr. Patel is a very great friend of mine and should be shown right up."

"Of course, Mr. Nelson," she said. His face had the same courtly intelligence it had had yesterday, or half an hour before when she'd given him the chocolate. Did it matter so much that he was confused about where he was? That he didn't remember her?

She had bought a deck of cards; she and Paul played poker but she wasn't a good player and she knew her lack of interest and skill was a disappointment to him. He took the cards out of her hands and began to play solitaire. She took out her book, *Homage to Catalonia*, which she had bought because of Mr. Nelson. She hoped that he would see it and that he would be himself again and that they could talk about history and politics together.

When she got to the Siciliana, it was crowded, and her friend the waiter was too busy to pay much attention to her. He asked only if her husband was better. When she said yes, he said, *"Bene,"* and went on to another table.

Mr. Nelson put his hand on her forearm when he passed her in the hall.

"I'm terribly embarrassed about this morning. Not recognizing you. Taking you for a stranger. Taking this for a hotel. Your husband told me what I'd done. It's very distressing. My mind goes in and out. You could say very properly that I keep losing my mind."

She was angry at Paul for telling him. What possible good could come of that?

"Please don't worry, Mr. Nelson. It doesn't matter a bit."

"You're very kind," he said. "You must take me for an old fool."

She wanted to say, "No, Mr. Nelson, I think you're wonderful," but he was not American, and she knew that to say it would be wrong.

The next day was Sunday, and each of the three old men had a visitor. She had bought chocolates for Mr. Nelson, three Seckel pears for Mr. Castanopoulos and, as an afterthought, a bag of hard candies for Mr. Cox-Ralston, and another one for Paul. But when she saw that they all had guests, she was embarrassed to present her gifts, as if she were suggesting some pride of place for herself, earned by her being there with them, buying presents, when their current guests had not.

She was relieved to see that Mr. Nelson's guest was, in fact, as he had said, "an Indian sort of chap." He was wearing traditional dress, which looked rather like ivory cotton pajamas. He wasn't a young man, but it was hard to place his age exactly; certainly he was younger than Mr. Nelson, but his toes, visible in his sandals, showed that he was no longer young.

Mr. Castanopoulos beckoned Andrea with his finger. "This my daughter," he said. Andrea saw that she had bought her father Seckel pears. But they were more beautiful than the ones Andrea had bought, with a rosy blush at their base that absorbed itself into a sunny yellow as it moved toward the narrow tip. Andrea's were small and dun-colored; their tawny skin was speckled with light dots, like a sprinkling of cinnamon or pepper; they looked unsavory in comparison with the fleshy beauties that the daughter had brought, sitting demurely in their cups of purple tissue beside the pineapple.

"Thank you for being kind to my father," the woman said. "I live rather far away, in Hendon, so I can't make it here as often as I'd like." Andrea noted that her speech was unaccented, and that she was rather heavily made-up, in the way of European professional women, skirting garishness through a firm confidence in their appeal as women, unafraid that anything of importance could be lost to them by display.

"He has rather a thing about fruit," the woman said, under her breath, and she and Andrea laughed uneasily.

"He's a charming man," Andrea said, knowing she exaggerated. Mr. Castanopoulos was not a charming man, not like Mr. Nelson, but his story had interested her, and she was grateful for the gift of interest, of distraction, so she wasn't spending all her time thinking about Paul, worrying about their future.

She sat beside Paul, took out the candy she had bought for him, spread it on his table, and kissed his newly shaved face. He cocked his head in the direction of Mr. Cox-Ralston and his guest.

"Monty Python's come to call," he said.

She understood what he meant. Mr. Cox-Ralston's visitor had an appearance so outlandishly comic that it was hard to believe at first that it wasn't a costume, a mask, put on for a deliberate comic effect. His hair, entirely without gray, although he appeared to be in his seventies, stood up perpendicular to his scalp in a thick alarmed brush. His cheeks seemed permanently flushed, stained a berry color, and his teeth protruded so that his face was capable of one expression only: an abashed grin that despaired of modulation. Andrea's and Paul's eyes met and they stifled giggles, pretending to embrace so they could hide their faces in each other's shoulders. Andrea savored the moment; it was the first time she'd felt really close to Paul since he'd collapsed.

Mr. Cox-Ralston proceeded upon an uninterrupted monologue: about the callousness of his daughter, who had not come to visit him, the badness of the food, the neglect of the nurses, the doctor who had had to try three times to find a vein for his IV.

"Ah, James, my little brother, how I envy you the ease of your retirement. When you left the bank, you lost merely a job; when I left the world of cinema, I lost a world."

Andrea wanted James to say something in his own defense, but not a sound came from him; he nodded as if his brother had a perfect right to assert the superiority of his life, his loss.

"The nurse said there's a garden in the back of the hospital," Paul said. "Shall we try to find it? So that we don't need to say our garden tour of England was a compete bust."

"That's a wonderful idea," Andrea said, feeling there was no place for them in the ward since the other men had visitors.

She pushed Paul in a wheelchair. The wheels needed oiling and their progress was slow. Mr. Nelson's guest caught up with them.

"I am Mr. Khan," he said. "I am Mr. Nelson's friend. I wanted to thank you for being so kind to Bill," he said to Andrea.

"It's my pleasure," Andrea said. "He's a very interesting man."

"Life has, I am afraid, not been kind to him. He was a code breaker during the War, the Second War, I mean, so he stayed here in England. He was worried that his children would not be safe here in London during the bombing so he and his wife moved them out to a little cottage they had near the Epping Forest in the outskirts of London. He and his wife stayed in Hampstead. As it turns out, the cottage was bombed and the children and the nurse were killed. The children were eight and five. Whereas Bill and his wife were perfectly safe. She died in 1960. He was, I guess, about fifty then and he just sold everything up, chucked the lot, house, job, and traveled around the world. I met him then, in India; we'd had mutual friends from my days at Cambridge. I'd trained as a chemist; most of my professional life I worked in Sweden. Stockholm, Sweden. But when I retired I found Stockholm, as a city, rather boring. Not enough cultural enrichments and it seemed to me in age what is left is the pleasures of mind and the imagination. We'd corresponded very regularly, Bill and I, and met from time to time. We came up with the plan of renting a small flat and living together. We rub along rather well, or we did until recently, and then Bill began losing track of things somewhat, and now this sepsis has set in because of an operation on his knee that went bad, but I like to think we will rub along rather well for a while longer."

"I'm glad you have each other," Andrea said, and worried then if that was too American a thing to say.

Mr. Khan bowed slightly and said, "I, too, am very glad. And glad for the two of you, that you have each other." He bowed to Paul. "And I very much hope that you'll soon be feeling quite tip-top."

"Thanks a lot," said Paul, but in a way that indicated to the Indian man that he didn't want his company.

"I'll be running along then," Mr. Khan said. "Don't go," Andrea wanted to say, but she knew that Paul didn't want him.

She wheeled Paul into the garden. Up the brick wall climbed late cream-colored roses; marigolds, which had before this struck her as fussy and schoolmarmish, pleased her with their geometric pleasures now. She wanted to talk to Paul about Mr. Nelson and his eventful tragic life but she didn't know how to elicit the response she wanted from him, and she feared that the wrong response would disappoint her disproportionately. She wanted to say, "I think they're better than us, these men. I wonder if we'll be interesting to the young when we are old."

"The doctor says they might let me out tomorrow," Paul said. "A few days in the real world after that and then he hopes I'll be ready to fly."

"That's wonderful, darling," Andrea said, but to her surprise, her heart felt heavy.

"My husband may be going home from the hospital tomorrow or the day after," she said to her friend the waiter at the Siciliana, whose name she still didn't know. She didn't want to say "in hospital," as the British said it, and she considered that it might be more restrained to wait till the following day to tell him, when it would really be her last time there, a more appropriate time for the announcement. But she wanted to tell someone, someone who might express the regret she knew she had no right to feel.

He didn't disappoint her. "Oh, but that is terrible, that I will not be seeing you again."

"I'll send you a postcard from New York, "she said. "You must tell me your name."

"Paolo," he said.

"Paolo," she repeated. "My husband's name was Paul."

He bowed, as if the connection were important.

"It'll be splendid to have hubby with us once again," said Mrs. Romilly. "I don't think we've had such a good-looking young man with us all year. I must say, he's rather a dish, your Paul. Quite good for the morale."

She wanted to say, "I never thought of him as particularly good-looking," and she wondered what it was that had made her love him. She supposed it was his way of seeing the world, a slightly hard vision with a touch of acid that made her feel safe from ambush. But that wasn't all; it was that he took pleasure in ordinary things, in dailiness, and she had understood that most of life was ordinary, so his pleasure in it gave her hope. He was mistrustful of heroics. He had said, "I think I will have succeeded in life if when I die people say of me that I did some good and little harm."

But now she would have liked to say to him, "I'm not sure that's enough." But he was her husband, he would be the father of her child.

She had loved him, but she had never thought him beautiful. Not like Mr. Nelson with his fine skull and his generous, courageous mouth. But what would it have been like to live with Mr. Nelson?

She was thinking of that when she fell asleep. She dreamed of a place she knew was Scotland. She had never been to Scotland but in her dream the air was clear and rich, delightful to the lungs, the mountains were high and when snow fell on them it cast a rosy shadow.

When she got to the hospital, Paul was dressed and sitting up in his chair. The bag she had brought his things in was packed and sitting on the bed like a cadet ready for his first posting.

"I'm sprung," he said, "We're out of here." He stood up, twirled her around, and kissed her on the lips.

"Don't tire yourself," she said, embarrassed that Mr. Nelson could see them.

"We've just got to wait for Morton, the head quack they call him, to sign off on me. They think it will be half an hour."

"Let me just run down the street and get some goodbye presents."

"Sweetie, you've done enough. And I want to be ready to fly out of here the first second we can."

She knew she couldn't go against his wishes. His impatience was a sign of health and his health must be the thing that she most prized.

"I'll just say goodbye to everyone," she said.

"The farewell concert . . . leaving the fans crying for more," he said.

She began with Mr. Castanopoulos. He had wrapped two apples in paper towels and presented them to her, with a bow of the head.

"Gif my regods to Brodway," he said.

"We shall miss you terribly, terribly, my dear," said Mr. Cox-Ralston.

"I'll write," she said, trying to control what sounded like wildness in her voice.

"I'm afraid I'm not much up to writing," Mr. Nelson said. "I'd be glad to hear from you, but you mustn't be disappointed if I don't respond. It's not that I wouldn't be thinking of you. But the old eyes aren't what they were and my arthritis has made my handwriting impossible."

"Perhaps Mr. Khan could keep me up-to-date," she said, knowing they both understood that what she meant was "perhaps he'll let me know when you die."

"Ah, Mr. Khan, a very fine chap. He's my very close friend. A great man. It would be wonderful if you could meet him sometime. He's a chemist, lives in Stockholm. I haven't seen him in many, many years."

"I did meet him," Andrea said, and then regretted having embarrassed him.

"Oh, yes, of course, I've forgotten. I forget a terrible number of things, you know."

"Mr. Cox-Ralston, you must tell me some of the movies you were in so I can look for them," she said.

"Oh, my dear, I'm afraid you misunderstood. I wasn't *in* movies. I worked as a film projectionist. But, you see, that was heavenly, that was magical in its own way. You flipped a switch and there was light in darkness, you brought magic into people's lives and they couldn't even see where you were."

She saw Paul pretending to blow his nose to hide his laughter. He'd always thought Cox-Ralston was an old fool, and he was right, of course he was right, he was an old fool and an old fraud, but Andrea didn't want Paul laughing at him.

The nurse was going over the details of Paul's medications. She made herself pay attention. It was terribly important that they got this right. The doctor arrived, listened to Paul's chest with a stethoscope, and pronounced him right as rain.

"Goodbye, everyone," she said. She turned her back on them. What she wanted to do was walk down the hall backward, waving at them, blowing kisses, saying very loudly, so that everyone could hear, "I'll miss you, I'll miss you. You don't know how happy you've made me. I think I will never be happier. Yes, I know it: I will never be this happy again."

"God, what a relief to get out of that loony bin," Paul said when they were waiting for the taxi. "One compulsive liar, one fruit fetishist, one who's only on our planet two-thirds of the time. Jesus, what a nightmare."

Yes, Paul, she wanted to say, you might be right, what you say is quite probably right. Only there is another way of thinking of it, of thinking of all of them. Not as nightmare, but as triumph. They had triumphed, all of them, in their ways. Simply by living, simply by getting to their age. Mr. Nelson had triumphed over tragedy, and Mr. Castanopoulos had triumphed over disgrace, and Mr. Cox-Ralston had triumphed over mediocrity. And that was something, wasn't it? You couldn't say that it was nothing. Or that it was bad. And certainly not a nightmare. She knew that *nightmare* was the wrong word for what the two of them had seen. You are wrong, Paul, she wanted to say. I know that you are wrong. But she said nothing. She took his arm. He was her husband; he was young and well.

"I can't wait to get home," he said.

"It will be wonderful," she said to him.

She knew their life was just beginning.

Conversations in Prosperity

It is the last day in September, cool and dry. My friend and I are sitting in the park, a few feet from the gardens, admiring the cosmos and the columbines, which we know we are incapable of growing for ourselves. We are quite different, physically: she's tall and thin and blonde, and I am short and dark and fleshy. She's wearing khaki shorts, a sleeveless blue shirt, and a denim jacket. I'm wearing purple leggings and a red cotton sweater. I have my dog with me, a seven-year-old black Labrador.

An older woman, alone, a very nice woman in a gauzy flowered skirt, a silk jacket that zips in front, tan Rockport sneakers, stops to pet the dog. She talks about her own dog, long dead. A cocker spaniel. How she used to come to the park with her dog and her son in a stroller. How one time a man gave her dog the rest of his ice-cream cone. But grudgingly. "Take it if you want it so much," the man said to the dog.

"I wanted to say to the man, 'Well, at least be gracious about it,' but of course I didn't," the woman says to us. She wants to talk. I focus upon the hem of her skirt, hoping it will move, indicating she's ready to leave us. We don't want to talk to her, we want to talk to each other. We love each other and have too little time to sit and talk. So much, too much, in our lives. We position our bodies so the woman will understand that we don't want to talk, but in a way that, we hope, will indicate that it has to do with our affection for each other, not our rejection of her. She does go away. We feel a little bad, but not for long.

Then a young woman, with well-cut hair that falls like a black slash across her cheek, flowered Lycra running shorts, a bottle of water, steps up to pet the dog. She says, "You have the perfect dog. You're so lucky to have the perfect dog." If she looked different, if her hair were less well cut, if her shoes were dirty, we might interpret these words as madness, but we know they aren't mad. Only, perhaps, a sign of melancholy. It's easier not to talk to her than the older woman, since it seems more likely that the future for her will be bright.

She moves away from us, not happier for having seen us.

Although we are quite different physically, my friend and I share a concern for virtue. My friend, who is a midwestern Protestant, carries in her heart a sentence a philosophy professor said to her once: "What have you done today to justify your existence?" And I, raised by Catholics who mixed a love of pleasure with a sense of endless duty, carry in my heart the words of Jesus: "Greater love than this no man hath, than that he lay down his life for his friends." We have talked about this to each other, and we understand that both these sentences take for granted that just living is not enough. Something great, something continually great must be done because this thing "life" is not to be taken for granted, consumed, like a marvelous meal or a day at the ocean. My friend has in fact devoted her life to serving the poor. She's a social worker; now she's working with children in Washington Heights. I have not put my lot with the poor, and my friend's saying that I am heroically committed to an ideal of language isn't, I know, enough for me. I have not laid down my life. But my friend, too, feels she hasn't done enough. Some days we are so sickened by the events of the world that we can't read the newspaper. Then we force ourselves to read it, on the phone, together. We hate our political opponents with a vengeance that there is no place for in the ideals of the liberal minded. It is always on our minds: we haven't done enough.

And so we can't quite brush away the two women who wanted to talk to us, to whom we refused to talk. We wish we could be other than we are. Or we wish we could be seen clearly for what we are really. Not, as everyone imagines, people who are endlessly sympathetic, endlessly dependable, but people who deeply resent invasions on our pleasure and our privacy. No one understands our hunger for solitude, or that we could quite easily and totally give ourselves over and became voluptuaries. When my friend had a short space between jobs she spent a day naked, eating the box of chocolates her co-workers had given her by way of farewell. She finished the whole box sitting on her couch watching the Simpson trial. She said no one would believe her if she told them. As no one understands when I describe the days spent with the phone off the hook eating Milano cookies and reading *People* magazine. They say my friend and I only do these things occasionally, that we need to do them because normally we are so productive and responsible. What they don't understand is that we would like to be doing those other things quite often. Maybe all the time. That we would if only we could believe that we could get away with it. If these were things of which it would be impossible for us to stand accused.

I may be speaking only about myself. I think that, much sooner than I, my friend would give up luxury and put her shoulder, as she always does, to the wheel.

I might not.

Both of us have things to do the next day that we don't want to do. A visit to the country. A friend who has lived in a foreign city for years and is back in town. Both of us say yes too much, because we *do* like people, we really do, but usually not as much as we first thought we would. Or when they're not around, we don't like them as much as when we were with them, and certainly, we don't look forward to seeing them again. And there are always too many people with whom it would be moderately pleasant to spend time. We are not the kind of people who have to speak to women in the park who seem approachable because of the kind eyes of their dog.

My friend says that when she saw the movie *Il Postino,* she knew she would do exactly what Pablo Neruda did. Have an intense, deeply felt friendship with the postman. Then, leaving the island, fail to write. Then come back for a visit to the island, but too late, after the postman was already dead.

We talk about the sickening sense that you have betrayed someone simpler, finer than yourself.

The truth that for a certain time, it was right to say you loved them.

Realizing too that while you never thought of them, your face was always in their heart, behind their eyes.

My friend says, "I've never been left."

I say, "I haven't been left since I was twenty."

As we say this, we are not proud. We understand that what is missing in us is the impulse to surrender. We speak of another friend of ours who has been left, again and again. Dramatically. Midnight scenes involving things thrown out of windows. Furniture removed when she's gone to work. She has been left, and left greatly. I think of her when she dances with a man. She puts her head back, exposing her throat, as if she were ready for the knife. When I see her do it, I envy her the beauty of the gesture. And I envy the man who is her partner. If I were a man I would fall at her knees. Or put a knife to her throat. Perhaps both. Perhaps both, simultaneously.

My friend and I agree that we are both too old now to be left dramatically. Or at all. We've chosen good men, accomplished men with a secret streak of passivity which we may be the only ones to see. These men make a still center around which we move, purposefully, anxiously, believing we are doing good.

I ask my friend if she thinks it's a good thing for a man to love someone like us.

Or for a son to have us as a mother.

She tells me her son once said, "The thing about you, Ma, is that emotionally, you're very low maintenance."

We realize that no one we can in good faith call a friend is one of the poor. We know only one person who doesn't have health insurance. One who won't get social security. We both worry about these people and hope that if they're in need we'll have the wherewithal to help. By wherewithal we mean both money and goodwill.

My friend tells me about a woman whom she works with who has three children, a husband out of work, a mother with Alzheimer's in a nursing home, an alcoholic father in another nursing home. My friend says, "I think that I should genuflect to her. But there's nothing I can do for her. Nothing at all."

No one we know well doesn't have some sort of household help. A cleaning woman.

I tell my friend that when I was young no one I knew had household help, and that in the years when no one I knew had household help, I was left by men, or boys, over and over.

I suggest that it would be too simple to say this has to do with age and money.

But I don't know how else to explain it.

I confide that my closest male friend, J., had a cancer scare this summer. The day before he left for a month-long holiday, his doctor phoned and said the minute he came back, he had to schedule a biopsy. He was about to get on a boat to sail around the Caribbean. He did get on the boat, he went sailing, and he told the friend he was sailing with about his cancer scare. But he didn't tell me, although I'm the person he usually confides in, because he knew I was trying to finish a book and he didn't want to distract me.

When he finally told me after the book was finished, and the biopsy had come back negative, I was grateful that he hadn't told me before. Then I was appalled. I say to my friend, "I often think I'm not really capable of love. Or capable of real love."

I repeat to her for the thousandth time the story about my daughter and me when we were in a riptide. I didn't try to save her. I saved myself. Someone else saved my daughter.

My friend (the friend with whom I'm having the conversation) tells me that I panicked, that it doesn't mean anything about my character. And that I wouldn't have felt like that about our other friend's not telling me about his cancer scare if I hadn't been finishing a book.

I don't believe her.

I know that one day it will be clear to everyone: I am incapable of love.

We stop for a cappuccino, and though we know it's overpriced, we don't for a minute consider not buying it. $2.75. Too much, but nothing, really, in our lives. On the tables there are bowls full of packets of sugar. I tell my friend that if I were one of the poor, I'd load my pockets with these packets of sugar; it would make a big difference. Perhaps I'd allow myself a coffee—not a cappuccino like this, but a plain coffee in a plain coffee shop—eighty-five cents—once a month. Each time I did this, I'd fill my pockets with sugar. I'd have to choose a different coffee shop each time because if I were one of the poor, I'd be noticed.

But, my friend says, if we lived in a really poor country, there wouldn't be packets of sugar on the tables.

Because of the conversation we are having, we pick up the movie *The Story of Adele H.* from the video store. We can hardly bear to watch it. The daughter of a famous man, Victor Hugo, Adele puts herself in the place of the desperate. For love. For unrequited love. She condemns herself to wandering. To starvation. Beneath our pity and our fascination, there is gratitude. Because she has done it, we need not.

The next day, I copy a line from a book I'm reading, and mail it to my friend. It says, *Ready to be someone else in order to be loved, she would abandon herself to ridicule and even to madness.*

Under the words I write,

Adele H., but not us —

Today it is the fifth day of October. My friend meets me in front of my son's school. A little paradise, this school, where children can be happy as they learn. A private school, with a very high tuition. Leaning against the building is a woman wearing a white clown's wig, bell-bottomed jeans, a blue bra, and no shirt. I have neglected to mention that it's raining and she appears to be at least seventy. And that she's not wearing shoes.

My friend and I don't say anything about her.

No one entering or leaving the building appears to look at her.

It is not possible that anyone entering or leaving the building will speak to her.

It is also impossible to invent anything that might approximate her history.

My friend and I don't say anything about her because we both know she's the woman we're afraid of becoming.

The one we fear becoming when we have lost our prosperity.

The one we really are.

The Healing

Veronica loved to hear, and then go over in her mind, the story of how her uncle Johnny Nolan came to marry Nettie Bordereau. They had met when he was working as a lifeguard at a hotel in the Adirondacks. She was a chambermaid, and they'd been thrown together because they were the only two young people who went into town for Sunday Mass. Nettie confessed afterward—not to the priest, but to Johnny—that she'd made a point of being in the station wagon that brought people to Mass because she'd had her eye on him since Memorial Day and saw that he never missed a Sunday. He'd promised his mother, he'd told Nettie later on, and she'd liked that. She told him that not only was he good-looking, he was reliable.

Johnny went back to New York after Labor Day, and she went back to Watertown. But every weekend he made the nine-hour trip to see her. He was starting a job with the telephone company, a linesman. The lifeguard job was just an interval between Korea and the job he thought would be his for life. It was a perfect time for him to get married, and the Nolans were pleased enough with Nettie. They admired her liveliness; they thought it would be good for Johnny, who, they were afraid, had a tendency to be lazy. But there was something about her quickness—which they attributed to her being French Canadian—that made them feel inadequate, apologetic, dull.

She and Johnny married in February. She wore a blue suit with a fur collar which made her look like an expectant little animal. The Nolans found the fur collar at once exciting and in bad taste. They were relieved when the couple announced they would live in Long Island City. Delia, Johnny's mother, Veronica's grandmother, had been a widow fifteen years; she liked to have her sons around her. She'd had seven, but had lost one in the war and one had moved to Baltimore. It never occurred to her that any of the three daughters would move away.

All the sons had married well, all six of them, but of the three daughters, only Veronica's mother had married. Aunt Noreen had become a Sister of the Good Shepherd. It was a cloistered order, so they never saw her. The other girl, Aunt Maddie, lived at home. She worked for the telephone company too. Or, she had worked there first, which was how Johnny had got the job. She was an operator. People said she had a good telephone voice on account of her having been musical. At family parties she played the piano while everyone sang. Veronica had never heard her sing.

Veronica knew her grandmother liked her best of all the grandchildren. It wasn't just that she was the youngest by three years; she was only nine, but she knew her having been singled out had nothing to do with her age. "You're nobody's fool," her grandmother had said to her once, when she'd heard about what Veronica had done when the butcher tried to shortchange her.

She was afraid of Moe Schultz with his bloody hands and his red cheeks that made you think there was blood too close under the surface, too much blood, and it would come spurting out at any minute, all over the place if someone crossed him, if he got too excited. And then he had a German accent. He had come from Germany. Veronica didn't know exactly when, but she knew that when you thought of Germany, you had to think of blood, of soldiers, of dead bodies, white, in piles. So she was standing up to all that when she looked at the coins, greasy, grown fattish themselves from the touch of Moe Schultz's fingers. She thought that there would be smears of blood on the coins if you put them under a microscope.

There should have been a quarter and two dimes in her hand, forty-five cents, and instead he had put only two dimes there. She felt in her flat palm, dry, warm, the absence of the quarter, which was of all coins the one that she liked best. Pennies were a children's coin, inconsequential. Nickels seemed coarse to her and common, workaday, dependable, but without uses, capable of purchasing nothing that could bring excitement or real joy. You would have to think, think hard, about spending a nickel. "He counts every last nickel," was something she had heard people say. She could imagine a gray-faced man with begrudging eyes and tired felt hat and gloves with no fingers. She imagined him at night, when he came home from work to his ugly room in a boardinghouse, a room with no pictures, maybe even no window, or if there was one it brought no light. He would come home, take off his rodent-colored hat, hang his jacket, also rodent colored, on the coat tree (he would have no closet) and before he sat down at the table that, except for the bed and the dresser, was the only furniture in the room, he would reach into his pockets, lint covered perhaps because the linings of his pockets had begun to shred, and take out three or four nickels that he would add to others in a box that he took from the dresser, a flimsy box that would break one day from the weight of all those coins.

Dimes seemed to her deceitful; she would never have been surprised if, handing over a dime one day, a shopkeeper would say: "But these won't do at all, you know, don't you know they're worth nothing." Dimes in their lightness, their flimsiness, made her question the whole idea of worth. It seemed an impossible question to her—what was something worth—and she resented dimes for making her consider it.

Quarters, though, were the coins of the great world. She always imagined them with high, piled, shining hair, in furs, trailing behind them a scent that was strong but not floral, making their way through anything, taking with ease and calm assurance what they knew to be their rightful place. Sometimes she couldn't imagine anything a quarter wouldn't buy, so desirable, so complete in its attractions, did each seem in itself.

So when Moe Schultz put into her hand only the two greasy dimes, she felt the absence of that quarter, strongly, as if she'd been deprived of a delicious meal that had been promised, that she had every right to expect, and had been presented instead with a plate of dry leaves. She felt the absence of the quarter in her mouth in just that way; the lack of it made her begin to salivate. And she saw the blood on Moe Schultz's hands, around the outlines of his nails, and she thought of the soldiers in their brown coats and the piles of corpses, and her body, too light to contain it, was filled with wave after wave of swelling anger. She had no choice but to speak.

"Excuse me, Mr. Schultz, I think you've given me the wrong change."

"I've given you what is owing," he said, staring her down with his brown eyes, also meat colored, also overfed by blood.

"I got one and three-quarters of a pound of hamburger, that's a dollar twenty-five, and a quarter pound of bologna, that's twenty cents, which makes a dollar forty-five."

"You got two pounds of hamburger. Give it to me. I weigh."

She knew that he would put the meat on the scale and then put his fat thumb beside it and it would look like she was wrong.

"I think you made a mistake, Mr. Schultz. I think you forgot I only asked for a pound and three-quarters."

He took the quarter from the cash register, whose keys he pushed with a violence Veronica knew was meant for her. He threw the quarter on the sawdust-covered floor, beside her shoes. She looked at the coin, shining though defiled, beside her round-toed navy oxford. She tried to think of a way to get the coin without looking clumsy, without, as her aunts would say, "giving him the satisfaction." She would not give him the satisfaction. So she bent at the knees, keeping her spine straight, keeping her eyes on the butcher, although he had turned his back on her. But she knew he could see her in the mirror that covered the shop's wall. She reached for the coin without taking her eyes from the butcher's enormous back. Not looking at the floor, not once, she fingered the coin, scooped it up, and put it in her pocket, not saying goodbye as she pushed open the door and heard, upon her leaving, the falsely cheerful tinkle of the bell.

It must have been Mrs. Gallagher who told her grandmother about it. She was glad the news had come to her grandmother rather than her mother, because it was the kind of news that would have made her mother feel afraid. Her mother was not a strong person. Veronica sometimes felt that in the process of being born, she and her brothers had pushed out all their mother's strength and left it in a bloody heap on the hospital floor. And their mother had not recovered. Her mother wore glasses all the time; Veronica had no image of her mother without glasses, and they made her eyes look swimming, as if they were always on the verge of tears. She wore her hair in a bun at the nape of her neck, but little wisps of hair were always escaping, and she was always, nervously, ashamedly trying to put the stray hairs back into place. Her chest under the apron, limp and floral, that she always wore, seemed caved in, as though someone had given her a blow to the back where her waist was, and she had never again been quite able to straighten up.

She was afraid of so many things: things she had failed to do and things she could not possibly keep from happening. You could never leave the house without her running in once more to be sure she'd turned the oven off or not left the iron plugged in. When a high wind came you could see the look of terror on her flushed face. She didn't trust the house to keep them; when she asked Veronica's father to double-check the windows, he was cruel, and he said he would not, she must practice self-control.

Her father was afraid of nothing, but nothing pleased him either. He was never happy, and he resented others' happiness, particularly his wife's in those rare moments when she had some. If he came home from work and saw her and the children playing cards on the dining room table, he threw down his coat and accused her of indulging herself rather than seeing to his dinner. Soon he was in a rage. He responded to Veronica's excellent report cards as if they were a trick she'd pulled to show him up. Her mother would give her a nickel for an ice-cream cone as a reward; her father predicted her brains would bring her nothing but bad luck.

He might have been a bit afraid, Veronica sometimes thought, of her grandmother. Veronica's mother would deliver the good report cards to Delia and Delia would say, "Isn't that great, then," and her father would have to pretend to be pleased.

Delia told Veronica she must study hard, that if she studied hard the world was her oyster. Her grandmother used phrases that pleased Veronica but which she in no way understood. She had never seen an oyster, but she knew it was a kind of fish, something like a clam, and she knew that it was gray. What that had to do with the world, or something good about it, was nothing she could imagine. Another time Delia had said, "I wouldn't be too quick about marrying. Marriage isn't all beer and skittles." She had no idea what skittles were and she hated the taste and smell of beer. She associated it with her father and her father's anger when he drank, so maybe the angry behavior of men was what her grandmother was talking about. But she was saying marriage wasn't beer and that other thing, so what could she possibly have meant?

Her puzzlement about the things her grandmother said added to her unease about Delia's favor. Delia liked her for things like standing up to Moe Schultz and preferring what she called "sums" to dolls and dress-up. Veronica was pretty sure that Delia assumed it was because she was "practical" rather than "dreamy", that she liked adding numbers. What she would never know, because Veronica would die before she let her know, were the dreams that went on in her head when she was adding numbers. That she wanted the quarter, not only because she was angry at being cheated, but because she wanted *who* the quarter was. That she liked writing numbers in a column because each of them was a person: two was a prince, five a jaunty boy, and eight a tender mother. Seven was a card-sharp and a cowboy, six was a fool who deserved nothing but to be deceived. And somehow the new number that could be born by adding the others up brought to her a world of couplings, connections she would dwell on endlessly. If her grandmother knew all that she would never take Veronica with her on errands.

So between feeling bad that her grandmother had chosen her on false grounds and sad about how the way her coming into life had sapped her mother's strength and hopeless that everything she did seemed to her father a theft from his account, she often wished she could be somewhere else, brought up among some other people. She was mostly alone, watching things, making up stories. The only sense of rightness came from being with her grandmother, when Delia called her "partner." And even then, when she heard those words, she felt that she had stolen grace.

Her aunts and uncles didn't like her except for Johnny, who did like her, because she was happy to listen when he spoke about Korea. And she liked the slippers he'd brought back, and the paper parasols and the tops and the toys made out of paper that no American children could figure out. She thought they were meant to be looked at rather than played with. The word "toy," she thought, must be a mistranslation. She was sure Johnny had misunderstood. She never told him that; she always asked him to take out his things from Korea and show them to her. This made everyone think she was showing off; she could tell they wanted to say something about it to her, but they were too afraid of Delia to let their dislike of Veronica show. But the Bordereaus, Nettie and her brother Phil (his real name was Philippe), didn't see any need to change anything they did because of something about Delia. They said, right out, and no one stopped them, "That kid gives me the creeps," and "What the hell's she staring at like that?"

There were a lot of Bordereaus around after a while, because within a year of Nettie's marrying Johnny her whole family had moved to Queens from Watertown. There was Phil, an electrician, and an older widowed sister, Adele, who was a nurse. A practical nurse. "An L.P.N.," Nettie had said, quickly, casually, pretending it was something she wasn't really proud of. For a long time, Veronica thought Nettie was saying "elpienne," that it was one of her French words, and Veronica thought it had something to do with the Alps, that Adele was some kind of mountain climber, although this was hard to understand because she was very fat and always complained about her sore feet. But by not asking, by listening—although the way it happened was a mystery to her—Veronica learned that L.P.N. were initials standing for licensed practical nurse. She didn't know either when or how she found out that an L.P.N. wasn't a real nurse, they didn't get paid as much, they couldn't give injections, and they almost never worked beside the doctors.

Phil and Adele and Mrs. Bordereau moved into the top floor of a house two blocks from Delia's. It was a house built on a slab of concrete; there was no grass at all, only one slab in the front and another one in the back, which Phil said was a relief because if there was anything he didn't need it was mowing. The house was very dark on account of something called blackout shades, which weren't really black, but dark green, and Veronica knew they had something to do with the war, but she didn't know what.

Mrs. Bordereau almost never left the house. She wore a white net over her hair and her glasses had no rims. Light bounced off them more than ordinary glasses. She made up special medicines and gave people "treatments" but no one ever went to her except Veronica and her family. Nettie said it would take a while for her to build things up, but then you wait and see, there'd be lines up the block, like in Watertown. Veronica did not believe her.

But for some reason, Delia *did* believe in Mrs. Bordereau's medicines. She took a bitter liquid in a spoon every morning and she had "treatments" for her back three times a week. She paid a dollar for the medicine and another dollar every week for treatments. Veronica was surprised: Delia was careful about money and two dollars a week seemed like a lot, particularly when she couldn't understand what happened in the treatments or what was in the liquid in the brown bottle with the cork for a stopper, wrapped in white paper and a rubber band.

With Delia getting medicine from Mrs. Bordereau and Phil coming by sometimes to take Aunt Maddie to the movies, the Bordereaus and the Nolans saw quite a lot of each other, enough for Veronica to know how much they didn't like her. Except for Mrs. Bordereau, who never said a word.

For a long time she believed they had no reason to dislike her. But then something happened and she knew they had a reason and she knew exactly what it was. She had seen something; she had seen something she wasn't supposed to see.

It was the middle of the afternoon. If they wanted to do something they didn't want anyone to see, Veronica thought, they should have waited till the sun was down. Anyone could have seen what she'd seen if they'd happened to be passing by. It was an accident that she was the one passing.

And she didn't move away because she didn't understand what she was seeing. She knew it was Philippe Bordereau's back; she could tell by his hair and his green work shirt that said "Phil" above the pocket in yellow script thread. He was pressing Aunt Maddie up against the side of the piano, the side that was like a little wall, narrow and solid; she had put her hand against it sometimes when Aunt Maddie played; she'd liked it very much that she could feel the music.

She knew it was Aunt Maddie because she could see her shoes, which always looked like Minnie Mouse shoes to Veronica. The shoes were pointy, but not pointy enough. Aunt Maddie had heavy legs and big hips. She wasn't fat, everyone said that, but she was a large woman. "Handsome," people said. The top of her body was smaller than the bottom half. Her feet went with the top of her body; they were too small for her legs, and although Aunt Maddie bragged about being a size five shoe, Veronica thought she shouldn't have talked about it. Sometimes it made her look down on grown-ups when she, a child, knew better than the grown-up the category of thing that should not be said.

Phil Bordereau was moving his hips in a circle, urging Aunt Maddie's back up against the piano's side. Veronica was thinking that it must have hurt Aunt Maddie; she didn't know why she was letting him go on doing it. She thought it must be a kind of kissing, although their mouths weren't joined. She could see Aunt Maddie's face (her eyes were closed) and Phil's wasn't near it.

Suddenly Phil moved away from Aunt Maddie. When he did that, she could see Veronica. "Phil," she said and pointed.

"Jesus Christ," Phil said and walked out the front door, letting it slam behind him.

Aunt Maddie walked past Veronica, up the stairs to her room. Veronica could see that the front of her dress was wet, as if she'd peed on herself. She couldn't imagine what Phil had done to Aunt Maddie that would make her pee. Whatever it was, she knew it was, more than anything that had happened to her, something she couldn't talk about.

She was pretty sure Phil had told Nettie about it. About what Veronica had seen. She got the idea when the two of them backed her into a corner.

"Now listen here," they said, "we want to talk to you. We want to say something."

She thought it was a little foolish that they believed those sentences were different from each other, that both of them were required. It made her feel, for a second, that she didn't have to take them seriously. But they stood very close to her, and kept taking steps even closer, so she had to take little steps back if she didn't want her feet crushed. They did that until none of them could go any further because Veronica was standing with her back against the wall.

Nettie shook her finger in Veronica's face. It was very close to her eye; she had to keep blinking it was so close.

"Curiosity killed the cat, you know," she said and then the two of them walked away. Veronica could tell they felt satisfied. As if they'd accomplished something. She wanted to tell them they'd accomplished nothing, nothing new had happened on account of what they'd done. She was never going to say anything, but it wasn't because of them, it was because of who she was and the things she'd always known. Long before she'd ever heard of them.

Delia stopped by to get Veronica. "Come with me, partner," she said. "We're going to take your Aunt Maddie over to Mrs. Bordereau's for a treatment. She's been a bit under the weather."

For a minute Veronica felt bad that Delia had asked her and not her mother. But she wanted to go too much to think about it for long. It would be interesting to go to Mrs. Bordereau's and find out what a treatment was and what it meant that Aunt Maddie was under the weather. She liked that about words, that they could hide what they meant, but not forever. In her experience you could always find out what they meant. Like when Nettie said, "Curiosity killed the cat." It meant they were mad at her for having seen Phil and Aunt Maddie when he did that thing to her that made her pee. It had nothing to do with cats, just as what was wrong with Aunt Maddie had nothing to do with weather. But you had to make the picture first. First you had to see a cat looking into something, then you had to see something springing out of it, maybe a bigger cat, a tiger, and jumping at its throat. Then you saw the cat dead. And you saw Aunt Maddie under a heavy, wet cloud, pressing her down, covering her almost entirely, until all you saw was her thick ankles and her little feet in their not-quite-pointy shoes.

"Ready, partner?" said Delia, pressing her foot down on the gas pedal. Her grandmother always wore only one kind of shoe, the shoe that all old ladies wore, black, with a rounded toe and a little heel and laces.

"Ready, partner," Veronica said.

"We'll get your Aunt Maddie and be on our way."

Aunt Maddie did not look well. She'd had a flu for weeks that Delia said "she couldn't shake." She was under the weather, and Veronica understood that; today was the kind of weather she most disliked, a winter morning. The sky was gun colored and the air tasted of rust. Old ice stuck to the sidewalk and the edges of the road. Delia said you had to be careful on this kind of road: you never knew when a slippery patch would come up. Maybe that was why she drove so slowly, or maybe it was because Aunt Maddie's stomach was upset.

Aunt Maddie looked heavy in her tweed coat. When she got out of the car, she took the white scarf from around her neck and wrapped it around her head, as if they were walking a long distance. But it wasn't a long distance, only a few steps up the concrete slab that led to the Bordereaus' house.

Nettie was waiting for them at the door. She'd opened it before they were halfway up the staircase.

When they were in the living room, Nettie said, "What's the little one doing here?"

"She's keeping me company," Delia said.

"Well that's a funny business," said Nettie, but she was afraid to look at Delia when she said it.

"There's no funny business about anything," Delia said, and Veronica thought this would make it impossible for Nettie to say anything back. But she was wrong.

"Suit yourself," she said.

The living room had nothing in it but what could be used. There were no pictures, no plants, no statues, no doilies or antimacassars. The floors were wooden; there were three hooked rugs, blue and olive green. There was a wooden table without a cloth and around it four wooden chairs without cushions so that Veronica thought it would be uncomfortable to sit on them even for the length of a meal. There was a TV and in front of it an olive green leather chair with a matching hassock, and another chair, covered in tweed, that looked exactly like Aunt Maddie's coat.

Mrs. Bordereau sat at the dining room table, on one of the hard chairs. But she was sitting on two pillows, so she was high up, like a bird on a perch or a queen on a throne. On the table in front of her were scissors, a clear, shallow bowl of water, cotton balls, a jar half full of a greenish ointment, a saucer with a white powder, paper bags, rubber bands, a corked brown bottle.

She looked as she always did, like a doll or a very neat, very dressed-up child, and the things spread out in front of her looked like some kind of child's game. She indicated, pointing, that Nettie should take the coats. She stood up. Veronica thought it was possible that she'd become taller than Mrs. Bordereau since the last time she saw her.

Mrs. Bordereau walked into the bedroom without saying anything. Aunt Maddie followed. Then Nettie went in, carrying a rubber sheet. It was mole colored and when the door opened and then closed a sharp smell came into the room.

"I'm getting the hell out of here," Nettie said, putting on her coat, patting the fur collar as if it were a small animal she loved, but not too much.

Delia reached into her pocketbook and took out a pack of cards. A rubber band that was too thick, too inelastic for the cards so that they bent a bit under its pressure, went around the pack. Delia took the rubber band off the cards and hung it around her wrist. When she dealt the cards, the rubber band, which was light blue, swung in what seemed to Veronica an inconvenient way.

She and Delia played hand after hand of casino. There was no noise from the other room. The clock ticked loudly; it was only a face with no border, and it was so high on the wall that it was hard to read. Delia and Veronica said only, "You won," or "I'll take that one." Two hours passed.

Then the bedroom door opened and they could hear the sound of weeping. Mrs. Bordereau went to the phone which was on a table near the front door. She dialed a number. She said something in French. Then she went into the bedroom and closed the door. They no longer heard the sound of weeping.

Nettie burst into the room rushing, bringing the cold of the outside with her. She didn't say anything to Delia or Veronica. She went into the bedroom and closed the door. Then she was dragging Aunt Maddie, who was crying.

Delia rose up and said, "What have you done to her?"

Nettie's look was full of hate. "Oh, innocent," she said. "No time to talk about it now. We'll take her to the hospital. We'll go in my car. You sit in the back with her."

In seconds they were all out the door, and Veronica could hear first the car starting and then the sound of it going down the street.

In a straight line, a line made by a series of red dots, some larger and some smaller, was a trail of blood that led from the bedroom to the front door. Mrs. Bordereau was on her knees, wiping the dots up with a wet cloth. She went into the bedroom and came out with a brown paper parcel tied with string which she brought into the kitchen. Then she went into the room again and came out carrying the rubber sheet. She walked into the bathroom with it and closed the door. Veronica could hear the sound of water filling up the bathtub. She heard the rubber sheet go plop into the water. Mrs. Bordereau came out, wiping her hands on the apron.

Then she sat down at the dining room table across from Veronica. They were both sitting the same way, with their hands folded in front of them, waiting for the next thing to happen. The clock ticked and the sounds bounced back and forth between the surfaces of the wooden floor and the hard wooden chairs.

Veronica felt herself beginning to cry. She didn't know whether she was crying because she was afraid or because she didn't know what to do. And she didn't know what she was afraid of, if she was afraid. Was it the trail of blood, the way Aunt Maddie looked? Or was it being alone with Mrs. Bordereau? She understood, finally, that not knowing what to do made her the most afraid. She wished more than anything that Delia hadn't taken her cards with her.

A rod of light slipped through the crack in the venetian blinds and glanced off Mrs. Bordereau's glasses. This made Veronica cry afresh.

"Why do you cry for?"

When Mrs. Bordereau spoke, Veronica realized she had never heard her voice before. She had an accent. Veronica guessed it must be French, but it did not sound like movies about Paris.

Veronica shook her head.

"You mustn't cry," said Mrs. Bordereau. "If people see you crying dey will tink you are remorseful."

Remorseful. The word, beautiful, heavy, cushioned, and enveloping and therefore different in its texture from everything in the room, consoled Veronica for a minute. The word stopped her tears. But it was only the sound of it that did that. The sound was purplish, or no, dark blue; it moved slowly like a royal robe. But the meaning was sharp; it pressed the surface of her skin and settled its blade in the organs of her stomach. She wanted to go to the bathroom. But she was afraid to move.

Remorseful.

Mrs. Bordereau was looking straight ahead of her, not at Veronica who sat a little to the left of where her gaze stopped. Mrs. Bordereau knew things about her. She understood that there were things wrong with Veronica and, looking at her, with her white hair in a net, and her glasses, Veronica knew she wasn't a person who spoke if she believed there was a chance she might be wrong.

Remorseful. It was a kind of being sorry. Veronica was very sorry. She wanted to tell Mrs. Bordereau everything she was sorry about. I'm sorry, I'm sorry, she wanted to say. I wish I was not the person who I am. I'm sorry I see things and I make up stories to myself. I'm sorry I make my father angry and my mother tired, that I stole her place with my grandmother and that my grandmother loves me too much because she thinks I'm something that I'm not. I'm sorry I saw Philippe and Aunt Maddie and the dots of blood. I am remorseful and I will change my ways. I will not see too much and I will not make up stories. I will not take a place that is not mine; I will not see the things I am not meant to see, and if I see them I will tell myself that I have not.

The clock ticked and the rays of light grew shorter on the wooden floor. Veronica believed that everybody had forgotten where she was, that they would not remember until the thing that was happening to Aunt Maddie was over. She did not know how long she had to sit across from Mrs. Bordereau, but she knew she couldn't move because Mrs. Bordereau knew everything and she must prove to her that she had understood, she was remorseful, but she would not let people know that she was, because that was the sort of thing you kept a secret, that other people shouldn't know.

Mrs. Bordereau's eyes had closed. She was asleep but her hands were still folded in front of her. Veronica believed that both of them could stay there forever. It was quite possible that nobody would come for her. She could not for the life of her imagine what the right thing was to do.

When the bell rang downstairs, the force of it frightened her. It was sharp, it was a sound of iron. Mrs. Bordereau opened her eyes. She got up and walked to the door. Veronica stayed still. She knew it would be Delia. Her grandmother would tell her something, she did not know what, but she knew it would change her life. But that was wrong. The change had happened. It was already much too late.

Eleanor's Music

"Do be sure, dearie, that you get the plain yogurt for your father. I brought home vanilla by mistake last week and he was ready to call out the constabulary."

"*Entendu,*" Eleanor called back, straightening her collar in front of the spotted mirror in the hall. How like her mother to use the phrase "call out the constabulary." It was the kind of charming phrase that was all too rare in this overwhelmingly crude world; soon that kind of charm, that kind of light playfulness, would be lost entirely.

How she loved her mother! Still perfectly beautiful at eighty-six. The only concession she'd made to her age was a pair of hearing aids. "My ears," she called them. Everything her mother touched she touched carefully, and left a little smoother, a little finer for her touch. Everything about her mother reminded Eleanor of walking through a glade, from the chestnut rinse that tinted what would be silver hair, to the shadings of her clothes. Each garment some variety of leaf tone: the light green of spring with an underhint of yellow, the dark of full summer, occasionally a detail of bright autumn: an orange scarf, a red enamel brooch. Wool in winter, cotton in summer: never an artificial fiber next to her skin. What her mother didn't understand, she often said, was a kind of laziness that in the name of convenience in the end made more work and deprived one of the small but real joys. The smell of a warm iron against damp cloth, the comfort of something that was once alive against your body. She was a great believer in not removing yourself from the kind of labor she considered natural. She wouldn't own a Cuisinart or have a credit card; she liked, she said, chopping vegetables, and when she paid for something she wanted to feel, on the tips of her fingers, on the palms of her hands, the cost.

Some people might consider these things crotchets or affectations, but Eleanor considered them an entirely admirable assertion of her mother's individuality. As she considered her father's refusal to step outside their Park Avenue apartment without a jacket and tie, regardless of the heat of the day or the informality of occasion. And, she supposed, it might be said that his continuing to smoke a pipe when there was clear evidence that it was hazardous to his health could be interpreted as a stubborn self-indulgence. But she always liked hearing him say to a born-again nonsmoker, "At my age I have the right to not listen to a bunch of damn fools who want to tell me I can live forever."

No, they were marvelous, her parents. She adored them, as she adored the apartment on Park Avenue where the three of them had lived since Eleanor was three. Except for the years she'd been married to Billy. Then she had lived downtown.

She had been shattered when Billy had told her he was leaving but it had just seemed natural to let him keep the apartment and for her to move back in with her parents, "until you're back on your beam," as her father said. It was eighteen years later, and she'd never moved out.

She knew that many people thought it odd, to say nothing of unhealthy, for her to be living with her parents at the age of fifty-one. "Health," said her father, "is the new orthodoxy. The new criterion by which we are judged of the fold or outside it. In the old days, they just tested people by trying to drown them, and if they survived they were drowned because it was proof they were of the devil's party. But that's too good for the health nags."

So she didn't listen any longer to the whispers she might once have overheard: that there was something wrong with her going on living with her parents. She had long ago given up that last residue of her embarrassment, which at one time, like a pile of dried leaves, could be set adrift by the slightest wind, and would flutter inside her, cause her to place her hand, splayed-out and flat, against her chest. Something had damped the pile, she liked to think of it as a gentle, constant, nourishing rain. The pile of leaves never flared up now. No, she never thought of it at all.

She enjoyed her life. She liked her job, teaching music at the Watson School, directing the chorus and the a cappella singers. She knew that the girls found her a little old-fashioned, a little stiff, but she believed that they were secretly pleased to have in her a sign of unchangeable standards; she allowed them to tease her, occasionally, but would not give in to their demands to include one rock-and-roll song at the Christmas concert, and she refused to disband the bell ringers, although it was, each year, increasingly difficult to find candidates. She deliberately stopped the repertory of the chorus at Victor Herbert, although one year she had allowed a Johnny Mercer song—"Dream, when you're feeling blue, dream and they might come true." She'd been surprised that, to the girls, that song was from the same out-of-memory basket as Purcell or Liszt—it had happened before they were born and was therefore apart from them. But that was her job: to instill in them, gracefully she hoped, a sense of the value of tradition, of the beauty of the past. If that meant she wasn't one of the most popular teachers, well, she had long ago learned to live with that. She had her votaries, one or two a year: never the most popular girls and, increasingly, not the most talented.

But she had something that the other teachers didn't have: she had a professional life. She was a member of the chorus of the Knickerbocker Opera Company, a small company that had three performances a year: *Amahl and the Night Visitors* at Christmas, a Gilbert and Sullivan in late February, and in early May one of the operas in the common repertory—*Carmen, Lucia di Lammermoor.* She wasn't paid much, but she was paid. She felt this distinguished her, and she thought of the words "distinguished" and "distinction." Being in the company allowed her to attach both words to herself. She was not an amateur, like many of her friends whose relationship to the arts was a species of volunteerism.

Her friends were dear to her, essential, old friends, some from when she was a student at Watson herself, some from Bryn Mawr, newer friends, one young colleague who was struggling with the fledgling string quartet, others from her book group. She was proud that her friends ranged in age from her parents' compatriots to a twenty-five-year-old ex-student, now an investment banker who sang in a Renaissance quintet and traced her devotion to music straight to Eleanor.

And there was Billy. People thought it was peculiar that she should be such close friends with her ex-husband, as they thought it was peculiar that she lived with her parents. But she was proud of that as well: she considered the shape of her life not peculiar, but original; she lived as she liked; real courage, she believed, was doing what you believed in, however it appeared.

Of course, if it had been up to her, she and Billy would never have split. And some people might find that peculiar too, that she would have been willing to go on with a marriage that had no physical side to it—or no, that wasn't right, because many of the pleasures she and Billy enjoyed were physical, winter skiing in Colorado, swimming in Maine in summer, ballroom dancing in their class on the West Side. She thought it was such a narrow understanding, to think that in a relationship between man and woman, "physical" and "sexual" were precise synonyms. She firmly believed that they were not.

And she didn't believe that her relationship with Billy, even now, was devoid of a sexual component. She knew he appreciated her as a woman, and that his appreciation was that of a man. He had come to her, weeping, confessing that his problems in bed with her had nothing to do with her, or with him for that matter: it was just the way he was; he had fallen in love with Paul, and realized for the first time the way he had always been, the way he had always been made, what he had been afraid of, had repressed, but could no longer. Because love had come his way.

"Love," she had said, as if she'd just picked up, between two fingers, an iridescent, slightly putrefying thing. "And what do you call what we have for each other, devotion, loyalty, shared interests, shared values, joy in each other's company, what do you call that if not love?"

She didn't say, "Don't you know that I would die for you," because although she meant it, she didn't want to mean it, and certainly, she would never say it. It sounded too operatic. Opera was the center of both their lives, she as a singer, he as an accompanist, but she had no interest in living at the intense, excessive temperatures opera suggested.

He had knelt before her (a gesture that was far too operatic for her tastes) and took her hands. "Of course I love you, Eleanor. I will always love you. You are my dearest friend, and always will be. But this is of another order."

"Get up, Billy," she said. "You must do what you think you must. I'll stay with Ma and Pa until you come to a decision."

She was sure he'd come around, come to his senses, show up with flowers, take her to an expensive dinner, where they would eat luxuriously, drink an extravagant wine, and not mention what she thought of as "his little lapse." But no, it didn't happen; he moved in with Paul, or rather Paul moved in with him, and she moved in with her parents. It seemed sensible; she had the option of moving in with her parents and he had no other way of staying in New York. He taught music at St. Anselm's, the boys' school that was the brother school to Watson. And Paul was a conductor. He led the Knickerbockers; Eleanor had never begrudged his talent. That paid very little, though, and he survived by doing legal proofreading. He'd never, as far as Eleanor could see, been able to support himself in any reasonable way. So it was better that Billy kept the apartment; anything else would have been vindictive. And above all, she didn't want a vindictive parting.

That had been eighteen years ago; she had been thirty-three. She and Billy had been married for nine years. A *marriage blanc*. That was a nicer way of putting it than using the word "unconsummated." On their wedding night, he'd said he just wasn't ready, and he had never been ready, and she had never felt free to bring it up. She'd thought they were happy, and she didn't miss what she'd never known. He was affectionate; they shared a bed, and held each other, sometimes, in the mornings. She found him beautiful; sometimes she was moved to weep at the sight of his back when he was shaving. But she would never tell anyone the truth of her marriage, and she would never speak to Billy about it: she couldn't see the point.

They still had lunch together every sixth Sunday, and of course they saw each other at the Knickerbocker Opera, where she was in the chorus and he was rehearsal pianist. They had never, officially, divorced.

The chive-colored scarf that she tied around her neck was a present from him on her last birthday. Really, Billy was wonderful at knowing what would suit her; his gifts were always exactly right. If she bought a new pair of shoes, he noticed, and was complimentary; he would take her hand and tell her that she still had the alabaster hands of a Canova statue.

If she changed the shade of her lipstick he'd comment, disappointed. He said, "Eleanor, my love, you must promise me that no matter what, you will be the one I can count on not to change in the slightest bit."

She had been glad to promise. And, looking in the mirror, she could be satisfied with her looks. With her *look.*

"Eleanor Harkness has a kind of timeless elegance." She had never actually heard anyone say that about her, but she imagined it was the kind of thing that people thought.

She believed—she hoped it wasn't vanity—that she was fortunate in her looks, that she still had the right to think of herself as a good-looking woman. Good-looking in a way that brought with it neither danger nor corrupting adulation. "Neither Madonna nor whore," she'd said to herself once, of herself, feeling a thrill in the harshness of the sharp words, uttered in silence, resonant only to her own ears. She believed she had the kind of features she would have chosen for herself: small, neatly made, her eyes gray-green, a modest, well-cut nose, a moderate mouth with a generous enough underlip. "A witty mouth," Billy had said once, and she had treasured that.

She patted her hair one last time in front of the mirror. She was particularly fond of her hair—beginning to gray now, but still arranging itself, when she took it out of its pins, in vibrant, abundant waves. But she never let it down in public: she clasped it to the back of her head with bone or tortoiseshell or amber clips and pins. No one saw her hair as she saw it as she sat in front of the dressing table that had been her grandmother's: carved cherry, with clusters of oak leaves and acorns forming an arch across the top. It was a secret thrill: to pull the last bone pin out of her hair and watch it fall down her back. Occasionally, she might have wished to do that for a man, that set piece of ancient feminine allure, but she had come to understand that what she would really have liked would be to do it not in a bedroom, but on a stage.

If she had any disappointment in her life, it was that her music had not come to more. But she had refused to dwell on it. As her mother always said, "It does no good to sit in the damp dark smelly places of the mind. It only leads to rot." But sometimes she allowed herself to wish she had performed more, that she could give recitals of lieder and songs of the French composers she so loved, Debussy, Fauré, Ravel. It had been ten years since she'd had a recital; when her beloved teacher died, she had taken it as a sign and didn't look for a replacement. She could never have borne the kind of singer's life that required so much pushing and striving. She was pleased to think of herself walking lightly, gracefully, into a space that seemed provided for her. Not the star of the company, but a member of the chorus. That was pleasing, that was satisfying. She was a fortunate woman. She knew it wasn't vanity that shaped this self-assessment. It was, rather, a habit of mind she had inherited from her parents. She was certain that acknowledging such an inheritance could never be thought a form of pride.

It was a perfect autumn morning, and she took pleasure not only in the weather but also in her being perfectly dressed for it. She knew that her panty hose were not silk, but they felt silky, nearly the color of her flesh, but a shade or so lighter. And riding lightly over them, the satin lining, a lighter shade of chive than the fine wool of her skirt itself and the scarf Billy had given her. Her blouse, of course, was silk; at first glance it seemed gray, but looked at more closely, examined for a while, it was obvious that it had been dipped in a bath of bluish green. A shade to complement both her eyes and the loden of her cape, in its turn set off by Billy's scarf. The sun made the mica flecks in the pavement sparkle, she wanted to say, like diamonds; she was pleased by the sounds the heels of her Ferragamo oxfords made—so comfortable for walking but, because they were Italian, not earnest looking. The sky was slate blue and the yellow maples flashed against it as if they'd been scooped out of a plane of light the slate concealed and shielded. A perfect day to walk across Central Park, this Saturday, October seventeenth. Children played with large balls in bright primary colors; rash boys skated dangerously: girls, their dress another kind of danger, sauntered, smoking, tipping back their soda cans for the last sweet drops.

She knew that Fairway would be crowded, but even the crowding was, today, enjoyable. She imagined assignations at the cheese counter—surely the blonde thirty-year-old and the bearded ginger-haired fellow holding a green bicycle helmet would meet up once again for drinks, for dinner, maybe—who knew—for life. The cheese man gave out samples, try this try this, this Brie is from Belgium, don't be prejudiced, it's cheap but good, and this Asiago—he kissed his fingers to his reddish lips—I envy you if you're trying it for the first time.

She bowed her head when he offered her a piece as if she were a knight taking upon herself the tribute of a king. Yes, half a pound, she said, and half a pound of Port Salut. She bought three kinds of dried bean—pinto, fava, cannellini, modest and sensible as old jewels in their barrels. Her mother was planning to make a hearty soup. She bagged two pounds of McIntosh apples with the smell of autumn on them. Where, she wondered, did they grow? Into her cart she carefully placed endive, arugula, free-range eggs. The yogurt, plain, that her mother had told her to be sure of. She would take a cab home. What she had bought would be too much to carry through the park.

She put all the food away, keeping out for her lunch and mother's the Port Salut and two of the largest apples.

"Mustn't linger. Rehearsal," she said, wiping her lips with the flax-colored napkin her mother had laid out. She brushed her teeth, put on some lipstick, and made her way downtown.

The Knickerbocker Opera Company rehearsed in the basement of Holy Paraclete Episcopal Church on Thirty-second Street and Madison Avenue. Eleanor took the Lexington Avenue bus downtown, glad to find one of the single seats vacant; she preferred not having to share a seat, which so often meant either having to shift to let the inside person out or stepping over the person on the aisle. She was looking forward to having a cup of tea with Billy before rehearsal, tea with lemon to keep her voice clear. He would order, as he always did, a Coke, a habit she found boyishly endearing in so sophisticated and cultivated a man.

She was the first to arrive. She saw him frown, as he always did when he walked into a restaurant, as if he were at once displeased to be in the room at all and concerned that the person he was meant to meet might never arrive.

She hadn't seen him since the tenth of June, their wedding anniversary: he hadn't, of course, forgotten. He and Paul had spent the summer at the house in Maine that had been his parents', where he and Eleanor had spent their summers when they were married. She had often wished that Paul would betake himself to an artist's colony—preferably in Europe—one summer and that Billy would invite her to Maine once again. It had never happened; each year she would listen to Billy's groans about what had fallen off or broken down at "the old manse." It was a rare instance of insensitivity on his part not to imagine that such a recitation might be painful for her. She spent her summers, as she had as a child, in her parents' cottage on Cape Cod.

He looked young and fit and tan in gray wool trousers, oxford shirt, blue blazer. There were lines around his eyes, but they suited him, made him look less provisional, less the eternal boy. She thought how much better-looking a couple she and he made than he and Paul. Paul had put on weight, and the look that was, in his youth, romantic and bohemian had become, in middle age, merely slovenly. She was sure that this change must be a grief to Billy, who cared so very much about the look of things.

"How's every little thing, old girl," he said, kissing her cheek.

"Right as rain, old boy."

"I see you kept yourself out of the Wellfleet sun. No chance of your marring your alabaster perfection to catch a few rays."

"I think we all need to be careful about skin cancer with the ozone layer thin as it is. Not that Pa would think of sunblock."

"How are the terrible two?"

"Very well indeed: they send their love."

"Dearest, I want you to be the first to know. Paul will make the announcement. Instead of doing *Iolanthe* this spring, we've commissioned a new work."

Eleanor's heart sank. She had little taste for contemporary music and Billy knew it. She wiped the corner of her mouth.

"It's a very fine piece by a young composer, a protégé of Paul's. The commission is a great thing for him."

She didn't want to ask where the money came from to pay this protégé. Instead she said, "What a fine thing for Paul to have done."

"Yes," Billy said, "I think it is. He's quite young, this fellow, twenty-four, but he has an extraordinary gift, he can write lyrically and satirically at the same time. A bite, but an aftertaste of sweetness. This piece is called *The Dream of Andy Warhol*. Andy Warhol relives the highlights of his life in the moments before his death."

"Andy Warhol?" she said, not even trying to conceal her shock. "An opera about Andy Warhol? Hardly a suitable subject, I'd have thought."

Billy's face reddened. He wiped his mouth, very much as she had just done, with the white cloth napkin.

"Try and keep an open mind, there's a good girl. We'll be passing out the score today. Must dash."

He left her to pay the check, which was, she thought, most unlike him.

She was never sure how many of the Knickerbockers knew that she and Billy had been married. She never wanted to bring it up herself, because she wasn't certain if she wanted it known or not. Billy was universally loved by all the singers for his kindness and admired for the suppleness and flexibility of his accompaniment, so luster would attach to her if it were known that she had been his wife. On the other hand, everyone knew that he and Paul were partners, so humiliation would attach to her, inevitably, as a woman who had been left. But to be left for a man was not the same—by a long chalk, she had always told herself—as being left for another woman. And she found it hard to determine which would attach to her more securely: luster or humiliation. So she had held herself back from the other people in the chorus; after twenty-five years of being a member, there was not one of them she could call a friend. Even those she had thought of as close acquaintances had left the chorus, because they had reached a certain age, the age at which their voices weren't up to certain musical demands. She was one of the older members now—but that was all right, she liked to think that she maintained a nice balance: she kept her reserve but she was friendly to everyone. If, occasionally, she picked up a whiff of resentment, she reminded herself that musical people were temperamental and self-centered, and that it had nothing to do with her.

She was asking Lily Streicher, who had been to Tuscany, how her summer was, when Paul walked in, dressed in navy pants, a yellow shirt (untucked, Eleanor noted, to hide his belly), and black loafers that made his feet look like thick fish, steaming in a too narrow pan, on the verge of spilling over the sides. The look of his feet in their ill-fitting shoes made her own feet feel hot; she wiggled them slightly in her Ferragamos.

He was carrying a stack of scores and he laid them dramatically on the top of the piano.

"Something exciting, boys and girls. Papa has quite a special treat."

There was a stir among the singers; Eleanor felt complacent in her secret knowledge.

"I've commissioned an opera for us. By the next genius among us; we've stolen a march on the MacArthurs. I'll pass out the score and Billy will play some bits for you. It's called *The Dream of Andy Warhol.* I'll allow the composer to fill you in. It's my honor to introduce him. Ladies and gentlemen: Desmond Marx."

Certainly, there wasn't a gasp when the young man walked through the door, but there was something like it in the feeling that spread through the air. It was as if a Bronzino had walked in, Eleanor thought, one of those arrogant courtiers in velvet and satin with the full lower lip and dissolute, commanding stare. Desmond Marx was beautiful: there was power in his beauty, and he knew it. His black jeans were creased perfectly, as if they'd just been pressed; his shirt, a bluish violet open at the neck, spread itself lightly, easily, over his muscular torso; he wore loafers—the same loafers Paul was wearing, but without socks, and his feet were thin and shapely in the loafers whereas Paul's looked overstuffed.

"Hi," he said, looking challengingly at the chorus. "Well, as Paul told you, my opera is called *The Dream of Andy Warhol* and I know perfectly well it's a lot different from the kind of thing you do. Maybe a little bit shocking for you. But I think Warhol was a great visionary, the person who had the clearest vision of his time and ours, its violence, its strangeness, and this is my vision of his vision. I like to think it brings out the pathos and the grandeur of this artist. And I look forward to your responses."

"Billy, if you would," said Paul.

Billy and Paul looked at each other, Eleanor thought, like a pair of cats that had swallowed the cream. She wondered where this Desmond Marx was living; Billy had said he was staying with them. It was, as she very well knew, a one-bedroom apartment. She wondered if they had recently got around to buying a foldout couch.

Eleanor didn't know if everyone feared, as she did, the harsh, atonal sound so typical of contemporary music. But Billy was right; Desmond Marx had a lyric touch, and the melodies were sweet and haunting.

"Turn to the first scene in the Factory, the second place where the chorus comes in," Paul said.

There was the sound of turning pages. Someone giggled. Eleanor didn't know why at first, and then her eye fell on the second page of the section that the chorus was meant to sing. She took her glasses off and put them on again. Surely she couldn't be reading what she thought she saw.

"Fuck me, suck me fuck me suck me." The words were peppered all over the page like a noxious mildew.

Someone else giggled. One of the tenors coughed.

"Anyone have a problem?" Paul said, challengingly.

Did she imagine it or was everyone looking at her? She'd been in the chorus longer than any of the others, except Randy Brixton, the tenor who had coughed. And nothing would make Randy Brixton speak up; he was pathologically disinclined to conflict. He would give way if anyone so much as asked him anything, so much as indicated he might have to assert himself. Randy would be no help. She looked around at everybody in the chorus, trying, in her teacherly way, to make eye contact. But no one would look up from the score.

"I don't know whether I have a problem, which would suggest something stemming from a personal set of circumstances, but I believe there's a problem with the Knickerbocker chorus, taking into consideration our history and the nature of our audience, singing words like these."

"Anyone else like to respond to this outburst?" Paul said. She had always known he disliked her, but he had made a point of being coldly correct with her. She tried to get Billy's eye. Surely Billy would back her up. But Billy had his eye on the score; he was turning pages, as though he were looking for something real.

"I'd hardly call it an outburst, Paul. You asked for response. I'd assumed it was a question asked in good faith."

It was as if a knife had been thrown down on the ground between them. Mumblety-peg, she thought, remembering a game she'd played in her childhood. One of those words that didn't sound like what it was. Which was certainly not the case with the ones on the page she was holding.

Silence shimmered in the air like an iron ring. Paul was indicating by his particular silence—a silence that was separate from the others as if it had been traced with a chalk line—that what she had just said wasn't worthy of a reply. And that was, she felt, the most insulting thing that he could do. The pusillanimity of her fellow choristers appalled her. She felt it was time to take a dramatic stand; that, she believed, would put some spine into some of them at least.

"I cannot bring myself to use such language," Eleanor said.

"You can't bring yourself. Then I suppose we'll have to do without you. But let me make this clear: you will sing in this opera, or you will not sing with us at all. This season or any other."

"You can't do that."

"Oh yes, my dear, I'm the director and I can. And many, I'm sure, would support me in saying that it's a bit overdue. You might have made a graceful exit as many of your cohort have, but you've outstayed your welcome. Your taste is as tired as your voice. It's time to leave now, Eleanor. Pick up your toys and go."

She waited a few seconds, certain that someone would come to her defense. But no one raised eyes from the score or the ground at their feet. And Billy was looking into space, as if she had already left the room and he was waiting for the next thing that would happen.

She understood that there were no words that would do anything but weaken her position. She made her way to the front of the chorus—she was, unfortunately, in the third row—and heard her heels making a sharp clack-clack on the gray linoleum floor.

She closed the door and flung her cape around her shoulders, pleased at the military suggestions of the gesture. She was afraid her face must be bright red: heat climbed up it as she thought of Paul's crude words, his vulgar insults. She was certain that Billy would be behind her in a moment; certainly, even if he didn't stand up to Paul, he wouldn't allow her to make her way home like this, entirely unsupported.

But as she climbed the last stair, opened the heavy door, and found herself shocked at the brightness of the day, she began to realize that Billy was not going to follow. Why had it been so difficult for her to admit, always, that he had always been a coward? And why had she tried for so long to deny what Paul was, what he had always been, an insignificant and stinking little turd. She banished the word from her mind; she would not sink to his level. Or to the level of the little Bronzino, the Bronzinetto, she called him to herself. Desmond Marx. Composer of that preposterous atrocity. *The Dream of Andy Warhol.* She'd have liked to call it instead *The Nightmare of the Modern Age.*

She must have been walking very fast, propelled by her rage, her shock; before she knew it she was in front of her building. Had she really walked forty blocks in half an hour? She could smell her sweat underneath the wool of her cape, the silk of her blouse, and it shocked her with its robust meatiness. She had never before associated such a smell with her own body.

She couldn't bear to wait for the elevator, propelled as she still was with rage. She burst into the apartment, hardly able to get her key into the lock. "Anybody home?" she called. Her mother's bedroom door was closed. Well, she would open it; she felt, today, she had a right. It was something she never did, but now she couldn't help herself. She had to tell her mother.

She knocked three times, but didn't wait for a response. At first, she couldn't tell whether or not her mother was there; the heavy velvet drapes were closed and she could barely make out her mother's shape under the satin coverlet. But then her eyes got used to the light and she saw her mother, lying on her back, her mouth open. On the night table beside her bed were her hearing aids, and in a glass, one on top of the other, the two halves of her dentures. Her mother's open, toothless mouth made her head look like a skull.

Had she known, had she ever considered, that her mother was toothless, that her mother wore false teeth? When had that happened? How was it that in all the years that they had lived together it was something she never knew? The rage that had consumed her body now spilled over to her mother. Why had her mother kept this from her? And how could she allow herself to be like this? It was against everything her mother stood for, to be lying here, in the middle of the afternoon, the drapes closed against the brilliant autumn sun, impervious to every sound, impervious to her shocking appearance.

She knew that she must leave the room. But she allowed herself to look at her mother for a few more seconds. Her mother was very old. Her mother's life was almost over. She was, lying on her back, cut off from light and sound, her countenance a corpse's, trying out the position she would, quite soon now, Eleanor realized, be permanently taking up.

There was something she wanted to say, but she didn't know exactly what the words might be. "It's over, it's finished." Was that what she wanted to say? But whom would she say it to? Her mother was deaf; her mother was asleep—she supposed it was peacefully—and her father was nowhere around.

She had been stolen from, and the thief had been not only thief but assailant. She resisted the impulse to go to the mirror and see whether, as a result of the assault, her looks had changed. That would be ridiculous, that would be—her mother's word, always used mockingly—"dramatic." This was her life, it was not an opera, and she would live it as she always had, as her parents always had: with dignity, on her own terms. And yet there had been this theft—must she think of herself now as impoverished, as her parents had never had to do?

And how could she name the thing whose absence made her feel so utterly bereft. It wasn't something with one name—and if it was impossible to name, it must be irreplaceable. She couldn't resist the impulse any more: she must look at herself in the mirror to see if the loss was visible.

She patted her hair. Of course it looked the same, of course her face was identical to the one she had seen only a few hours before. She need not feel humiliated; humiliation was a trick of the eye, and she would be sure, always, that when eyes fell on her they would see something admirable, something fine. She could do that. It might not even be so difficult; she might even make it into something of a game she played with herself: this covering up, this patching over.

She made her way into the living room, the room her mother had made so delightful, had made her own, so high and airy and refined, and yet so simple, so easy to be one's self in. One's best self.

In a little while, her mother would walk in, fresh, rested from her nap; together they would set the table for an early dinner, beginning with the soup her mother had made, that Eleanor had bought the ingredients for. Things would go on; life would go on.

Above all, she must not let her mother know what had happened, that she was suffering. It was beautiful, her mother's world, and Eleanor knew that the most important thing that she could do now would be to play her part, so that her mother wouldn't know that the world she still believed she was inhabiting had disappeared. Had been stolen.

There would be no need to tell her mother what had happened to her today. There would be no need to tell anyone. No one in the chorus knew anyone she knew—and Billy would never say anything. It suddenly occurred to her that there might be a difficult moment the next time she and Billy met. Perhaps it would be better to say nothing of what had taken place today. As for the other people, her friends, her colleagues, she would simply say that she had decided to resign from the company. And when people asked her why she'd say, "The time has come, the walrus said." Something light, something amusing. The kind of thing her mother would have said.

Three Men Tell Me Stories
About Their Boyhoods

Three different men have told me these stories, if they can be called stories. Perhaps it's better to say: three men have told me these *things*, and when I heard them, each of them was bathed in the same light. Yes, I heard them, but the words created pictures—or perhaps not pictures, it is better to say an atmosphere. And so it's not wrong to say the words were bathed in a particular light.

Everything these men say has to do with boys moving in rooms of adults. Uncomprehending boys, trying to understand. Rooms with no or little natural light. Rooms lit by lamps. Lamps lit by adults, dimmed by adults.

Has any child ever performed the action of dimming a light? Has any child ever felt he has had too much of brightness? Even if a blinding light were shone in the eyes of a child, he would only cover his eyes. A gesture adults think of rarely. They close their eyes, but they don't cover their eyes with their hands. Not as a rule.

The beginning of what the first man tells me happens in Belgium in the 1920s. A wealthy house in the city of Antwerp. A house owned by Americans living in Europe. The man is an American now, living in America, but he began his life as an American boy brought up in Europe.

His father is the European representative of the Swift meatpacking company, based in Chicago. But the family is far from Chicago, far from the smell and noise of the stockyards, of the elevated trains. They are in Antwerp, in a house where you can hear the click of civilized, decorous heels on the outside pavement, a house of wealth where servants move noiselessly up and down carpeted staircases, where the light, in every season, always falls through drawn curtains and always takes on something of their brown. Whatever season, whatever the texture of the fabric, the curtains are always brown.

No one is happy in the house because at the center of it is a tyrannical father, who sits in a chair that the son thinks of as something like a throne. Later, when the son, a grown man, inherits the chair he will see that it is not very large and is nothing like a throne at all. But that will be much later.

The son knows that his father is the source of all the misery in the house, although his father is always nice to him. He admires his son's lightness of body, which is like his own. But to everyone else, the mother, the older brother, the sister, the servants, he is a humiliator. Many days he opens his mouth only to humiliate. He fires servants, particularly young girls, for minor infractions, and then the mother has to hide them, until he forgets and it is all right to bring the servant back out to the light of day.

In this dark house, the only source of light for the boy is his sister, with whom he plays upstairs in the nursery, supervised first by nannies, then by governesses. When the sister is ten and the boy is seven, she is hit by a car on the streets of Antwerp and killed. After her death, no one in the house speaks of her and only forty years later does the boy, middle-aged, realize how deeply the loss of this sister has affected him. How everything, every decision in his subsequent life, has flowed from that.

The summer that the boy is twelve, the family goes back to America, to visit their families and for a holiday to the Far West. Their first stop is Moline, Illinois, the mother's hometown. While they are there the father, who is known to be suffering from an enlarged heart, dies. An excessively methodical man, he somehow dies without a will, and somehow the family is suddenly poor. The older brother, who played on the Belgian Olympic tennis team, must change his life. By day, he must work in the Swift meatpacking plant and by night play tennis for money with rich men in an exclusive tennis club. He is allowed to be a member, and not to pay, because it is clear that, despite certain circumstances, he has the right breeding. And it is perfect for the rich men that they be challenged by, and lose money to, someone so well-bred.

The boy and his mother spend the summer in Moline. The boy is not sad, he is happy. He is happy because of the rich, uncultivated trees and the white houses with porches. Most of all, he is happy because of the open doors of Moline. The open doors of a Midwest summer. The screen doors that open and bang shut as children walk in and out of each other's houses, as mothers say, "Go on upstairs, he's in his room playing with his trains. Do you want some lemonade to drink?"

Is he happy because in America the enlarged heart of his father, the tyrant, was made to explode?

He believes nothing is closed to him in America. All doors, like the screen doors of Moline, will always be open to him.

But he is not allowed to stay in America. His mother says they must go back to Belgium where they have, at least, a house. A house he hates as he hates Europe for its closed doors, its locked doors, its frightened children, who must wait in rooms whose light is never clear and never generous, to be taken somewhere, to walk, never alone, on streets that do not look as if they should be dangerous, but where, nevertheless, it is possible for one of them to die.

The second man tells me about being a boy, also in the Midwest, but in the thirties. One day, the boy is standing in a room in the family house, a house of the Indiana dunes, a house built by his father, who is stern but not a tyrant. A house doubtless, with a screen door like that beloved by the first man. The boy learns from his mother (usually smiling but not smiling now) that his father has a brother he has hidden from his three sons.

This frightens the boy because he is not only a son but a brother, the youngest of three, and he loves his brothers, particularly the middle one, his protector. It frightens him more than he can bear to imagine a time when his brothers would not speak of him. When he has this fear, he is standing in brown-stained light. The light that permeated the large prosperous house in Antwerp.

The boy is nine years old, and so his mother doesn't tell him the whole story till he is ready to leave home for the army, nine years later. So for nine years, until he hears the story, when he thinks of his father and his father's brother, he is bathed in that brown light.

Only as he is about to go to the world war, to a possible heroic death (a death which does not come), his mother tells him the story.

The two brothers were orphaned, and they were left a pool hall as their only inheritance. The plan was that they would take turns going to college. One would stay home and manage the pool hall and make sure it was earning properly, and the other would go off to Purdue. The older, my friend's father, went off first. My friend's mother tells him that perhaps this was the natural way of doing things, but that it was too bad the boys were so young they didn't see the possibilities of trouble. Perhaps it should have been done the other way; perhaps running the pool hall was too much responsibility for the younger brother. Perhaps he should have been allowed to go off to college to mature. Especially since he was very handsome and eager to please. Catnip to women, my friend's mother said.

Bad things began to happen. The younger brother fell in love with the landlady of his boardinghouse. He was eighteen and she was thirty-five. He began drinking and gambling. The pool hall had to be sold. The older brother had to come home from Purdue, but by the time he arrived back home the younger brother had run off with his landlady, whereabouts unknown. I can hear the whistle of the train in the air of Illinois as they escaped. When the boy, or the young man, hears this story he can see the landlady's full body, her corsets, her straw or feathered hat. And the young handsome man, reaching in his pocket for a flask, or maybe a pint bottle.

He went from bad to worse. He married the landlady but she left him. He became involved with mobsters. He hit the skids. Then, somehow, my friend's mother didn't know how, he pulled himself together. He got work in a bank as a clerk. Then he was promoted; he became what was known as a repo man, repossessing the assets of the failed.

Then he met Hazel, who was a buyer at Indianapolis's largest department store. After two years, he told her the story of what he had done to his older brother, and his grief at their estrangement. He loved his brother and he knew he had done wrong.

She said he must write to his older brother. But the older brother was not inclined to forgive. He'd been robbed of a college education and forced to work in the hellish steel mills of Gary, Indiana, instead of behind a desk, wearing a white collar. But his wife, my friend's mother, said that it was a terrible shame that brothers shouldn't speak. She reminded him that blood was thicker than water. She reminded her husband that the brothers had loved each other. He agreed that the younger brother and his wife should be allowed to visit. He made no promises about what would happen after that.

But when the two men meet they fall into each other's arms like sisters. My friend doesn't know what was said; whether or not forgiveness was asked for and granted.

The families visit back and forth. Usually because the older brother has children and the younger one does not, the younger couple does the traveling. But once Hazel invites the whole family for a slap-up weekend in Indianapolis. She takes them to a restaurant that has a real pond in its lobby, full of live lobsters which are caught, right there, then prepared and served to the guests. Hazel orders lobster and champagne all around. She insists that the three sons of her brother-in-law be given, in her presence, and at her expense, their first taste of champagne.

My friend and his two older brothers are abashed in their stiff shoes, their stiff suits, their stiffly brushed hair. They're overawed at the opulence of this restaurant, the tinkling of cocktail glasses, the women with furs slung around their shoulders and jewels dangling from their ears. My friend says he was in love with everything and everyone; he believed his family was the most desirable in the world.

One time the uncle takes them to the racetrack: the whole family, my friend and his brothers and his parents. Hazel doesn't go along. He provides everyone with betting money. Ten dollars apiece for the grown-ups. Five for each child. But it isn't a good time because after his uncle bets he begins trembling, his whole body shakes and his face goes gray. This is when the brown light permeates again; when my friend, aged eleven, observes his glamorous uncle, trembling. They win a hundred dollars, but it doesn't matter. They've seen what they didn't have to see. But none of them ever speaks about it. The visits take up their old pattern: the younger coming to the older, to the house the older built in Ogden Dunes, Indiana, overlooking Lake Michigan, which, particularly in summer, is a pleasant place.

The younger brother prospers as a repo man until he gets bored. He decides to open a little bookie operation, investing his wife's savings. Soon he's wiped out by mobsters. Hazel writes my friend's family that the younger brother has lost all interest in life, that he sleeps most of the day and sits in the living room in the darkness weeping. She says the older brother and his family should stay away until the younger brother pulls himself together.

But he never does. He dies in a year, of a blood clot in the leg. Hazel moves to Florida but doesn't contact the family. Except one letter to the mother saying she has remarried and it was the worst mistake of her life but she deserves her unhappiness for betraying the memory of her own true love. Years later, they learn of her death from strangers who say they found the address going through her papers.

The third story isn't placed in the Midwest. It happens in New York, in the forties, during the war. Like the story of the uncle, this one has to do with mobsters, not the small-time mobsters of Indianapolis, but the big-time mobsters of New York.

The man with mob connections who is the center of the story isn't big-time, isn't even a full-time mobster. His name is Earl and he's a business associate of my friend's father; they both work in the garment district. But somehow Earl has much more money than my friend's father. He owns a car. He lives in Manhattan, on Central Park West. My friend admires the way Earl dresses, particularly his black-and-white shoes. He loves it when he and his family travel from the Bronx to eat with him in restaurants. Or sometimes he picks my friend and his father up in his car and they go for jaunts. Often they go to Colony Records in Times Square and Earl buys stacks and stacks of 78s. My friend is impressed; his parents buy only one record at a time, and that rarely.

It is through Earl that my friend, age nine, first hears Billie Holiday and the Ink Spots, and although they frighten him a little, they excite him too. He knows they are the signs of a world more daring and truthful than any inhabited by his parents. When he hears this music, he sees lights and gleaming streets, he hears the slamming of cab doors and the shaking of cocktail shakers. Also the silence when these people, these cab riders and cocktail drinkers, who have gone too far, and tried too much, are simply made to disappear from sight.

My friend knows that living in Manhattan is the better thing to do, better than living in the Bronx. His parents whisper about the source of Earl's wealth, but they're not specific, and the boy knows they're afraid to be.

Earl is divorced and this is different from anyone the boy and his parents know. He has a son the boy's age, although the boy has never met him because he lives with his mother. One day, Earl invites them to come to his apartment for his son's ninth birthday party. My friend doesn't want to go for three reasons. He doesn't know the boy, he doesn't want to go to a birthday party with his parents, and he'll have to wear a suit. His parents say he has no choice: they're grateful to Earl, they owe him. They don't say what for.

The boy is thrilled by entering a building on Central Park West, with its suggestion of Europe. By being shown in by a doorman who acts as if he thinks they're rich. But above all by walking into the sunken living room in Earl's apartment, something he has seen only in movies.

Because none of the children know each other, they attach themselves to their parents, particularly their mothers. My friend focuses on these mothers' hair, piled high, their filter-tipped cigarettes with lipstick prints left on the butts in the ashtrays, their finely made shoes. They speak more quietly than his mother and he knows it is money that makes them quiet and different. The adults barely speak to each other. Each family inhabits a discrete solar system, no one knows what to say or what to do because although there is cake in the middle of the table, which is set with party hats, horns, and snappers at each place, the birthday boy has not arrived.

Because of this, the light in the elegant apartment, with its thick, gravy-colored drapes, is darkish brown. The boy stands in the brown light, near his mother, and says nothing.

Earl stays in the kitchen, shouting into the telephone. He is shouting at his ex-wife, shouting because the boy has not arrived. Occasionally one of the men disappears into the kitchen to say something to him, but comes out quickly and whispers something to his wife. Nobody says anything to any of the children.

Eventually, one by one the families leave. My friend doesn't remember how this happened. Only a few words picked up from his parents' conversation on the subway home. Words entirely new to him: Reno, alimony, custody. And a way of referring to a person he has never heard: "his EX."

What do these stories have in common, beyond the fact that they happened to boys of about the same age in America?

That's it, you see. America! Where the light is always meant to fall clear, straight down to the plain wood of the floor, straight from the sparkling windows. Oh, the Puritans, the Shakers. Oh, the Federalist Builders, spurred on by the light of the Enlightenment. The truth shall make you free. Stand in the light and take your place in it.

As if there were nothing that could not be brought to light.

What the parents of these boys work for, what all parents brought up in, or believing in, or hoping for prosperity work for, is this: that there shall be a curtain, always shut, between light and darkness. That boys will play, grow, flourish in the light that travels through the sparkling glass. And on the other side, the curtain will be fixed and always drawn.

But on the other side of what? The space where their children live? The other side of living space? The parents never understand that such boundaries don't remain fixed. That what they think of as a boundary is only an envelope of brownish light. And that whatever they do, behind the curtain they think of as so concealing, there are stirrings, rumblings. Rumblings that the boys—drawn by the pull away from their own childhood—will approach. They must look. Or not look, glance. Or peer.

With half-closed eyes, the boys approach the small rent in the blackout curtain, which is not black after all, but darkish brown. Peer through. As they continue to peer, the rent will seem to become larger. They will keep their hands still at their sides, as they've been told. They will touch nothing, move nothing.

They are good boys.

Peering, they will see only shadows moving in half darkness, certainly a danger to themselves. Moving in sadness, in disorder. Speaking words that can only cause harm.

The boys stand still as if they have been shot. They cannot move away and they will not move forward. Not yet. The grace of immobility. This much will be allowed them.

They can change nothing; nothing they do can touch all that goes on. One day they will have no choice but to inhabit the abode where those things happen. But for now their feet are placed on the hardwood floor, and although they are standing in a brownish light, the sun still strikes their shiny hair, slicked down, out of politeness. For now, they may stand where they are. They know it is just for now.

They know some things but do not know them fully. They know that they have been deceived and that they can no longer trust their safety to the ones who have deceived them. Yet they must. They have no choice.

Something is in store for them. This is the only thing they understand.

Vision

Temporarily, my vision is impaired. This is of no importance to the story.

It is of no importance to the story; it is not a permanent affliction; it will pass. But while it does not pass, the act of sustained looking, which more than I knew was central to my life for—what? joy, information, solace, rest—is now a difficulty. So I do not do it much. Vision has become abstract. Seeing as idea. While I am thinking of seeing, rather than *seeing*, a memory floats up into the area behind my eyes where I need not see but may see if I wish. Also the memory in this case is a story, so I can choose to put aside the whole matter of seeing: I can hear.

I hear my mother's best friend telling a story as my mother and I sit beside her on a stone front porch. The situation of the story indicates I must know something about sex; the flavor of the memory reveals that I am still a child. I must be twelve years old.

What do we need to know about my mother and my mother's friend? Their looks? Their voices? Harder, impossible, perhaps, to describe voices. Always, one must go outside the frame to other issues: money, history. Between my mother and her best friend there are schools, dollars, rooms, linens, doctors, a variety of forks, musical instruments. My mother's friend grew up in privilege, and this explains her voice. But now she has sometimes less money than we do, sometimes as much, but never more. This can make her sometimes inaudible but never adds to her buffed consonants an edge. My mother's voice, shaped in a house of scarcity, impatience, anger, passions laid out like the evening meal, hurts me sometimes because it can provide me with no bolster, sometimes strengthens me because it lets me know that all my life behind me and within my blood there is the brute, inflexible, impermeable force of instinct, given in this case the name of mother love.

What are they wearing? My mother's friend is wearing some garment signifying a genteel, overdetermined recoil from sex. It will be flocked, or lightly dotted. Printed without distinction blue and white. I will dress my mother in one of the two dresses of my childhood love. Apple green cotton with a print of branches and a durable round flower—zinnia, hollyhock—the branches and the flowers both in white. Or perhaps her bluish purple sundress so I can see her buoyant upper arms. Both dresses are wonderfully resistant to the touch: starched, ironed by her, they cry out their bifurcated cry: we are delicious, we will not succumb.

It must be summer. We are sitting on a porch. The porch is not familiar, so we must be on vacation.

My mother is a widow and I am her only child; we always take vacations with at least one of my mother's childless friends. The cynical contemporary reader says: the mother takes another grown-up to spare her the boredom of enforced aloneness with her child. But it is not this; it is the opposite of this. It is her pity for her childless friends that presses on my mother's always originally constructed sense of duty. It urges her to share me with her friends. Most of her friends seem never to have married or to be older than she, so that their children could be my parents. She is old to be the mother of a child herself.

We always have a very happy time. We choose places with lakes or mountains, sometimes both. A drive six to eight hours in duration, long enough so that we feel the glamour of a journey, but not so long that we turn upon each other with sour questions, accusations, or regret.

My mother's friend is speaking now. "We didn't have a porch on our house; I was looking out the windows of the living room. There was a window seat. The people across the street had just moved in and didn't seem to want to know the neighbors; I had never seen the woman, she had no children, and she never left the house. We'd seen the husband leaving in the mornings. Well, he looked like any other husband, and at that age I did not give men a thought.

"It was August when she started coming on the porch. I know that it was August; in July mother and I went to my grandmother's. Every summer we did that; that's how I know that it could not have been July. Each morning she would come onto the porch wearing her wrapper. I was very shocked by that: no woman I had ever known would have dreamed of appearing even at her breakfast table in a wrapper. And her hair was down, down on her shoulders. No woman I ever knew would have done that. Her wrapper was light pink with a pattern of large red birds: peacocks, I guess. Or they might have been herons. Herons, yes. She was behind the screen and I looked out through the window. I could see though that on her lap she held a paper sack. Slowly throughout the morning she'd take pears out of the sack and eat them. Perfectly still she sat, except to reach inside the sack and get a pear, and then of course to eat. Other than that she was motionless. The trees were wonderful in summer on that street: tall, wide old elms. Beeches. All the houses were quite cool even though it was southern Illinois, which has a southern climate, and if you stepped out from the shelter of the trees the heat was killing. So there was not at all a great deal of activity out on the street, no reason to be looking out there. But she just sat there looking, eating. And I noticed she was getting bigger. So I kept watching her. All the time that she sat there, I sat and watched her. On the window seat I sat. I brought a book with me so when my mother asked I could say I was reading.

"One day my mother said: 'You know that woman is about to have a baby.'

"I was innocent; I must have known that children came from the body of a mother. Yet I hadn't seen a hint of it, and so I hadn't thought of it. It was all hidden; everything was hidden in those days. When women were pregnant you couldn't tell; it was the way they dressed. But once I found out the woman was going to have a child, it was one of those things like a key to a puzzle so everything begins to make sense, you see everything, you can't imagine why you didn't see it. Every day I felt I could see her getting bigger and bigger. It was almost as if she grew as I watched her, like one of those speeded-up films where the flower blooms before your eyes. Except of course we didn't have them in those days.

"But I just watched her sitting, looking out at the street, the street that was nearly always empty, watched her eating those pears, one after another, growing bigger before my eyes.

"Then one day she didn't come out on the porch, and we could see a great commotion going on across the street there. I don't know if we heard anything: I don't remember. Just the doctor going in and once the husband on the porch to smoke a cigarette. And then the doctor leaving. I sat the whole day watching. I kept thinking she would come back out, but with the baby now, not eating pears, not now she had a baby, and not looking out at nothing on the street, but feeding the baby, tending it, seeing that it was comfortable.

"But she died. She died and the baby was born dead too. We didn't see them take her out; they must have done it in the night. And then quite soon the man sold up the house and moved away. We always thought that there was something shady there."

Now I can remember that at this point in the story I became dissatisfied. My mother's friend's voice changes. The rapt, clouded, reverent tone turns coy: she makes the thing a joke. She giggles. "After that I was afraid of eating pears. I thought the pears had done it, made her pregnant, killed her and the baby. For years, you couldn't get me to go near a pear."

As I listen to her speaking, I do not believe her; I do not believe her now. I do not know how much she could have known, a lonely child on a street of heavy trees, holding her book as a deception, looking, looking. But I know she did not think it was the pears.

Here are the things I do not know:

What did the woman see as she looked at the empty street?

Was she happy with the child within her womb? Was she trying, filling herself with pears and staring down the empty street, the street down which her husband walked to work each morning, was she trying to connect the secret child, whose face she could not know, with the whole outside world?

Did she know the girl across the street looked at her? Was she grateful?

Did she speak English?

Was she really married to the man?

If she had lived to her new status as a mother, would she have spoken to the neighbors?

Did every aspect of the episode take place in silence?

Did the girl think she had killed the woman and the baby by her failure to keep them in sight?

Did the girl invent the whole thing? Was there a pregnant woman who came on the porch each morning and ate pears and looked out to the empty street and died in childbirth, giving birth to a dead child? Or was it the girl's vision of the life of women which so frightened her that, sitting on a porch herself, fifty years later, she must turn it to a joke: the rapt girl looking, and the woman growing large looking at nothing, knowing or not knowing she is seen, invisible in death, taken away, out of the sight of the so faithful watching girl who as a woman will not marry, will tell the child of someone else about it, and will turn her vision to a joke for fear of disappearing, being made to disappear?

from TEMPORARY SHELTER

Temporary Shelter

He hated the way his mother piled the laundry. The way she held the clothes, as if it didn't matter. And he knew what she would say if he said anything, though he would never say it. But if he said, "Don't hold the clothes like that, it's ugly, how you hold them. See the arms of Dr. Meyers's shirt, they hang as if he had no arms, as if he'd lost them. And Maria's dress, you let it bunch like that, as if you never knew her." If he said a thing like that, which he would never do, she'd laugh and store it up to tell her friends. She'd say, "My son is crazy in love. With both of them. Even the stinking laundry he's in love with." And she would hit him on the side of the head, meaning to be kind, to joke, but she would do it wrong, the blow would be too hard. His ears would ring, and he would hate her.

Then he would hate himself, because she worked so hard, for him; he knew it was for him. Why did she make him feel so dreadful? He was thirteen, he was old enough to understand it all, where they had come from, who they were, and why she did things. She wanted things for him. A good life, better than what she had. Better than Milwaukee, which they'd left for the shame of her being a woman that a man had left. It wasn't to be left by a man that she'd come to this country, that her parents brought her on the ship, just ten years old, in 1929, when they should have stayed home, if they'd had sense, that year that turned out to be so terrible for the Americans. For a few months, it was like a heaven, with her cousins in Chicago. Everybody saying: Don't worry, everyone needs shoes. Her father was a cobbler. But then the crash, and no one needed shoes, there were no jobs, her mother went out to do strangers' laundry, and her father sat home, his head in his hands before the picture of the Black Madonna and tried to imagine some way they could go back home.

"And I was never beautiful," his mother said, and he believed that that was something he would have to make up to her. Someday when he was a man. Yes, he would have to make it up to her, and yet she said it proudly, as if it meant that everything she'd got she had got straight. And he would have to make it up to her because his father who'd lived off her money and sat home on his behind had left them both without a word. When he, Joseph, was six months old. And he would have to make it up to her that she had come to work for Dr. Meyers, really a Jew—once you were one you always were one—though he said he was a Catholic, and the priests knelt at his feet because he was so educated. And he would have to make it up to her because he loved the Meyerses, Doctor and Maria. When he was with them, happiness fell on the three of them like a white net of cloud and set them off apart from all the others. Yes, someday he would have to make it up to her because he loved the Meyers in the lightness of his heart, while in his heart there was so often mockery and shame for his mother.

He couldn't remember a time when he hadn't lived with the Meyers in White Plains. His mother got the job when he was two, answering an ad that Dr. Meyers had put in the *Irish Echo*. No Irish had applied, so Dr. Meyers hired Joseph's mother, Helen Kaszperkowski, because, he had explained with dignity, it was important to him that the person who would be caring for his daughter shared the Faith. Joseph was sure he must have said "The Faith" in the way he always said it when he talked about the Poles to Joseph and his mother. "I believe they are, at present, martyrs to the Faith." He would speak of Cardinal Mindszenty, imprisoned in his room, heroically defying Communism. But the way Dr. Meyers said "The Faith" made Joseph feel sorry for him. It was a clue, if anyone was looking for clues, that he had not been born a Catholic, and all those things that one breathed in at Catholic birth he'd had to learn, as if he had been learning a new language.

But of course no one would have to search for clues, the doctor never tried to hide that he was a Jew, or had been born a Jew, as he would say. He would tell the story of his conversion calmly, unfurling it like a bolt of cloth, evenly, allowing it to shine, allowing the onlooker to observe, without his saying anything, the pattern in the fabric. He had converted in the 1920s, when he had been studying art, in Italy, in a city called Siena. Joseph had looked up Siena in Dr. Meyers's atlas. He had been pleased when Dr. Meyers came into the library and found him there, rubbing his finger in a circle around the area that was Siena, touching the dark spot that marked it, as if he were a blind child. He was seven then, and Dr. Meyers took him on his lap. How comfortably he fit there, on Dr. Meyers's lean, dry lap, a lap of safety.

Not like his mother's lap, which he had to share with her stomach. Holding Joseph on his lap and not afraid to kiss a little boy the way all of Joseph's uncles were, Dr. Meyers showed him the pictures in the book of Cimabue and Simone Martini and explained to him the silence and the holiness, the grandeur and the secrecy. He used the pictures for his business now, his business in liturgical greeting cards, holy pictures, stationery. The business that had bought him this house and all these things. And Joseph understood why he had left his family (his family said he could never see them again) and all he had been born to. For the quiet sad-faced mothers and their dark commanding baby sons.

He understood it all; so did Maria. They had loved it all, the silence and the grandeur, since they had been small, before they went to school when Dr. Meyers took them with him to Daily Mass, the only children there, kneeling together, looking, very still as every other person rose and went up to Communion. They made up lives for all the people, and they talked about them even when they no longer went to Daily Mass; when they were older, in the parish school, they talked about those people. The woman who was always pregnant (they said "expecting," thinking it more polite) and the crippled woman, and the Irish man who wore a cap, and the old, the very old Italian lady dressed entirely in black who sat at the very back of the church and said the Rosary out loud, in Italian, during the whole Mass, even during the silence of the Consecration. But the person they thought of most and considered most theirs was the very small woman who was extremely clean. They imagined her in her small house alone (they were sure she lived alone), brushing her hat, her black felt hat with the feather band around it, brushing her purple coat with its velvet collar and buttons of winking glass, polishing her old lady's shoes till they looked beautiful. Then putting on her hat without looking in the mirror because if she did she would have to see the horror that was her face. For on the side of her nose grew a shiny hard-skinned fruit, larger than a walnut, but a purple color. Joseph and Maria talked about it, never once mentioning it to Dr. Meyers. They thought that the woman must be a saint, because, despite the terrible cross God had given her, her face was as sweet as an angel's.

Joseph thought that Maria, too, must be a saint because she never lost her patience with his mother, although she lost patience with everything else. His mother was terrible to Maria; every day of her life she was terrible. If he didn't know how good a woman his mother was, and how much she loved the Meyerses and how grateful she was to them, he would think she hated Maria. That was how she acted. It was mainly because Maria was sloppy, she really was, his mother was right, much as he loved her, much as he thought Maria was a saint, he knew his mother was right. She left the caps off of pens so that the pockets of her skirts turned black; she threw her clothes around the room, she dropped her towels on the floor, she scrunched up papers into a ball and threw them into the wastebasket, and missed, and didn't bend to put them properly into the bin; she made her bed with lumps, sometimes the lumps were just the blankets or the sheets, sometimes they were her socks or underwear or books she'd fallen asleep reading. As if she didn't understand you made a bed for the look of it, not just so that if someone (Joseph's mother) asked if you had made your bed you would be free to answer yes.

He wondered what Maria thought about his mother. They never spoke about her. No, once they had spoken about her, and it would have been much better if they'd never had the conversation. Once his mother had said such awful things, called Maria a pig, a slut, a hussy, a disgrace, and she'd just stood there, going white. Although she always had high coloring, this day she had gone dead white and made her body stiff and clenched her fists beside her body as if she wanted, really very badly wanted, to hit Joseph's mother and all her life was put into her fists, keeping them clenched so they would not. She had excused herself and left the room, walking slowly as though she had to show them, Joseph and his mother, that she didn't need to run. And Joseph for once had shouted at his mother, "Why are you so horrible to her?" And his mother had shouted, opened her lips, showed her strong yellow teeth; her tongue spat out the words, "How dare you take her part against me. The filthy, filthy pig. They're all alike. Fine ladies, with someone like me to clean up their shit. And you too, don't forget it. You're not one of them, you're *my* flesh and blood, whether you like it or you don't. They'll leave you in the end, don't you forget it. In the end I'll be the only thing you have."

She couldn't be right, the Meyerses would not leave him. So he left his mother sobbing in the kitchen and went upstairs to where he knew Maria would be sitting, still and white as if she had shed blood. He knocked on her door and then walked in. He saw her sitting as he knew she would be, and he sat down beside her on her bed.

"I'm sorry she's so mean. You should do something. You should tell your father."

"No," she said. "If I say something, he might say something to her, and she might want to leave, or he might make her leave, and you'd leave too."

He should not have come into her room; he wished he hadn't heard it. And wished later that he hadn't heard, been made to hear, the conversation at the table, Dr. Meyers talking to them both, Maria and his mother, calmly, saying that he understood both sides and that they must be patient with each other. Our Lord had loved both sisters, Martha and her sister Mary, there was room for all beneath the sight of God.

What he said made nothing better. His mother said she just did it for the girl's own good, these things were important in a woman's life, she, Helen Kaszperkowski, knew that. And then Maria said she would try to be better at these things. And Dr. Meyers lifted up his knife and fork and said, "Good, good." And Joseph knew he had no home, there was no place that was his really, as Maria's place was with her father. He was here or he was there, but it was possible, although he felt himself much happier beside the Meyers, that his mother had been right and it was beside her that he must find his place, must live.

But what was it, that happiness he felt beside the Meyers if it was not where he belonged? He thought about the things the three of them did together. The train into the city and the dressing up, the destination always one of those high, gray-stoned buildings with the ceiling beautiful enough to live on, carved or vaulted, and the always insufficient lights. The joy those buildings gave him, the dry impersonal air, the rich, hard-won minerals: the marble and the gold, where no wet breath—of doubt, of argument or of remorse—could settle or leave a trace. And how the voice of Dr. Meyers came into its own; the thick dental consonants, the vowels overlong and arched, belonged there. Everybody else's speech offended in those rooms, seemed cut off, rushed, ungiving and unloved. But Dr. Meyers's voice as he described a painting or a pillar wrapped around whatever he called beautiful and made it comfortable and no longer strange. It belonged then to Joseph and Maria; Dr. Meyers had surrounded it with their shared history and let its image float in slowly, like a large ship making its way to harbor, safely to its place inside their lives.

And then there were the treats, the lunches at the automat, the brown pots of baked beans or macaroni, the desserts at Rumpelmayer's and the silly games, the game they played with cream puffs. "It is important," Dr. Meyers would say in Rumpelmayer's, in the room that looked just like a doll's house, pink and white and ribboned like a doll, "it is important," he would say, making his face look pretend-serious, "to know exactly how to eat a cream puff. When I was in Paris, very great ladies would say to me, '*C'est de la plus grande importance savoir manger une cream puff comme il faut.*' He would keep on his pretend-serious face and cut into one cream puff deliberately, carving up pieces with the right mix of pastry and cream, then popping them into his mouth like Charlie Chaplin. "But, my children," he would say, "it takes a lot of practice. You must eat many cream puffs before you can truly say you know how to eat them *comme il faut.*"

Then he would order one cream puff for each of them and say, "That's good, you're getting the idea, but I don't think it's quite yet *comme il faut.*" So, with a pretend-serious face he would order another for them, and then another, then when he could see them stuffed with richness and with pleasure at the joke he would say, "Ah, I think you're getting there. You are learning the fine art of eating cream puffs *comme il faut.*"

Then they would go to the afternoon movies, the Three Stooges, Laurel and Hardy, movie after funny movie, and Dr. Meyers laughed the hardest, laughed till he coughed and they hit him on the back, then laughed at how hard they were hitting him. And then they would walk outside. Outside, where, while they had pleased themselves in warmth and darkness, the sky had grown somber. And quickly, sharply, they left behind the silly men who fought and shouted just to make them laugh. They'd wend their way through the commuters to St. Patrick's for the five thirty, the workers' Mass. And pray, amidst the people coming from their offices in suits, the women, some in hats, some taking kerchiefs from their handbags, all of them kneeling underneath the high dark ceiling where the birettas of dead cardinals hung rotting; always they chose a pew beside the statue of Pope Pius, waxy white, as if he were already dead. Then, blurred by the sacraments and silenced, they walked to Grand Central, boarded the train, too hot or too cold, always, and looked out the windows, pressed their cheeks against the glass and played "I Spy."

And at home Joseph's mother waited, served them dinner when they arrived, served them in anger for she knew they had left her out. Once they invited her to come with them to the Metropolitan Museum. Dr. Meyers showed her the Ming vases and her only comment was "I'd hate to have to dust all those," and Dr. Meyers laughed and said it was extraordinary how one never thought of all the maintenance these treasures took, and then his mother smiled, as if she had said the right thing. But he could see Maria look away, pretending not to be there for his sake, and his heart burned up with shame, and he was glad that Dr. Meyers never asked his mother to come along again, and he knew it was one more thing he would have to make up to her when he was grown-up and a man.

What was Maria thinking when she pretended not to look and not to be there? Sometimes he couldn't keep the thought away, the thought that those two hated each other. It must not be true. His mother said she was doing things for Maria's own good, and Maria never said a thing about his mother. But could they both be lying to him? No, not lying, but the sin, as Father Riordan called it, of concealing truth. A venial sin, but did they live it? It was more likely that his mother lived in sin, in venial sin of course. God forbid that she would live in mortal sin. But was her unkindness venial sin? And the way she found wrong everything about Maria? Why did she hate Maria's hair?

As far as he could see and understand there could be nothing in Maria's thick black hair to hate. His mother acted as if Maria's hair were there to balk, to anguish, to torment her. "Nobody thinks of me," she would say after she had begun, "and that disgusting hair. Nobody thinks of what it means for me, that hair all over the place. In the shower, in those brushes. Think of it, she never cleans them out. I tell her and I tell her, and she leaves it in there, that disgusting hair until I don't know what use it is to her, a brush in that condition, and I clean it out myself. Because he likes things right, likes her to have things right, although he don't mind if somebody else does it for her. To tell the truth, that's the way he likes it best, some fat Polack cleaning up after the princess."

How could she stay with them, the Meyers, hating them so? She did it for him, so he could grow up here, in this house, with these "advantages." The large house with its high walls full of pictures. Scenes of European streets and buildings. Drawings by people hundreds of years dead. Velasquez. Goya. The house with its green lawn and dark enshadowed garden and its vivid shocks: the daylilies, orange-yellow; purple lupins; columbines with veins like blood. And the things that Dr. Meyers taught that she knew she could not teach her son: poetry and how to use a fork, the names of emperors and which tie went with which suit, and all the lessons. All the lessons that Maria got, Joseph got too: piano, French, and in the summer, tennis. "The teacher comes for one, he comes for two," said Dr. Meyers, shrugging. "Still he has to come." He said it as if it were a joke, the statement final and yet supplicating, and the lifted shoulders. Joseph knew, though no one had told him, that Dr. Meyers learned this kind of sentence, how to say it, from his grandfather the rabbi. Joseph heard the words like that, the tone of them, when he and Maria sneaked into the synagogue for Yom Kippur.

It was something Maria had wanted badly. She was not like him. When something rose up before her eyes as if it were a figure on a road she was approaching, she would run to it the way she always ran, headlong and holding nothing back, the way she ran in games, and in the garden on a summer night, just for the pleasure. How beautiful she looked then after running, her hair falling out of her barrette, the sweat that beaded in the cleft above her lip like seed pearls, her white cheeks flushed as if a wing had touched them, a wing dipped in roses. Or in blood. No one could beat her when she ran; it was one reason why the other children in the neighborhood didn't want to play with her. She had to win, and she held nothing back. It didn't bother Joseph; he was glad to let her win. He understood her rages when she lost; the things she said were horrible; sometimes she hit him hard, wanting to hurt. He knew just what she felt. She felt that it was meant for her to win, so when she lost it was as if some plan had been spoiled or some promise broken. And then she was so sorry afterward, she came to him with such important gifts, wonderful gifts, thought up in heaven. Sometimes they were too good; what she had done was not so bad that she should give them. Like the time she went into her savings to buy him a fountain pen just like her father's, from the jewelry store in town. Because when he had beaten her in tennis she'd hit him on the back so hard he'd fallen over, and his teeth had bitten through his lip.

"It's too much," he said, though she knew how he loved it: the black shiny bottom and the silver top. "Real silver," she said, "here, look at the mark." And then they both got scared. "Don't use it where anyone can see it. Not your mother and not anyone at school. The nuns will ask you where you got it. Keep it someplace secret." And he had, for he was good at that, was best at keeping secrets. No one had ever found the pen. Or found the thing she had no right to give him: the gold necklace with the Jewish star that was her mother's mother's.

Maria's mother had been Jewish too, but renounced it to marry Dr. Meyers. She'd died soon after Maria was born, puerperal fever, it was called; Joseph imagined she had turned completely purple. He and Maria often looked at her pictures. It was the only thing he envied that she had: pictures of the absent parent. He had no pictures of his father; his mother talked with happiness about the day she burnt them up. "I held a match to them and—*pfft*—goodbye." One day Maria said, "Maybe one of my mother's sisters had a baby in Milwaukee on the day that you were born. Then the hospital had a mix-up, you know you hear of these things all the time. And that baby was you, and the baby that your mother had is living now with my aunt." She spat on the floor. "It serves them right." She'd never seen her aunt, her mother's favorite sister, who had told Maria's mother that she had no sister, her sister was dead.

Joseph had been frightened when she'd made that story up, frightened that she really believed it. Frightened too, because he wanted to believe it. And knew what that meant: he wished his mother not his mother. And he wanted to run downstairs, run down to his mother, ask was there something he could do to help her, sit beside her, tell her about school, remind her Dr. Meyers said he had the seeing eye, the clever hand, that Dr. Meyers said he was training him to take over the business one day, so the Lord would be honored with things of beauty. See, Mother, Joseph wanted to say, I have the seeing eye, the clever hand. You will never have to worry about money. I will take care of you, and everything you suffer now I will make up to you when I become a man.

But he did not do that; he sat instead beside Maria, looking at the photographs, thinking about the dark, sad-faced woman who had never held her child, who left her brothers and her sisters and her parents to marry Dr. Meyers. His people, too, had refused to speak to him, but he could bear it, Dr. Meyers could, you could see it in his eyes that could go cold. Maria's, too, could do that. She didn't have her mother's eyes, light brown as if they had once been Maria's blazing color, but she had wept so for her family that they had faded.

It was after Maria had given Joseph her grandmother's necklace that she got the idea: they must go into the synagogue. He could imagine how she'd thought it up, alone, at night in bed, her eyes wide open in the dark, awake and lying on her back in the first cold of autumn. It must have been then she decided that she would ask Moe Brown. Moe Brown who owned the candy store and loved her. He always gave her an extra soda free, and he gave one to Joseph too. She'd told Moe both her parents had been born Jewish. "But they gave it up," she said, as if it was a car they had got tired of. It frightened Joseph to hear her say it like that, so lightly, when it was the most important thing Dr. Meyers had ever done, had won for himself the salvation of his soul, the fellowship of Christ, a place in heaven.

But she had been right to talk about it that light way. It made Moe feel that he could talk about it, it was not so terrible. "The way I figure, honey," Moe said, "is live and let live. But personally I don't get it. Once a Jew always a Jew. Ask the late Mr. Hitler."

"Oh, if the Germans won the war, my father and I would have been sent to concentration camps. We would have died together," Maria said, her eyes getting tearful. Which was the kind of thing that made Moe love her. And made Joseph feel if that had happened, he would go with them, Maria and her father, and would die with them, suffer their same fate. But what would happen to his mother?

Moe had no idea that when Maria asked him all those things about the temple and the services she was planning to sneak in. Joseph had no idea himself, and when she told him, he was shocked. Didn't she know that Catholics were forbidden to attend the services of other faiths? And they would be sure to be found out. Moe said that there were people in the back collecting tickets.

"Listen, dodo," she said, "we'll wait till it's started. Way started. Then we'll sneak up to that balcony Moe said there was. With the people that have no tickets. Everyone'll be paying attention to the service. It's a very sad day. The day of atonement."

"But we won't know what to wear or what to do. I don't have one of those little hats."

"A yarmulke," she said, casually, as if she'd used the word every day of her life. "It's a reform temple. You don't need one."

"It's a terrible idea," he said, stamping his foot and feeling close to tears, because he knew he couldn't stop her.

"All right, don't go. I'll go myself. It's not your heritage anyway."

He couldn't let her go. To let her go meant he was not a part of her, her life, her past, her family. And then suppose she got in trouble. He could not leave her alone.

The plan worked perfectly. They waited ten minutes after the last person had gone into the temple. Carefully, they opened up the heavy door and saw the staircase to the balcony, just as Moe had described it. No one saw them climb the stairs or sit in the last seat in the back. How happy she seemed then, her face filmed with the lightest sweat, the down above her lips just moistened, her eyes shining with the look he knew so well: her look of triumph. They watched below. The man who sang, whom Moe had called the cantor, had the most beautiful voice Joseph had ever heard. The cantor's voice made him forget Maria. He rode the music, let it carry him. The sadness and the loneliness, the darkness and the hope. The winding music, thick and secret. Like the secrets of his heart. The secrets he had had to keep from everyone, that he would have to keep forever. When he felt Maria pulling at his arm, he realized that for the first time in his life when he was with her he had forgotten she was there.

"Let's go," she whispered silently.

"Why?" he mouthed at her. He didn't want to go.

"I hate this. I'm leaving."

He knew he must leave with her. It was the reason he was here, to be with her, and to protect her if danger came. He couldn't leave her now, and she had broken it, the ladder of the music. He had lost his footing; now he must drop down.

When they got outside, she ran away from him. He ran after, knowing he couldn't catch her, waiting for her to be out of breath. When he caught up to her, he saw that she was crying.

"I hated it. It was so dark and ugly. It was disgusting. Let's not talk about it ever again. Let's just forget we ever did it."

"Okay," he said. He let her run home by herself.

But he did not forget it, the dark secret music, like the secrets of his heart. The music that traveled to a God who listened, distant and invisible, and heard the sins of men and their atonement in the darkness and in darkness would forgive or not forgive. But would give back to men the music they sent up, a thick braid of justice and kept promises and somber hope.

He knew she didn't like it because it was nothing like the music that she loved, the nuns' high voices that had changed her life, that made her know that she would never marry but would join them, singing in the convent, lifting up to God those voices which except for these times were silent the whole day. That day in the convent she was far away from him, and knew it, and looked down at him from the lit mountain on whose top she stood, and kept him from the women's voices, rising by themselves into the air, so weightless, neither hopeful nor unhopeful, neither sorrowing nor free from sorrow, only rising, rising without effort above everything that made up life. You never saw the faces of the women who made these sounds that rose up, hovered high above their heads and disappeared. You saw only the light that struck the floor, shot through the blue glass and the red glass of the windows, slowed down, thickened, landing finally as oblong jewels on the wooden floor. He saw Maria rise up on the breaths of the faceless nuns, rise up and leave him, leave the body that ran and knocked down, that lay on the grass. The body she loved that did always what she told it, that could dance and climb or run behind him and put cool hands over his eyes and say "Guess who?" as if it could be someone different. But in the chapel she rose up and wanted to leave the body life that she had loved. Leave him and all their life together. The men singing in the temple did not want to rise up and leave. And that was why he liked them better. And why she did not.

They heard the nuns' music the day Sister Lucy was professed. Sister Lucy who had been Louise La Marr and who had worked for Dr. Meyers. For five years she had been his secretary. "She was, of course, much more than a secretary. I deferred to her in so many questions of taste," Dr. Meyers had said. Neither Joseph nor Maria remembered her very well; they had been seven when she entered Carmel, and she'd not made much of an impression. "God, when I think she was right there, right in my father's office, and I didn't talk to her. I didn't pay attention to her. But that's the way it is with saints, from what I've read," Maria said.

Maria had begun reading all the books she could get about cloistered nuns. She would come to Joseph, holding in her hands the story of a Mexican woman who had seen the Virgin Mary, a French woman a hundred years dead, a Spanish woman whose father had been a count, and say, "Listen to this. Do you think it sounds like me?" Of course it would sound nothing like her, but he saw how much she wanted it and he'd say, "I think so. Yes. The part when she was young, our age, sounds like you."

Then she would slap the book against the outside of her thigh, the front, the back, twisting her wrist. Then she would lie down on his bed or on the floor and put her hands behind her head and look up dreamily toward the ceiling. "I know they'll let me write to you in Carmel," she would say, "so don't worry. We'll always be best friends. Even though we'll never see each other again. Except through the grille. The last time we'll see each other without the grille will be the day of my profession." Then she would rise away from him, rise up into that world that was the breath of all those women, whose faces were never seen by men.

It was the end of everything, he understood now, her idea to join the convent. It was the first thing of hers he couldn't be a part of, the first thing that she kept back. He'd always known that there were things she hadn't told him before, things she thought about his mother, for example. But he had understood that. Always before, when they were together something pushed forward, pushed against him. She was always running toward him, running away from something else, something she didn't like, or was afraid of, or was bored by, or despised. And then, whatever she ran from became theirs: they opened it, like a surprise lunch, devoured it, took it in. Nothing was wasted; nothing could not be used. With her the hurts, the slights, the mockery of boys who found his life ridiculous, his mother's mistakes and tricks and hatreds, his sense that he was in the eyes of God unworthy, and in the eyes of man a million times inferior to the Meyers, all meant nothing when he was with Maria. Over all that she threw the rich cloak of her fantasy and all her body life.

Now she was taking back the cloak. Bit by bit she pulled it, leaving naked the poor flesh of all his doubts and failures and his fears. She began spending hours with Sister Berchmans, who had terrified them both. But now Maria said that Sister Berchmans was her spiritual adviser and a saint. Maria said that Sister had confided to her that she knew she frightened the children, but it was because she felt she must be distant to avoid establishing particular affections for her students, which would get in the way of her life with God. Maria said she wouldn't be surprised if Sister Berchmans entered Carmel, although it was nothing the nun had said, it was an idea that Maria had picked up "from certain hints which I'm not free to tell you."

For the first time, he disliked Maria, when she made her lips small and her eyes downcast and spoke of Sister Berchmans and the letters Sister Lucy had sent her "which I don't feel free to show." To punish her, he became friends with Ronald Smalley, who collected rocks and vied with Joseph for the eighth-grade mathematics prize. When he came home one day, holding a crystal of rose quartz, she mooned around him asking what he did at Ronald's house. "Nothing," he said, to taunt her.

"You're disgusting," she said, stamping her foot. "You don't even care that I had a completely disgusting time here all alone on this rotten Sunday while you were off with your stupid friend and his disgusting rocks."

But to please her he gave up Ronald. And she was pleased, and he was pleased to know that he had pleased her. For she had no friends; she could not keep a friend. When she tried to make a friend, the friendship ended sharply, and with grief. For no one but he understood her, he felt, and for the gift of her was willing to put up with her tempers and her scenes. For he knew that to keep them together she kept silent about his mother, kept silent so he would not be sent away. So she was his. His and her father's. And now Sister Berchmans's, who must keep herself for God.

But he suspected it was Sister Berchmans at the back of everything. Her white face looking out at him from her white coif. What did she see when she looked at him? And what had she told Dr. Meyers? Or did she never dare to speak to Dr. Meyers; had she spoken only in confession to Father Cunningham, who did the nun's bidding like a boy?

Joseph knew it was her fault. Because Maria told her things, and she had got things wrong. He knew the nun had spoken in confession, and then Father Cunningham had come to Dr. Meyers, and now everything was gone. He looked up at his mother, now, holding the Meyerses' laundry.

"Look, it's not the end of the world. For me, it's a good thing. Listen, Butch, for both of us. A house to call our own. With my name on the deed. No one else's, only mine. And yours, someday, if you don't leave your mother in the lurch."

They were sending him away, though they were keeping on his mother. Every day his mother could come back here to their home, the white house with the green shutters, the green-striped awning in the summer and the screened-in porch that in the winter turned into a house of glass. But how could he come back? He would have no part in the house now. What had been his room would become—what? What did they need a new room for, what could they do with his when they already had so many? The library and Dr. Meyers's study, Maria's room, the playroom (now their toys were gone and workmen years ago set up a Ping-Pong table there), his mother's laundry room, her sitting room (though never once in all the years had she had a guest). Would the Meyerses move from the house themselves? Would they buy some place smaller, thinking to themselves, "Now Joseph and his mother are not here the house is wrong for us"? No, they would never leave the library with its bookshelves specially made, the deep shadowy garden with its daylilies and columbines, the willow that grew roots into the plumbing that Maria made her father promise never to cut down. No, they would never leave the house. It was their home.

But he had thought it was his home. What would he be allowed to take from this house with him? They had come, his mother often told him (he could not remember coming here), with nothing. And where had all the things he had lived with come from? The dresser and the beds, the Fra Angelico Madonna, the picture of the squirrel by Dürer and the horse by Stubbs, the paperweight that dropped white snow on the standing boy? He asked his mother which of all these things were theirs.

"You've got a head on your shoulders, I'll tell you that," she said. "It's good stuff, the stuff in your room. I've got an eye for things like that, and I can tell you. Ask him to tell you, when he takes you on this little trip with the priest. Ask him if you can take the stuff in your room. But don't tell him that I told you first."

Dr. Meyers had arranged for Joseph and himself to go on a weekend retreat with the Passionists in Springfield, Massachusetts. He had told Joseph's mother he would tell Joseph about his decision, his decision that they would have to leave the house. But he had asked Joseph's mother to keep quiet, to let him tell Joseph himself. But she had not kept quiet. She had told him: they are sending you away.

"I guess they want to get rid of you before the two of you get any bright ideas. Of course, she'd be the one to think it up, but you'd be the one to get the blame."

His mother was right: Maria was the one with bright ideas, ideas that rose up, silver in a dark sky, shimmered and then flew.

"It's like he just noticed what you've got between your legs. Like he just figured out she don't have the same thing between hers. Or maybe he needed the priest to tell him."

Put the clothes down, Mother, he wanted to say. You have no right to touch them. You are filthy, with your red hair that you dye one Sunday night a month, with your fat body and your ugly clothes, your red hands and your yellow teeth. And with your filthy heart. The thing he had between his legs, his shame, that did things he could not help, that left the evidence of all he wished he could not be, the body life that he, because he was her son, was doomed to. And his mother knew, she found the evidence, the sheets, showing the thing he could not help, there in the morning. It all happened while he slept, and not his fault, even the priest said not his fault. But still it happened, all because he was her son. And now they knew, and they were sending him away. Because they did not want him in the house now with Maria. But Maria had nothing to do with all that. She hovered above it, like a nun, a saint. He prayed that they would never tell her, she would never know the things they knew about him. Perhaps if he left and said nothing they would not tell.

"I guess you're okay to be her playmate, but God forbid anything else. And for a husband, let's face it, he's got something better in mind than some dumb Polack whose mother washed his shitty underwear for ten years straight."

Why wouldn't she stop talking? He wanted something terrible to happen. She wouldn't be quiet till he said something to make her.

"Maria doesn't want to get married," he said, quietly so she would not know how he hated her and how he dreaded living with her by themselves in some house that belonged to her alone. "She's going to be a nun."

Joseph's mother snorted. Her lips lifted and she showed her yellow teeth. He thought of Maria's mother in the photograph, her sad face frowning, looked at his mother, snorting, throwing laundry into the machine and wondered how it was that he could be her son.

"Wise up, buddy. There's no convent in the world that would take that one."

He was almost as tall as his mother. She could say anything about him, terrible things, he wouldn't answer back. But she could not say things about Maria.

"Sister Berchmans said they'd take her when she finished school."

"The nun tell you that?"

"No, but I know it's true."

"Yeah, and you can buy the Brooklyn Bridge for fifteen bucks. Listen, nobody tells you this, or tells them it, because they're too polite. But they don't take Jews in the convent. And she'll always be a Jew."

"You made that up. Who told you that?" he said. Now he was shouting at his mother. Now he clenched his fists. It was the first time in his life that he had clenched his fists at her. And it just made her laugh.

"Just look at them, those nuns. Just look at all their faces. Ever see a face like hers? Just think about it. She'll find out and get her heart broken to boot, but it'll be too late. All his money won't be able to buy her way in. 'Cause they don't let them in."

She poked her finger at his chest. *They. Don't. Let. Them. In.* Each word the blow she wanted it to be. Could she be right? They wouldn't be so terrible. Was it the word of God? The God who sent unbaptized babies down to limbo? Who would separate a mother and a child because no water had been poured. He mustn't think about it. It was the sacrament of baptism he thought of. The indelible, fixed sign.

Was there a sign on them because their blood was Jewish? No, it couldn't be. He would find out from Dr. Meyers. He would ask him a clever way. This weekend at the monastery, when they were alone.

He packed his suitcase for himself. Pajamas, underwear, a shirt, his slippers. Then he packed an extra pair of pajamas. In case it happened. That thing in the night.

Maria was angry when they left. She dreaded being home for a whole weekend with Joseph's mother. But where could she go? She had no friends. She couldn't go to Sister Berchmans. For a moment Joseph was glad, then he hated the thought of her alone with his mother. He was glad when Dr. Meyers left her money for the movies and suggested she go to the library. She brightened at the thought of that. Then she would go to Moe's, she said, "and get a double black-and-white and think of you two fasting."

Her father pretended to slap her, then kissed her on both cheeks. "What will become of you? I ask myself. I suppose you will have to live with your father forever."

Maria smiled her pious smile and looked at Joseph, as if they two knew the truth. But Joseph looked away. Over Maria's shoulder he could see his mother.

They drove four hours to the monastery, speaking easily of things, of school and politics, of Dr. Meyers's days in Europe, of his promise one day to show Joseph Chartres.

"One day you may decide that you would like to go away to school. Remember, you have only to ask. I know what it's like to be a young boy. You can always come to me, you know, with any problem."

No I cannot, he thought, you are sending me away. The home you call yours I called mine. And now I have no home.

"Thank you," he said, and looked out the window where the rain was turning the gray pavement black.

A lay brother named Brother Gerald showed them to their room. Two iron beds and on the green walls nothing but a crucifix.

"Well, no distractions. That can certainly be said. Better a bare room than an excrescent display of Hallmark piety," said Dr. Meyers, flipping the gold clips of his suitcase. He hung up his shirts and put his shaving kit out on the bed. "And now to supper, whatever that will be. Certainly not as good as what your mother cooks."

Why had his mother told him? Every second now, he had to wait for Dr. Meyers's words. Each bite of food might bring those words closer, every step around the grounds. Each time Dr. Meyers laid a hand on Joseph's shoulder, he was sure it was the time. But Saturday went by, the early Mass, the Rosary, Confessions, Vespers, dinnertime. And when it was his turn to speak to the retreat master, Joseph sat dumbly, listening to Father Mulvahy talk about bad companions and the dangers of the flesh. He knew what dangers of the flesh were. They could make you lose your home. He thought about the garden, deep in shadow. He thought about Maria and his mother's words. Perhaps he should ask Father Mulvahy if she'd told the truth. But he did not know how.

"Joseph, I have something difficult to tell you," Dr. Meyers said, Sunday after Mass, when Joseph thought the time was wrong. Fresh from Communion, polished by the glow of silence, of the Sacrament, they walked to the refectory alone.

"In some ways, Joseph, you are like my son. I've always loved you as a son. And because I love you as a son, I fear for the salvation of your soul. I pray for it, I pray for it every morning, as I do for my own daughter's."

Dr. Meyers kept his hand on Joseph's shoulder. Their feet made ugly sounds in the wet grass. He thought of Maria, of the gift of her ideas and words. He thought of the gold star, the secret gift nobody knew she gave him. Was his living in the house a danger to their souls? It could not be. Dr. Meyers must have got it wrong.

"Your nature, Joseph, is not passionate, like my Maria's. Nevertheless, you are a young man now. And to put difficulties in a young man's path is a cruelty I hope I would not be guilty of."

You are guilty of the cruelty of sending me away. Of separating me from everything I love. Of sending me to live alone, in ugliness and hatred with the mother whom I cannot love.

Joseph nodded soberly when Dr. Meyers said, "I thought it best," and ended with the news of his gift to Joseph and his mother of the house.

"But you must never be a stranger, Joseph. You are like our family. Our home is yours."

But you have sent me from your home, my home. I have no home. There is no place for me.

"Thank you, sir," he said.

"You're a good boy, Joseph," said Dr. Meyers, squeezing his shoulders. "For you I have no fears. But what will happen to Maria?"

He felt his spine light up, as if a match had been struck at the base. A hot wire went up into his skull, and then back down his spine.

"I think she'll become a nun," said Joseph, looking daringly at Dr. Meyers.

Sadly, Dr. Meyers shook his head. "Think of how she is. There is no convent that would have her."

Joseph felt his throat go hot like melting glass. It could not be that what his mother said was right. It could not be that they knew the same thing, his mother and Dr. Meyers, knew this thing he and Maria did not know.

Why did they know and never tell their children? They were cruel, the both of them. The cruelty he thought was just his mother's, Dr. Meyers shared. He might have thought that he kept silent out of kindness, but it was not kindness. It was fear.

But Joseph knew what he would do. He would get Dr. Meyers to send him away to school. He would not see Maria. He would write to her. And his letters would make her think of him in the right way. Make her think of him so she would love him, want to live with him, the body life, and not the life that rose up past the body, not the life of Sister Berchmans and the white-faced nuns. He would make her feel that only with him could her life be happy. He would make her want to marry him before they went to college. He would do that so that she would never know that they would never let her have it. He would marry her before she could find out that because of her blood they would keep back from her her heart's desire.

"I would like to go away to school," he said to Dr. Meyers.

"Of course, Joseph," Dr. Meyers said. "We can arrange anything you want."

Delia

People talked about how difficult it was to say which of the O'Reilley girls was the best-looking. Kathleen had the green eyes. She came over by herself at seventeen. She worked as a seamstress and married Ed Derency. The money that she earned, even with all the babies—one a year until she was thirty-five—was enough to bring over the three other girls. Bridget had black hair and a wicked tongue. She married a man who was only five feet tall. She had no children for seven years; then she had a red-haired boy. Some believed he was the child of the policeman. Nettie was small; her feet and her ankles were as perfect as a doll's. She married Mr. O'Toole, who sang in the choir and drank to excess. She had only daughters. Some thought Delia the most beautiful, but then she was the youngest. She married a Protestant and moved away.

In defense of her sister, Kathleen pointed out that John Taylor looked like an Irishman.

"He has the eyes," Kathleen said to Nettie and to Bridget. "I never saw a Protestant with eyes like that."

"Part of the trouble with Delia all along is you babied her, Kathleen," Bridget said. "You made her believe she could do no wrong. What about the children? Is it Protestant nephews and nieces you want?"

"He signed the form to have them baptized," said Nettie.

"And what does that mean to a Protestant?" Bridget said. "They'll sign anything."

"He's good to the children. My children are mad for him," said Kathleen.

"Your children are mad entirely. Hot-blooded," said Bridget. "It's you have fallen for the blue eyes yourself. You're no better than your sister."

"He's kind to my Nora," said Kathleen.

Then even Bridget had to be quiet. Nora was Kathleen's child born with one leg shorter than the other.

"There was never any trouble like that in our family," Bridget had said when she first saw Nora. "It's what comes of marrying outsiders."

John Taylor would sit Nora on his lap. He told her stories about the West.

"Did you see cowboys?" she would ask him, taking his watch out of the leather case he kept it in. The leather case smelled like soap; it looked like a doll's pocketbook. When Nora said that it looked like a doll's pocketbook, John Taylor let her keep it for her doll.

"Cowboys are not gentlemen," said John Taylor.

"Is Mr. du Pont a gentleman?" asked Nora.

"A perfect gentleman. A perfect employer."

John Taylor was the chauffeur for Mr. du Pont. He lived in Delaware. He told Nora about the extraordinary gardens on the estate of Mr. du Pont.

"He began a poor boy," said John Taylor.

"Go on about the gardens. Go on about the silver horse on the hood of the car."

Delia came over and put her hands on top of her husband's. Her hands were cool-looking and blue-white, the color of milk in a bowl. She was expecting her first baby.

"Someday you must come and visit us in Delaware, when the baby's born," she said to Nora. She looked at her husband. Nora knew that the way they looked at each other had something to do with the baby. When her mother was going to have a baby, she got shorter; she grew lower to the ground. But Delia seemed to get taller; she seemed lighter and higher, as though she were filled, not with a solid child like one of Nora's brothers or sisters, but with air. With bluish air.

Delia and John Taylor would let her walk with them. She would walk between them and hold both their hands. Their hands were very different. Delia's was narrow and slightly damp; John Taylor's was dry and broad. It reminded Nora of his shoes, which always looked as if he were wearing them for the first time. They knew how to walk with her. Most people walked too slowly. She wanted to tell them they did not have to walk so slowly for her. But she did not want to hurt their feelings. John Taylor and Delia knew just how to walk, she thought.

After only two weeks, they went back to Delaware.

"She's too thin entirely," said Bridget.

"She's beautiful," said Nora. Her mother clapped her hand over Nora's mouth for contradicting her aunt.

Delia never wrote. Nora sent her a present on her birthday, near Christmas. She had made her a rose sachet: blue satin in the shape of a heart, filled with petals she had saved in a jar since the summer. She had worked with her mother to do the things her mother had told her would keep the smell.

Delia sent Nora a postcard. "Thank you for your lovely gift. I keep it in the drawer with my linen."

Linen. Nora's mother read the card to her when the aunts were to tea at their house.

"Fancy saying 'linen' to a child," said Bridget. "In a postcard."

"She has lovely underthings," said Nettie.

"Go upstairs. See to your little brother, Nora," said her mother.

"When they came back to New York, he gave her twenty-five dollars, just to buy underthings. Hand-hemmed, all of them. Silk ribbons. Ivory-colored," said Nettie.

"Hand-done by some greenhorn who got nothing for it," said Bridget.

Now Nora knew what Delia meant by linen. She had thought before it was tablecloths she meant, and that seemed queer. Why would she put her good sachet in with the tablecloths? Now she imagined Delia's underclothes, white as angels, smelling of roses. Did John Taylor see her in her underclothing? Yes. No. He was her husband. What did people's husbands see?

She was glad the aunts had talked about it. Now she could see the underclothes more clearly. Ivory ribbons, Nettie had said. Delia's stomach swelled in front of her, but not as much as Nora's mother's. And Nora's mother was going to have a baby in May, which meant Delia would have hers first. March, they had said. But Delia's stomach was light/hard, like a balloon. Nora's mother's was heavy/hard, like a turnip. Why was that, Nora wondered. Perhaps it was because her mother had had five babies, and this was Delia's first.

When her mother wrote to Delia, Nora dictated a note to her too. She asked when John Taylor's birthday was. She thought it was in the summer. She would make him a pillow filled with pine needles if it was in the summer. In July, the family went to the country for a week, and her mother would give her an envelope so she could fill it with pine needles for her Christmas gifts.

March came and went and no one heard anything of Delia's baby. Nora's mother wrote, Nettie wrote, even Bridget wrote, but no one heard anything.

"She's cut herself off," said Bridget. "She hasn't had the baby baptized, and she's afraid to face us."

"First babies are always late," said Kathleen. "I was four weeks overdue with Nora."

"Perhaps something's happened to the baby. Perhaps it's ill and she doesn't want to worry us," said Nettie.

"Nothing like that used to happen in our family," said Bridget, sniffing. "Or anyone we knew in the old country."

"What about Tom Hogan? He had three daft children. And Mrs. Kelly had a blind boy," said Nettie.

"If you'd say a prayer for your sister instead of finding fault with her, you might do some good with your tongue, Bridget O'Reilley, for once in your life," said Kathleen.

"If she'd of listened to me, she wouldn't be needing so many prayers," said Bridget.

"God forgive you, we all need prayers," said Kathleen, crossing herself.

"What's the weather in Delaware?" said Nettie.

"Damp," said Bridget. "Rainy."

"They live right on the estate," said Kathleen. "They eat the same food as Mr. du Pont himself."

"Yes, only not at the same table," said Bridget. "Downstairs is where the servants eat. I'd rather eat plain food at my own table than rich food at a servant's board."

"Will we not write to her, then?" said Nettie, to Kathleen mainly.

"Not if she's not written first. There must be some reason," said Kathleen.

"It's her made the first move away," said Bridget.

"If something was wrong, we'd hear. You always hear the bad. She must be all wrapped up. Probably the du Ponts have made a pet of her," said Kathleen.

Nora remembered that John Taylor had said that on Mrs. du Pont's birthday there was a cake in the shape of a swan. And ices with real strawberries in them, although it was the middle of November. And the ladies wore feathers and looked like peacocks, Delia had said. "They're beautiful, the ladies," John Taylor had said. "You should know, tucking the lap robes under them," Delia had said, standing on one foot like a bird. "God knows where you'd of been if I hadn't come along to rescue you in good time." "You've saved me from ruin," John Taylor had said, twirling an imaginary mustache.

Nora remembered how they had laughed together. John and Delia were the only ones she knew who laughed like that and were married.

"Do you think we'll never see Delia and John again?" said Nora to her mother.

"Never say never, it's bad luck," her mother said. She put her hand to her back. The baby made her back ache, she said. Soon, she told Nora, she would have to go to bed for the baby.

"And then you must mind your aunt Bridget and keep your tongue in your head."

"Yes, ma'am," said Nora. But her mother knew she always minded; she never answered back. Only that once, about Delia, had she answered back.

When Nora's mother went to bed to have the baby, the younger children went to Nettie's, but Nora stayed home. "Keep your father company," her mother had said. "At least if he sees you it'll keep him from feeling in a house full of strangers entirely."

But even with her there, Nora's father walked in the house shyly, silently, as if he was afraid of disturbing something. He took her every evening, since it was warm, to the corner for an ice cream. She saw him so rarely that they had little to say to one another. She knew him in his tempers and in his fatigue. He would walk her home with a gallantry that puzzled her, and he went to sleep while it was still light. He woke in the morning before her, and he went away before she rose.

Bridget made Nora stay outside all day when her mother went into labor. She sat on the front steps, afraid to leave the area of the house, afraid to miss the first cry or the news of an emergency. Children would come past her, but she hushed them until they grew tired of trying to entice her away. She looked at her hands; she looked down at her white shoes, one of which was bigger than the other, her mother had said, because God had something special in mind for her. What could He have in mind? Did God change His mind? Did He realize He had been mistaken? She counted the small pink pebbles in the concrete banister. She could hear her mother crying out. Everyone on the block could, she thought, with the windows open. She swept the sand on the middle step with the outside of her hand.

Then in front of her were a man's brown shoes. First she was frightened, but a second later, she recognized them. She did not have to look up at the face. They were John Taylor's shoes; they were the most beautiful shoes she had ever seen.

"Hello, Nora," he said, as if she should not be surprised to see him.

"Hello," she said, trying not to sound surprised, since she knew he did not want her to.

"Is your mother in?"

"She's upstairs in bed."

"Not sick, I hope."

"No. She's having another baby."

John Taylor sucked breath, as if he had changed his mind about something. The air around him was brilliant as glass. He looked around him, wanting to get away.

"How is Delia?" said Nora, thinking that was what her mother would have said.

"She died," said John, looking over his shoulder.

"And the baby? Is it a boy or a girl?"

"Dead. Born dead."

"Do you still drive a car for that man?" she said, trying to understand what he had told her. Born dead. It did not sound possible. And Delia dead. She heard her mother's voice from the window.

"I'm on holiday," said John, reaching into his pocket.

She was trying to think of a way to make him stay. If she could think of the right thing, he would take her for a walk, he would tell her about the cars and the gardens.

"How've you been, then?" she said.

"Fine," said John Taylor.

But he did not say it as he would have to an adult, she knew. He did not say it as if he were going to stay.

"Nora," he said, bending down to her. "Can we have a little secret? Can I give you a little present?"

"Yes," she said. He was going away. She could not keep him. She wanted something from him. She would keep his secret; he would give her a gift.

He reached into his pocket and took out a silver dollar. He put it in her hand and he closed her hand around it.

"Don't tell anyone I was here. Or what I said. About Delia, or about the baby."

It was very queer. He had come to tell them, and now she must not tell anyone, she thought. Perhaps he had come this way only to tell her. That was it: he had come from Delaware to tell her a secret, to give her a gift.

"I won't say anything," she said. She looked into his eyes; she had never looked into the eyes of an adult before. She felt an itching on the soles of her feet from the excitement of it.

"I'll count on you, then," he said, and walked quickly down the street, looking over his shoulder.

She went into the house. Upstairs, she could hear Bridget's voice, and her mother's voice in pain, but not yet the voice of the baby. She lifted her skirt. She put the silver dollar behind the elastic of her drawers. First it was cold against her stomach, but then it became warm from the heat of her body.

The Only Son of the Doctor

Louisa was surprised that she was with a man like Henry, after all she had been through. She liked to tell him that he was the best America could come up with. She told all her friends about his father, who had built half the houses in the town where Henry lived, who had gone broke twice but had died solvent; about the picture of his eighteenth-century ancestor, dumb as a sheep but still a speculator; about his mother, who had founded the town library. And she told them—it was one of her best stories now—that when she had agreed to go to bed with him, he had said to her, "Bless your heart."

It was to expose him that she had wanted to meet him in the first place. There had been a small piece about him in the *Times*, and she had not believed that he could be what he seemed, a country doctor who ran a nursing home that would not use artificial means to keep the old alive. The story said he was in some danger of being closed down; the home was almost bankrupt.

If things looked simple, Louisa's genius was to prove that they were not. She wrote to the doctor about his home, hoping to unmask him and his project. The *Times* had been almost idolatrous; they described reverentially his devotion to the aged. They described the street where he lived as if they had dreamed of it over the Thanksgiving dinners of their childhood. Louisa drove the 120 miles from New York hoping to see behind the golden oaks a genuine monstrosity, hungering to discover, in the cellar of the large farmhouse the doctor had converted, white skeletons behind the staircase, whiter than the Congregational church that edified the center of the village. At the very least, she hoped to find the doctor foolish, to catch him in some lapse of gesture or language so that she could show the world he was not what he seemed.

When he opened the door to her, she saw that his face was not what she had expected. The eyes were not simple: blue, of course they were blue, but they were flecked with some light color, gold or yellow, warning her of judgment, of a severeness at the heart of all that trust. And she knew he was a man who was used to getting whatever woman he wanted. She could tell that by the way he closed the door behind her, by the way he led her into the living room.

"Tell me about yourself," she said, pressing the button of her tape recorder. "Tell me how you came to such work."

His voice was so perfectly beautiful that she felt she had suddenly stepped into a forest where the leaves were visible in moonlight. He said he was devoted to stopping the trend of prolonging agony. That was what had made her love him first: those words "the trend of prolonging agony." It made change sound so possible; there was such belief implicit in that construction: that life was imperfect but ordinary, and not beyond our reach.

He had thought he would be an actor, he said, after college. He said his dream was to play light comedy; he had wanted to be Cary Grant. But she could see his gift was not for comedy. His gift was for breaking news. She knew, sitting in his living room, that his was the voice she would have preferred above all others to speak the news of her own death. He said he had decided to take up this work, after years of practice as an internist in Boston, because he had seen how impossible it had been for his mother to die well. So he had come back to his hometown, where his father had built half the houses, where his mother had founded the library, to start an old-age home.

He asked Louisa for her help in keeping the home alive, for it was, as the *Times* had suggested, in danger of bankruptcy. The piece she wrote about him and his work brought floods of contributions. She talked her friends into helping him with a fund-raising campaign. His own efforts had been small, and local, and hopelessly inefficient. He wrote all the fund-raising letters himself, at a huge black manual typewriter. He was always writing letters, always meeting with the board of directors. The board was made up of townspeople: the lawyer, the minister, the principal of the high school. When she came up from the city to speak to the board, to advise them on the first steps of their fund-raising campaign, her differentness from them made her feel like a criminal. Later she would be able to sit with them at the doctor's table and joke or help them peel potatoes. But that first meeting of the board made her think of the city mouse–country mouse tales she had read as a child. Sitting around her at the doctor's table, all those people made her feel edgy and smart-alecky and full of excessive cleverness suspiciously come by. She felt as if she were smoking three cigarettes at once. They turned to her with such trust; they were so impressed by her skills; they were so sure that she could help them. Their trust made them seem very young, and it annoyed her to be made to feel the oldest among them when in fact she was the youngest by fifteen years. The night of that first meeting of the board, she went to bed with the doctor because he seemed the only other adult in town.

By the time the campaign was over and the committee had raised its money, she had got into the habit of spending her weekends with him. They never said that she would do this; she simply called on Thursdays to say what train she would be taking Friday. And he would say: "This is what I've arranged for us. We'll have the Chamberlains on Saturday; Sunday we'll take a picnic lunch to the river."

It was partly his voice that made her love doing these things. His voice made everything simpler; it could reclaim for her pleasures she had believed lost to her forever. Her first husband had told her she was a disaster with tools. The doctor (his name was Henry; she did not like his name; she did not like to use it, although she admitted it suited him) taught her simple carpentry. He made it possible for her to ask questions that were radically necessary and at the same time idiotic: "When you say joist, what exactly do you mean? How does a level work?" He made it possible for her to work with things whose names she understood.

She had learned, particularly in the years since her divorce, when people had invited her for weekends out of kindness, that it was impossible for a person living in the country to take a city guest for a walk without reproach, implied or stated. She could see it in the eyes of whatever friend she walked with, the unshakable belief in the superiority of country life. People in the country, she thought, believed it beyond question that their lives had been purified. They had the righteousness of zealots: born again, free at last.

This had kept her out of the country. The skills she prized and possessed were skills learned in the city: conversation, discrimination. She remembered a story she had read as a child about a princess who had to go into hiding on a farm. How she suffered at the hands of the milkmaid, who set up tests that the princess was bound to fail: the making of cheeses, jumping from hayloft to haycart, imitating the calls of birds. The milkmaid took pleasure in convincing the princess of the worthlessness of the princess's accomplishments. And she did convince her, until a courtier arrived. The milkmaid was tongue-tied; she fell all over her feet in the presence of such a gentleman, while the princess poured water from a ewer and told jokes. Louisa saw herself as the princess in the tale, but the courtier had never come to acknowledge her. Always she was stuck in the part of the story that had the princess spraining an ankle on the haycart, unable to imitate the cry of the cuckoo! On the whole, she had found it to be to her advantage to decline invitations to any place where she would be obliged to wear flat shoes.

But she loved simply walking in the country with Henry. He had a way of walking that made her want to take month-long journeys on foot with him. He did not spend time trying to get her to notice things—bark, or leaves, or seasonal changes. He would walk and talk to her about his mother's father, about his days in the theater, about his work with the aged. He would ask her advice about the wording of one of his letters. Always, when they were walking, he would soon want to go home and begin writing a letter. So that for the first time in her life it was she who begged to stay outside longer, she who did not want to go indoors.

And his house was the most perfect house she had ever known. It had been his family's for generations. The living room had thirteen windows; he kept in a glass-and-wood cabinet his great-grandmother's wedding china. But his study was her favorite room. He had a huge desk that he had built himself, and on the desk was a boy's dream of technology: an electric pencil sharpener, a machine that dispensed stamps as if they were flat tongues, boxes for filing that seemed to her magic in their intricacies. He had divided his desk by causes; it was sectioned off with cardboard signs he had made: nuclear power, child abuse, migrant workers. He never mixed his correspondences. But the neatness of his desk was boyish—not an executive neatness, but the kind of neatness that wins merit badges, worried over, somewhat furtive, somewhat tentative, more than a little ill at ease.

And he had pictures of ships on the wall of his study. Ships! How she loved him for that! It was impossible that any other man she had ever known well—her father, her husband, any of her lovers—would have had pictures of ships. All the men in her life had doted on the foreign, which was why they were interested in her. Why, then, was Henry interested? Sometimes she was afraid that he would realize he had made a mistake in her, that he would wake up and find her less kind, less generous, less natural, than the women he was accustomed to loving. She was afraid that he had misunderstood her face because he liked it best after sex or early in the morning. He liked her best without makeup, and he didn't notice her clothes. Other men had loved her best when she was dressed for the theater or parties. Henry preferred her naked, with her hair pulled back. This disturbed her; it made her feel she was competing in the wrong event. She could never win against girls who dashed down to breakfast after taking time only to splash cold water on their eyes. She had some chance against women who invented their own beauty. But he would dress her in his shirts; he would kiss her before she had washed her face. Now she did not wear makeup when she was with him—he had asked her not to so simply. How could she refuse such a desire, spoken in the voice she loved? But she was afraid that she could lose his love, in some way she could not predict, if he loved her for herself the first thing in the morning.

And it troubled her that she could not predict in Henry the faults that would cause her one day not to love him. Would she one day grow tired of his evenness; would she long for storms, recriminations? She felt she had to ask him about his wife; they had gone on for months saying nothing about her. What kind of woman would leave such a house, such furniture? Henry said only that she was living in New Mexico, she had a private income, they wrote twice a month. He said nothing that would allow her to look into herself for the wife's faults, to see in Henry the wife's objections. In time she grew grateful for his reticence. She was, for the first time, safe in love. He did not look, for example, at other women in restaurants. He did not see them. Perhaps it was because she and Henry spent so much of their lives away from each other. It made her gentler, that lack of access. It made him, she thought, less curious.

She asked him once if he had ever thought of asking her to come and live with him. He looked at her strangely; she could tell that he had not thought of it. That look surprised her, and it embarrassed her deeply. And then she began to feel that look as an extreme form of neglect. They had been together for six months; they had been in love. And he had not thought of living with her. He said (one of those truths he thought there was no reason not to tell), "I just don't think of you as making much impression on a house. I don't think of you as caring about it."

"Of course I do. I like having a beautiful place to live."

"Yes, but I mean you don't become attached to a house itself. You become attached to the things in it."

There was no way she could prove him wrong. She would have to do something so extreme that everything in her life would have to change utterly. She would have to build herself a house in the woods and live in it for years to prove to him that she cared about houses. And she was ready to do it; she awoke next to him at four in the morning and she thought that that was just what she would do. She would quit her job; she would stop seeing him. She would build herself a house to prove to him that she cared about houses. In the morning she laughed to think of herself writing a letter of resignation, buying lumber, but she was frightened that because of him she had entertained, even for a moment, such a fantastic renunciation. She saw that loving someone so calm, so moderate, that being loved so plainly and truthfully, could lead to extremes of devotion, of escape.

He accused her of being unable to resist the habit of separating sheep from goats. It was a loving accusation. He told her that her habit of sheep and goats had lifted from him a burden; he did not have to look so clearly at people when he was with her. She made a list of the phrases he used to defend the people she criticized: "good sort," "means well," "quite competent at his job," "very kind underneath it all." He put the list on the corkboard above his desk. He said he kissed it every morning that she was not there. He touched it for good luck, he said, before writing a letter.

One Thursday in August when she called he said, "My son is with me." She had made his son one of the goats. Partly it was an accident of their ages; his son was nearly her age and she resented him for it. But it was a class resentment as well, and a historical one. Henry's son—with, she thought, using a phrase her mother might have used, all the advantages—had gone the way of the children of the affluent sixties. He had dropped out. Dropped out. It was such a boring phrase, she had always thought, such a boring concept. Dropped out. And yet she resented his hitchhiking through Denmark while she was working as a waitress or in the library to support her scholarship, resented him for not carrying on his father's line, for not having an office by this time, with pictures of ships. And she did not comprehend how he could resist all this. All this: she meant the house with all the windows, the attic full of old letters, the grandmother who was named for her great-aunt, killed during the Revolution. Before Louisa met him, she decided the boy was thickheaded. She could not be sympathetic to this boy who had left his father. When his father was the man she loved.

On the train up, she tried to remember what Henry had told her about his son. There had been the same reluctance to talk about his child as there had been to talk about his wife, and she had been as grateful. He had said something about the boy's hitchhiking through Denmark. And there was something about a fight. She remembered now that there was some reason for her wanting to forget it. She had not liked Henry's part in it.

The family had been vacationing in Europe and Henry's son had refused to return home. He was fifteen at the time, and he wanted to spend the year in Scandinavia, hitchhiking around, earning money at odd jobs. Why Scandinavia? she had asked, searching for some detail that would make the boy sympathetic. It simply took his fancy, Henry had said. He had, of course, insisted that his son come home and finish high school. His son had refused. Finally, after a week of silence, the boy had said, "Well, there's only one thing to do. We'll have to go outside and fight."

"What did you do?" Louisa had asked, with that combination of thrill and boredom she felt when she watched Westerns.

"I let him go."

Of course. What had she wanted him to do? Arrange some display of paternal weapons? He would not be the man she loved if he had forced his son to succumb to his authority. But why was she so disappointed? How would her own father have acted toward her brother? Her brother, a lawyer now with three children, would never have had the confidence for such defiance. He would have known, too, physical anger at his father's hand. Such knowledge would have prevented risk. Louisa resented Henry's son for knowing, at fifteen, that he could survive without the sanction of his parents. She wanted to tell that boy what a luxury it was— that defiance, that chosen poverty. She wanted to tell him that with less money and position, he could never have been so daring. She wanted to tell him he was spoiled. By the time the train pulled into the station, she was terribly angry. She realized that she had ridden for miles with her hands clenched into fists.

She was exceptionally loving in her embrace of Henry. He told her, with some excitement, that Eliot had spent the last few days painting his barn. He said, with a gratitude that touched and frightened her, that his barn was now the most beautiful in the county. He told her what good stories Eliot had to tell, about Alaska, about South America. She closed her eyes. Nothing interested her less than stories about men in bars, and fights, and roads and spectacular views, and feats of idiot courage. She knew she would have nothing to say to his son. Would this make Henry stop loving her? By the time they were in front of the house, she knew she was wrong to have come.

He was sitting at the kitchen table with his legs spread out, at least halfway, she thought, into the room. Henry had to step over his son's legs to get to the table. She followed behind Henry, stepping over his son's black boots. She hated those boots; there was something illegal-looking about them. They were old; the leather was cracked so that it looked not like leather but like the top of a burned cake. It was an insult to Henry, she thought, to wear boots like that in his house.

"Eliot, I'd like you to meet Louisa Altiere. Louisa, my son, Eliot Cosgrove."

"Hey," said Eliot, not looking up.

Louisa walked over and extended her hand.

"I'm very glad to meet you," she said.

He did not take her hand. She went on extending it. With some aggressiveness she thrust her hand almost under his nose. He finally shook her hand. She wanted to tell him that she had got better handshakes from most of the dogs she knew.

"Why are you glad to meet me?" he said, looking up at her for the first time.

"What?"

"I mean, people say they're glad to meet somebody. But how do you know? You're probably really a little ticked off that I'm here. I mean, you don't get to spend that much time with Henry. And here I am cutting into it."

"On the contrary, I feel that knowing you will enable me to know your father better."

"Watch out, Eliot," said Henry. "Watch out when she says things like 'on the contrary.'"

The two men laughed. She felt betrayed, and excluded from the circle of male laughter. Henry had put his feet up on the table.

"I'll go and unpack," she said, feeling like a Boston schoolteacher in Dodge City. She wondered if Henry had told his son what she was like in bed.

She looked at the barn through the window of Henry's bedroom. She used to like looking at it; now it bulked large; she resented its blocking her view of the mountains. She kept walking around the bedroom, picking things up, putting them down, putting her dresses on different hangers, anything so that she would not have to go downstairs to the two men. My lover, she was thinking, and his son.

Henry had a drink waiting for her when she did go down. He stood up when she walked into the room. How much smaller he was than his son. It did not have to do entirely with Eliot's being born after the war and having more access to vitamins. She had loved Henry for being so finely made that his simplest gestures seemed eloquent. Once she had wept to see him taking the ice cubes out of the tray. She remembered his telling her that when Eliot was a child they called him "Brob," for "Brobdingnagian."

While Henry talked to her about his work on the Child Abuse Committee and the letters he had received from a prominent U.S. senator, Eliot sat at the table, whittling. It distracted Louisa so much that she was not exactly able to understand the point of Henry's letter. She stared at Eliot until he put down his knife.

"I thought whittling was something that dropped from a culture when people became literate," she said.

"What makes you think I'm literate?" said Eliot, throwing the pop top of his beer can over her head into the garbage.

"I assume you were taught to read."

"That doesn't mean I'm still into it."

Henry put his head back and laughed, a louder laugh than she had ever heard from him.

She spent the rest of the afternoon shopping and making dinner. Bouillabaisse. She was glad of the time it took to sauté and to scrub; it meant she did not have to be with Henry and Eliot. And the dinner was a success. But while Henry praised Louisa, Eliot sat in silence, playing with the mussel shells. Then Henry turned his attention to his son. They spoke of old outings, old neighbors. They laughed, she was disturbed to see, most heartily about a neighbor's wife who had gained a hundred pounds. They imitated the woman's foolishness in clothes, the walk that forgot the flesh she lived in. They talked about their trips to Italy, to the Pacific Northwest.

Louisa saw there was no place for her. She cleared the table and washed the dishes slowly, making the job last. They were still talking when she rejoined them at the table. They had not noticed that she had left.

Henry mentioned the meeting he would have to go to after supper. He was the chairman of a citizens' committee to stall a drainage bond. Louisa was annoyed that Henry had not told her he would be away for the evening, had not told her she would be alone with Eliot. Perhaps he had guessed she would not have come if she knew.

"I think it's good that you and Eliot will have the time alone. You'll get to know each other," said Henry when he was alone with her in the bedroom, tying his tie.

After Henry left, she took her book down into the living room, where Eliot sat watching a country and western singer on television. She was embarrassed to be sitting in a room with someone at seven thirty on a Saturday night, watching someone in a white leather suit who sang about truck drivers.

"When did you first become interested in country music?" she asked.

"A lot of my friends are into it."

She opened her novel.

"You don't like me much, do you?" he said, after nearly half an hour of silence.

His rudeness was infantile; no one but a child would demand such conversation. All right, then, she would do what he wanted; she would tell the truth, because at that moment she preferred the idea of hurting him to the idea of her own protection.

"I don't think you deserve your father."

The boy stopped lounging in his chair. He sat up—she wanted to say, like a gentleman.

"Don't you think I know that?" he said.

She turned her legs away from him, in shame and in defeat. How easily he had shown her up. He could work with honesty in a way that she couldn't. He reminded her that he was, after all, better bred; that she was what she had feared—someone who had learned the superficial knack of things but could be exposed by someone who knew their deeper workings. She did not know whether she liked him for it; she thought that she should leave the house.

"I'm sorry," she said. "I had no right to speak to you like that."

"The real secret about my father is that nobody's good enough for him. But he keeps on trying. His efforts are doomed to failure."

Did he say that? "His efforts are doomed to failure." Of course he did. He was, after all, the son of his father. And she saw that he had to be what he was, having Henry for a father. She saw it now; such a moderate man had to inspire radical acts.

"Forgive me," she said. "I was very rude."

He was not someone used to listening to apologies. She wanted to touch his hand, but she realized that for people connected as they were, there was no appropriate gesture.

"Once I was in Alaska, riding my bike through this terrific snow-storm. And I had a real bad skid. I fell into the snow. I think I musta been out for a couple of minutes. I thought I was going to die. When I came to, I could hear the sound of my father's typewriter. I could hear him at that damn typewriter, typing letters. I was sure I was going to die. I was sure that was the last sound I'd hear. But someone came by in a pickup and rescued me. Weird, isn't it?"

She could see him lying in the snow, wondering whether he would survive, thinking of his father. Hearing his typewriter. Was it in love or hatred that he had heard it? She thought of Henry's back as he wrote his letters, of the perfect calm with which he arranged his thoughts into sentences, into paragraphs. And what would a child have thought, seeing that back turned to him, listening to the typewriter? For Henry needed no one when he was at his desk, writing his letters for the most just, the most worthy, of causes. He was perfectly alone and perfectly content, like someone looking through a telescope, like someone sailing a ship. She thought of this boy, four inches taller than his father, fifty pounds heavier, wondering if he would die, hearing his father's typewriter. But was it love or hatred that brought him the sound?

She began to cry. Henry's son looked at her with complete uninterest. No man had ever watched her tears with such a total lack of response.

"I'll say good night, then. I'm taking off in the morning. Early. I'll leave about four o'clock," he said.

"Does your father know?"

"Sure."

"And he went to the meeting anyway?"

"It was important. And he's going to get up and make me breakfast."

"What about tonight?"

"What about it?"

"Don't you want to stay up and wait for him?"

"He'll be late. He's at that meeting," said Eliot, climbing the stairs.

"I'll wait up for him," said Louisa.

"Far out," said Eliot—was it unpleasantly?—from the landing.

She read her novel for an hour. Then she went upstairs and looked at herself in the mirror. She took out all the makeup she had with her: eye shadow, pencil, mascara, two shades of lipstick, a small pot of rouge. She made herself up more heavily than she had ever done before. She made her face a caricature of all she valued in it. But it satisfied her, that face, in its extremity. And it fascinated her that in Henry's house she had done such a thing. Her face, no longer her own, so fixated her that she could not move away from the mirror. She sat perfectly still until she heard his key in the door.

The Neighborhood

My mother has moved from her house now; it was her family's for sixty years. As she was leaving, neighbors came in shyly, family by family, to say goodbye. There weren't many words; my mother hadn't been close to them; she suspected neighborly connections as the third-rate PR of Protestant churches and the Republican Party, the substitute of the weak, the rootless, the disloyal, for parish or for family ties. Yet everyone wept; the men she'd never spoken to, the women she'd rather despised, the teenagers who'd gained her favor by taking her garbage from the side of the house to the street for a dollar and a half a week in the bad weather. As we drove out, they arranged themselves formally on either side of the driveway, as if the car were a hearse. Through the rearview mirror, I saw the house across the street and thought of the Lynches, who'd left almost under cover, telling nobody, saying goodbye to no one, although they'd lived there seven years and when they'd first arrived the neighborhood had been quite glad.

The Lynches were Irish, Ireland Irish, people in the neighborhood said proudly, their move from the city to Long Island having given them the luxury of bestowing romance on a past their own parents might have downplayed or tried to hide. Nearly everybody on the block except my family and the Freeman sisters had moved in just after the war. The war, which the men had fought in, gave them a new feeling of legitimate habitation: they had as much right to own houses on Long Island as the Methodists, if not, perhaps, the old Episcopalians. And the Lynches' presence only made their sense of seigneury stronger: they could look upon them as exotics or as foreigners and tell themselves that after all now there was nothing they had left behind in Brooklyn that they need feel as a lack.

Each of the four Lynch children had been born in Ireland, although only the parents had an accent. Mr. Lynch was hairless, spry, and silent: the kind of Irishman who seems preternaturally clean and who produces, possibly without his understanding, child after child, whom he then leaves to their mother. I don't know why I wasn't frightened of Mrs. Lynch; I was the sort of child to whom the slightest sign of irregularity might seem a menace. Now I can place her, having seen drawings by Hogarth, having learned words like *harridan* and *slattern*, which almost rhyme, having recorded, in the necessary course of feminist research, all those hateful descriptions of women gone to seed, or worse than seed, gone to some rank uncontrollable state where things sprouted and hung from them in a damp, lightless anarchy. But I liked Mrs. Lynch; could it have been that I didn't notice her wild hair, her missing teeth, her swelling ankles, her ripped clothes, her bare feet when she came to the door, her pendulous ungirded breasts? Perhaps it was that she was different and my fastidiousness was overrun by my romanticism. Or perhaps it was that she could give me faith in transformation. If, in the evenings, on the weekends, she could appear barefoot and unkempt, on Monday morning she walked out in her nurse's aide's uniform, white-stockinged and white-shod, her hair pinned under a starched cap, almost like any of my aunts.

But I am still surprised that I allowed her to be kind to me. I never liked going into the house; it was the first dirty house that I had ever seen, and when I had to go in and wait for Eileen, a year younger than I, with whom I played emotionlessly from the sheer demand of her geographical nearness and the sense that playing was the duty of our state in life, I tried not to look at anything and I tried not to breathe. When, piously, I described the mechanisms of my forbearance to my mother, she surprised me by being harsh. "God help Mrs. Lynch," she said, "four children and slaving all day in that filthy city hospital, then driving home through all that miserable traffic. She must live her life dead on her feet. And the oldest are no help."

Perhaps my mother's toleration of the Lynches directed the response of the whole neighborhood, who otherwise would not have put up with the rundown condition of the Lynches' house and yard. The neighbors had for so long looked upon our family as the moral arbiters of the street that it would have been inconceivable for them to shun anyone of whom my mother approved. Her approvals, they all knew, were formal and dispensed *de haut en bas*. Despising gossip, defining herself as a working woman who had no time to sit on the front steps and chatter, she signaled her approbation by beeping her horn and waving from her car. I wonder now if my mother liked Mrs. Lynch because she too had no time to sit and drink coffee with the other women; if she saw a kinship between them, both of them bringing home money for their families, both of them in a kind of widowhood, for Mr. Lynch worked two jobs every day, one as a bank guard, one as a night watchman, and on Saturdays he drove a local cab. What he did inside the house was impossible to speculate upon; clearly, he barely inhabited it.

My father died when I was seven and from then on I believed the world was dangerous. Almost no one treated me sensibly after his death. Adults fell into two categories: they hugged me and pressed my hand, their eyes brimming over with unshed tears, or they slapped me on the back and urged me to get out in the sunshine, play with other children, stop brooding, stop reading, stop sitting in the dark. What they would not do was leave me alone, which was the only thing I wanted. The children understood that, or perhaps they had no patience; they got tired of my rejecting their advances, and left me to myself. That year I developed a new friendship with Laurie Sorrento, whom I never in the ordinary run of things would have spoken to since she had very nearly been left back in the first grade. But her father had died too. Like mine, he had had a heart attack, but his happened when he was driving his truck over the Fifty-ninth Street Bridge, at five o'clock, causing a traffic jam of monumental stature. My father had a heart attack in the Forty-second Street Library. He died a month later in Bellevue. Each evening during that month my mother drove into the city after work, through the Midtown Tunnel. I had supper with a different family on the block each evening, and each night some mother put me to bed and waited in my house until my mother drove into the driveway at eleven. Then, suddenly, it was over, that unreal time; the midnight call came, he was dead. It was as though the light went out in my life and I stumbled through the next few years trying to recognize familiar objects which I had known but could not seem to name.

I didn't know if Laurie lived that way, as I did, in half darkness, but I enjoyed her company. I only remember our talking about our fathers once, and the experience prevented its own repetition. It was a summer evening, nearly dark. We stood in her backyard and started running in circles shouting, "My father is dead, my father is dead." At first it was the shock value, I think, that pleased us, the parody of adult expectation of our grief, but then the thing itself took over and we began running faster and faster and shouting louder and louder. We made ourselves dizzy and we fell on our backs in the grass, still shouting "My father is dead, my father is dead," and in our dizziness the grass toppled the sky and the rooftops slanted dangerously over the new moon, almost visible. We looked at each other, silent, terrified, and walked into the house, afraid we might have made it disappear. No one was in the house, and silently, Laurie fed me Saltine crackers, which I ate in silence till I heard my mother's horn honk at the front of the house, and we both ran out, grateful for the rescue.

But that Christmas, Laurie's mother remarried, a nice man who worked for Con Edison, anxious to become the father of an orphaned little girl. She moved away and I was glad. She had accepted normal life and I no longer found her interesting. This meant, however, that I had no friends. I would never have called Eileen Lynch my friend; our sullen, silent games of hopscotch or jump rope could not have been less intimate, her life inside her filthy house remained a mystery to me, as I hoped my life in the house where death had come must be to her. There was no illusion of our liking one another; we were simply there.

Although I had no friends, I was constantly invited to birthday parties, my tragedy giving me great cachet among local mothers. These I dreaded as I did the day of judgment (real to me; the wrong verdict might mean that I would never see my father), but my mother would never let me refuse. I hated the party games and had become phobic about the brick of vanilla, chocolate, and strawberry ice cream always set before me and the prized bakery cake with its sugar roses. At every party I would run into the bathroom as the candles were being blown out and be sick.

Resentful, the mothers would try to be kind, but I knew they felt I'd spoiled the party. I always spent the last hour in the birthday child's room, alone, huddled under a blanket. When my mother came, the incident would be reported, and I would see her stiffen as she thanked the particular mother for her kindness. She never said anything to me, though, and when the next invitation came and I would remind and warn her, she would stiffen once again and say only, "I won't be around forever, you know."

But even I could see there was no point trying to get out of Eileen Lynch's party. I didn't say anything as I miserably dressed and miserably walked across the street, my present underneath my arm, a pair of pedal pushers I was sure Eileen wouldn't like.

Superficially, the Lynches' house was cleaner, though the smell was there, the one that always made me suspect there was something rotting, dead, or dying behind the stove or the refrigerator. Eileen's older sisters, whose beauty I then felt was diminished by its clear sexual source, were dressed in starched, high dresses; their shoes shone and the seams in their stockings were perfect. For the first time, I felt I had to admire them, although I'd preferred their habitual mode of treatment—the adolescent's appraisal of young children as deriving from a low and altogether needless caste—to their false condescending warmth as they offered me a party hat and a balloon. Eileen seemed unimpressed by all the trouble that had been gone to for her; her distant walk-through of Blind Man's Bluff and Pin the Tail on the Donkey I recognized as springing from a heart as joyless as my own.

Throughout the party, Mrs. Lynch had stayed in the kitchen. After the presents had been opened, she appeared, wearing her nurse's uniform and her white hose, but not her cap, and said to all of us, "Will ye come in and have some cake, then?"

It was the cake and ice cream I had known from all the other birthday parties and I closed my eyes and tried to think of other things—the ocean, as my mother had suggested, the smell of new-mown grass. But it was no good. I felt the salty rising behind my throat: I ran for the bathroom. Eileen's guests were not from my class, they were a year younger than I, so I was spared the humiliation of knowing they'd seen all this a dozen times before. But I was wretched as I bent above the open toilet, convinced that there was nowhere in the world that I belonged, wishing only that I could be dead like my father in a universe which had, besides much else to recommend it, incorporeality for its nature. There was the expected knock on the door. I hoped it would be Mrs. Lynch instead of one of Eileen's sisters, whose contempt I would have found difficult to bear.

"Come and lay down, ye'll need a rest," she said, turning her back to me the way the other mothers did. I followed, as I always had, into the indicated room, not letting my glance fall toward the eating children, trying not to hear their voices.

I was surprised that Mrs. Lynch had led me, not into the child's room but into the bedroom that she shared with Mr. Lynch. It was a dark room, I don't think it could have had a window. There were two high dressers and the walls were covered with brown, indistinguishable holy images. Mrs. Lynch moved the rose satinish coverlet and indicated I should lie on top of it. The other mothers always turned the bed down for me, and with irritation, smoothed the sheets. Mrs. Lynch went into the closet and took out a rough brown blanket. She covered me with it and it seemed as though she were going to leave the room. She sat down on the bed, though, and put her hand on my forehead, as if she were checking for fever. She turned the light out and sat in the chair across the room in the fashion, I now see, of the paid nurse. Nothing was said between us. But for the first time, I understood what all those adults were trying to do for me. I understood what was meant by comfort. Perhaps I was able to accept it from Mrs. Lynch as I had from no other because there was no self-love in what she did, nothing showed me she had one eye on some mirror checking her posture as the comforter of a grief-stricken child. She was not congratulating herself for her tact, her understanding, her tough-mindedness. And she had no suggestions for me; no sense that things could change if simply I could see things right, could cry, or run around the yard with other children. It was her sense of the inevitability of what had happened, and its permanence, its falling into the category of natural affliction, that I received as such a gift. I slept, not long I know—ten minutes, perhaps, or twenty—but it was one of those afternoon sleeps one awakes from as if one has walked out of the ocean. I heard the record player playing and sat up. It was the time of the party for musical chairs.

"Ye'd like to join the others then?" she asked me, turning on the light.

I realized that I did. I waited till the first round of the game was over, then joined in. It was the first child's game I can remember enjoying.

My mother didn't come for me in the car, of course. I walked across the street so she and Mrs. Lynch never exchanged words about what had happened. "I had a good time," I said to my mother, showing her the ring I'd won.

"The Lynches are good people," my mother said.

I'd like to say that my friendship with Eileen developed or that I acknowledged a strong bond with her mother and allowed her to become my confidante. But it wasn't like that; after that time my contacts with the Lynches dwindled, partly because I was making friends outside the neighborhood and partly because of the older Lynch children and what happened to their lives.

It was the middle fifties and we were, after all, a neighborhood of second-generation Irish. Adolescence was barely recognized as a distinct state; it was impossible to imagine that adolescent rebellion would be seen as anything but the grossest breach of the social contract, an incomprehensible one at that. *Rebel Without a Cause* was on the Legion of Decency condemned list; even Elvis Presley was preached against on the Sunday mornings before he was to appear on the *Ed Sullivan Show.* So how could my neighborhood absorb the eldest Lynch kids: Charlie, who left school at sixteen and had no job, who spent his afternoons in the driveway, souping up his car. Or Kathy, who'd got in trouble in tenth grade and then married, bringing her baby several times a week, assuming that Eileen, at ten, would be enchanted to take care of it. She wasn't of course, she viewed the child with the resentful gaze she cast on everything in life and refused to change its diapers. Rita, the third daughter, had gone to beautician school and seemed on her way to a good life except that she spent all her evenings parked with different young men in different cars—we all could see that they were different, even in the darkness—in front of the Lynch house.

I was shocked by the way the Lynches talked to their parents. In the summer everyone could hear them: "Ma, you stupid asshole," "Pop, you're completely full of shit," "For Christ sake, this is America, not fucking Ireland." Once in the winter, Charlie and Mrs. Lynch picked Eileen and me up from school when it was raining a gray, dense, lacerating winter rain. In the backseat, I heard Mrs. Lynch and Charlie talking.

"Ye'll drop me at the supermarket, then."

"I said I'd pick these kids up. That was all."

"I just need a few things, Charlie. And I remember asking ye this morning and ye saying yes."

He slammed the brakes on and looked dangerously at his mother. "Cut the crap out, Ma. I said I have things to do and I have them. I mean it now."

Mrs. Lynch looked out the window, and Charlie left us off at the Lynch house, then drove away.

People said it was terrible the way the Lynches sat back, staring help-lessly at their children like Frankenstein staring at his monster. My mother's interpretation was that the Lynches were so exhausted simply making ends meet that they didn't have the strength left to control their children, and it was a shame that children could take such advantage of their parents' efforts and hard lot. The closest she would come to criticiz-ing them was to say that it might have been easier for them in the city where they didn't have the responsibility of a house and property. And such a long commute. But it was probably the kids they did it for, she said. Knowing how she felt, nobody said "shanty Irish" in front of my mother, although I heard it often on the street, each time with a pang of treachery in my heart as I listened in silence and never opened my mouth to defend.

Everyone for so long had predicted disaster for the Lynches that no one was surprised when it happened; their only surprise was that it hap-pened on such a limited scale. It was a summer night; Charlie was drunk. His father had taken the keys to the car and hidden them so Charlie couldn't drive. We could hear him shouting at his father, "Give them to me, you fucking son of a bitch." We couldn't hear a word from Mr. Lynch. Finally, there was a shot, and then the police siren and the ambulance. Charlie was taken off by the police, and Mr. Lynch wheeled out on a stretcher. We later found out from Joe Flynn, a cop who lived down the street, that Mr. Lynch was all right; Charlie'd only shot him in the foot. But Charlie was on his way to jail. His parents had pressed charges.

Then the Lynches were gone; no one knew how they'd sold the house; there was never a sign in front. It was guessed that Mr. Lynch had men-tioned wanting to sell to someone in the cab company. Only the U-Haul truck driven by Kathy's husband and the new family, the Sullivans, arriv-ing to work on the house, told us what had happened. Jack Sullivan was young and from town and worked for the phone company; he said he didn't mind doing the repairs because he'd got the house for a song. His father helped him on the weekends, and they fixed the house up so it looked like all the others on the street. His wife loudly complained, though, about the filth inside; she'd never seen anything like it; it took her a week to get through the kitchen grease, she said, and they'd had to have the exterminator.

Everyone was awfully glad when they were finally moved in. It was a relief to have your own kind, everybody said. That way you knew what to expect.

Watching the Tango

One should not *watch* the tango. Or at least not in a theater like this, one so baroque and so well cared for, so suggesting plutocrats and oil money or money made from furs: Alaska, some cold climate, underpopulation, paying women to come out. They watch the tango, these two lovers, because they have heard from friends that it is good to watch these dancers, and seats were available on quite short notice. And they must do things on short notice, for they are illicit lovers; he is married, and her job has those long hours: it is hard to get away. They are longing for the lights to go out so they can hold hands. Someone they know is in the row behind them; they must wait for darkness.

They do not know what to expect but they have, of course, associations with the tango. Underlit and fundamentally quite dirty dance halls in parts of some large city fallen now into decay. The lights go out. They hear the sounds of an accordion, and overrich violins. He takes her hand, plays tunes on the palm of it. Her eyes close out of pleasure and she feels herself sink down and yet be buoyed up. And it encourages her to give herself up to these impossible joke instruments, their tasteless sounds.

The dancers come onto the stage. They are not young. First the men dance with each other. And the women, to the side, each dance alone in circles, as if they didn't notice, didn't care. Then suddenly, like the crack of a whip, the couples come together. Mere formality is seen to be the skeleton it is; limbs intertwine, the man's hand on the woman's back determines everything: the stress is all. The dancers are seductive, angry, playful, but it does not matter. All their gestures are theatrical, impersonal: the steps matter, and the art, which is interpretive. None of the couples is the same.

What are these women doing with their middle age? Theirs is not a body type familiar to us North Americans. Long and yet heavy-limbed, with strong, smooth athletes' backs, the high arched feet of the coquette, these bodies have not kept themselves from the fate of those of the simply indolent. Beneath the skirts, covered with beads and sequins, are soft stomachs, loose behinds. Can it be that when they are not here dancing these women are lounging, reading illustrated Spanish romances that look like comic books: heavy-lidded blondes succumbing, ravished, their words appearing over their heads in balloons like the words of Archie and Veronica? Are they eating chocolates, these women, these dancers? How late do they sleep?

It is impossible to invent for them an ordinary life. Of course they sleep all day. And where? Their bedrooms are quite easy to imagine. Dark and overfull: the hair pomade, the bottles of gardenia, jasmine; the pictures of the dying saints. The dolls stiff on the dresser tops, their skirts lace or crocheted, look out upon the scene like smug and knowing birds. What have they witnessed? Tears and botched abortions, abject and extravagant apologies, the torpid starts of quarrels, joyous reconciliations unconvincing in the light of day. The light of day, in fact, must never enter. The dark shiny curtains stay closed until late afternoon. Outside the closed door the house life goes on like another country. Some old woman—mother, servant, it hardly matters—dusts and polishes the furniture with oil that smells of roasting nuts. She does not knock to say "Still sleeping? Rise and shine!" She does not dare. She is professionally quiet.

The woman who is watching the tango takes her lover's hand and brings it to her lips. He does not know exactly why, but she can see that he has understood the springs of such a gesture. Sorrow. "You all right?" he whispers. "Yes." She is thinking: we will never dance together among friends. It makes her want to cry: she so envies the spectacle of these couples before them, so free of responsibility. They sleep late, they make love, they dance among their friends. But they do not look happy.

Happiness seems as irrelevant to them as sunlight, medicine, or balanced meals. Yet they do not suggest the criminal. They are infinitely, reverently law-abiding. You can see how they would love a dictator. But what is this: a woman dancing amorously with another woman? And a man, seething with anger, dangerously dancing by himself? What now? Here he comes with a knife. Of course he kills her. More in love than ever with her dead, he carries her offstage, kissing her all the while with a real tenderness.

They had talked before at supper, the two lovers, about violence between women and men. The statistics, she said to him, are up: more women now are violent to men. Oh good, he said, like lung cancer. How far we've come. Still, many more men are violent to women than women are to men, she said. And men can kill women with a blow of the fist. Don't forget that, she told him. Thanks, he said. I'll keep it in mind. Once he told her that he had hit a woman. She was completely on his side.

A short, dyed blonde appears onstage holding a microphone. The lovers, listening, do not know Spanish, yet they understand this woman has been betrayed. By whom? She is at least in her mid-fifties. The sex she suggests is quite unsavory. Money may have changed hands. Did a young man in tight black pants grow tired of the way he had to earn his free time? So he could be out gambling with his pals while the singer sang her heart out. Worse, with a young girl who made fun of her. The singer is right; it is terrible. She knows better. But she will make the same mistake again. The woman watching thinks of the singer dyeing her secret hairs, gray now, perhaps with a small brush. The thought of it raises in her a terrible pity. She begins to be afraid of growing old.

Intermission now. In the red lobby with its stone festoons, the lovers must pretend to be talking casually. In fact, every word he says increases her desire, and she doesn't want to go back to the theater, to the dark, where she cannot see his face, so beautiful and so arousing to her. But there is nowhere else to go. Adulterous, they are orphans. They sit in restaurants; they walk around the streets.

His friends come up. Almost never when the lovers are together do they speak to anyone except themselves. It is odd; the woman feels they are speaking in a foreign language. "We have visited Argentina," the man who is her lover's friend says, and it sounds to her like a sentence in a textbook. The four of them hear the bell and walk together down the aisle back to their seats.

A new couple has joined the dancers. Older, heavier, afraid of risks, as if they know there are things not easily recovered from, not ever, they move funereally and with no sense of play. But their somberness has not destroyed the others' spirits. Over in the corner are the madcap couple, jumping, laughing like jitterbuggers. He loudly slaps her behind. The male dancer to their left has an expression of balked chastity. "That one's a spoiled priest," the woman tells her lover. "I've seen that face on thousands of rectory walls." "And the old guy owns the nightclub," says her lover. "He has my marker for seventy-five grand." The dancers are becoming individuals, which makes them to the woman, oddly now, less interesting. She feels that, knowing them, she has to take them seriously. And she doesn't want that. She wants to lose herself in the cheap music and to dream about her lover's body.

The finale brings out all the dancers' passion to assert their differences. The musicians, too, are ardent. The woman watching with her lover thinks: the lights will go on, we will leave each other for the hundredth time. Thousands of times more we will kiss each other blandly at the train station, in case his neighbors are around.

He says, "Their children probably don't dance the tango. Maybe no one will when they are dead."

"We will," she says. "We'll do it for them."

They take hands with the lights on. Suddenly gallant and protective, they see everyone—the dancers, the musicians, the sad singers—all of them valorous, noble, worthy, and capable of the most selfless love.

"We'll do it one day," she says. "One day we'll dance the tango."

They walk outside the theater holding hands with the rash courage of new converts, soldiers, gamblers, pirates, clairvoyants. The rain keeps them beneath the theater marquee where they kiss as if it didn't matter or as if it were the only thing that did. They see one of the dancers arguing with someone—his real wife?—a sparrow in a kerchief and brown shoes. Impatiently, he opens his umbrella, leaves her there—she has no coat, no pocketbook—and walks away. She stands with the self-conscious stoicism of one who knows she has no choice. A minute later he returns, beckons, and she runs to the umbrella. He is wearing patent leather shoes. His dancing shoes? They will be ruined.

"Let's go now," the watching woman says to her lover. She doesn't want to see the other dancers coming out. She doesn't want to have to worry.

Agnes

"Well, it's the same old story. It's the woman pays. You see it every time," said Bridget, closing her pocketbook with a click, Nora could see, of dreadful satisfaction.

"Anybody could have seen it coming. But you don't, I guess," said Nettie.

"And whose fault was it but her own?" Bridget asked.

"Poor soul, there was few enough moments of joy she had on earth. And God have mercy on the dead. There'll be no more talk of it in my kitchen," said Kathleen.

Nora looked up at her mother, thinking her a coward to make the conversation stop. She had contempt for every one of them, her two aunts and her mother. And her father too, pretending he was sorry about Agnes's death. For they had never liked her, any of them, although at least her mother had been kind to her. Nora had not liked Ag herself.

Ag was a disappointment, for she was the only woman any of them knew who lived in sin, and she made such a dowdy appearance. Really, Nora felt, and anyone with sense would have agreed with her, if you were going to be somebody's mistress, you should look—how? You should be overdressed and overly made-up with loud dyed hair that was itself a challenge, a large bosom and a shocking, sticking-out behind, a waist you drew attention to with tight, cinched belts. You should smoke cigarettes and leave them in the ashtray marked with your dark lipstick, piles of them so people would count them when you were gone, and make remarks. But Agnes looked, Nora had always thought, like a wet bird, with her felt navy blue hat in winter, her straw navy-blue hat in summer, with her damp hands that she kept putting to her face as if she were afraid that if she didn't keep checking, she'd find her face had fallen off.

Sometimes, though, the difference between Ag's fate and her appearance raised in Nora a wild hope. Ag looked as damaged as Nora with her one short leg knew herself to be. But Ag provided a suggestion that it could be possible to live a life of passion nonetheless. How could this be anything to Nora but a solace? At thirteen, she dreamed identically to her girlfriends. Rudolph Valentino would carry her off somewhere, his eyes gone vague and menacing with love. He would hold her at arm's length, staring at her face, unable to believe in his good fortune. They would lie down together on soft sand. He would not have noticed her leg, and when she tactfully brought it up he would laugh, that laugh that could have been a villain's but was not, and say, "It is as nothing with a love like ours."

Sometimes in the middle of this vision, Nora grew embarrassed at herself and angry, and her anger grew up like a bare spiked tree against an evil sky; it grew and spread until it became the only feature in the landscape. "Fool," she called herself, for everybody knew that no one would forget her leg, it was the first thing anybody saw about her, it was the thing the merciful looked past, remarking on her hair, her eyes; the thing that most people could not get past, so that they did not look at her. She would never be beloved, carried off. She would take a commercial course, forget the academic that the teachers told her she belonged in, forget that stuff, for she would always be alone, and when her parents died she would live in the house alone. She would always support herself so she would never have to rely on her four brothers. At such moments, a last resort but one she dared to trust, Ag's face would swim up among the others in her mind. For Nora knew her uncle Des could have had anybody, but he'd stuck with Ag. Ten years he'd stuck with her, and all that time she'd asked for nothing. Supported him and said okay when he said he would never marry, that he had no patience for the priests and couldn't be tied down. Still he stayed with her, and the example of Ag and her uncle suggested to Nora that if she could bring a man to see that she would ask for nothing, she too could have a passionate life.

But in the end, there was no comfort in it, for the life so obviously weakened Ag and made her hungry for respectability. Ag was no help to her, and Nora grew resentful of the cruelly false hint Ag did not know she proffered. She could only just bring herself to be civil to Ag, and she allowed her parents to believe that she judged Ag's morals as harshly as her aunt Bridget did.

Now she felt bad about not having liked Agnes, and it was typical of Agnes, she was great at making everyone feel bad. She came into a room like the end of the party: no one could enjoy themselves with her around; nobody could relax. She should have seen it and kept away. But she didn't see it, of course, and kept on coming. You could say, perhaps, that it was Uncle Des's fault: he should never have brought her in the first place, acting as if it was respectable. But she came more than he did: three times to his one, although the sisters always knocked themselves out asking him to come and knocked themselves out when he got there.

Nora knew her uncle Desmond was a bootlegger. She'd heard the word before. It was a queer word, she thought, "bootlegger," it sounded innocent like "shoemaker" or "fireman," far more innocent than names of other jobs: "chauffeur," "handyman," that men in her family without much comment seemed to hold. But because of Des there were odd night stirrings, brisk events involving whispers and rushed trips downstairs to the coal cellar and then up again and downstairs in a greater rush, and Nora being told to keep the children back, but told not one thing else. And then the arguments, the terrible dangerous anger when her father came home and was told: Des had to hide some of his liquor in the cellar, he could be killed or be arrested, there was not another blessed place.

Edmund Derency paced, he literally pulled his hair, he told his wife her brother was a thief, a wastrel, and he didn't give a tinker's damn for her or for her family, and they would lose it all, lose everything for him, and because of his damn laziness and trickery it all would go for nothing, the trip over and the years of work so they could have what they had now: the house, a girl in high school, jobs in the government you kept forever unless they found out about something like this, and then it was all gone.

Look at the house, Kathleen, he said, take a good look at it, remember it so you can think of it when us and all the kids are living on the street because of your damn brother and his damn fast tricks.

But then it was over, Des was back with money in his pocket and a gift for everyone, a radio big as a piece of furniture that even her father could not resist. Nor could he keep up his grudge against Des, spectacularly handsome in his shirtsleeves, the sight of him a gift, like a day at the beach for all the children issued fresh, as if it was the thing they all deserved, they knew it now, but had been all along afraid to wish for. When Des put his hands on Ed Derency's shoulders and said, "God, Edmund, I'd have shot myself in the foot rather than do this to you and Kath. If there had been a God's blessed way out of it. But they were on my neck, and I don't need to tell you of all people what that could have meant."

"Not another word, Des. What else would family be for? God knows they're trouble enough at the best of times, if you take my meaning."

There were the two of them, drinking her uncle Desmond's whiskey, the very bottles Nora's father had threatened to smash up with an axe, winking, their arms around each other, men together, as if women and all that had to do with them—the children and the houses and the family meals—were just a bad joke that had been forced upon their kind. Nora hated them for that, she hated what was clearer to her daily: the adult world of false seeming, lies and promises you couldn't trust an inch. There was Des, just having made a joke, or laughed at one, about the weight of women on the world, singing "I'll Take You Home Again, Kathleen" while her mother played the piano for him, tears dropping on her fingers while she played. And the aunts crying in their chairs and Agnes sitting there patting her eyes with a twisted-up handkerchief as if she were afraid that if she made a noise or if her tears fell on the furniture she would be a nuisance. Nora hardened her heart against her uncle, against all of them, and turned away when he sang the song he used to sing to her when she was little: "With someone like you, a pal good and true / I'd like to leave them all behind."

She thought with anger how she once had loved it, what a fool she'd been, a fool he'd made her, and the family'd allowed. He knew that he had lost her, and he made his eyes go sad. "There's no more time for your old uncle now you're a young lady, is there?"

How could anybody look so sad? He needed all her comfort. She was about to say, "Oh, Uncle Des," and put her arms around him, smell the smell of his tobacco and the starched collar he always wore. But something in his look gave him away, some insecurity. He looked around the room, hedging his bets, looking toward the younger children, giving up: they were all boys. But in that moment he had lost her, and she shrugged her shoulders and said, "I have lots to do. With school, you know, and all."

Afterward she was glad she had done it. For that was the last time he had come with Agnes; it all happened not long after that: he must have known. Must have known when they made him sing "I'll Take You Home Again, Kathleen" a second time, and he looked at all of them, especially at Agnes though, and said, bringing his fist down on the radio, "We'll all go back. I swear it to you. It's the one reason I'm in this rotten business. If I make a killing, it's back home in triumph for the lot of us. First class. We'll turn them green."

He hadn't meant a word of it. Two weeks later he was on the train to California with his brand-new wife.

"Well, it's ridiculous, he's never even brought the girl around. How could he have just upped and married somebody we've never met? You must have read it wrong, the letter. Let me have a look at it," said Bridget.

She read the piece of paper—hotel stationery—as if she were a starving person looking in a pile of rot for one intact kernel. Then, Nora could see, she hated herself for her fool's work and looked around her for someone to blame.

" 'Twas fast, like, you'd have to say that," Nettie said timidly. "Perhaps they had to."

"I'd say Des would know better than that," said Edmund Derency, "I'd say that for him."

The sisters turned upon him then, their eyes hard with the fury of shared blood.

"You never knew him," Kathleen said with tight lips to her husband. "There's something he's keeping from us. The woman could be sick, dreadfully sick. Or dying, and he wouldn't want the three of us to know."

Ed Derency threw down his newspaper. "She's a rich girl whose family threw her out for marrying a greenhorn. That's as sick as she is."

"And how will he support a wife in California? He'd got nothing put away. Too generous," said Kathleen.

"And Agnes Martin to count on with the money she got wiping the noses of the Yankee brats," said Edmund.

"She worked for the finest families in New York, Ed Derency, don't you forget it," Bridget said.

"Since when are you on Ag's side?" he asked.

"What will happen to Ag now?" said Nettie.

"I hate to think of it," said Edmund.

"No one's asking you to think of it," Bridget said. "It's none of your affair. Someone should phone her."

"I'll telephone her," said Kathleen, rising as if she'd waited to be asked. "I'll invite her for Sunday dinner."

Nora ran upstairs to the bathroom, shut the door behind her, and ran the water in the sink as loudly as she could. She dreaded the thought of Ag and wished her mother had the courage to cut her off. There was nothing they could do for her, nothing that anyone could do. She hoped Ag knew that and would have the sense to stay away. But then she knew Ag wouldn't, and her vision of Ag sitting in the living room and hoping for a scrap of news hardened Nora's heart. She'd be damned if she'd be nice to Ag; if Ag had pride, she'd stay away. But if she'd had the pride, she'd never have taken up with Uncle Desmond and embarrassed everyone and put herself in this position so she would be hurt. She'd be better off dead, Nora said to herself, enjoying her cruel face in the mirror.

When Ag arrived, she looked no different; if she'd spent nights weeping, it had left no mark. She talked of Desmond's marriage, his departure, reasonably, as if it were something they had discussed together and agreed to.

"He pointed out to me," Ag said, "that really he had no choice but to marry her. 'She's not like you and me, Ag,' he said. 'She was brought up with the silver spoon. I couldn't do it to her, leave her in the lurch. She stood up to her parents for me. She lost everything. She wasn't like the two of *us*. She really had something to lose.'"

Ag said this proudly, with a pride Nora had never seen in her when she'd had Desmond actually with her. And Nora hated her because Ag didn't see how she'd been taken in. Desmond had gone off with another woman, had given her everything that Ag had wanted from him, and Ag acted as if he'd given her a gift. Disgust welled up in Nora, and at the same time fear; she wanted Ag to know what had happened to her, but she didn't want anyone to say it. She was petrified every second that Bridget would open up her mouth.

But the visit passed with not much more than the usual discomfort; Ag had always been so troublesome a presence that her new estate hardly made a difference.

"Do you think we've seen the back of her at last?" asked Bridget.

"There's no one else for her on holidays and things. In charity, I'd say we'd have to ask her," Kathleen said.

"Charity my foot," said Ed.

"You talk big, Ed Derency, but you'd be the last to turn her out. Or have her sitting by herself on Christmas."

"It's just February, Kath. Let's see what the year brings," said Nora's father, but Nora couldn't tell whether or not he meant it kindly. She could see that they felt relieved that Agnes hadn't come apart over Desmond's leaving; their relief had made them quiet. They discussed Ag's folly, her gullible swallowing of the story Des had fed her, less than they might have, or than they'd discussed anything else she'd ever done. They were quiet because they were cowards, and they couldn't say a word about what had happened without putting Desmond in a light which even their love couldn't render flattering.

Agnes phoned whenever Desmond wrote her.

"Well, at least he keeps in touch with her, that's something," Kathleen said.

It was from Ag and not from Desmond that they learned Desmond's wife had had a baby. Desmond's letters were about weather, about his new job in a haberdasher's, about how a customer who worked in Hollywood had said that Des should have a screen test. Not a word about his wife, as if she were a temporary measure, and the important things in life were weather, scenery, the movie industry, the cut of clothes. It was only from Ag that they learned how he met his wife. Des was her father's bootlegger; her father was a big lawyer in New Jersey. Tenafly, Agnes had said. No one could tell Nora how it happened: that he went from chatting the girl up, leaning his foot on the running board of some big car, and then the next thing, they were on the train to California. Was it that it was obvious to everyone but her how it had happened? Or was it that she was the only one who had the sense to know that the time in between was the real clue, the real important time, the time that held what she and Agnes needed to know: what had happened that had made Des give this woman easily the thing Ag wanted and would never get, or ask for, or after a while think of as any possibility at all.

Agnes was cheerful at the news of Desmond's baby's birth. She had become, Nora could see, more family to him than his own family. Her new responsibility gave her a pride of place that she had never had, as if she'd landed a good job at last and reveled in the title. Nora saw that all this made the sisters hate her, and she knew that Agnes didn't have the sense to see. Proudly, without apology, she brought them news of him as pretext for a visit. She came often, for Desmond called her often for advice: she was a children's nurse, and Des said, Ag reported proudly, his wife had never been around a baby in her life.

"I even wondered if I should go out there. Lend a hand, you know. Poor thing, she sounds so overwhelmed. You see it all the time. She's very young, you know."

Bridget put her full teacup heavily down in her saucer. They all knew she was about to say something terrible, but for this once no one tried to shift the conversation to distract or stop her. Nora saw that they wanted Bridget to do the dreadful thing, to hurt Ag, that they—her mother and Nettie, with their famous reputations, in her mother's case for being kind, and in her aunt's for being too cheerful to think a bad thing about anyone—wanted now for Agnes to be hurt. Nora saw that only she did not want it, but she was afraid, not strong, a child, and to prevent it you had to be stronger than all that hating of the three of them, than all that wish to hurt. She saw them look at Bridget, and saw her take it as a sign.

"She's young, all right, but you're not, Agnes. Old enough, I'd say, to know better. Stay out of where you're not wanted. The minute she finds out about you, she'll stop you herself. Have a little pride for once in your life. Tell him you're not his free advice bureau. Tell him to pay some greenhorn girl himself."

After Bridget had said what they had wanted her to say, Nora could see that they were sorry. She saw Nettie desperately looking at Kathleen to say something to smooth things over.

"Of course she didn't really mean that she was going to go out there, Bridget. It was just a way of talking, like. A way of saying that she wished them well."

Ag neither confirmed Kathleen's words nor denied them: she had sense enough to let the matter drop, to let Bridget sniff silently, convinced that she was right, but too much of a lady to press home her point.

In the end what bothered Nora most was how right Bridget had been. Desmond's wife found out about Ag and brought all communication to an end.

She had come upon a letter Des was writing to Agnes. "She's awfully pretty, Ag, but very young and doesn't understand a thing. It's very often now I long for our good old chats." Underneath this, which had been written in Des's formal copperplate, was scrawled in a back-slanting script: "I have found this in my husband's desk, and having informed him of my discovery, he has agreed that from this moment all communication between you two must cease. There is a child to be considered after all." And she had signed her name: Harriet Browne O'Reilley. Underneath her signature, as if she were continuing a conversation, Ag had scratched: "This is the thing I cannot bear." And then she hanged herself.

Nora made herself imagine it: the letter with the three different handwritings, the things that Ag had done between the time she'd put the pen down and the time she'd tied the dressing-gown sash around her neck and kicked the chair away. She imagined Ag had done some ordinary things: made tea, perhaps, or washed out stockings. She knew Ag had never been upset or agitated: killing herself must have seemed to her simply the next thing to be done, like boarding a bus or shopping for a pair of shoelaces. "This is how it is," she must have said. "And I will do this now." Nora could see just how it was, Agnes's small efficient movements canceling her pain. Each night Nora would think of Ag before she went to sleep. She didn't want anyone else to think about her. She resented that she had not been the one to find her. It should have been Nora, not a neighbor breaking down the door with the police, afraid because they hadn't seen Ag leaving the apartment. It should have been herself, not the police, who'd called up Des in California. It should have been she, not her mother, who took the instructions from Des about the disposition of the body. No, not that: Des should not have been consulted. Nora should have made the plans. She would have stood up to the priest who refused Ag a Christian burial. She would have made up a story to fool him; she would have found a way to hide the circumstances of Ag's death. She would have seen to it that Ag had a proper funeral, that everyone came to pay respects and brought in Mass cards and took holy pictures with Ag's name on the back of them to put into their prayer books so that they'd remember her at Mass.

She would have done far better than her mother, who set out for the police station, her eyes apologetic and her posture cringing and came back having made the arrangements with an undertaker who was Presbyterian to have the simplest coffin and to send the bills to Des. She understood her mother's anger, and her shame, but her mother had got it wrong, she was angry and ashamed for the wrong thing, as Ag had died for the wrong thing, and left it to the wrong person to pick up all the pieces.

Kathleen said nothing about Ag when she came home from making the arrangements, and it was months before the family said a word about her. When Agnes's name came up in family conversation, Nora could see everybody take Des's part; it was easy, she thought with contempt, to know what they would say. They wanted to make a lesson from it, sew it up, as if it could be useful to their lives. Whereas the truth was only she had anything to learn of it. The lesson was not anything the women thought. It was much worse than anything they mentioned. The truth was that Ag was right to hang herself, except she should have done it earlier. The truth was women like that were better off not being born, and if you saw you had a girl child growing up like that you'd be best drowning it straight off, holding its head under the water till the breath went out of the doomed creature, so you'd save it all the pain and trouble later on.

The Magician's Wife

Unlike most of her friends, Mrs. Hastings did not think of herself first as the mother of her children. She was proudest of being Mr. Hastings's wife. So that in their old age it grieved her to see her husband known in the town as the father of her son, Frederick, the architect, who was not half the man his father was, for beauty, for surprises. Frederick had put up buildings, had had his picture taken with mayors outside city halls, with the governor outside office buildings. She ought to have been proud of Frederick, and of course she was, really, and he was very good to them; they would not be half so well-off without him. She valued her son as she valued the food she had cooked, the meals she had produced, very much the same since the day of her marriage.

Her husband had added to his salary by being a magician. Not that he hadn't provided perfectly well for them; still it was something else that life would have been meaner without, the money he had made on magic. How had it first started? That was one of the arguments she had with his mother. His mother said he had always been that way, putting on magic shows in the barn as a boy. But she knew it hadn't started that way; she remembered the way it had. It was on their honeymoon. They saw a vaudeville show in Chicago, and there was a magician, the amazing Mr. Kazmiro, whose specialty was making birds appear. That night on the way to the hotel, Mrs. Hastings could see her husband brooding over something. When he brooded his eyes would go dull, the color of pebbles, and she could see him rolling the idea from one side of his brain to the other as you would roll a candy ball from one side of your mouth to the other if you had a sore tooth. In the morning (it shocked her, how handsome he was in his pajamas) he said, "May, let's go shopping." They went down to the area behind the theater where the shops sold odd things: white makeup in flat little tins, wigs for clowns or prima donnas, gizmos comedians used. It was in one of those stores that he bought his first trick; she remembered it was something with balls and hoops and wooden goblets with false bottoms. She never looked too closely at his tricks—not then, not ever. It had shocked her how much the trick cost, ten dollars, but she had said nothing. It was her honeymoon. She never said anything about the expense except to ask what it was about these things that cost so much money. Her husband said it was a highly skilled business, that each of his tricks was the work of craftsmen. But that was how he got started, she remembered, on the fourth day of their honeymoon. No matter what his mother said, it had nothing to do with his life before he got married, his magic.

Once he had performed for the Roosevelts. It was 1935 and one of the Roosevelt grandchildren was recovering from measles. The boy was crotchety and there was nothing you could do to please him, one of the servants had said, one who had seen Mr. Hastings entertaining at the county fair in Rhinebeck. It was a wicked night, she remembered. It thundered and flashed lightning so that the lights flickered on and off. When the telephone rang, they thought it was a joke, some lady calling to ask if Mr. Hastings would care to come over to Hyde Park and do a small performance for a sick child. Her husband and children had thought it was a joke, for one minute. Of course her husband would be called to entertain the President, of course the car, the big black car driven by a man in a uniform, would come for him. She remembered how her husband had talked to the chauffeur, as if he had been brought up to order servants about. She remembered what her husband had said, not looking at the man in the uniform, but not looking at his feet either, looking straight ahead of him. She remembered he had said, "Do you mind if I bring my wife?" and the chauffeur had said, "As you wish, sir," and opened the door. That was the gallantry of him, so that she would get to meet Franklin Roosevelt, and Eleanor, who was as plain as she looked in her pictures and had a voice that was an embarrassment; but she was, as Mrs. Hastings said to the people whom she told about it, "Very gracious to us, and a real lady."

All the vivid moments of her life had been marked by her husband's magic. Not only the Roosevelts—although how would she ever have met the Roosevelts if she had not married Mr. Hastings?—but the moments that heightened the color of everyone's ordinary life. There was a show for each of her birthdays and anniversaries, for each important day of each child's life. On one occasion Frederick had sulked and said, "It's my party and everyone's paying attention to *him*." And she had told him he should thank his lucky stars not to have a father like everyone else's, dull as dishwater, and that any other boy would give his eyeteeth to have a father who could do magic. And Frederick said—where did he get those eyes, those dull, brown, good boy's eyes, they weren't hers, or his father's—Frederick said, "Not if they really knew about it."

Frederick was not nearly so handsome as his father, particularly when his father was doing magic. Mrs. Hastings remembered the look of him when he was all dressed up, with his hair slicked back and his mustache. He looked distinguished, like William Powell. She knew all the women in the town envied her her husband, for his good looks and his beautiful manners and his exciting ways. Once Mrs. Daly, the milkman's wife, said, "It must be hard on you, him spending all his spare time practicing in the basement." It was well-known that Mr. and Mrs. Daly had had separate bedrooms since the birth of their last child. Mrs. Hastings wanted to tell Mrs. Daly about the trick her husband had played on her in bed one night, pulling a pearl from the bodice of her nightgown, putting it in his mouth and bringing out a flower. But that was exactly the kind of detail Mrs. Daly wanted, which Mrs. Hastings had no intention of giving her. So she turned to Mrs. Daly and said in her highfalutin voice—her husband said, "Okay, Duchess," when she used it on him—"He always shows me everything while he's working on it," which was partly true, although he would never show her anything until he was sure it worked. But it was true enough for someone like Mrs. Daly, who slept in a single bed near the window, true enough to knock her off her high horse.

How could she be lonely up in the kitchen with the knowledge of him below her doing things over and over with scarves and boxes and cards and ribbons. She could imagine the man she loved, alone, away where she could not see him, practicing over and over the tricks that would astound not only her but every person they knew. Why would she prefer conversations at the kitchen table about money or food or what who wore when? She thought it a great and a kingly mercy that he kept his job as a machinist, which he hated, instead of quitting to work full-time as a magician, which he sometimes talked about. When he talked about it, a little flame of fear would go up in her, as if someone had lit a match behind one of her ribs. But she would say, "Do whatever you want. I have faith." What she liked really, though, was that during the day he went to his job, like anyone else's husband, but he spent his nights doing magic. He would come up the stairs every night in triumph, and every night he wanted her because, he said, she was the best little wife a man ever had; and every night she wanted him because she could not believe her good fortune, since she was, compared with her husband, she knew, quite ordinary.

And the years had passed as they do for everyone, only for her it was different. Her years were marked not only by the birth and aging and ceremonies of children, but by the growth of her husband's art. After 1946, for example, he gave up the egg and rope tricks and moved into scarves and coins. His retirement was nothing that he feared. He did not go around like other men, taking a week to do a chore that could have been done in an hour. Nor did she go around like other women, saying, "I can't get him out of my hair; he doesn't know what to do with himself." She loved being the wife of a retired husband as she had never loved being the mother of young children. She loved hearing him take long steps from one end of the basement to the other, loved the times she could hear him standing still, could hear, she thought, his concentration coming up to her through the ceiling, could see it seeping through the floorboards like waves of visible heat. She would never, never interrupt him, but she always knew when it was the last second of his work and she would hear his step on the stairway, would hear him say, "Got any beer?" And she would say, "I've had it waiting." It was the happiest time of her life, the years of his early retirement.

But then his eyes began to go. At first it was rather beautiful, the way his eyes misted over. It was like, she said to herself, a lake the first thing in the morning. He wore thicker glasses with a pink tint which the doctors said were more restful. They would have made any other man look foolish, but not her husband, with his fine, strong head, his way of holding his shoulders. Even at his age his looks were something other women envied her for. She could see the envy in the way they'd look at her as she walked with him in the evening.

She began to notice how queerly he held things, the funny angle at which he held the newspaper. Now she would hear him in the basement, snorting with frustration, using words that she imagined he used only on the job, not words for her or the house. And worst of all, she could hear him drop things; sometimes she would hear things break. She would pretend to be sewing or reading when he came looking for the broom or the dustpan.

The doctors said nothing would reverse the process, so, as time passed, there were more and more things he couldn't do. But the miracle of it was that the losses did not enrage him as, she knew, they would have enraged her. He simply accepted the loss of each new activity as he would have accepted the end of a meal. Finally one night he said to her, "Listen, old girl, you're my only audience now. I'm blind as a bat, and one thing nobody needs is a half-blind magician."

Did she like it better that he did his tricks only for her now, in the living room? Or had she liked it better sitting in the audience, watching the wonder of the people around at what he could produce from the most surprising places. On the whole she thought she liked it better watching the stupefaction, the envy. But it was in her nature, that preference. She had not as nice a nature as his. It was his nature to take her hand and say, after he had done a trick she had seen five hundred times, perhaps, and was not tired of, "I only make magic for *you* now." Making his almost total blindness into a kind of gift for her, a perfect glass he had blown and polished.

On the whole she blamed Frederick for what happened on the Fourth of July, although she knew the idea had come from the grandchildren. Sometimes her husband would take them down to the basement with him to show them some of the equipment. Sometimes he would do tricks for them, the simpler ones that he had done almost from the beginning and knew so well that he didn't have to see to do them. She understood the children's enchantment with him and his magic; he was a perfect grandfather, indulgent, full of secret skills. Of course she understood their pride—there was no one like him. But she didn't understand Frederick's going along with their damn fool idea. His great virtue had always been his good sense. Why did he put his father up to it, without even asking her?

It was tied up with the grandchildren and the way they were so proud. They wanted their friends to see that their grandfather was a magician, so they egged him on to give a show at the Fourth of July Town Fair. Finally Frederick got behind them.

At first she thought it would be all right because of the look on her husband's face when he talked about it, because she knew what gave him that look: the prospect of once again astonishing strangers. Nothing could make up for the loss of it, and it was something she could not give him. Sitting in that living room, honored as she was by the privacy of this intimate performance for her only, no matter how much she loved him, she had seen it all before.

And so she had to tell him what a good thing it was, how proud she would be, what a miracle he was in the lives of his grandchildren. At first she thought he would do only old tricks, and she felt safe. The audience would love him for his looks and because he was Frederick's father. She pressed his suit herself, weeks before; she pressed it several times just for practice. She looked through all her dresses to find the one that would most honor him. Finally she decided on her plainest dress, a black cotton with short sleeves. It was an old woman's dress but, being without ornament, the dress of an old woman who knows herself to be in a position of privilege. She would braid a silver ribbon into her long hair.

As the weeks went on, all ease was drained from her, a slow leak, stealing warmth, making the center of her chest feel full of cold air as if she had just walked into a cave. It was not the old tricks, the ones he almost didn't need eyes for, that he was doing. He was trying to do the newer, more complicated ones. She knew because of the household things he asked for: ribbon now instead of string, scarves instead of cotton handkerchiefs. When he showed her the act, as he always did before the performance, she saw him fumble, saw him drop things that he did not see so that the trick could not possibly go right. But she saw, too, that sometimes he was unaware that he had not done the trick properly. Sometimes the card was not the right card, the scarf the wrong color. All the life in her body collected in one solid disk at the center of her throat when she saw him foolish like that, an old man. But she would not tell him. It was not something that she could do, to say to him: your best life is entirely behind you—you are an old man. She could not even suggest that he do the simpler things. It was not in her; it had never been in her, and she understood what he was doing. He was risking foolishness to get from his audience the greatest possible astonishment, the greatest novelty of love.

She could not sleep the night before, looking at his sweet white body, the white hairs on the chest that still had the width and the toughness of the young man she had married. She poured boiling water over her finger so she had to go to the fair with her hand in a bandage. That annoyed Frederick, who said, "Today of all days, Mother."

Frederick was looking very foolish. He was wearing red, white, and blue striped pants and a straw boater which, with his thinning hair, his failure of a mustache, was a grave tactical error. His father came down wearing his white suit, blue shirt, red bow tie and provided, by his neat, hale presence, all the festivity Frederick had worked so hard to embody.

They had set up a stage on the lawn of the courthouse. First some of the women in the Methodist choir sang show tunes. Then the bank president's daughter, dressed like Uncle Sam, did her baton routine, then somebody played an accordion. Then Frederick got up onstage. All his business friends whistled and stamped and made rude noises. She was embarrassed at the attention he was bringing to himself.

"Now I don't want to be accused of nepotism," he said. (It must have been some joke, some business joke; all the men laughed rudely as she imagined men laughed at dirty jokes.) "But when you have a talent in the family, why hide it under a bushel? My father, Mr. Albert Hastings, is a magician extraordinaire. He had the distinction of performing before Franklin Delano Roosevelt. And as I've always said, what's good enough for the Roosevelts is good enough for us."

The men guffawed again. Frederick stretched out one of his arms. "Ladies and gentlemen, the amazing Hastings."

Albert had been backstage all the time. She was glad he had not been with her to sense her fear, perhaps to absorb it. A woman behind her tapped her on the shoulder and said, "You must be very proud." Mrs. Hastings put her finger to her lips. Her husband had begun speaking.

It was the same patter he had used for years, but there was a new element in it that disturbed her: gratitude. He kept telling the audience how good it was to allow him to perform. *Allow* him? He would never have spoken like that, like a plain girl who has finally been asked to dance, ten years ago, five even. She hoped he would not go on like that. But she could see that the audience loved it, loved him for being an old man. But was that the kind of love he wanted? It was not what she thought he was after.

One of the grandchildren was onstage helping him. He made some joke about it, hoping that no one would doubt the honesty of his assistant. For the first trick the child picked three cards. It was a simple trick and over quickly. The audience applauded inordinately, she thought, for it was a simple trick and he used it first, she knew, simply to warm them up.

The second trick was the magic bag. It appeared tiny, but out of it he pulled an egg, an orange, grapes, and finally a small bottle of champagne. "I keep telling my wife to take it to the supermarket, but she won't listen," he said, gesturing at her in the first row of the audience. She got the thrill she always had when he acknowledged her from the stage. She began, for the first time, to relax.

The next trick was the one in which he threaded ribbons through large wooden cards. He asked his grandson to hold the ribbons. It was important that they be held very tightly. She could see her husband struggling to see the holes in the cards through which the ribbon had to be threaded. She could see that he had missed one of the holes, so when he pulled the ribbon, nothing happened. It was supposed to slip out without disturbing the cards. But he pulled the strings and nothing moved. He looked at the audience; he gave it an old man's look. "Ladies and gentlemen, I apologize," he said.

Then they applauded. They covered him with applause. How she hated them for that. She could feel their embarrassment and that complicity that ties an audience together, in love or hatred, in relation to the person so far, so terribly far away on the stage. But it was not love or hate they felt; it was embarrassment for the old man, and she could feel their yearning that it might be all over soon. To hide it, they applauded wildly. She sat perfectly still.

If only the next trick would go well! But it was the scarf trick, the one he had flubbed in the living room. She felt as though she could not breathe. She thought she was going to be sick. She should have told him that it had not worked. She should not have been a coward. Now he would be a fool to strangers. To Frederick's business friends.

"Ladies and gentlemen, I have a magic box, a magic cleaning box. I keep trying to get my wife to use it, but she's a very stubborn woman."

She knew what was supposed to happen. You put a colored scarf in one side of the box and pulled a white one out of the other side. But in the living room he had pulled out the same colored scarf that he had put in. But she had not told him. And he had not seen the difference.

He did the same thing now. At least it was over quickly. He held up the colored scarf, the scarf he thought was white, and twirled it around his head and bowed to the audience. He did not know that the trick had not worked. The audience was confused. There was a terrible beat of silence before they understood what had happened. Then Frederick started the applause. The audience gave Mr. Hastings a standing ovation. Then he disappeared backstage with a strange, old man's shuffle she had not seen him use before.

Frederick got up on the stage again. He was saying something about refreshments, something about gratitude to the women who had provided them. She was shaking with rage in her seat. How could he go on like that, after the humiliation his father had endured? And it was his responsibility. How could he go on talking to the audience, about games, about prizes, when that audience had witnessed his father's degradation? Why wasn't he with his father, to comfort him, to cover his exposure, when it had been his fault, when it was Frederick, through thickheadedness, or perhaps malice, who had caused his father's failure in this garish public light?

"Let me get you some supper," said Frederick, offering his mother his arm. He was nodding to other people, even as he spoke to his mother.

She turned to her son in fury.

"Why did you allow him to do this?"

"Do what?"

"This performance. This failure."

"He got a big kick out of it. He's a good sport," said Frederick.

"Everyone saw him fail," said Mrs. Hastings through closed teeth.

"It's all right, Mother. He thinks he did fine."

"It was a humiliation."

He shook his head and looked at her but with no real interest. He walked slightly ahead of her, too fast for her; she could see him searching the crowd for anyone else to talk to. He looked over his shoulder at her with the impatience of a young girl.

"Shall I fix you a plate?" he asked.

"You'll do nothing for me after what you've done to your father."

He stopped walking and waited for her to catch up.

"You know, Mother, Father is twice the person you are," he said, not looking at her. "Three times."

She stood beside him. For the first time in his life, Mrs. Hastings looked at her son with something like love. For the first time, she felt the pride of their connection. She took his arm.

The Imagination of Disaster

I am aware of my own inadequacies, of course, but if this happens, no one will be adequate: to be adequate requires a prior act of the imagination, and this is impossible. We are armed; they are armed; someone will take the terrible, the unimaginable, vengeful step. And so we think in images of all that we have known to be the worst. We think of cold, of heat, of heaviness. But that is not it; that does not begin to be it. A mother thinks: how will I carry my children, what will I feed them? But this is not it, this is not it. There will be no place to carry them, food itself will be dangerous. We cannot prepare ourselves; we have known nothing of the kind.

But some days I think: I should prepare, I should do only what is difficult. I think: I will teach myself to use a gun. I hide behind the curtain, and when the mailman comes I try to imagine his right temple in the gunsight as he goes down the sidewalk. How sure one must be to pull the trigger, even to kill for one's own children, for their food, their water, perhaps even poison. The imagination is of no use.

The imagination is of no use. When I run two miles a day, I make myself run faster, farther, make myself feel nauseated, make myself go on despite my burning ribs. In case this one day will be a helpful memory, a useful sensation. Of endurance and of pain. My daughter comes and asks my help in making clay animals. On days like this, I want to say: no, no clay animals, we'll dig, we'll practice digging, once your father was a soldier, he will teach you to use a gun. But of course I cannot do this; I cannot pervert her life so that she will be ready for the disaster. There is no readiness; there is no death in life.

My baby son is crying. Will it be harder for males or females? Will they capture boy children to wander in roving gangs? Will my son, asleep now in his crib, wander the abashed landscape, killing other boys for garbage? Will my daughter root among the grain stalks, glistening with danger, for the one kernel of safe nourishment? Ought I to train them for capitulation? I croon to him; I rock him, watch the gold sun strike a maple, turn it golder. My daughter comes into the room, still in her long nightgown. Half an hour ago, I left her to dress herself. She hasn't succeeded; she's used the time to play with my lipstick. It is all over her face, her hands, her arms. Inside her belly is another tiny belly, empty. Will she have the chance to fill herself with a child, as I have filled myself with her and with her brother? On days like this I worry: if she can't dress herself in half an hour, if she cannot obey me in an instant, like the crack of a whip, will she perish? She can charm anyone. Will there be a place for charm after the disaster? What will be its face?

When the babysitter comes, I get into my car. She can make my daughter obey in an instant; she can put my son to sleep without rocking him, or feeding him, or patting him in his crib. On days like this I think I should leave them to her and never come back, for I will probably not survive and with her they will have a greater chance of surviving.

To calm myself I read poetry. When it comes, will the words of "To His Coy Mistress" comfort me, distract me as I wait to hear the news of the death of everything? I want to memorize long poems in case we must spend months in hiding underground. I will memorize "Lycidas," although I don't like Milton. I will memorize it because of what Virginia Woolf said: "Milton is a comfort because he is nothing like our life." At that moment, when we are waiting for the news of utter death, what we will need is something that is nothing like our life.

I come home, and begin making dinner. I have purposely bought a tough cut of meat; I will simmer it for hours. As if that were an experience that would be helpful; as if that were the nature of it: afterward only tough cuts of meat. I pretend I am cooking on a paraffin stove in a basement. But I cannot restrain myself from using herbs; my own weakness makes me weep. When it comes, there will be no herbs, or spices, no beautiful vegetables like the vegetables that sit on my table in a wooden bowl: an eggplant, yellow squash, tomatoes, a red pepper, and some leeks. The solid innocence of my vegetables! When it comes, there will be no innocence. When it comes, there will be no safety. Even the roots hidden deep in the earth of forests will be the food of danger. There will be nothing whose history will be dear. I could weep for my furniture. The earth will be abashed; the furniture will stand out, balked and shameful in the ruin of everything that was our lives.

We have invited friends to dinner. My friend and I talk about our children. I think of her after the disaster; I try to imagine how she will look. I see her standing with a knife; her legs are knotted and blue veins stick out of them like bruised grapes. She is wearing a filthy shirt; her front teeth are missing; her thick black hair is falling out. I will have to kill her to keep her from entering our shelter. If she enters it she will kill us with her knife or the broken glass in her pocket. Kill us for the food we hide which may, even as we take it in, be killing us. Kill us for the life of her own children.

We are sitting on the floor. I want to turn to my friend and say: I do not want to have to kill you. But they have not had my imagination of disaster, and there can be no death in the midst of life. We talk about the autumn; this year we'll walk more in the country, we agree. We kiss our friends good night. Good night, good night, we say, we love you. Good night, I think, I pray I do not have to kill you for my children's food.

My husband puts on red pajamas. I do not speak of my imagination of disaster. He takes my nightgown off and I see us embracing in the full-length mirror. We are, for now, human, beautiful. We go to bed. He swims above me, digging in. I climb and meet him, strike and fall away. Because we have done this, two more of us breathe in the next room, bathed and perfect as arithmetic.

I think: Perhaps I should kill us all now and save us from the degradation of disaster. Perhaps I should kill us while we are whole and dignified and full of our sane beauty. I do not want to be one of the survivors; I am willing to die with my civilization. I have said to my husband: Let us put aside some pills, so that when the disaster strikes we may lie down together, holding each other's hands and die before the whole earth is abashed. But no, he says, I will not let you do that, we must fight. Someone will survive, he says, why not us? Why not our children?

Because the earth will be abashed, I tell him. Because our furniture will stand out shamed among the glistening poisoned objects. Because we cannot imagine it; because imagination is inadequate; because for this disaster, there is no imagination.

But because of this I may be wrong. We live with death, the stone in the belly, the terror on the road alone. People have lived with it always. But we live knowing not only that we will die, that we may suffer, but that all that we hold dear will finish; that there will be no more familiar. That the death we fear we cannot even imagine, it will not be the distinguished thing, it will not be the face of dream, or even nightmare. For we cannot dream the poisoned earth abashed, empty of all we know.

Out of the Fray

She looked out of the window of a plane with pleasure for the first time in her life. The land gave way to water, and there was a minute when it was not possible to say where it left off and air began. The word *ozone* came to her mind, that comforting and fleshless territory where the mere act of breathing was a joy and every issue grew abstract. Now she could feel this, Ruth knew that she had changed her life.

Always before when any plane she flew on became airborne, she'd searched around for the stranger she would choose to die with. As a young woman, she'd picked people whose faces or clothes or postures indicated they would face death interestingly, or flippantly, or with some wit. After she had children, she looked for someone who seemed as if he would keep his head—if the children were with her, she'd want the practical help of such a person; if she were alone she'd want to go over the details of her life insurance and discuss the prospects of half-orphans finding psychological wholeness in maturity. But now she was with Phil, and they were on their way to London. It was a business trip for him; he worked for a human rights organization whose headquarters was in London, and he suggested Ruth come along: it would be, he said, their last vacation before marriage. Soon he would be her husband. She remembered that when she was with her first husband, she'd still searched planes, and that memory made her squeeze Phil's arm, guilty that these stray pieces of information could so reassure her, that she needed reassurance. But it was an odd decision that they'd made, to marry. It struck everyone they knew as at best unnecessary, and it made them feel apart from other people. Like orphan children in a foreign country they'd become solicitous, protective, unnaturally alert. Phil felt something more, though, he was almost childishly proud of their decision, as if it were an original, brave idea. For the last month, he'd taken her to meet people he'd known in grammar school or worked with for six months in college. She felt it made the people cynical and bored, and she didn't blame them; he'd been married twice before and left a woman he had lived with. It would be for her a second marriage, and she had been reluctant to agree.

"How," she said, refusing him at first, "how can we do it, knowing what we know?"

"But what about the kids?" he'd said. "How can they go around saying 'that guy my mother lives with'?"

"You like 'my stepfather'?"

"I do," he'd said. "It sounds like something you can count on."

And she had wanted that, that the children could count on him, somehow, even if he and she broke up. If they were married, she could name him in her will as the person to have custody in case both she and her ex-husband died. She had quite amicable relations with her children's father; still, she felt it would be odd to get him to agree to naming her paramour as the person in charge of their children's fate. If she could say "my husband" to her former husband, she could put the idea to him in language that had dignity and weight. It was important to her, this relation between language and the facts that it encircled. She was a science writer. She'd wanted to be a scientist herself; genetics was the field she had chosen. But quickly she learned that she lacked the kind of imagination that real scientific distinction called up; what she was good at was taking the findings—often brilliant, often crucial—of men and women who could not communicate what they had found, and making of them something articulate and shapely and still true. And so it bothered her that, in marrying, she was making a promise she couldn't keep. She felt like a child crossing her fingers behind her back: she felt it for both herself and Phil. When she thought of their marrying, she saw them as children, standing before a judge, their fingers crossed behind their backs, saying, "I promise I will never leave you." When what they meant was, "I will try."

Before they left for London, Phil had himself measured for a custom-tailored suit. My wedding suit, he'd called it. And he gave the children a hundred dollars each to buy new clothing for the wedding. Elena was fourteen; she was delighted with the prospect of new clothes. But Jacob was eleven; he told Phil he'd just broken his Walkman and asked if he couldn't use the hundred dollars for a new one instead. Phil never got angry with the children, but Jacob could see that he had hurt him and pretended he'd said what he said as a joke. When Phil pretended to believe him, Ruth felt herself fill with a surprising love that made the walls of her heart, which was a muscle after all, feel thin and stretched like a balloon filled up with water. She remembered thinking of heavy water, water with an extra molecule, made only artificially and never to be put in contact with living things. You could poison plants by watering them with heavy water; it could be dangerous if drunk.

Was Philip dangerous? She couldn't understand how a man so lovable, so tactful, and so generous of heart had left three women. It was an odd position she was in in her relation to his past. She didn't want to seem merely inquisitive, although there was an element of gossip in her desire to know the details of her predecessors. But there was more: there was something much worse. What she really wanted was to have him paint pictures so unflattering that they were little murders: then she could bury the mutilated carcasses herself and never fear. But she knew the way of it, everyone did: people began, in great hope, love affairs, and then things soured and went bad. And so she and Phil spoke remarkably little about the women in his life, and his friends had been more than reticent. After three disasters, she suspected they had lost the energy for one more round of reassurances: she was infinitely better than the others, they could see that now for the first time Phil was really happy, they were glad she was around.

They were driving through London in a taxi, the exciting route past Marble Arch. The massive green of Hyde Park, the enlivened whiteness of the buildings made Ruth feel daring. "We're really here," she said to Phil. "We've made it."

"We always make it, darling," he said. "And we always will."

She kissed him on the mouth so that he would not feel her doubting.

"Tell me again how you met Sylvie," she said. They were on their way to visit Sylvie MacGregor, who was divorced from Jack MacGregor, Phil's oldest friend.

"It must have been, what, I guess 1965. Jack and I had just come from the San Gennaro Festival. I'd won two prizes, throwing rubber balls and knocking over ducks or one of those games. I'd won a bottle of wine and a breakaway cane. For some reason we decided to drive up to Tanglewood. Well, I know why we did it, we were trying to pick up girls. Tanglewood is a terrific place to pick up girls. So I was walking with this cane. And when Sylvie saw me, she said I must be tired, did I want to sit on her blanket with her and her friend. I pretended to be a cripple for the whole day—I didn't want to embarrass her. It's no wonder she chose Jack instead of me.

"Three months after that she'd married Jack; Jack and I were both working for Lindsay then. In the fall of 1967, Jack went across the country with the McCarthy campaign, and late the following January he told Sylvie he'd met someone else and was leaving. Sylvie tried to kill herself. She called me just in time. I went with her to Roosevelt Hospital in the ambulance and let her come back to my apartment. It was just after my first divorce."

Ruth imagined that apartment, ugly in the willed, self-punishing style of the abodes of men who have left women. But, he told her, Sylvie brought it around wonderfully. She made him meet her at furniture stores, look carefully at swatches of fabric. She arranged for everything: the curtains, the deliveries. "But she didn't go too far," he said. "She never made me feel she was taking over, she made me feel it was my place."

"And were you lovers?"

"No. One night I suggested it, and she said, 'That's not the kind of thing I want.' I was actually a little relieved. She'd be quite something to take on: all that devotion. One of the reasons she was so devastated by Jack is that she'd given him everything, she'd had no reserve.

"She really fell apart," said Phil, "and people were ridiculous about it. They thought she was exaggerating. You know, that was the time everyone was leaving everyone. But only Sylvie got suicidal. And then she made this terrible decision: to grow old. All our friends were wearing long skirts or tight jeans, and she began wearing tweeds and cashmeres, putting her hair in a chignon. She couldn't stay in New York, it was no place for her, nobody understanding her, and her always being afraid of running into Jack or the new woman. She's Belgian, but she didn't want to go back. So she decided on London.

"I remember the night she left. I took her to the airport. We were three hours early—you know how I am—so we had too many drinks, which she said she wanted; she wanted to sleep the flight through. But when she landed in Heathrow, she got the news: Bobby Kennedy had been shot. She got hysterical in the airport; when you meet her you'll see how extraordinary that must have been. It was as if someone had taken her marriage to Jack, which she'd decently buried, dug it up and hacked it to pieces publicly. She phoned me, really out of control. I told her to come right back and stay with me. But she said she wouldn't. 'I just wanted to hear a friendly voice,' she said, 'And now I must get started.'"

"And she did," said Ruth, "she did get started."

"In a way, yes, of course she did. She got a flat in Clapham and had a small piano moved in. Three days a week she took lessons—she'd never touched the instrument in her life before—with some terribly hard-up young student at the conservatory. Then he got married and went to Sweden, and she began taking lessons with Miss Taub.

"You'll meet Miss Taub, no doubt," Phil said. "She must be seventy if she's a day. She and Sylvie became best friends almost immediately, and she took Sylvie into her circle, although Sylvie's the youngest of the group by twenty years. And she has this job, she runs some sort of institute for the blind. So she's become a kind of fixture on the South Bank, this beautiful, rather remote woman, taking old women and blind people to concerts. You'll see, we'll have at least one night with Miss Taub, and possibly a blind person. I never know what to do with those occasions."

"Why?"

"Well, I always feel that my physical health and whatever youth I have is a kind of affront to them. Besides, I'm always afraid I'm going to step on the guide dog's tail and start him howling in the middle of something pianissimo."

"Phil, guide dogs don't howl. They're used to people stepping on their tails."

"It would be just my luck to get one that's hypersensitive."

They drove out of the impressive part of London; just into Clapham it was easy to imagine people living ordinary lives, taking their shoes to the shoemaker's, getting quick meals from Indian takeouts, going to movies because they were too tired to read. Ruth wondered what Sylvie had looked like when Phil had first known her. She remembered the first thing Phil had told her about Sylvie, something her ex-husband had said, that she had always wanted to be an old woman, and she'd turned herself into one so she could have the life she wanted. Ruth had been puzzled by Phil's tone in telling her: he'd sounded angry. She had assumed that he was angry for the whole estate of men: in refusing to fight against aging, in embracing it prematurely, Sylvie was taking herself out of the game. "I won't play," she'd said, and left the other players feeling foolish. Yet Phil considered her one of his dearest friends.

"You know," he said as they approached her street, "you can ask Sylvie anything about me."

Ruth didn't say what she was thinking, that the problem was that she knew too much about Phil already, that the only real information she wanted was impossible to get: she didn't want more history, she wanted guarantees. "You will be happy now," she wanted someone to say, "I promise." Perhaps that was what she'd wanted from Sylvie, but her first glance as Sylvie opened the door told her she wouldn't get it. Sylvie had taken pains to show that her allegiance was with a past which was more real, more vivid to her, than the thin present in which she felt herself required now to live.

Her flat was based on the idea of home of single women who had come to London from the Continent after the war. Modestly, wisely, they had bought the first luxuries available in the early fifties; as if they didn't want to seem too brash they concentrated on light browns and cream colors. Accents of gold might show themselves from time to time—some braid on a throw pillow, a detail of a tapestried chair. Pale green lamps threw their genteel and muted lights on objects neutral as shells. Only occasionally a porcelain box, a cigarette case, a small dish for nuts or candy would cry out that it was un-English and suggest some difficult, exciting European life that had been left for good.

At first Ruth thought that Sylvie had chosen her clothing along the same lines, and as a kind of camouflage to beauty. But then she looked more closely and saw that those careful clothes—the dun-colored blouse, the olive green loose skirt, the beige shoes with a thin chain on the instep—represented Sylvie's real understanding of the nature of her beauty. Ruth wondered if, like a tall woman who wears high heels, Sylvie underscored her unfashionableness to turn it into an asset. She was, after all, nearly fifty, and by choosing to dress older than she was, there was no need for her to acknowledge that she was no longer young. Ruth felt arriviste in her red flowered skirt, blue shirt, jade beads, an outfit she'd been pleased with in the hotel mirror.

Sylvie offered them drinks and brought out little plates of sandwiches. She disappeared again and again into the kitchen, bringing out dishes of odd, Germanic foods: pickled or salted, all desirable because they looked distinctly unnutritious. She seated herself across from Ruth, her spine an inch or two away from the chair back, and said, "Now you must tell me all about your children." But Ruth grew tongue-tied; her children seemed out of place in the flat. You wouldn't like them, Ruth thought, catching Sylvie's bright and overeager eye. You'd think them spoiled and greedy and uneducated.

"It's so hard to describe one's children," she said, defeatedly. "One never knows if one's being at all realistic."

"Anything you said about them would sound like bragging," Phil said. "Only it would be the truth."

"How enchanting," Sylvie said. "Phil's a born father, Ruth, don't you think?"

"None of the potential mothers seemed to think so," Phil said. "I was game."

The personal tone seemed almost obscene to Ruth among the artifacts of Sylvie's flat; she blushed for Phil's misjudgment. But Sylvie went on to talk about the other wives, the other women, as if it were the most natural thing in the world. The conversation led naturally to people they had known, and Ruth could see Sylvie straining not to talk about old times, times Ruth had not been a part of, but her efforts to update their talk made Ruth feel childish, as if the grown-ups had kindly taken the time to ask her how she liked her school. She'd been through this before, meeting Phil's friends, but it was different with Sylvie. The smooth surface of Sylvie's life, her presentation of herself, left no foothold for Ruth. She jumped up eagerly when Phil said they must leave for dinner; then she felt her action made her appear greedy, and she told Phil to sit down again, they needn't rush. But Sylvie arose then, slowly, as if she were walking out of the ocean, and said, "No, let's go now. It's horrible to be late, don't you think so, Ruth?"

"No, Ruth is unable to be on time," said Phil. "If she happens to be early, she'll do something—wallpaper the bathroom or begin to learn to play the flute—anything to avoid the terrible fate of being on time."

"How extraordinary, Phil, and you so anxious always about lateness," Sylvie said. "This must be love at last."

They walked into the street wrapped in a garment of bonhomie that Phil, Ruth saw, believed was genuine and beautiful and that to her was a hair shirt.

Phil had been right; Sylvie had made arrangements for them first to have dinner, then to go to the Schubert lieder in the Purcell room with Miss Taub. One of the people from the Institute for the Unsighted had been asked but, Sylvie explained, at the last moment she had got the flu.

"Ah, here's Miss Taub," said Sylvie when they approached the restaurant. "She makes rather a fetish of being early, but through the years I've managed to indulge her when I can. Tonight she's had to wait."

Miss Taub kissed Phil and gave her hand to Ruth. It was appropriate, of course; she'd known Phil, and it was her first meeting with Ruth. Of course, it was appropriate, but it was one more brushstroke, Ruth felt, in the group portrait: the two older women, eminently civilized, being courted safely, tenderly by Phil, and Ruth apart, spread out and representing Nature. Sylvie floundered visibly in trying to keep the conversation nonexclusionary, entertaining, smooth. Then, all at once, she gave Ruth a look of pure unhappiness. "See, I am drowning," the look said, "and it is your fault." At once Ruth saw that she had been impossible. The pain in Sylvie's eyes was genuine. Its disproportion drew out the maternal side of Ruth: she would not let this woman, who had so clearly suffered, suffer more. She sat up straight, then leaned her elbows on the table. She talked about her children and asked Miss Taub's advice about their music lessons. Phil turned on Ruth his look of bliss. She knew that they had triumphed, but the triumph had been brought about by Sylvie, who had let herself appear, to this unpleasant stranger, intimately weak.

"*Bonne chance,*" Miss Taub said, as they put her in a taxi. "I know we will meet again."

And Ruth hung on her lover's arm, because the words seemed like a blessing and a talisman, and in her gratitude for them she felt suddenly weak as if she could, without Phil's arm, fall down or faint.

Sylvie had invited them to lunch Saturday at her flat, but she phoned in the morning to ask if she could take them, instead, to a restaurant near her office. The institute librarian, she explained, was sick, and many of the members could use the library only on Saturdays. She could leave one of the members in charge while they lunched, but they could not be leisurely, she said, not half so leisurely as they'd have liked.

Phil had a meeting in the morning; he told Ruth that he would meet her at the institute at one o'clock. But when Ruth arrived, Sylvie told her Phil had telephoned; the meeting would be indefinitely long, and they would have to lunch without him.

Ruth looked around her in a kind of panic. The blind people walked around the room, so even-paced and so sagacious she could have gone down on her knees. And Sylvie walked slowly, certainly, among them, touching some of them on the shoulder, saying their names, as a queen might walk among her castle staff. She introduced Ruth to the man who would sit at the desk while they lunched.

"How lucky you are to have our Sylvie to lunch," he said, his smile courtly beneath his merely damaged gaze.

"Yes, I'm only sorry my friend is tied up and can't join us," Ruth said, then felt she'd been tactless. "I mean, it's terrible that on a day like this he has to work."

"Your friend?" laughed Sylvie. "Your fiancé, you mean. They will be married, Ted, within two weeks."

"Taking your honeymoon before," he said, but he could not sound worldly. Ruth smiled, then realized he couldn't see her, so she laughed too loudly. Some people sitting at the tables looked toward her with the self-righteous stares of interrupted readers. That the stares were sightless was irrelevant, the censure was the same, and Ruth apologized to Sylvie and to the man Ted, whom she had wanted to praise by her laughter.

"Not at all," he said. "There's nothing worse than a library prig."

"Take your time," he said to Sylvie, who said she would. But when she got outside, she said to Ruth, "Ted's such a dear, and wonderfully intelligent, but if a crowd should gather at the desk, he simply couldn't cope."

As they walked, Ruth wondered if Sylvie suspected, as she did, that

Phil had invented his overlong meeting so that the two women could be alone. For herself, she felt he had erred badly; the small ease she had gained with Sylvie at dinner days before had vanished. She felt, as they walked, that she followed in Sylvie's majestic wake, an undistinguished tug behind a schooner.

After they had ordered, Sylvie asked her about her work, apologizing for her ignorance in science. Then, without transition she said, "Have you ever met my husband, Jack MacGregor? Phil still sees him, I believe."

"Yes, but he lives in California, and I haven't met him yet."

Ruth was shocked by Sylvie's question and embarrassed to hear her call Jack "my husband." They had been divorced seventeen years; Jack had teenage children by the woman he'd left her for.

"We never write, it's such a shame. We've quite lost touch. I'm utterly dependent upon Phil for news of him. Strange, isn't it? You'd think that one would keep in touch with someone so important in one's past. It's lucky I have Phil, or Jack could die without my knowing."

Sylvie patted the corners of her mouth with her stiff napkin, then folded her hands as if to say, "What is it exactly that you want to know?" Ruth tried to read the beautiful, pale face, but it was blank and formal. A poker face, Ruth thought, and then realized at once how it was between them. She sat across from Sylvie like an inexperienced player before a seasoned gambler. Sylvie had, Ruth saw now, the professional's immaculate composure. The formality of every gesture was a weapon and a code. Concealment was the métier, the game untitled and the stakes unnamed. The purpose of the game itself became known only gradually. It was to get the green player to reveal her hand. Then the professional, seemingly prepared to throw down everything, would discard, in fact, only selected single cards—the obvious, the garish pictures—which could distract the green player from the game's real feat: everything valued or thought important had been kept back.

Ruth felt herself dig in, take root, grow obdurately stable. She asked Sylvie about Belgium, her childhood, her emigration to America. It seemed to Ruth that Sylvie quite purposefully drained all these topics of interest in order to return the conversation to its natural center: Phil. But Ruth knew that she could resist, for lunch was not meant to go on too long. They were both grateful to leave each other. When they parted, they did not kiss.

Ruth watched Sylvie walk down the street, unhurried and assured.

And yet her back was angry, and she thrust her neck a shade uncomfortably forward as she walked. Phil well might say that she was happy, but watching her progress, Ruth saw the effort and the cost. She understood that Sylvie's life had been finished when Jack left her; she walked now as one dead. A blow that others might recover from, she never would; the damage that was temporary for some had been for Sylvie quite final. And the recovery of others, somehow, made it worse. It put everyone into a falsifying light, for if Sylvie's response was just, then others were deficient; if they were sane and sensible, then her life was a waste.

She walked around the squares of Bloomsbury feeling for no reason that she must kill time. The chestnuts held their flowers jealously, like precious candelabras that had been in the family for years. Some roses were beginning, others would be over in a day. The image of Phil's body kept floating before her eyes, and then parts of his body only: the torso, the back, the legs. She began running to the hotel, terrified that when she got there the room would be empty. It was not. She found Phil on the bed, reading a six-week-old copy of the *New Statesman;* others were spread out on the floor around the bed. He was touched and gladdened by her eagerness, though she suspected he mistook its causes and believed Sylvie had eased her mind about his past.

They would spend their last evening with Sylvie. Phil apologized when he told Ruth, but it seemed to be the only night Sylvie was free, and they had a piece of luck: they could get tickets for *Antony and Cleopatra.* "Fine," Ruth said. "Really, that's wonderful." She was thinking that she wanted to be home with her children. Their presence was a forced balance to her always. If they were here, she thought, the figure of Sylvie might not have loomed so menacingly, so symbolically; with the children along, she felt she might have been less cruel.

"I've always liked the character of Enobarbus," Phil said, after the play as they drank gin on Sylvie's settee. "I'd like to have seen him played by Ray Bolger."

They made up their ideal cast of *Antony and Cleopatra,* and the time went pleasingly and fast. But Ruth could sense behind it all, like a perfume at once menacing and seductive, Sylvie's dread that they would leave. She kept thinking up little strategems so they would linger: she wrote down things she'd love for them to send her from New York; she asked questions about the children to which she already knew the answers. She kept offering them different foods, and when they refused, running into the kitchen to see what else she had to offer. But in the air there began to arise another scent: the thin, high one that was merely Phil's anxiety about packing, about missing planes. Both women knew that was the scent that must be followed, and they rose at once.

"Next time I see you, you will be married," said Sylvie, holding Ruth's hands. "I wish you every happiness," she said, handing them a gift. It was a miniature of a woman, blonde and blue-eyed, in a low-cut yellow dress. "It is from my family."

Phil had tears in his eyes as he thanked Sylvie, but Ruth could only wonder what gift Sylvie had given the other women as they parted. Were they all treasures from her family? Had Phil taken them with him when he left the women? Were they even now in his apartment, in his office, objects that she hadn't questioned, that he'd got in just this way?

"Things change, my friend, but we are constant," Sylvie said, as she kissed Phil goodbye.

She smiled at Ruth as she looked over Phil's shoulder, and Ruth felt herself forced to return the smile in kind.

She sat in a chair across the room and watched Phil as he slept. Usually she was a sounder sleeper than anyone she slept with. She wondered whether any man had watched her as she watched Phil now; she could not imagine it.

The light that came from the streetlights made the room seem unchangeable: an object in history, a work of art. Phil's back was to her, and his posture made him boyish. The fine shoulders were the shoulders of a boy, the few dark hairs made a pattern she wanted to follow with her lips. She could not bear anymore to be merely looking, and she wondered if she lay against him if she would wake him up. She decided to take the chance; he seemed deeply asleep. She took her nightgown off because she wanted to feel the softness of her breasts against the hard curve of his back. He did not waken. She moved away, back to the chair. She wanted to be watching him again.

She understood that if he left her it would be like death and wondered when it happened how she would go on.

The Other Woman

She was lying in the spare room in the single bed at three in the morning. It was hot, and her sense of moral failure made her head go queer. She was not asleep, and yet you would have to say she was dreaming. Images behind her eyes buzzed and skipped as in a nightmare.

Two hours before, she had been lying in bed next to her husband. They were reading; sometimes her husband's hand would fondle her belly or scratch her thigh. He would read her a sentence from a book about England; she would look up from her magazine. They would read each other sentences; they would say, "You should read this."

She was reading a story about an adulterous affair. The woman had been left by her lover (who adored her), who went back to his wife. It was the sight of his children's hands as they slept, he had said, that made his decision for him. He loved the woman; he would go back to his wife. Because of the hands of his children as they slept.

She lay back, her arms behind her head, looking at her naked breasts and the curve of her waist. What does this body mean to me? she wondered, and ran her palms along the high bones of her pelvis. How peculiar it was, she thought, looking at her husband, that her body had the power to excite him, to make him lay down his book and turn to her, cupping her buttocks in his hands, wanting her like that. Her sense of the oddness of it all made her distant from him, but she began to feel his desire soothe her; it became a dwelling she could rest inside, and she thought as she met his desire with her own familiar body, How easy it is to be faithful! For it was not his body that excited her (it had never been men's bodies that had excited her), but the idea of him, of all that he was and was to her, that made her rise to meet him, desire for desire. It was the oddness of it all, and the familiarity.

He always became invigorated after sex, with a pure, inappropriate energy. She drew the quilt around her bare shoulders and settled down in the bed. It was sleep she wanted, sleep to flow over her. But she could see the muscles of his back twitching with impatience, like a horse's flanks sucking in and out. The magazine was still on the bed, and she threw it benevolently in his direction. "Read that story," she said. "You'll like it." And she brought the covers over her head so that she could be in darkness. She was content. He was engaged; she had earned the delicious feeling of cool sheets around her shoulders, of roundness, of being what we so rarely feel ourselves to be—in exactly the right place, doing what it is we are meant to do at that moment. The air conditioner hummed soothingly nearby; it was possible to sleep.

She became aware of the peculiar sensation that occurs when the interface between a dream and the world is violated. In her dream she was in a car, driving; outside the dream the bed was shaking with awkward, uneven spasms. She woke in a resentful confusion.

The sight she saw was the one that to her, even in a state of full wakefulness, was most finally disturbing. Her husband was weeping. He was a strong man, even in the obvious senses, and she depended on that. The strength of his body and its predictability were a center for her more random life.

In the years she had known him, he had been sick twice; he had wept four times. She remembered these incidents distinctly. When he wept, his weeping was torn out of his body. She could weep and be engaged in other activities; she could walk and weep or weep and pack a suitcase. But when he wept, his entire body was taken up with it, so that he needed her for physical support.

She sat up quickly and was annoyed by her breasts, bobbing so foolishly, so irrelevantly, as she moved to put her arms around him for comfort only. This now was the function of her body, and the other, earlier one, the one she was reminded of by her breasts, vexed her; it seemed peculiar that she had the same body for comfort as for excitement. It was as though she were divided in some final, harmful way.

She put her arms around him and put his head against her breast. She began to swim up past sleep and became aware that she did not know the reason for his weeping. She stroked his hair and spoke so quietly that her own voice was unfamiliar to her. But her words were coos and nonsense syllables—ancient language she had learned somewhere, in some life. For the moment, she did not want to ask him anything; she did not want to use her language for that.

She looked at his face and wiped his eyes with the sleeve of the nightgown that she had taken from under her pillow. She had never seen anyone look as he did—it was a look of such pure grief, a look of no extraneous emotions. His face looked ancient, as though it bespoke a great sorrow that had not spent itself in mourning. It was the face of a mother holding a dead child, of a wife whose husband has been drowned. One expected such a look from women, but this—this was her husband, a man, and that made it more terrible.

His sobs had stopped and he lay with his head against her in silence.

"My darling," she said. "What is it?"

"The story," he said.

"The story?"

She was surprised, for it was she who lived in stories and he who lived in the world.

"It was when the children were babies," he said. His children both were in their teens now, but still his children, and her husband's love for them, she had come to understand, was the deepest thing in his life. You could not say that it was a love that could come between him and her, because his love for her was outside that center of him, the center that was his love for his children. She had borne no children, and so she had no place in that center. It was as if he and his children stood somewhere at the bottom of a well, in a spot so dark, down so far, that she could not see it. It was not like his past, his divorce, which was another kind of darkness to her, because this with his children continued into her life, into all their lives. But it was a darkness she could live with, for they were children and she was a woman. That difference, she had come to understand, made it all right.

"It was when the children were babies," he said. "There was a woman. I never told you about her." And he began to weep again.

The area under her breast grew cold and stony. She wondered how he could leave his head there.

"I had never loved anyone so much," he said. "She was going to leave her family. We were going to go away. I had never loved anyone so much. I hated my wife; all that was nothing. And then I looked at the children, and I knew that nothing on earth could make me leave them."

"And the woman?" she said, almost sick with the effort it took her to go on holding him.

"She went back to her husband. That was the terrible part—how I failed her. I had never loved anyone so much."

He wanted her to weep with him, to sympathize, for her flesh to warm with his sorrow; and all she could think was, Why must you tell me this? You must not tell me this. How can you expect me to comfort you for this?

Suddenly he sighed, a great sigh, the release of a burden. "It was a very long time ago," he said, exhausted, and he wept sleepily against her. But her body was tense with effort. She was his wife, and a wife must do this, must hold her husband in sleep and keep him from his sorrow.

But the idea of hurting him came to her mind like the thought of a delicious confection. She wanted to push him away from her, to let him lie there in the dark, wanting her, in shame, in need. She wanted to say, How you have hurt me! But she held him in her arms and stroked his head until she heard his gentle breathing. Once he was asleep, she could no longer endure the touch of his skin on her skin.

She put on her nightgown and went into the other room. She did not want to open the window for fear of waking him, so she lay in the hot, dusty air, conscious of sweat beginning to form arcs under her breasts. And she thought of her husband, who had loved a woman so much that after all these years her loss was his deepest sorrow. He would never weep like that for her. Often she had imagined her husband's response to her death. And she had always seen him accepting it as a part of their lives, going on, his mourning taking a practical turn. He would think of her, perhaps, in the garden.

For she had been his wife, and their love had known no obstacles. They had met, loved, been free to marry. Their love was even, sweet, and temperate, like milk in a brown bowl on a shelf in a fragrant pantry. But, it seemed to her now, such a love might be too mild—toothless, without the edge of frustration to eat its way into his life. Like the other. And so he would never love her so much, so much as he had loved the other woman. Even when she died he would not mourn her so deeply. He could not, for their love had been born of ease and was happy. His love for the other woman had been born of sorrow, and so he would never love her so much as he had loved the other woman.

And how could he ask her for comfort? The coldness under her breast grew until her body was entirely filled with it. And through her mind, in anger, in exhaustion, beeped two sentences: He will never love me so much. How can he ask me for comfort?

She lay on top of the spread, stretching her limbs out as far away from her body as she could. Her sex was open—utterly vulnerable, she thought.

She began to fall into a sleep that was harsh, like rusted wires.

She heard the door open. Her husband came into the room, and even in the dark she could see that he was frightened; she could smell his fear in the darkness. But his fear did not move her; inside her were the cold light and the words that buzzed and skipped: He will never love me so much. How can he ask me for comfort?

"I had a terrible dream," he said. He was sweating. She did not tell him to continue, but he lay down beside her and said, "They were in a car. The children and the other woman. The car exploded. I woke up weeping. You weren't there."

"I was restless," she said. "I didn't want to wake you."

She wanted to get up and walk away from him—anywhere, outside into the air. But she stroked his hair and said in a voice that was thick with effort, "Come here. It was only a dream."

She thought surely he would discern the strain in her voice, in her hands. And she was torn between the desire for him to know what he had done to her and the desire to keep it from him, to absorb his sorrow into herself. But since she was a woman, her body had been bred to deceit.

How easy it was for her, quite mechanically, with no connection to herself, to soothe her husband, to be a comfort to him. And he settled into her false comfort, pressing against her body for relief. She knew that he would never know what she was feeling, and knowing this, she had never loved him so little.

Billy

I wasn't home when the call came saying that Billy had died. The woman left the message with my son. Extraordinary, really, to leave such a message with a boy, a ten-year-old. "Just tell your mother Bill McGovern died. I'm his landlady. We found her number in his room, it was the only one we found there. But there's nothing that she needs to do. We buried him already. Just to let her know." She said that Billy had become a hermit in his room. She told my son that they'd kept asking him to come downstairs, for holidays and things, but he'd always say no. "Just send me up a plate," he'd say.

My son reported all this flatly; he is the serious one of the three, the youngest; it was unfortunate the woman got him. He would worry. Worry that someone he never heard of died with his mother's phone number in his room. He is a modern child, the son of modern, divorced parents; he would imagine Billy was my lover. And so I wanted to tell him about Billy, to relieve him, for it would be awful for a boy like him to think of a dead person as his mother's lover. But I didn't know where to begin the story. Or how to tell it once I'd started. To make a story of a life, you had to shape it, and there was no shape to Billy's life, that was the problem. I thanked my son and sent him to his room to join his brothers.

I'd known Billy all my life. His mother was my mother's best friend. I loved Veronica McGovern. She brought into my childhood books, classical records, prints of the old masters, and a hint that there was somewhere a world—which she had once inhabited and now only imagined—where people had intelligent conversations in low, untroubled voices, where no one ever worked too hard or got too tired. She flipped the switch of my imagination, lighting up those rooms that are a refuge from the anger and miscomprehension of the adult world. She saved me from the isolated fate of the bright, undervalued child. She spared me years of bitterness. But she ruined her son's life as certainly as if she'd starved him in infancy; he would probably have been much better off if she'd abandoned him at birth.

Veronica had always lied about her age; she was eleven years older than my mother, though we never knew it till her death. She'd married at eighteen and had Billy a year later; my mother had had me at thirty-one. So although Billy and I were technically in the same generation, he was twenty-two when I was born. I thought him handsome when I was growing up; some nights he didn't come home and Veronica wrung her hands and mentioned the name Roberta. It was such a serviceable name and yet the woman cast so lurid a glow. She lived in the Village; she was a dancer; when Billy was with her he didn't come home. I had no idea what Billy and Roberta did the nights that he was with her; I had no idea that it was *what* they did that caused Veronica's distress; I was young enough simply to see not sleeping in one's own bed as an emblem of danger.

Billy would come home after these nights at around lunchtime; my mother and I would be sitting at Veronica's kitchen table and at the sight of him we would fall silent. He shimmered with the glow of sex, though at the time I wouldn't have known to call it that. There was always a beat of silence when we saw him in the doorway, like the silence between merry-go-round tunes. Then he would say, "Hello, Mother." Veronica would light a Herbert Tareyton cigarette and tell him to bring a chair from his room. There were only three chairs in the kitchen, a setup left over from the days when Charlie McGovern, Veronica's husband, Billy's father, who died when I was nine, was still alive.

I'd grown up on tales of Charlie McGovern's binges and disappearances, and Billy had been pointed to as an example of what can happen when a single mother spoiled a child. My father disappeared when I was two; it was handy for my mother to have so ready an example. "Spoiled." It is a terrible word, suggesting meat gone iridescent, but in Billy's case, it has always seemed apt. My mother explained that Veronica had never said no to Billy. Life with Charlie devastated her and she wanted to keep Billy by her side. In return for his loyalty she indulged him and convinced him that the world was too gross to value him correctly; in time, he believed it an unfit place for him to walk in as a man.

I only knew Charlie McGovern as a drunk, but in the twenties he had been a millionaire. To a child in the early fifties, the twenties were like the fall of Rome, something much too distant to think of concretely or even to believe in. Had Veronica McGovern been a flapper? Impossible to connect that sweet, wounded, muted, and above all genteel creature with the Jazz Age, but when she spoke about the early days of her marriage, it was all bathtub gin and the Black Bottom and rides in rumble seats and staying up till dawn. She mentioned that Charlie always bought her perfumed cigarettes and stockings with her name embroidered just at the top. Hearing about those stockings caused a river of electric joy to run through every nerve in my six-, seven-, eight-year-old body; it was one of those pieces of information children instantly know to be crucial, some essential clue to the incomprehensible maze of adult life, although they cannot place quite the significance of the small jewel so casually presented. I decided that at least I knew that Veronica and Charlie had once been in love, the love, perhaps, of people in the movies. But what had come of it? No two people could less suggest what my idea was of the love between men and women: Charlie so clearly embodying ruin in his bathrobe with its sash of fraying rope, Veronica devoting her physical existence to concealing any hint of sex.

She clearly thought about how she looked: her impression of well-bred decay could not have been achieved by accident. I remember my shock when I realized as a quite young child that Veronica wore no brassiere. I fell asleep once in her lap and awoke with my arms around her torso. She must have sat perfectly still all the time I slept. Pretending to be still half asleep, I ran my fingers up and down her back as if it were a clavichord. I kept playing her back, not knowing what it was I missed. When I realized what it was it came to me to pity her, for it was pitiable that she had nothing to show for her womanhood, nothing like my mother's fine, high bolster of a bosom I had always been so happily able to trust. She wore 4711 Cologne—an androgynous scent in an age when the sexes shared almost nothing. Her shoes were a generation out-of-date: round-toed and laced and made to match some prewar dream. She was personally fastidious, but when three of her bottom teeth fell out she couldn't bring herself to see a dentist, but filled in the gap with strips of wax.

And so, of course, it was shocking when Billy came home from a night with Roberta. I can see now that Veronica must have tried to incorporate her son's girlfriend into the fabric of her frail domestic life. She would ask about Roberta in a tentative, good-humored way, and Billy would reply in vague terms, but without bad spirits. I don't know if the women ever met, but Roberta must have tried in some ways to ingratiate herself, for I remember a birthday card she sent Veronica. On the front of the card, a smiling sausage said, "I wish you the happiest birthday ever." On the inside of the card, the same sausage, now fatter and smilier, said, "And that's no Baloney!"

It seemed to me then that the birthday card was a clue to what was between Billy and Roberta, for Billy was by profession a cartoonist. He drew bosomy showgirls in the laps of sailors, or forlorn sex-starved schlemiels looking with longing at signs saying "Exotic Dancers." I don't know whether Billy made a living from cartooning before I was old enough to notice such things, but by the time I could understand, it was clear to me that he lived off his mother. She taught third grade in a public school in Harlem; she was a passionate teacher and she loved her work. I realize now that she never talked about her students' being black; given her nature, it is possible she didn't notice. When she came home from school, Billy was often still in bed. This *did* distress her. When she mentioned the fact to my mother, it was the only time I ever heard anything in her voice to suggest that something in her life had gone awry.

By the time I was twelve, Roberta was off the scene for good and Billy had hit the skids in earnest. He'd lost his looks; the dashing, slightly wicked ladies' man had turned into a fat mick with two days' growth of beard most of the days he cared to come out of his room. I don't know how often he left his room when he and his mother were alone in the apartment, but when my mother and I arrived, he was never visible, nor could he be counted upon to appear. When he did join us, he was affable and sometimes witty, but his interest in us was limited, and he clearly longed to be back in his room.

The year I turned fifteen, I spent a week with Veronica and Billy while my mother was in the hospital for an appendectomy. I realized gradually that I'd become interesting to Billy; it was my first hint that I might in any way engage a grown-up male. And although I could see that Billy was no prize in the particularities of his condition, his membership in the estate of adult malehood had its potency. I flirted with him—it was dreadful of me, of course, but then who ever thought of teenage girls as anything but savage. He took me bowling and bought me a beer. I didn't like it after the first few daring sips and asked for a Coke. He laughed and said I was a cheap date. I was alarmed and not a little bit insulted. I knew it was sex I was playing with, and not in its nicest aspects. I didn't know that calling someone a "cheap date" was a joke or a compliment; I was mistaken in the meaning of the words, but the unease I felt was right.

Billy and I walked out of the bowling alley, feeling the smoky blue air we'd just left behind to be the norm. Even the tainted air of the Bronx seemed too pure for Billy and me; I felt that we were seething with corruption. As we walked down the street, we ran into some of Billy's friends. They were as corpulent as he, and as ill-shaven; only it seemed they had been born to the bodies they were now inhabiting; it was clear to me that Billy had stepped down into his.

"Hey, Len, I want you to meet my girlfriend," Billy said, putting his arm around my shoulder.

Some genius made me go along with Billy; I was outraged at his suggestion, but I wanted to protect him from his friends. Clearly, if there were sides, I belonged on Billy's.

His friend Len, who wore a short-sleeved checked shirt and had a tattoo of an anchor on his forearm, snorted, "Guess you're robbing the cradle, for a change."

"I'm only kidding, Len," he said. "This is my mother's best friend's kid. I used to change her diapers."

These words angered me as his suggestion of our coupling hadn't. Both were false, but one falsehood elevated me to an honorific, if shameful position; the other simply reduced me to a child. And since I was much closer to being a child than a sexual adventuress, I resented Billy's revision. I wanted to tell them that it wasn't true that Billy'd changed my diapers, that he'd never done a helpful thing in his life. But Billy hadn't moved his hand off my shoulder, and I felt the urgency of his need for my loyalty thrum through his fingers. And so I looked sullen, but didn't move away.

"I bet you'd like to change her diapers now," Len snorted. His two friends snorted along with him, caricatures of simpleminded, fleshly hearted sidekicks.

"Knock it off, Len," Billy said, stepping between the men and me, suddenly my gallant protector.

"Okay, Billy," Len said. "I didn't mean nothing by it. Just run along home to your mommy and forget it."

Then they were gone, moving away from us in a collective shift of bulk. For a moment, I was afraid Billy was going to cry.

"No one understands what it's like for me," he said, not looking at me. "Living with my mother. Living off her. I know I'm a mess but I can't help it. She made me a mess and the army finished the job. You know I'm on veteran's disability. You know that, don't you? I don't live off my mother. I pay my share of the rent. And don't you forget it," he said, shaking his finger at me.

"I won't," I said, in a frightened voice. I'd never lived with adult males; their rage was as foreign to me as space talk, and as terrifying.

"Listen, I'm sorry. I'm not myself these days. You know what I used to be like. Do I seem myself to you?"

"No," I said. I had no idea what could possibly be the right answer to that question.

"Let's go get a soda," he said. "I think you understand me. And by the way, don't say anything to my mother about meeting up with Len. She doesn't understand that kind of thing. You know, she was never in the army," he said, as if he were clearing up a misapprehension.

We went into an ice-cream parlor and both ordered hot fudge sundaes. Billy told me about his disability; it was lupus; he'd contracted it in Biloxi; he'd never even been sent overseas because of it. It meant he could never go out in the sun, he said; too much sun could make him look like a monster in half an hour. He never quite explained what would happen and I hadn't the nerve to ask.

THE STORIES OF MARY GORDON

"I like talking to you," he said. "You know how to listen. Always remember this: there's nothing more attractive to a man than a woman who really knows how to listen to him."

This was precisely the sort of information I most wanted; it made me willing to listen to him, to hang on through the long, self-pitying narrations to the bright, occasional sentence that would let me into the secret world of men. After a week, my mother came home from the hospital. Veronica was so grateful to me for "getting Billy out of himself" that she bought me a volume of Christina Rossetti. I'd asked for E. E. Cummings, but she said she'd wait till Christmas for that. Meanwhile, wouldn't I try Christina Rossetti, try to make a friend of her? I did as Veronica said, I read Christina Rossetti, but it was fifteen years before I could see her as anything but maudlin. Veronica kept her word, though, even after I told her I didn't like Christina Rossetti. She gave me Cummings's collected poems as a Christmas gift. I explained to her that I liked Cummings better because he wasn't a phony. I could have died when I saw the look on her face. Never had anybody looked so sad, so wounded, so unhopeful. And I had done it. I could never take it back. I had done what Billy must have done a thousand times, and it disturbed me to feel so much kinship with him.

Soon after my time at Billy and Veronica's, I got my first boyfriend. It wouldn't have occurred to me to be grateful to Billy; I couldn't have known that it was his attentions that had given me the confidence to present myself as a desirable female. And so with the perfect heartlessness of a young girl in love for the first time, I couldn't bring myself to speak to Billy. I wouldn't go with my mother to Veronica's house. If Billy phoned and asked for me, I commanded my mother to say I was in the shower, or sick or sleeping. "Tell him I'm with my boyfriend," I said meanly to my mother, wanting at once to punish Billy for his presumptions, and to flaunt my status before his damaged countenance. Teenagers are pack animals; instinctively they turn on the wounded member and fall upon him, then run off. Occasionally, I would answer the phone when Billy called and I'd be forced into a conversation. Realizing the perfunctoriness of my presence, Billy would try to get my attention by telling dirty jokes. How completely he misunderstood our fragile, temporary bond! It wasn't the brute facts of sex I was interested in, had ever been interested in. What I'd valued in Billy's conversation was a clue to the rules of courtship. That courtship could potentially end in the kind of thing Billy told jokes about and could only outrage me. I was disgusted, and I lost what little faith I had in him as a source of information that could do me any good.

Veronica died when I was twenty; Billy, then, must have been forty-two years old. The cable between his house and ours was cruelly cut; he had no reason, really, to regularly get in touch with us. On holidays, his birthday, my mother made obligatory calls, but the news of his life was too dispiriting to encourage any but the smallest contact. For, as far as we could figure, he did nothing. He had no work, no friends. He said his mother had been right, his friends were no good. He said he felt better off just keeping to himself. We heard from neighbors of his that he'd grown obese, that he sometimes passed out at the local bar and had to be carried home—no mean feat since he was reported to weigh two hundred seventy-five pounds. The neighbors said he'd been told he was diabetic, so he was eating and drinking himself to death.

The last time I spoke to him was the night before my wedding. He'd been invited, but he hadn't sent back the little card that said "_____ will _____ attend." We were sure that he wouldn't come; perhaps we wouldn't have invited him if we'd thought there was a chance of his coming. We only heard from him when he was drunk; he'd call and talk about his mother with a sentimental tenderness the sources of which had never been obvious while his mother had lived. His relationship to her had been marked by a grudging deference that could turn to rudeness like the crack of a whip. And she had curved herself into a shape that would obtrude into his life as little as possible until he needed her reassurance that his failures were attributable not to his own deficiencies but to the sheer corruption of the brutish world.

Billy was the last person I wanted to speak to on the night before my wedding. I'd decided I hated my veil; I'd been hysterical for hours, and not in much mood to be polite. But I knew that this large and complicated wedding could only be paid for by my doing my bride's job of graciousness. Think of Veronica, my mother said, but what she meant was, think of all I've just done for you. And she *had* done everything, and done it well; it was surprising that she'd done it at all considering how much she disliked my fiancé.

I could tell Billy was drunk the moment he started speaking.

"I'll bet you're a pretty little bride," he said.

"All brides are pretty, Billy," I said impatiently.

"And what's the lucky man like?"

"Handsome, smart, and madly in love with me."

"And what's he like in bed? Oh, I forgot, you're not supposed to know that. White for a virgin. White. But what color's the groom wearing?"

"Black, Billy. The men don't matter at a wedding."

"Just tell me one thing, honey. I just want you to tell me one thing. Did I ever have a chance?"

"A chance?"

"A chance with you. I mean, did you ever think about me?"

I felt filled up with disgust. To imagine that that gross, drunken creature thought of taking the place of my perfect, princely husband-to-be! I couldn't bear to talk to him another second.

"I've got to go, Billy. I've got a lot to do."

"Sure, honey. I'll call you up sometime."

"Sure, Billy, my mother has my new number."

But of course he never called, and I would never call him. He knew of my divorce; my mother made a round of what she felt were de rigueur informing calls; it took a year, but in the end she got through everyone in her address book.

I think of Billy now as I make dinner for the children. I think of him eating by himself on holidays, in furtiveness, in shame, off the landlady's plate. I wonder why he didn't kill himself straight out. What could life have been to him, what could his waking after noon each day have signaled but one more round of fresh defeats? I wonder, too, with the inevitable egotism of the living, if he thought of me after I was divorced, if he imagined a place for himself here, with my sons, in a house as fatherless as his had been. And I hate the thought of him thinking of me, of us, like that.

I would like to blame somebody. Billy or Veronica. Roberta or the landlady. I would like, even, to take the burden of his ruin on myself, to imagine that had I not stayed in their house when I was fifteen, his life might have been different. I would like to point to one specific moment, one incident embedded in his history and say: Here everything went wrong.

But I cannot find a moment solid, powerful enough to blame. It seems impossible that anything could have been other than it was. I call my sons for dinner. Irritable, I tell them they should make more friends. They are fourteen, twelve, and ten: they regard my suggestion with various tones of incomprehension. Too soon after supper, it seems to me, they disappear into their rooms.

I realize I must say something to them. I don't want to; anger takes me over: I blame their father for his absence. Were he here now I could say, "What should we do? What do I have to tell them?" There is no one to turn to. My mother is in her room now in the home run by the Visitation Sisters, in the plain, unyielding senile fog that has become her habitation, and will always be, until her death. There is no one but me to speak to the children. There is no one who knew Billy and knows them now but me.

The apartment seems too big although our problem in reality is that we are quite cramped. But the ceilings loom, the walls push out, refusing shelter, the no-wax linoleum glares up. I walk into their bedroom where they sit in the unreal half-light of TV, aquarium, beneath the ever-changing posters: now Police, Graig Nettles, Sting. I tell them I would like to talk to them, when they are ready. Astonishingly, they turn off the TV. They have been waiting.

"I wanted to tell you about Billy," I tell them. And I do say something, tell the outlines of his life, abstract the epochs, as if I were giving a lecture on prehistory: the Pleistocene, the Paleolithic. I speak about the army days, and his cartooning, and the final, long demise.

"He sounds like a complete fuckup to me," says my oldest son. "A real loser."

"You're being a little hard," I say. "Things weren't easy for him." I neglect to fill in the details; it would not be tactful to speak to three fatherless boys about the devastations of a father's abandonment.

"So, things are hard for everyone. Big deal," my oldest son says. He is the unforgiving one. My strongest ally in refusing to forgive his father.

"Why do you think it happened to him?" asks my second son, the scientist.

"I don't know," I tell him. "That's what's hard to figure out."

But all this time I have known that the worried eyes of the youngest were fixed on us, needing reassurance, frightened of the spectacle of Billy's life, seeing it, of the three of them, most vividly.

"It couldn't happen to people like us, though, could it?" he asks. He is speaking for the group.

They gather from the far corners of their diverse positions here, with me in the still center. Do they want to know the truth? Will the truth help them?

I am thinking of Veronica. I think that what she did was tell the truth to Billy, but too early, and too much. The world is cruel, she told him, it is frightening, and it will hurt you. She told him this with every caress, with every word of praise and spoon of medicine. And he believed her. Well, of course he would. She was telling the truth; she was his mother.

I will not tell these boys the truth. To protect them, I will dishonor Billy. I will make him out a monster and a sport. I will deny his commonality to the three who sit before me, waiting for an answer. Not the truth, but something that will let them live their lives.

"No," I tell them. "It doesn't happen to people like you. Billy wasn't like you. He was not like you at all."

Safe

I

The morning starts with a child's crying. By arrangement I ignore it, by arrangement, my husband, who does not see the morning as I do—the embezzler of all cherished wealth, thief of all most rare and precious—gets the child and brings her to me. Still asleep, I offer her my breast, and she, with that anchoritic obsession open only to saints and infants, eats, and does not think to be offended that her mother does not offer her the courtesy of even a perfunctory attention, but sleeps on. There is a photograph of the two of us in this position. My eyes are closed, the blankets are around my chin. My daughter, six months old, puts down the breast to laugh into the camera's eye. Already she knows it is a good joke: that she is vulnerable, utterly, and that the person who has pledged to keep her from all harm, can do, in fact, so little to protect her. Is a person, actually, who can swear that never in her life has she awakened of her own accord. Yet, miraculously, she feels safe with me, my daughter, and settles in between my breast and arm for morning kisses. This is the nicest way I know to wake up. I have never understood people who like to be awakened with sex: what one wants, upon awakening, is something gradual, predictable, and sex is just the opposite, with all its rushed surprises.

I carry my daughter into the bathroom. My husband, her father, stands at the mirror shaving, stripped to the waist. How beautiful he is. I place my cheek on his back and embrace him. The baby plays at our feet. In the mirror I can see my arms, my hands around his waist, but not my face. I like the anonymity. I take my nightgown off and go into the shower. Every time I take a shower now, I worry about the time when water will be rationed, when I will have to wash in a sink in cold water. My mother knew a nun who, after twenty-five years in the convent, was asked what gift she would like to celebrate her silver jubilee. She asked for a hot bath. What did that mean about the twenty-five years of her life before that? All her young womanhood gone by without hot baths. I would not have stuck it out.

I step out of the shower and begin to dry myself. I see the two of them looking at me: man and child, she in his arms. She stretches out her arms to me in that exaggerated pose of desperation that can make the most well-fed child suggest that she belongs on a poster, calculated to rend the heart, urging donations for the children of a war zone or a famine-stricken country. I take her in my arms. She nose-dives for my breast. My husband holds my face in both his hands. "Don't take your diaphragm out," he says. Just ten minutes ago, I fed my child; just last night I made love to my husband. Yet they want me again and again. My blood is warmed, then fired with well-being. Proudly, I run my hands over my own flesh, as if I had invented it.

II

The baby is predictable now. We know that she will want a nap at nine fifteen, just after we have finished breakfast. I put her in her crib and wait until I hear her even breathing. Does she dream? What can she dream of, having lived so little? Does she dream of life inside my body? Or does she dream for the whole race?

My husband is in bed waiting for me. Deep calls to deep: it must have been sex they were talking about. I want him as much as ever. Because of this, because of what I feel for him, what he feels for me, of what we do, can do, have done together in this bed, I left another husband. Broke all sorts of laws: the state's, the church's. Caused a good man pain. And yet it has turned out well. Everyone is happier than ever. I do not understand this. It makes a mockery of the moral life, which I am supposed to believe in.

All the words of love, of sex and love, the simple words; have, take, come, now, words of one syllable. Behind my eyes I see green leaves, high, branching trees, then rocks that move apart and open. Exhausted, we hold each other, able to claim love. The worst thing about casual sex is not being able to express love honestly afterward. One feels it, but knows it to be false. Not really love. Yet, is it not inevitable to love one who has proffered such a gift?

We drift into sleep, knowing the baby's nap will not last long. She cries; the day begins for real. I am taking her into the city to see an old lover.

III

Of all the men I have been with, M—— found me consistently, astonishingly, pleasing. We had five months together in a foreign city, London, where he was almost the only one I knew. I was married then, to my first husband, who did not praise, who thought of me as if I were colonial Africa: a vast, dark, natural resource, capable, possibly, of civilization. As it turns out, I did not want his civilization—a tendency colonialists have discovered to their sorrow.

M—— is, as they say, well-bred, but with him the phrase has real meaning. Only centuries of careful marriages could have produced, for example, his nose. There are no noses like it in America, which got only the riffraff for its settlers, or those who must fear beauty as a snare. His nose is thin and long, the nostrils beautifully cut, the tip pointed down slightly to the full, decisive lips. He is the blondest man I have ever been with—this, in combination with his elegant, well-cut clothes, made him a disappointment naked. Really fair men always look foolish without their clothes, as if they ought to know better.

M—— likes to pretend that I have been married so many times he can't keep track. In letters, he tells me he imagines me inviting the milk-man, the postman, the butcher into bed to thank them for their services. I write that there are no milkmen in America, the postman is a woman, and I buy meat in the supermarket. Don't quibble, he replies, suggesting my gynecologist, my lawyer, the man who does my taxes.

It is all praise, it is all a reminder of my power, and I thrive on it, par-ticularly as we spoke last time we saw each other openly about the pleas-ures of friendship without the intrusions of sex. I was newly married then, and he took no small pride in the court adviser/Dutch uncle tone he spoke in when he warned me against the dangers of infidelity. I told him he needn't worry; I had learned my lesson; I wanted to have a child. And besides, my husband made me happier than I had ever been. So then you're safe, he said, as safe as houses. I didn't like the image: I knew the kind of houses that were meant: large and wide and comfortably fur-nished: it made me see myself as middle-aged, a German woman with thick legs and gray bobbed hair.

It is with a high heart that I ride down on the bus on a spring morn-ing. The countryside is looking splendid: frail greens against a tentative blue sky, the turned earth brown and ready. M——'s nose is not his only benefice: his manners, too, are lovely. They are courtly, and I dream of my daughter meeting him at Claridge's one day for tea, when she is twelve, perhaps, and needing flattery. I look at her in my arms, proud of what I have come up with. This rosy flesh is mine, this perfect head, this soft, round mouth. And of course, I think we make a charming picture, rightly observed, and I count on M—— for the proper angle.

The city pavements sparkle and the sun beams off the building glass. We get a taxi in a second—I am covered over with beneficence, the flatter-ing varnish of good luck. But my luck changes and we are stuck in traffic for forty-five minutes. M—— hates lateness—he thinks it is rudeness—and I know this will get the day off to a bad start.

He is waiting for me in the sculpture garden of the Museum of Mod-ern Art. He does not look pleased to see me, but it is not his way to look pleased. He says he hates his first sight of people he loves: they always expect too much from his face and it makes him feel a failure.

I apologize nervously, excessively, for being late. He steers us silently toward the cafeteria. I am wearing the baby in a front pack sling, when I take her out and give her to M—— to hold, she screams. He asks me what she likes to eat. "Me," I say, but he is not amused. "Get her some yogurt," I say, feeling foolish.

"And you?" he asks.

"Oh, anything," I say.

"You always say that," he says, frowning, "and you always have something specific in mind. You've lost an earring."

He looks at the baby. "Your mother is always losing earrings in the most extraordinary places, at the most extraordinary times." She looks him squarely in the eye and screams. He moves off with a shudder.

Finally, the yogurt pleases the baby, and her good temper is restored. I ask M—— about his visit, and he is noncommittal, uninformative. I begin to fear that he has crossed the ocean to see me. He wants to talk about the past, our past; he keeps bringing up details in a way that makes me know he thinks about me often. He keeps taking my hand, squeezing it in studied, meaningful patterns of pressure, but I keep having to pull my hand away to take things from the baby, or to hold her still. Besides, I don't want to hold his hand. Not in that way. I begin to feel unsettled, and start chattering, diverting much of my foolish talk to the baby, a habit in mothers I have always loathed.

"I've got us theater tickets for tonight," says M——. "And you must tell me where you would most like to have dinner."

I look at him with alarm. "I can't possibly go to the theater with you. I have to get home with the baby. You should have said something."

"I thought you'd know that's what would happen. It's what we always did."

"I never had a baby before. Or a marriage, not a real one. Surely you must know we can't go on a *date*."

"Obviously I don't know anything about you anymore. Come on, let's look at the pictures."

I try to put my arms through the sling, but it is a complicated arrangement if one is trying to hold the baby at the same time, and I know she will not go with M——. He stands behind me, helping me to put my arms through the straps. His hand brushes my breast, but instead of moving his hand away, he cups my breast with it.

I am covered over in panic. For the first time in my life, I am shocked by a man's touch. I understand for the first time the outraged virgin, for I am offended by the *impropriety* of such a gesture, indicating, as it does, a radical misunderstanding of my identity. He cannot have free access to my body, not just because it is mine, but because it stands for something in the world, for some idea. My body has become symbolic. I laugh at the idea as soon as it occurs to me, and M—— looks hurt, but I continue to laugh at the notion of myself as icon. My actual virginity I gave up with impatience and dispatch; an encumbrance I was eager to be rid of. Now, fifteen years later, I stand blushing.

We try to look at pictures, but it is no good, the baby cries incessantly. Besides, we really do not want to be together anymore. He puts me in a taxi and tries to embrace me, but the baby is strapped to me and all he can manage is a chaste and distant kiss on the cheek. It is the first time I have disappointed him; and I feel the failure all the way home. The baby falls asleep the minute she gets on the bus; she was crying from exhaustion. I do not know what I was thinking of, making this expedition. Or I know precisely what I had been thinking of, and cannot now believe I was so foolish.

IV

It is evening. My husband and I are going to dinner at our favorite restaurant. The girl who is taking care of the baby is a girl I love. Seventeen, she is the daughter of a friend, a woman I love and admire, a woman of accomplishment whose children are accomplished and who love her. E—— is beautiful, a beauty which would be a bit inhuman if she understood its power, and were it not tempered by her sweetness and her modesty. I know her well; she lived with us in the summer. I was relieved to be unable to assume a maternal role with her; I believed, and still believe, that she sees me as a slatternly older sister, good at heart but scarcely in control. She plays the flute; she gets my jokes; she speaks perfect French; she does the dishes without being asked. The baby adores her. We can leave telling her nothing but the phone number of the restaurant. She knows everything she needs to know.

It is not a good dinner. I want to tell my husband about M—— but cannot. It is not his business; spouses should never be able to image their fears of their beloved's being desired by another. And I may want to see M—— again. I am distracted, and my husband knows me well enough to know it. We are both disappointed for we do not have much time alone.

We do not linger over after-dinner drinks, but come home early to find E—— in the dark, crying. My husband leaves her to me; he has always said that a woman, however young, does not want to be seen in tears by a man who is not her lover. In the car, I ask her what is wrong.

"It's R——," she says, her first boyfriend, with whom I know she has broken up. "It's awful to see him every day, and not be able to talk to him."

"Mm," I say, looking at the dark road.

"It's just so awful. He used to be the person in the world I most wanted to see, most wanted to talk to, and now I rush out of classes so I don't have to pass him in the halls."

"It's hard."

"Was it like that for you? First loving someone, then running away from the sight of them?"

"Yes, it happened to me a lot." I conjure in my mind the faces of ten men once loved.

"Do you think people can ever be friends when they fall out of love with each other?"

"I suppose so. I've never been able to do it. Some people can."

She looks at me with anguish in the dark, cold car. "It's such a terrible waste. I can't bear it, I don't think. Do you think it's all worth it?"

"I don't think there's an alternative," I say.

"What a relief it must be that it's all over for you."

So this is how she sees me: finished, tame, bereft of possibilities. I kiss her good night, feeling like that German woman with thick legs. Lightly, E—— runs through the beam of the headlights over the grass to her house. I wait to see that she is in the door.

Her urgent face is in my mind as I drive home, and M——'s face and the face of ten loved men. I realize that I am old to E——, or middle-aged, and that is worse. The touch of M——'s hand on my breast gave me no pleasure. That has never happened to me before.

I have never thought of myself as old; rather I fear that I am so young-seeming that I lack authority in the outside world. I feel the burdens of both youth and age. I am no longer dangerous, by reason of excitement, possibility—but I cannot yet compel by fear. I feel as if the light had been drained from my hair and skin. I walk into the house, low to the ground, dun-colored, like a moorhen.

My husband is in bed when I return. I look in at the baby. Under her yellow blanket her body falls and rises with her breath. I wash my face and get into my nightgown. It is purple cotton, striped; it could belong to a nun. I think of the nightwear of women in films whose bodies glow with danger: Garbo, Dietrich, Crawford. Faye Dunaway, who has a baby and is not much older than I. I see my husband is not yet asleep. He takes me in his arms. I ask, "Do you ever think of me as dangerous?"

He laughs. "Let me try to guess what you've been reading. *Anna Karenina? Madame Bovary? Vanity Fair?*"

"I'm serious. I'll bet you never think of me as dangerous."

He holds me closer. "If I thought of you as dangerous, I'd have to think of myself as unsafe."

I pull him toward me. I can feel his heart beating against my breast. Safe, of course he must be safe with me. He and the baby. Were they unsafe, I could not live a moment without terror for myself. I know that I must live my life now knowing it is not my own. I can keep them from so little; it must be the shape of my life to keep them at least from the danger I could bring them.

In a few hours, the baby will awaken, needing to be fed again. My husband takes my nightgown off.

The Dancing Party

"I know why you're in this mood," says the angry wife, "I just wish you'd admit it."

They drive in darkness on the sandy road; she has no confidence that he will find the house, which they have only seen in daylight. And she half wishes he would get a wheel stuck in the sand. She would be pleased to see him foolish.

"I'm in a bad mood for one reason," says the husband. "Because you said to me: Shape up. No one should say that to someone: Shape up."

"I could tell by your face how you were planning to be. That way that makes the other people at a party want to cut their throats."

"Must I sparkle to be allowed among my kind?"

"And I know why you're like that. Don't think I don't. It's because you watched the children while I swam. For once."

"Yes, it's true, the day was shaped by your desires. But I'm not resentful. Not at all. You must believe me."

"But I don't believe you."

"Then where do we go?"

"We go, now, to the party. But I beg you: Please don't go in with your face like that. It's such a wonderful idea, a dancing party."

The house is built atop the largest dune. In daylight you can see the ocean clearly from the screened-in porch. The married couple climb the dune, not looking at each other, walking far apart. When they come to the door, they see the hostess dancing with her brother.

How I love my brother, thinks the hostess. There are no men in the world like him.

The hostess's brother has just been divorced. His sister's house is where he comes, the house right on the ocean, the house she was given when her husband left her for someone else. Her brother comes here for consolation, for she has called it "my consolation prize." And it *has* been a consolation, and still is, though she is now, at forty-five, successful. She can leave her store to her assistants, take a month off in the summer, and come here. She earns more money than her ex-husband, who feels, by this alone, betrayed. She comes, each morning, to the screened-in porch and catches in the distance the blue glimpse of sea, the barest hint, out in the distance, longed for, but in reach. She'd brought her daughters here for the long, exhausting summers of the single mother. Watched their feuds, exclusions, the shore life of children on long holiday, so brimming and so cruel. But they are grown now, and remarkably, they both have jobs, working in the city. One is here, now, for the weekend only. Sunday night, tomorrow, like the other grown-ups, she will leave. The daughter will be in her car, stuck in the line of traffic, that reptilian creature that will take her in its coils. Exhausted, she will arrive in her apartment in Long Island City. She will wait till morning to return her rented car.

I will not be like my mother, thinks the daughter of the hostess. I will not live as she lives. How beautiful she is, and how I love her. But I will not live like that.

She lifts an angry shoulder at the poor young man, her partner, who does not know why. She is saying: I will not serve you or your kind. I will not be susceptible.

She sees her mother, dancing, not with her brother any longer, but with another man. She sees her mother's shoulder curving toward him. Sees her mother's head bent back. Susceptible. Will this be one more error of susceptibility? Oh, no, my mother, beautiful and still so young, do not.

Shore up and guard yourself. As I have. Do not fall once more into those arms that seem strong but will leave you. Do not fall.

The daughter leaves the young man now to dance with the best friend of her mother. This woman has no husband and a child of two. The mother with no husband and a child of two dreams of her lover as she dances with the daughter of the hostess. She thinks: I have known this girl since she was five. How can it be? I have a child of two; my best friend has a daughter who lifts her angry shoulder and will drive away on Sunday to the working world. Do not be angry at your mother, the mother with no husband wants to say. She is young, she is beautiful, she needs a man in her bed. The mother with no husband thinks of her own lover, who is someone else's husband and the father of the two-year-old child. Someday, she thinks, it is just possible that we will live together, raise together this boy of ours, now only mine. She longs for her lover; she spends, she thinks in anger, too much life on longing. But she chose that. Now she thinks about his hair, his rib cage, the feel of his bones when she runs her fingers up his back, the shape of his ear when she can see him in the distance. She thinks: He is torn, always. When the child was conceived she said, being nearly forty: I will have it. There is nothing you need do. He said: I will stand with you. He came on the first day of their son's life and visits weekly—uncle? friend?—and puts, each month, three hundred dollars in a small account and in a trust fund for college. Says: I cannot leave my wife. The mother with no husband longs sometimes to be with her lover in a public place, dancing, simply, like the married couple, without fear among the others of their kind.

The scientist has come without her lover. He has said: Oh, go alone. You know I hate to dance. She phoned her friend, a man in love with other men. Come dancing with me. Yes, of course, he says. He is glad to be with her; he too is a scientist. They work together; they study the habits of night birds. They are great friends. The lover of the scientist is brilliant, difficult. In ten years she has left him twice. She thinks now she will never leave him.

The daughter of the hostess puts on music that the angry wife, the mother with no husband, and the scientist don't like. So they sit down. Three friends, they sit together on the bench that rests against the wall. They look out the large window; they can see the moon and a newly lit square white patch of sea. They like each other; they are fortyish; they are successful. For a month each summer they live here by the ocean, a mile apart. The angry wife is a bassoonist of renown. The mother with no husband writes studies of women in the ancient world. These women, all of them, have said to each other: What a pleasure we are, good at what we do. And people know it. The angry wife has said: You know you are successful when you realize how many people hope that you will fail.

And how are you? they ask each other. Tired, say the two, the angry wife, the mother with no husband, who have young children. I would like to have a child, the scientist says. Of course you must, say the two who are mothers. Now they think with pleasure of the soft flesh of their children, of their faces when they sleep. Oh, have a child, they tell the scientist. Nothing is better in the world.

Yes, have a child, the hostess says. Look at my daughter. See how wonderful. The daughter of the hostess has forgotten, for a time, her anger and is laughing with the young man. Asks him: Are you going back on Sunday? Would you like a ride? The hostess thinks: Good, good. My daughter will not drive alone. And maybe he will love her.

I am afraid of being tired, says the scientist to her three friends.

You will be tired if you have a child, they say to her. There is no getting around it. You will be tired all the time.

And what about my work?

You will do far less work. We must tell you the truth.

I am afraid, then, says the scientist.

The widow sits beside them. And they say to her, for she is old now: What do you think our friend should do?

The widow says: Two things in the world you never regret: a swim in the ocean, the birth of a child.

She says things like this; it is why they come to her, these four women near the age of forty. She has Russian blood; it makes her feel free to be aphoristic. She can say: To cross a field is not to live a life. To drink tea is not to hew wood. Often she is wrong. They know that, and it doesn't matter. She sits before them, shining, like a bowl of water colored, just for pleasure, blue. They would sit at her feet forever; they would listen to her all night long. She says: I think that I have made mistakes.

But they do not believe her.

She says: In my day we served men. We did not divorce. I do not think then we knew how to be good to our children and love men at the same time. We had wonderful affairs. Affairs are fine, but you must never fall in love. You must be in love only with your husband.

But only one of them has a husband. He is sitting, drinking, talking to another man. His wife would like to say: Look at the moon, don't turn your back to it. But she is tired of her voice tonight, the voice that speaks to him so cruelly, more cruelly than he deserves. She would like to say: Let's dance now. But she doesn't want to dance with him. Will I get over being angry, she wonders, before the party ends? She hopes she will and fears that she will not.

The widow greets her friend across the room. They have both understood the history of clothes. And so they watched, in the late 1960s, the sensitive and decorative march of vivid-colored trousers and light, large-sleeved printed shirts, of dresses made of Indian material, of flat, bright, cotton shoes. So, in their seventies, they greet each other wearing purple and magenta. As they kiss, the gauzy full sleeves of their blouses touch. Tonight to be absurd, the widow's friend has worn a feather boa. Her husband, her fifth husband, stands beside her, gallant and solicitous for her and for her friend.

The widow says to her old friend, pointing to the four women sitting on the bench: I think they've got it right. Their lovely work.

The friend says: But look, they are so tired, and so angry.

The widow says: But we are tired at that age, and angry. They will have something to show.

Who knows, the widow's friend says, turning to her husband. Dance with me, she says, I think this one's a waltz.

He kisses her, for she has made him laugh. They dance, they are the only ones now dancing with the hostess's daughter and her friends. The music has gone angular and mean, it seems to the four women on the bench. The hostess's daughter thinks: Perhaps, then, I should marry a rich man. I am not ambitious, but I like nice things.

The mother without a husband thinks about her lover. Of his mouth, his forearms, his way of standing with his knees always a little bent, the black hairs on the backs of his small hands.

The hostess thinks: Perhaps I will ask this new man to stay.

The scientist thinks: I will live forever with a man who hates to dance.

The daughter of the hostess thinks: I love my mother, but I will not live like her.

The widow thinks: How wonderful their lives are. I must tell them so that they will know.

Her friend thinks: If this man dies I will be once more alone.

The angry wife wishes she were not angry.

Suddenly a funny song comes on. It has a name that makes them laugh, "Girls Just Want to Have Fun." The daughter of the hostess claps her hands and says: No men. The women, all of them: the hostess and her daughter, the scientist, the mother with no husband, the angry wife, the widow and her friend, stand in a circle, kick their legs in unison, and laugh. And they can see outside the circle all the men, ironical or bored-looking, the kindly ones amused. They all look shiftless there, and unreliable, like vagabonds. The two old women cannot bear it, that the men should be unhappy as the women dance. The widow's friend is first to break the circle. She takes her husband's hand and leads him to the center of the room. The widow dances with the handsomest young man. The daughter of the hostess walks away. But the four women near to forty sit down on the bench. The angry wife can see her husband's back. His back is turned against her; he is looking at the moon.

Violation

I suppose that in a forty-five-year life, I should feel grateful to have experienced only two instances of sexual violation. Neither of them left me physically damaged and I cannot in truth say they have destroyed my joy of men. I have been happily married for fifteen years before which I had several blissful and some ordinary disappointing times with lovers. In addition, I am the mother of two sons, my passion for whom causes me to draw inward, away, when I hear the indiscriminate castigation of all males, so common and so understandable within the circles I frequent. I rarely think of my two experiences, and I'm grateful for that, for I don't like what they suggest to me about a world which I must, after all, go on inhabiting. And I don't like it when I start to feel in danger in my house, the Federalist house we've been so careful in restoring, in the town not far from Hartford where we've lived now for ten years, and when I wonder if, perhaps, safety is a feeling open to men alone. It is then, especially, that I am glad to be the mother only of sons.

I am thinking of all that now as I stand at the wooden counter cutting celery, carrots, water chestnuts, so unvegetative in their texture, radishes that willingly compose themselves in slices decorative as shells. Courageously, we've kept the kitchen faithful to its period: We have not replaced the small windows by large sheets of glass that would allow a brightness our ancestors would have shunned. Leaves make a border at the windows; farther out—beech, locust—they become a net that breaks up the white sky. I arrange the vegetables, green, orange white, white circled by a ring of red on the dark wood of the chopping board, as if I had to make decisions like a painter, purely on the basis of looks. As I handle the slices of vegetable, cool and admirably dry, I think about myself as a young woman, traveling abroad or "overseas" as my parents then called it, truly away from home for the first time.

At twenty-two, I must have thought myself poetical. This is the only thing I can surmise when I look at the itinerary of that trip—my parents' present to me after college graduation—that I took with my college roommate and best friend. Lydia had majored in economics like me, although like me she had adopted it as a practical measure, rejecting a first love (for her it had been art history, for me English). But we both prided ourselves on being tough-minded and realistic; we knew the value of a comfortable life, and we didn't want to feel we had to be dependent on a lucky marriage to achieve it. We'd both got jobs, through our fathers' connections, at large Manhattan banks; we'd take them up in the fall, and the knowledge of this gave us a sense of safety. We could be daring and adventurous all summer, have experiences, talk to people (men) we never would have talked to at home, reap the rewards of our secret devotion to the art and poetry we hadn't quite the confidence to give our lives to. We considered ourselves in the great line of student pilgrims admiring ourselves for our self-denial, traveling as we did with backpacks and hostel cards and a few volumes of poetry. Not for a moment did we understand the luxury of a journey made on money we had never had to earn, and that the line we followed was that of young people on the grand tour: a look at the best pictures, the best buildings, some introduction to Continental manners, the collision of which with our young natures would rub off the rough edges but leave our idealism smooth. We would return then to the place that had been held for us in the real life that had been going on without us, not forgetting us, but not requiring us yet.

Our plane landed in Amsterdam. We saw the Rembrandts and Vermeers, and the Van Goghs my friend thought, by comparison, jejune, and then we took an all-night train to Florence. We stayed in a cheap *pensione* with marble floors and huge mirrors and painted ceilings above the iron cots that were our beds. And in Piazzole Michelangelo, I met Giovanni, who sold Electrolux vacuum cleaners. Poor Italian, he was overmastered by the consonants of his employer's name and pronounced his product E-LAY-TRO-LOO. Luckily, he worked all day so my friend and I could see the Ufizzi, the Palazzo Pitti, the Duomo, the Museo San Marco, and I need leave her alone only at night when Giovanni drove me around Florence at breakneck speed and snuck me into his *pensione* until midnight, then miraculously got me back into mine. (Now I see he must have bribed the concierge.) He agreed to drive us to Ravenna, where I could do homage to Dante and my friend to the mosaics, but even after he'd done this nice thing for the both of us and paid for both our lunches, my friend was put out with me. She felt that I'd abandoned her for a man. She hadn't met anybody possible, the friends that Giovanni had introduced her to were coarse, she said, and she was afraid to go out alone at night, she was always being followed by soldiers. It wasn't her idea of a vacation, she said, sitting in her room reading Kenneth Clark. Punitively, she suggested that when we got to England, where we both could speak the language, we should split up and travel alone. It would open us up to experiences, she said. Clearly she felt she hadn't had hers yet, and I'd had more than my share.

I left Giovanni tearfully, vowing to write. He bought us chocolates and bottles of *acqua minerale* for the train. Then we were off, heartlessly, to our next adventure. We were both sick crossing the Channel; it made us tenderer to each other as we parted at Dover and hugged each other earnestly, awkward in our backpacks. She would go to Scotland, I to Ireland; in two weeks we would meet in London, stay there for a week, then travel home.

I decided to cross the Irish Sea from Wales, the home of poets. I would spend the day in Swansea and cross over at Fishguard to Rosslare. From Dylan Thomas's home, I would proceed on a pilgrimage to Yeats's. I felt ennobled but a bit lonely. It might be a long time, I knew, before I found someone to talk to.

Swansea was one of the least prepossessing cities I had ever seen: it might, despite the hints left by the poets, have been someplace in Indiana or worse, Ohio, where I was from. I decided to look for a pub where

Thomas must have got his inspiration. I found one that looked appropriate, ordered bread and sausages and beer, and read my Yeats.

So I was not entirely surprised to hear an Irish voice ask if it could join me, and was pleased to look up and see a red-haired sailor standing with a pint of beer. I was abroad, after all, for experience, to do things I wouldn't do at home. I would never have spoken to a sailor in Cleveland, but then he wouldn't have been Irish. I thought he'd noticed me because he saw that I was reading Yeats.

"Yer American, then," he said.

"Yes."

"Great place, America. What yer doin' in this part of the world?"

"I'm traveling," I said.

"On yer own?"

"Yes."

"Brave, aren't ye?"

"No, not especially," I said. "I just don't see that much to be afraid of. And an awful lot that's fun and exciting. I'd hate to think I'd let fear hold me back."

"It's a great attitude. Great. Ye have people over here in Swansea?"

"No."

"What brings ye here?"

"Dylan Thomas, the poet. You've heard of him?"

"I have, of course. You're a great poetry lover, aren't ye? I seen ye with the Yeats. I'm from the Yeats country myself."

"That's where I'm going," I said, excitedly. "To Sligo."

"Yer takin' the ferry?"

"Nine o'clock."

"What a shame. I won't have much time to show ye Swansea. But we could have a drink or two."

"Okay," I said, anxious for talk. "You must have traveled a lot of places."

"Oh, all over," he said. "It's a great life, the sailor's."

He brought us drinks and I tried to encourage him to talk about himself, his home, his travels. I don't remember what he said, only that I was disappointed that he wasn't describing his life more colorfully, so I was glad when he suggested going for a walk to show me what he could of the town.

There really wasn't much to see in Swansea; he took me to the

Catholic Church, the post office, the city hall. Then he suggested another pub. I said I had to be going, I didn't want to be late for the boat. He told me not to worry, he knew a shortcut; we could go there now.

I don't know when I realized I was in danger, but at some point I knew the path we were on was leading nowhere near other people. When he understood that I was not deceived, he felt no more need to hesitate. He must have known I would not resist, he didn't have to threaten. He merely spoke authoritatively, as if he wanted to get on with things.

"Sit down," he said. "And take that thing off your back."

I unbuckled my backpack and sat among the stalky weeds.

"Now take yer things off on the bottom."

I did what he said, closing my eyes. I didn't want to look at him. I could hear the clank of his belt as it hit the ground.

"What's this," he said. "One of yer American tricks?"

I had forgotten I was wearing a Tampax. Roughly, he pulled it out. I was more embarrassed by the imagination of it lying on the grass, so visible, than I was by my literal exposure.

"Yer not a virgin?" he said worriedly.

I told him I was not.

"All right then," he said, "then you know what's what."

In a few seconds, everything was finished, and he was on his feet. He turned his back to me to dress.

"I want ye to know one thing," he said. "I've just been checked out by the ship's doctor. Ye won't get no diseases from me, that's for sure. If ye come down with something, it's not my fault."

I thanked him.

"Yer all right?" he said.

"Yes," I told him.

He looked at his watch.

"Ye missed yer ferry."

"It's all right," I said, trying to sound polite. "There's another one in the morning." I was afraid that if I showed any trace of fear, any sense that what had happened was out of the ordinary, he might kill me to shut my mouth.

"I'll walk ye to the town."

I thanked him again.

"I'm awful sorry about yer missing the boat. It's too bad ye'll have to spend the night in this godforsaken town." He said this with genuine unhappiness, as though he had just described what was the genuine offense.

We walked on silently, looking at hotels blinking their red signs FULL.

"I'll be fine now," I said, hoping now we were in public, I could safely get him to leave.

"As long as yer all right."

"I'm fine, thank you."

"Would you give me yer name and address in the States? I could drop you a line. I'm off to South America next."

I wrote a false name and address on a page in my notebook, ripped it out and handed it to him.

He kissed me on the cheek. "Now don't go on like all these American ladies about how terrible we are to ye. Just remember, treat a man right, he'll treat you right."

"Okay," I said.

"Adios," he said, and waved.

I stepped into the foyer of the hotel we were standing in front of and stood there a while. Then I looked out onto the street to be sure he was gone. There was no sign of him, so I asked the hotel clerk for a room. I wanted one with a private bath, and he told me the only room available like that was the highest priced in the house. I gladly paid the money. I couldn't bear the idea of sharing a bathtub. It wasn't for myself I minded; I cared for the other people. I knew myself to be defiled, and I didn't want the other innocent, now sleeping guests, exposed to my contamination.

I traveled through Ireland for ten days, speaking to no one. It wasn't what I had expected, a country made up of bards and harpists and passionate fine-limbed women tossing their dark red hair. Unlike the other countries of Europe, there was nothing one really *had* to look at, and the beauty of the landscape seemed to wound, over and over, my abraded feelings; it made me feel even more alone. The greasy banisters of the urban hotels I stayed in sickened me; the glowing pictures of the Sacred Heart in the rooms of the private houses that, in the country, took in guests, disturbed my sleep. I felt that I was being stared at and found out.

And that, of course, was the last thing I wanted, to be found out. I've never said anything about the incident to anyone, not that there's much reason to keep it from people. Except, I guess, my shame at having been ravished, my dread of the implication, however slight, that I had "asked for what had happened," that my unwisdom was simply a masked desire for a coupling anonymous and blank. And so I have been silent about that time without good cause; how, then, could I ever speak of the second incident, which could, if I exposed it, unravel the fabric of my family's life?

My Uncle William was my father's only brother. He was two years older, handsomer, more flamboyant, more impatient, and it was said that though he lacked my father's steadiness, my father hadn't got his charm. Their mother had died when they were children, and their father drowned before their eyes when my father was seventeen and William nineteen. They agreed between them, teenage orphans, that my father should go off to college—he would study engineering at Purdue—and my uncle would stay home and run the family business, a successful clothing store my grandfather had built up and expanded as the town's prosperity increased and its tastes became more daring. When my father left for school it was a thriving business and it was assumed that with William's way with people, women especially (he planned to build his line of women's clothing; his first move was to enlarge the millinery department), it could only flourish. But in two years, everything was lost and my father had to leave college. The truly extraordinary aspect of the affair, to my mind, is that it was always my father who was apologetic about the situation. He felt it had been unfair, a terrible position to put Uncle William in, making him slave alone in the hometown he had never liked, while my father had been able to go away. William was really smarter, my father always said. (It wasn't true; even my mother, a great fan of Uncle William's and a stark critic of my father, corrected him, always, at this point in the story.) My father and my uncle agreed that it would be better for my uncle to go away; he'd put in his time and it was my father's turn; there was no reason for Uncle William to stick around and endure the petty insults and suspicions of uncomprehending minds.

In five years, my father had paid all the debts, a feat that so impressed the president of the local bank that he offered him a job. His rise in the bank was immediate, and it led to his move to Cleveland and his continued steady climb and marriage to my mother, the daughter of a bank president. I've never understood my father's success; he seems to trust everyone; wrongdoing not only shocks but seems genuinely to surprise him; yet he's made a career lending people money. I can only imagine that inside those cool buildings he always worked in, he assumed a new identity; the kind eyes grew steely, the tentative, apologetic yet protective posture hardened into something wary and astute. How else can I explain the fact that somebody so lovable made so much money?

In the years that my father was building his career, my uncle was traveling. We got letters from around the country; there was a reference in one, after the fact, to a failed marriage that lasted only sixteen months. And occasionally, irregularly, perhaps once every five years, there would be a visit, sudden, shimmering, like a rocket illumining our ordinary home and lives, making my father feel he had made all the right decisions, he was safe, yet not removed from glamour. For here it was, just at his table, in the presence of the brother whom he loved.

I, too, felt illumined by the visits. In middle age, William was dapper, anecdotal, and offhand. He could imitate perfectly Italian tailors, widows of Texas oilmen, Mexican Indians who crossed the border every spring. In high school, my friends were enchanted by him; he was courtly and praising and gave them a sense of what they were going away to college for. But by the time we had all been away a couple of years, his stories seemed forced and repetitious, his autodidact's store of information suspect, his compliments something to be, at best, endured. For my father, however, my Uncle William never lost his luster. He hovered around his older brother, strangely maternal, as if my uncle were a rare, invalid *jeune fille*, possessed of delicate and special talents which a coarse world would not appreciate. And while my father hovered, my mother leaned toward my uncle flirtatious and expectant and alight.

Once, when I was living in New York, his visit and my visit to Ohio coincided. I was put on the living room couch to sleep since my uncle had inhabited my room for two weeks and I would be home for only three days. At twenty-five, any visit home is a laceration, a gesture meanly wrought from a hard heart and an ungiving spirit. No one in town did I find worth talking to, my parents were darlings, but they would never understand my complicated and exciting life. Uncle William, in this context, was a relief; I had, of course, to condescend to him, but then he condescended to my parents, and he liked to take me out for drinks and hear me talk about my life.

One night, I had gone to dinner at a high school friend's. She had recently married, and I had all the single woman's contempt for her Danish Modern furniture, her silver pattern, her china with its modest print of roses. But it was one of those evenings that is so boring it's impossible to leave; one is always afraid that in rising from the chair, one is casting too pure a light on the whole fiasco. I drove into my parents' driveway at one thirty, feeling ill-used and restless, longing for my own bed in my own apartment and the sound of Lexington Avenue traffic. In five minutes, I was crankily settling onto the made-up couch, and I must have fallen instantly to sleep. I have always been a good sleeper.

It was nearly four when I realized there was someone near me, kneeling on the floor. Only gradually, I understood that it was my uncle William, stroking my arm and breathing whiskey in my face.

"I couldn't sleep," he said. "I was thinking about you."

I lay perfectly still; I didn't know what else to do. I couldn't wake my parents, I could see behind my eyes years of my father's proud solicitude for the man now running his hand toward my breast, scene after scene of my mother's lively and absorbed attentions to him. As I lay there, I kept remembering the feeling of being a child sitting on the steps watching my parents and their guests below me as they talked and held their drinks and nibbled food I didn't recognize as coming from my mother's kitchen or her hand. A child transgressing, I was frozen into my position: any move would mean exposure and so punishment. At the same time that the danger of my situation stiffened me into immobility, I was paralyzed by the incomprehensibility of the behavior that went on downstairs. Could these be people I had known, laughing in these dangerous, sharp, unprovoked ways, leaning so close into one another, singing snatches of songs, then breaking off to compliment each other on their looks, their clothes, their business or community success. My childish sense of isolation from the acts of these familiars now grown strangers made me conscious of the nerves that traveled down my body's trunk, distinct, electric, and my eyes, wide as if they were set out on stalks, now lidless and impossibly alert. Twenty years later as I lay, desperately strategizing, watching my uncle, I knew the memory was odd, but it stayed with me as I simulated flippancy, the only tactic I could imagine that would lead to my escape. My uncle had always called me his best audience when I'd forced laughter at one of his jokes; he'd say I was the only one in the family with a sense of humor.

"Well, unlike you, Uncle William, I *could* sleep, I *was* sleeping," I said, trying to sound like one of those thirties comedy heroines, clever in a jam. "And that's what I want to do again."

"Ssh," he said, running his hand along my legs. "Don't be provincial. Have some courage, girl, some imagination. Besides, I'm sure I'm not the first to have the privilege. I just want to see what all the New York guys are getting."

He continued to touch me, obsessive now and furtive, like an animal in a dark box.

"I'm not going to hurt you," he said. "I could make you happy. Happier than those young guys."

"What would make me really happy is to get some sleep," I said, in a tone I prayed did not reveal all my stiff desperation.

But, miraculously, he rose from his knees. "You really are a little prude at heart, aren't you? Just like everybody else in this stinking town."

And suddenly, he was gone. In the false blue light of four o'clock, I felt the animal's sheer gratitude for escape. I kept telling myself that nothing, after all, had happened, that I wasn't injured, it was rather funny really, I'd see that in time.

My great fear was that I would betray, by some lapse of warmth or interest in the morning, my uncle's drunken act. I longed for my parents' protection, yet I saw that it was I who must protect them. It had happened, that thing between parents and children: the balance had shifted; I was stronger. I was filled with a clean, painful love for them, which strikes me now each time I see them. They are gallant; they are innocent, and I must keep them so.

And I must do it once again today. They are coming to lunch with my uncle William. I will be alone with them: my husband is working; my children are at school. In twenty years, I've only seen him twice, both times at my parents' house. I was able to keep up the tone: jocular, toughminded, that would make him say, "You're my best audience," and make my father say, "They're cut from the same cloth, those two." It was one of those repayments the grown middle-class child must make, the overdue bill for the orthodontists, the dance lessons, the wardrobe for college, college itself. No one likes repayment; it is never a pure act, but for me it was a possible one. Today, though, it seems different. Today they are coming to my house, they will sit at my table. And as I stand at the kitchen window where I have been happy, where I have nurtured children and a husband's love and thought that I was safe, I rage as I look at the food I'd planned to serve them. The vegetables which minutes ago pleased me look contaminated to me now. Without my consent it seems, the side of my hand has moved toward them like a knife and shoved them off the cutting board. They land, all their distinction gone, in a heap in the sink. I know that I should get them out of there; I know I will; for I would never waste them, but for now it pleases me to see them ugly and abandoned and in danger, as if their fate were genuinely imperiled and unsure.

What is it that I want from Uncle William? I want some hesitation at the door, as if he isn't sure if he is welcome. I want him to take me aside and tell me he knows that he has done me harm. I want him to sit, if he must sit, at my table, silent and abashed. I don't demand that he be hounded; I don't even want him to confess. I simply want him to know, as I want the Irish sailor to know, that a wrong has been done me. I want to believe that they remember it with, at the least, regret. I know that things cannot be taken back, the forced embraces, the caresses brutal underneath the mask of courtship, but what I do want taken back are the words, spoken by those two men, that suggest that what they did was all right, no different from what other men had done, that it is all the same, the touch of men and women; nothing of desire or consent has weight, body parts touch body parts; that's all there is. I want them to know that because of them I cannot ever feel about the world the way I might have felt had they never come near me.

But the Irishman is gone and Uncle William, here before me, has grown old and weak. I can see him from the window, I can see the three of them. Him and my parents. They lean on one another, playful, tender; they have been together a lifetime. In old age, my parents have taken to traveling; I can hear them asking my uncle's advice about Mexico, where they will go this winter, where he once lived five years. They are wearing the youth-endowing clothing of the comfortably retired: windbreakers, sneakers, soft, light-colored sweaters, washable dun-colored pants. They have deliberately kept their health, my parents, so that they will not be a burden to me; for some other reason my uncle has kept his. Groaning, making exaggerated gestures, they complain about the steepness of my steps. But it is real, my father's muscular uncertainty as he grabs for the rail. They stand at my front door.

What happened happened twenty years ago. I've had a good life. I am a young and happy woman. And now I see the three of them, the old ones, frail, expectant, yearning toward me. So there is nothing for it; I must give them what they want. I open my arms to the embrace they offer. Heartily, I clap my uncle on the back.

"Howdy, stranger," I say in a cowboy voice. "Welcome to these parts."

Mrs. Cassidy's Last Year

Mr. Cassidy knew he couldn't go to Communion. He had sinned against charity. He had wanted his wife dead.

The intention had been his, and the desire. She would not go back to bed. She had lifted the table that held her breakfast (it was unfair, it was unfair to all of them, that the old woman should be so strong and so immobile). She had lifted the table above her head and sent it crashing to the floor in front of him.

"Rose," he had said, bending, wondering how he would get scrambled egg, coffee, cranberry juice (which she had said she liked, the color of it) out of the garden pattern on the carpet. That was the sort of thing she knew but would not tell him now. She would laugh, wicked and bland-faced as an egg, when he did the wrong thing. But never say what was right, although she knew it, and her tongue was not dead for curses, for reports of crimes.

"Shithawk," she would shout at him from her bedroom. "Bastard son of a whore." Or more mildly, "Pimp," or "Fathead fart."

Old words, curses heard from soldiers on the boat or somebody's street children. Never spoken by her until now. Punishing him, though he had kept his promise.

He was trying to pick up the scrambled eggs with a paper napkin. The napkin broke, then shredded when he tried to squeeze the egg into what was left of it. He was on his knees on the carpet, scraping egg, white shreds of paper, purple fuzz from the trees in the carpet.

"Shitscraper," she laughed at him on his knees.

And then he wished in his heart most purely for the woman to be dead.

The doorbell rang. His son and his son's wife. Shame that they should see him so, kneeling, bearing curses, cursing in his heart.

"Pa," said Toni, kneeling next to him. "You see what we mean."

"She's too much for you," said Mr. Cassidy's son Tom. Self-made man, thought Mr. Cassidy. Good-time Charlie. Every joke a punch line like a whip.

No one would say his wife was too much for him.

"Swear," she had said, lying next to him in bed when they were each no more than thirty. Her eyes were wild then. What had made her think of it? No sickness near them, and fearful age some continent like Africa, with no one they knew well. What had put the thought to her, and the wildness, so that her nails bit into his palm, as if she knew small pain would preserve his memory.

"Swear you will let me die in my own bed. Swear you won't let them take me away."

He swore, her nails making dents in his palms, a dull shallow pain, not sharp, blue-green or purplish.

He had sworn.

On his knees now beside his daughter-in-law, his son.

"She is not too much for me. She is my wife."

"Leave him then, Toni," said Tom. "Let him do it himself if it's so goddamn easy. Serve him right. Let him learn the hard way. He couldn't do it if he didn't have us, the slobs around the corner."

Years of hatred now come out, punishing for not being loved best, of the family's children not most prized. Nothing is forgiven, thought the old man, rising to his feet, his hand on his daughter-in-law's squarish shoulder.

He knelt before the altar of God. The young priest, bright-haired, faced them, arms open, a good little son.

No sons priests. He thought how he was old enough now to have a priest a grandson. This boy before him, vested and ordained, could have been one of the ones who followed behind holding tools. When there was time. He thought of Tom looking down at his father, who knelt trying to pick up food. Tom for whom there had been no time. Families were this: the bulk, the knot of memory, wounds remembered not only because they had set on the soft, the pliable wax of childhood, motherhood, fatherhood, closeness to death. Wounds most deeply set and best remembered because families are days, the sameness of days and words, hammer blows, smothering, breath grabbed, memory on the soft skull, in the lungs, not once only but again and again the same. The words and the starvation.

Tom would not forget, would not forgive him. Children thought themselves the only wounded.

Should we let ourselves in for it, year after year? he asked in prayer, believing God did not hear him.

Tom would not forgive him for being the man he was. A man who paid debts, kept promises. Mr. Cassidy knelt up straighter, proud of himself before God.

Because of the way he had to be. He knelt back again, not proud. As much sense to be proud of the color of his hair. As much choice.

It was his wife who was the proud one. As if she thought it could have been some other way. The house, the children. He knew, being who they were they must have a house like that, children like that. Being who they were to the world. Having their faces.

As if she thought with some wrong turning these things might have been wasted. Herself a slattern, him drunk, them living in a tin shack, children dead or missing.

One was dead. John, the favorite, lost somewhere in a plane. The war dead. There was his name on the plaque near the altar. With the other town boys. And she had never forgiven him. For what he did not know. For helping bring that child into the world? Better, she said, to have borne none than the pain of losing this one, the most beautiful, the bravest. She turned from him then, letting some shelf drop, like a merchant at the hour of closing. And Tom had not forgotten the grief at his brother's death, knowing he could not have closed his mother's heart like that.

Mr. Cassidy saw they were all so unhappy, hated each other so because they thought things could be different. As he had thought of his wife. He had imagined she could be different if she wanted to. Which had angered him. Which was not, was almost never, the truth about things.

Things were as they were going to be, he thought, watching the boy-faced priest giving out Communion. Who were the others not receiving? Teenagers, pimpled, believing themselves in sin. He wanted to tell them they were not. He was sure they were not. Mothers with babies. Not going to Communion because they took the pill, it must be. He thought they should not stay away, although he thought they should not do what they had been told not to. He knew that the others in their seats were there for the heat of their bodies. While he sat back for the coldness of his heart, a heart that had wished his wife dead. He had wished the one dead he had promised he would love forever.

The boy priest blessed the congregation. Including Mr. Cassidy himself.

"Pa," said Tom, walking beside his father, opening the car door for him. "You see what we mean about her?"

"It was my fault. I forgot."

"Forgot what?" said Tom, emptying his car ashtray onto the church parking lot. Not my son, thought Mr. Cassidy, turning his head.

"How she is," said Mr. Cassidy. "I lost my temper."

"Pa, you're not God," said Tom. His hands were on the steering wheel, angry. His mother's.

"Okay," said Toni. "But look, Pa, you've been a saint to her. But she's not the woman she was. Not the woman we knew."

"She's the woman I married."

"Not anymore," said Toni, wife of her husband.

If not, then who? People were the same. They kept their bodies. They did not become someone else. Rose was the woman he had married, a green girl, high-colored, with beautifully cut nostrils, hair that fell down always, hair she pinned up swiftly, with anger. She had been a housemaid and he a chauffeur. He had taken her to the ocean. They wore straw hats. They were not different people now. She was the girl he had seen first, the woman he had married, the mother of his children, the woman he had promised: Don't let them take me. Let me die in my own bed.

"Supposing it was yourself and Tom, then, Toni," said Mr. Cassidy, remembering himself a gentleman. "What would you want him to do? Would you want him to break his promise?"

"I hope I'd never make him promise anything like that," said Toni.

"But if you did?"

"I don't believe in those kinds of promises."

"My father thinks he's God. You have to understand. There's no two ways about anything."

For what was his son now refusing to forgive him? He was silent now, sitting in the back of the car. He looked at the top of his daughter-in-law's head, blonde now, like some kind of circus candy. She had never been blonde. Why did they do it? Try to be what they were not born to. Rose did not.

"What I wish you'd get through your head, Pa, is that it's me and Toni carrying the load. I suppose you forget where all the suppers come from?"

"I don't forget."

"Why don't you think of Toni for once?"

"I think of her, Tom, and you too. I know what you do. I'm very grateful. Mom is grateful, too, or she would be."

But first I think of my wife to whom I made vows. And whom I promised.

"The doctor thinks you're nuts, you know that, don't you?" said Tom. "Rafferty thinks you're nuts to try and keep her. He thinks we're nuts to go along with you. He says he washes his hands of the whole bunch of us."

The doctor washes his hands, thought Mr. Cassidy, seeing Leo Rafferty, hale as a dog, at his office sink.

The important thing was not to forget she was the woman he had married.

So he could leave the house, so he could leave her alone, he strapped her into the bed. Her curses were worst when he released her. She had grown a beard this last year, like a goat.

Like a man?

No.

He remembered her as she was when she was first his wife. A white nightgown, then as now. So she was the same. He'd been told it smelled different a virgin's first time. And never that way again. Some blood. Not much. As if she hadn't minded.

He sat her in the chair in front of the television. They had Mass now on television for sick people, people like her. She pushed the button on the little box that could change channels from across the room. One of their grandsons was a TV repairman. He had done it for them when she got sick. She pushed the button to a station that showed cartoons. Mice in capes, cats outraged. Some stories now with colored children. He boiled an egg for her lunch.

She sat chewing, looking at the television. What was that look in her eyes now? Why did he want to call it wickedness? Because it was blank and hateful. Because there was no light. Eyes should have light. There should be something behind them. That was dangerous, nothing behind her eyes but hate. Sullen like a bull kept from a cow. Sex mad. Why did that look make him think of sex? Sometimes he was afraid she wanted it.

He did not know what he would do.

She slept. He slept in the chair across from her.

The clock went off for her medicine. He got up from the chair, gauging the weather. Sometimes the sky was green this time of year. It was warm when it should not be. He didn't like that. The mix-up made him shaky. It made him say to himself, "Now I am old."

He brought her the medicine. Three pills, red and gray, red and yellow, dark pink. Two just to keep her quiet. Sometimes she sucked them and spat them out when they melted and she got the bad taste. She thought they were candy. It was their fault for making them those colors. But it was something else he had to think about. He had to make sure she swallowed them right away.

Today she was not going to swallow. He could see that by the way her eyes looked at the television. The way she set her mouth so he could see what she had done with the pills, kept them in a pocket in her cheek, as if for storage.

"Rose," he said, stepping between her and the television, breaking her gaze. "You've got to swallow the pills. They cost money."

She tried to look over his shoulder. On the screen an ostrich, dressed in colored stockings, danced down the road. He could see she was not listening to him. And he tried to remember what the young priest had said when he came to bring Communion, what his daughter June had said. Be patient with her. Humor her. She can't help what she does. She's not the woman she once was.

She is the same.

"Hey, my Rose, won't you just swallow the pills for me. Like my girl."

She pushed him out of the way. So she could go on watching the television. He knelt down next to her.

"Come on, girleen. It's the pills make you better."

She gazed over the top of his head. He stood up, remembering what was done to animals.

He stroked her throat as he had stroked the throats of dogs and horses, a boy on a farm. He stroked the old woman's loose, papery throat, and said, "Swallow, then, just swallow."

She looked over his shoulder at the television. She kept the pills in a corner of her mouth.

It was making him angry. He put one finger above her lip under her nose and one below her chin, so that she would not be able to open her mouth. She breathed through her nose like a patient animal. She went on looking at the television. She did not swallow.

"You swallow them, Rose, this instant," he said, clamping her mouth shut. "They cost money. The doctor says you must. You're throwing good money down the drain."

Now she was watching a lion and a polar bear dancing. There were pianos in their cages.

He knew he must move away or his anger would make him do something. He had promised he would not be angry. He would remember who she was.

He went into the kitchen with a new idea. He would give her something sweet that would make her want to swallow. There was ice cream in the refrigerator. Strawberry that she liked. He removed each strawberry and placed it in the sink so she would not chew and then get the taste of the medicine. And then spit it out, leaving him, leaving them both no better than when they began.

He brought the dish of ice cream to her in the living room. She was sitting staring at the television with her mouth open. Perhaps she had opened her mouth to laugh? At what? At what was this grown woman laughing? A zebra was playing a xylophone while his zebra wife hung striped pajamas on a line.

In opening her mouth, she had let the pills fall together onto her lap. He saw the three of them, wet, stuck together, at the center of her lap. He thought he would take the pills and simply hide them in the ice cream. He bent to fish them from the valley of her lap.

And then she screamed at him. And then she stood up.

He was astonished at her power. She had not stood by herself for seven months. She put one arm in front of her breasts and raised the other against him, knocking him heavily to the floor.

"No," she shouted, her voice younger, stronger, the voice of a well young man. "Don't think you can have it now. That's what you're after. That's what you're always after. You want to get into it. I'm not one of your whores. You always thought it was such a great prize. I wish you'd have it cut off. I'd like to cut it off."

And she walked out of the house. He could see her wandering up and down the street in the darkness.

He dragged himself over to the chair and propped himself against it so he could watch her through the window. But he knew he could not move any farther. His leg was light and foolish underneath him, and burning with pain. He could not move anymore, not even to the telephone that was half a yard away from him. He could see her body, visible through her nightgown, as she walked the street in front of the house.

He wondered if he should call out or be silent. He did not know how far she would walk. He could imagine her walking until the land stopped, and then into the water. He could not stop her. He would not raise his voice.

There was that pain in his leg that absorbed him strangely, as if it were the pain of someone else. He knew the leg was broken. "I have broken my leg," he kept saying to himself, trying to connect the words and the burning.

But then he remembered what it meant. He would not be able to walk. He would not be able to take care of her.

"Rose," he shouted, trying to move toward the window.

And then, knowing he could not move and she could not hear him, "Help."

He could see the green numbers on the clock, alive as cat's eyes. He could see his wife walking in the middle of the street. At least she was not walking far. But no one was coming to help her.

He would have to call for help. And he knew what it meant: they would take her away somewhere. No one would take care of her in the house if he did not. And he could not move.

No one could hear him shouting. No one but he could see his wife, wandering up and down the street in her nightgown.

They would take her away. He could see it; he could hear the noises. Policemen in blue, car radios reporting other disasters, young boys writing his words down in notebooks. And doctors, white coats, white shoes, wheeling her out. Her strapped. She would curse him. She would curse him rightly for having broken his promise. And the young men would wheel her out. Almost everyone was younger than he now. And he could hear how she would be as they wheeled her past him, rightly cursing.

Now he could see her weaving in the middle of the street. He heard a car slam on its brakes to avoid her. He thought someone would have to stop then. But he heard the car go on down to the corner.

No one could hear him shouting in the living room. The windows were shut; it was late October. There was a high bulk of gray cloud, showing islands of fierce, acidic blue. He would have to do something to get someone's attention before the sky became utterly dark and the drivers could not see her wandering before their cars. He could see her wandering; he could see the set of her angry back. She was wearing only her nightgown. He would have to get someone to bring her in before she died of cold.

The only objects he could reach were the figurines that covered the low table beside him. He picked one up: a bust of Robert Kennedy. He threw it through the window. The breaking glass made a violent, disgraceful noise. It was the sound of disaster he wanted. It must bring help.

He lay still for ten minutes, waiting, looking at the clock. He could see her walking, cursing. She could not hear him. He was afraid no one could hear him. He picked up another figurine, a bicentennial eagle, and threw it through the window next to the one he had just broken. Then he picked up another and threw it through the window next to that. He went on: six windows. He went on until he had broken every window in the front of the house.

He had ruined his house. The one surprising thing of his long lifetime. The broken glass winked like green jewels, hard sea creatures, on the purple carpet. He looked at what he had destroyed. He would never have done it; it was something he would never have done. But he would not have believed he was a man who could not keep his promise.

In the dark he lay and prayed that someone would come and get her. That was the only thing now to pray for; the one thing he had asked God to keep back. A car stopped in front of the house. He heard his son's voice speaking to his mother. He could see the two of them; Tom had his arm around her. She was walking into the house now as if she had always meant to.

Mr. Cassidy lay back for the last moment of darkness. Soon the room would be full.

His son turned on the light.

A Writing Lesson

Fairy tales, we have been told, have within them the content of all fiction. As an exercise, write the same story as a fairy tale, and then as the kind of fiction we are more used to.

If you are writing a fairy tale, you can begin by saying that they had built a house in the center of the woods. And they sat in the center of it, as if they were children, huddled, cringing against bears. He had to go outside, for food or fire; she never went out. He was clever, and hidden, and got by the bears when he was outside. The walls of the house were thick, and they were safe, sitting in the center.

If your story is not a fairy tale, begin by saying that the husband and the wife lived a life that was somewhat isolated. In the first paragraph, be sure that you introduce the other major character: the girl. Say, before you go any further, that the girl is strong and young and the man is a good man. Say at this point that the wife is frail and beautiful. The reader will know from the beginning that you mean the wife to win in the end, if you are writing the fiction we are familiar with. In a fairy tale, the prize usually goes to the young, the strong, the courageous, and the good. But perhaps even in fairy tales there is no possibility that the frail and the beautiful will not, in the end, win. And so you can apply your description of the characters to either of your stories.

You will, by this time, have prepared the reader for the end of the story and indicated the direction you would have his sympathies take. This both is and is not the technique of the teller of tales. The main feature of the technique is that the teller gets to the point.

Quickly, then, whichever mode you are writing in, let the reader know that the girl is someone else's wife, and should not be called a girl if the fiction you are writing is realistic. She is called a girl simply to distinguish her (and it is important that she be distinguished) from the man's wife, with whom, as things would happen, she has more in common than she can know or would admit. But you must let the reader see these similarities only gradually; it is part of the craft of concealment.

When you are writing the fairy tale, go on to say that the wife sat all day combing her beautiful hair. The man and the girl worked together, cutting up wood, tying it in bundles. Sometimes their fingers would touch and she would tell him with her eyes, "How I love you. It is unbearable to me." The man will understand, although the girl will not speak because she has seen the wife, pale and fragile, combing her beautiful hair.

This is the way to describe the situation if you intend to write a fairy tale. If you are writing realistic fiction, your approach will be different. It is possible to say that the wife did have beautiful hair and that the man and the girl worked together, but it must be a perfectly ordinary job; it will have nothing to do with bundling wood (wood should not even be mentioned); they can share an office, a secretary. And sometimes she *will* try to tell him something with her eyes. But if you are not writing a fairy tale, you must remember that the language of the eyes is silent, and often unheard or misunderstood. As a humorous touch, you can say that the girl once tried to tell him with her eyes, and he asked if she were ill. And so the girl will remain silent, for she has seen the wife with her husband, frail and tentative, sitting beside him at dinner, touching him often. And the sight will have moved her; such fragility, in any mode of fiction, must move any but the coldest hearts. But because outside of fairy tales, if you are not writing a fairy tale, the feelings of the characters are not always clear, you must make the point that the girl hated the woman, for the girl was a hewer of wood. That is to say, she believed that love was earned and could be lost, and the wife was loved for her beautiful hair. How the girl would have loved that: to be loved for her frailty, her hair, not to have to work at love like a cabinetmaker (you can see that we are using the image of wood without actually mentioning wood), but to be loved for what she was born with, what she had nothing to do with, what she could neither improve very much nor change very much. How she would have loved to be loved for what she could not do.

A problem now arises: How do you describe endurance, silence, in the language of the fairy tale? And how do you say that in the midst of her silence there was talk, a paradise of talk, a wilderness of talk, about everything else? And how do you describe his fine bright eye: a bird's? a horse's? For you, the craftsman, this will be a difficult problem. Perhaps you will have to leave all these things out of the fairy tale and put in their place definite, visible action.

In the fairy tale, something definite must happen: It is in the nature of the narrative. In the fairy tale, she will weep. The girl will weep in the woods and someone, someone old or magical, will hear. Something will happen, something outside her, so that her intention of silence will remain pure, and yet he will know. Something dramatic will happen, so that she can remain silent, but he will come to her, to her deathbed, to her bed of leaves, knowing.

Even in the course of the fiction we are familiar with, there is one central event around which the story centers, around which it fans, like a peacock's tail. You should be searching your narrative for a central event, a significant event. In the fiction we are familiar with, it is possible that the central event will be an event in the mind: a decision. For example, it would be perfectly consistent with the rules of fiction and with the character of the girl as you have created her, if you have her decide not to act but to keep her love a secret. You can refer back to the scene of the husband and the wife at dinner. You can depict the girl watching the wife afraid to eat anything until her husband has eaten something first, then giving him half her dinner. You may describe the fear that that engendered in the girl: you may discuss the fear that may exist in the heart of a strong person in the presence of vulnerability. You may mention, here, the girl's sense of superiority: she would, she knew, never wait to see what anyone was eating before she began to eat. And you may include here her sense that, being stronger than the wife, she was more able to bear loss.

The central event of a fairy tale often involves loss. The theme of the quest is also prevalent. In the fairy tale, for example, the girl can go to the man for help because she has lost something magical: a comb made of pearls, a ring in the shape of a lion's head. And they will search in the woods until it is dark, and then they will lie down with the animals.

In a story that is not a fairy tale, the difficulties in getting them into the woods alone may be distracting. He is married; she is married, so you can see the implications for your narrative. In addition, the image of a couple in the woods may be comic or prurient. And besides, the girl has decided that nothing of that nature will happen. You must convey that her decision involved some sorrow, but you must not say that the girl is weeping: it is not consistent with her character. You may make the wife weep; you could create a moving scene in which you describe the wife, combing her beautiful hair, weeping. Only you have decided that the girl will remain silent. So there is no reason for the wife to weep. But you may depict the wife weeping anyway: it will be beautiful and consistent with her character.

And the man? The man loved them both, each according to what he believed she needed, each according to his needs. The girl he loved in a paradise of talk, a wilderness of talk, and his wife he took to him, flesh to flesh. If we were to end the fairy tale, this would be a happy ending: each having what she needed, which was what he thought she needed: each happy. But, in realistic fiction, this apportionment will not satisfy the character of the girl as you have created her.

Perhaps even in the fairy tale, apportionment will not be enough for the girl, and she will turn into a kind of witch, stirring her love in a dark pot, over and over, with things from old nightmares: heads of animals, curious mangled limbs, herbs that are acrid, dangerous. Even this could lead to an event or an ending: the girl could bewitch the wife and take the husband. But you want the girl to be the hero of the story, and now the girl has become a witch, so you can see the problem for your narrative.

But the problem is not insuperable because the form of the fairy tale, unlike the realistic form, allows for the possibilities of transformation. So you can depict the girl transformed from a girl to a witch, and then you could transform her back to a girl, sadder, more silent, perfectly beautiful in the woods, having learned in her witchhood the language of animals. You can have her send the man and the wife off, having cured them of their enchantment, and leave her in the woods, full of secrets, full of lore. This will compel the reader with the attractions of the supernatural.

It is possible in realistic fiction as well to create the witch as hero, but you must place her in another moral context, and you cannot call her a witch. The use of multiple contexts is an option of the writer of the fiction we are now used to, but you must be sure that your values are clear to the reader. You must create a context in which you extol the values of silence and endurance. You must make the reader interested in the girl's interesting and understandable hatred; you must make him sympathize with her fear and her sense of superiority. You will praise the girl for swallowing her power like a spell she wants to forget, for loving, in spite of herself, the beautiful wife, fraily combing her beautiful hair by the window. And this is the image that will stay in the reader's mind. Of course you can see the problem for your narrative.

You must be sure that the reader can only interpret the story as you would have it interpreted. If you have written a fairy tale, it may be possible for the reader to find everyone a hero: the girl, the man, the wife. All may live on, each inhabiting his particular beauty. But if you are not writing a fairy tale, the center of your fiction is the avoidance of action, the will, steadfastly clung to out of love and hatred, not to change, but to be silent. This may be interpreted as cowardice or bravery, depending upon the context you have created. If it is cowardice, the wife will be the hero of the story, because the reader will have seen her do nothing cowardly. And if it is bravery, the reader will still remember the wife, sitting at her window, fraily combing her beautiful hair.

Once you have decided upon the path of your narrative and have understood its implications, go back to the beginning of the story. Describe the house.

The Thorn

If I lose this, she thought, I will be so far away I will never come back.

When the kind doctor came to tell her that her father was dead, he took her crayons and drew a picture of a heart. It was not like a valentine, he said. It was solid and made of flesh, and it was not entirely red. It had veins and arteries and valves and one of them had broken, and so her daddy was now in heaven, he had said.

She was very interested in the picture of the heart and she put it under her pillow to sleep with, since no one she knew ever came to put her to bed anymore. Her mother came and got her in the morning, but she wasn't in her own house, she was in the bed next to her cousin Patty. Patty said to her one night, "My mommy says your daddy suffered a lot, but now he's released from suffering. That means he's dead." Lucy said yes, he was, but she didn't tell anyone that the reason she wasn't crying was that he'd either come back or take her with him.

Her aunt Iris, who owned a beauty parlor, took her to B. Altman's and bought her a dark blue dress with a white collar. That's nice, Lucy thought. I'll have a new dress for when I go away with my father. She looked in the long mirror and thought it was the nicest dress she'd ever had.

Her uncle Ted took her to the funeral parlor and he told her that her father would be lying in a big box with a lot of flowers. That's what I'll do, she said. I'll get in the box with him. We used to play in a big box; we called it the tent and we got in and read stories. I will get into the big box. There is my father; that is his silver ring.

She began to climb into the box, but her uncle pulled her away. She didn't argue; her father would think of some way to get her. He would wait for her in her room when it was dark. She would not be afraid to turn the lights out anymore. Maybe he would only visit her in her room; all right, then, she would never go on vacation; she would never go away with her mother to the country, no matter how much her mother cried and begged her. It was February and she asked her mother not to make any summer plans. Her aunt Lena, who lived with them, told Lucy's mother that if she had kids she wouldn't let them push her around, not at age seven. No matter how smart they thought they were. But Lucy didn't care; her father would come and talk to her, she and her mother would move back to the apartment where they lived before her father got sick, and she would only have to be polite to Aunt Lena; she would not have to love her, she would not have to feel sorry for her.

On the last day of school she got the best report card in her class. Father Burns said her mother would be proud to have such a smart little girl, but she wondered if he said this to make fun of her. But Sister Trinitas kissed her when all the other children had left and let her mind the statue for the summer; the one with the bottom that screwed off so you could put the big rosaries inside it. Nobody ever got to keep it for more than one night. This was a good thing. Since her father was gone she didn't know if people were being nice or if they seemed nice and really wanted to make her feel bad later. But she was pretty sure this was good. Sister Trinitas kissed her, but she smelled fishy when you got close up; it was the paste she used to make the Holy Childhood poster. This was good.

"You can take it to camp with you this summer, but be very careful of it."

"I'm not going to camp, Sister. I have to stay at home this summer."

"I thought your mother said you were going to camp."

"No, I have to stay home." She could not tell anybody, even Sister Trinitas, whom she loved, that she had to stay in her room because her father was certainly coming. She couldn't tell anyone about the thorn in her heart. She had a heart, just like her father's, brown in places, blue in places, a muscle the size of a fist. But hers had a thorn in it. The thorn was her father's voice. When the thorn pinched, she could hear her father saying something. "I love you more than anyone will ever love you. I love you more than God loves you." *Thint* went the thorn; he was telling her a story "about a mean old lady named Emmy and a nice old man named Charlie who always had candy in his pockets, and their pretty daughter, Ruth, who worked in the city." But it was harder and harder. Sometimes she tried to make the thorn go *thint* and she only felt the thick wall of her heart; she couldn't remember the sound of it or the kind of things he said. Then she was terribly far away; she didn't know how to do things, and if her aunt Lena asked her to do something like dust the ledge, suddenly there were a hundred ledges in the room and she didn't know which one and when she said to her aunt which one did she mean when she said ledge: the one by the floor, the one by the stairs, the one under the television, her aunt Lena said she must have really pulled the wool over their eyes at school because at home she was an idiot. And then Lucy would knock something over and Aunt Lena would tell her to get out, she was so clumsy she wrecked everything. Then she needed to feel the thorn, but all she could feel was her heart getting thicker and heavier, until she went up to her room and waited. Then she could hear it. "You are the prettiest girl in a hundred counties and when I see your face it is like a parade that someone made special for your daddy."

She wanted to tell her mother about the thorn, but her father had said that he loved her more than anything, even God. And she knew he said he loved God very much. So he must love her more than he loved her mother. So if she couldn't hear him her mother couldn't, and if he wasn't waiting for her in her new room then he was nowhere.

When she came home she showed everyone the statue that Sister Trinitas had given her. Her mother said that was a very great honor: that meant that Sister Trinitas must like her very much, and Aunt Lena said she wouldn't lay any bets about it not being broken or lost by the end of the summer, and she better not think of taking it to camp.

Lucy's heart got hot and wide and her mouth opened in tears.

"I'm not going to camp; I have to stay here."

"You're going to camp, so you stop brooding and moping around. You're turning into a regular little bookworm. You're beginning to stink of books. Get out in the sun and play with other children. That's what you need, so you learn not to trip over your own two feet."

"I'm not going to camp. I have to stay here. Tell her, Mommy, you promised we wouldn't go away."

Her mother took out her handkerchief. It smelled of perfume and it had a lipstick print on it in the shape of her mother's mouth. Lucy's mother wiped her wet face with the pink handkerchief that Lucy loved.

"Well, we talked it over and we decided it would be best. It's not a real camp. It's Uncle Ted's camp, and Aunt Bitsie will be there, and all your cousins and that nice dog Tramp that you like."

"I won't go. I have to stay here."

"Don't be ridiculous," Aunt Lena said. "There's nothing for you to do here but read and make up stories."

"But it's for *boys* up there and I'll have nothing to do there. All they want to do is shoot guns and yell and run around. I hate that. And I have to stay here."

"That's what you need. Some good, healthy boys to toughen you up. You're too goddamn sensitive."

Sensitive. Everyone said that. It meant she cried for nothing. That was bad. Even Sister Trinitas got mad at her once and told her to stop her crocodile tears. They must be right. She would like not to cry when people said things that she didn't understand. That would be good. They had to be right. But the thorn. She went up to her room. She heard her father's voice on the telephone. *Thint,* it went. It was her birthday, and he was away in Washington. He sang "Happy Birthday" to her. Then he sang the song that made her laugh and laugh: "Hey, Lucy Turner, are there any more at home like you?" because of course there weren't. And she mustn't lose that voice, the thorn. She would think about it all the time, and maybe then she would keep it. Because if she lost it, she would always be clumsy and mistaken; she would always be wrong and falling.

Aunt Lena drove her up to the camp. *Scenery.* That was another word she didn't understand. "Look at that gorgeous scenery," Aunt Lena said, and Lucy didn't know what she meant. "Look at that bird," Aunt Lena said, and Lucy couldn't see it, so she just said, "It's nice." And Aunt Lena said,

"Don't lie. You can't even *see* it, you're looking in the wrong direction. Don't say you can see something when you can't see it. And don't spend the whole summer crying. Uncle Ted and Aunt Bitsie are giving you a wonderful summer for free. So don't spend the whole time crying. Nobody can stand to have a kid around that all she ever does is cry."

Lucy's mother had said that Aunt Lena was very kind and very lonely because she had no little boys and girls of her own and she was doing what she thought was best for Lucy. But when Lucy told her father that she thought Aunt Lena was not very nice, her father had said, "She's ignorant." *Ignorant.* That was a good word for the woman beside her with the dyed black hair and the big vaccination scar on her fat arm.

"Did you scratch your vaccination when you got it, Aunt Lena?"

"Of course not. What a stupid question. Don't be so goddamn rude. I'm not your mother, ya know. Ya can't push me around."

Thint, went the thorn. "You are ignorant," her father's voice said to Aunt Lena. "You are very, very ignorant."

Lucy looked out the window.

When Aunt Lena's black Chevrolet went down the road, Uncle Ted and Aunt Bitsie showed her her room. She would stay in Aunt Bitsie's room, except when Aunt Bitsie's husband came up on the weekends. Then Lucy would have to sleep on the couch.

The people in the camp were all boys, and they didn't want to talk to her. Aunt Bitsie said she would have to eat with the counselors and the K.P.s. Aunt Bitsie said there was a nice girl named Betty who was fourteen who did the dishes. Her brothers were campers.

Betty came out and said hello. She was wearing a sailor hat that had a picture of a boy smoking a cigarette. It said "Property of Bobby." She had braces on her teeth. Her two side teeth hung over her lips so that her mouth never quite closed.

"My name's Betty," she said. "But everybody calls me Fang. That's on account of my fangs." She opened and closed her mouth like a dog. "In our crowd, if you're popular, you get a nickname. I guess I'm pretty popular."

Aunt Bitsie walked in and told Betty to set the table. She snapped her gum as she took out the silver. "Yup, Mrs. O'Connor, one thing about me is I have a lot of interests. There's swimming and boys, and tennis, and boys, and reading, and boys, and boys, and boys, and boys, and boys."

Betty and Aunt Bitsie laughed. Lucy didn't get it.

"What do you like to read?" Lucy asked.

"What?" said Betty.

"Well, you said one of your interests was reading. I was wondering what you like to read."

Betty gave her a fishy look. "I like to read romantic comics. About romances," she said. "I hear you're a real bookworm. We'll knock that outa ya."

The food came in: ham with brown gravy that tasted like ink. Margarine. Tomatoes that a fly settled on. But Lucy could not eat. Her throat was full of water. Her heart was glassy and too small. And now they would see her cry.

She was told to go up to her room.

That summer Lucy learned many things. She made a birchbark canoe to take home to her mother. Aunt Bitsie made a birchbark sign for her that said "Keep Smiling." Uncle Ted taught her to swim by letting her hold on to the waist of his bathing trunks. She swam onto the float like the boys. Uncle Ted said that that was so good she would get double dessert just like the boys did the first time they swam out to the float. But then Aunt Bitsie forgot and said it was just as well anyway because certain little girls should learn to watch their figures. One night her cousins Larry and Artie carried the dog Tramp in and pretended it had been shot. But then they put it down and it ran around and licked her and they said they had done it to make her cry.

She didn't cry so much now, but she always felt very far away and people's voices sounded the way they did when she was on the sand at the beach and she could hear the people's voices down by the water. A lot of times she didn't hear people when they talked to her. Her heart was very thick now: it was like one of Uncle Ted's boxing gloves. The thorn never touched the thin, inside walls of it anymore. She had lost it. There was no one whose voice was beautiful now, and little that she remembered.

Eileen

"There's some that just can't take it," Bridget said. "No matter what they do or you do for them, they just don't fit in."

"You certainly were good to her, Kathleen," said Nettie, "when she first came over. No one could have been better when she first came over."

"That was years ago," Kathleen said. "We never kept up with her."

Nora thought of Eileen Foley when she had first come over, twelve years ago, when Nora was eleven and Eileen, twenty-one. They'd had to share a bed, and Kathleen had apologized. "There's no place for her, only here. I don't know what they were thinking of, sending her over, with no one to vouch for her, only the nuns. The Foleys were like that, the devil take the hindmost, every one of them. You'd see why she wanted to get out."

But Nora hadn't minded. She liked Eileen's company, and her body was no intrusion in the bed. Her flesh was pleasant, fragrant. Though she was large, she was careful not to take up too much room. They joked about it. "Great cow that I am, pray God I don't roll over one fine night and crush you. How'd yer mam forgive me if I should do that."

And they would laugh, excluding Nora's brothers, as they excluded them with all their talk about the future, Eileen's and Nora's both. It was adult talk; the young boys had no place in it. It was female too, but it was different from the way that Nora's mother and aunts, Bridget and Nettie, spoke, because it had belief and hope, and the older women's conversation began with a cheerful, skeptical, accepting resignation and could move—particularly when Bridget took the lead—to a conviction of injustice and impossibility and the inevitable folly of expecting one good thing.

They talked every night about what had happened to Eileen at work. She was a cook at a school for the blind run for the Presentation sisters. It was in the Bronx. In Limerick, she'd worked at the sisters' orphanage; she was grateful they had recommended her over here. She was proud of her work, she liked the people, worshipped the nuns that ran the place. She said she would have loved to be a nun, only for her soft nature. She was right about herself; she had a penchant for small luxuries: lavender sachets to perfume her underclothes, honey-flavored lozenges that came in a tin box with a picture of a beautiful blond child, a clothesbrush with an ivory handle, a hatpin that pushed its point into the dull black felt of Eileen's hat and left behind a butterfly of yellow and red stones. She would take these things out secretly and show them first to Nora, so that Nora felt that she possessed them too and considered herself doubly blessed: with the friendship of one so much older and with the passion of her observation of these objects she could covet, and could prize but need not own.

The nuns, Eileen told Nora often, had a terrible hard life. They slept on wooden pallets and were silent after dark; they woke at dawn, ate little, and were not permitted to have friends. Not even among each other; no, they had to be particularly on their guard for that. "Particular friendships, it's called," Eileen told Nora proudly. "They're forbidden particular friendships." She told Nora she'd learned all this from Sister Mary Rose, who ran the kitchen. It was not her praise that mattered to Eileen, though, but the words of Sister Catherine Benedict, the superior.

"She came up to me once, that quiet, I didn't know she was behind me. I was cutting up some cod for boiling, you know the blind ones have to have soft foods, as they can't cut, of course—and Sister must have been watching me over my shoulder all the time. 'You are particularly careful, Eileen Foley, and the Blessed Mother sees that, and she will reward you, mark my words. A bone left in a piece of fish could mean death for one of the children, so to cut up each piece with the utmost care is like a Corporal Work of Mercy for the poor little souls.'"

Eileen said that Sister Catherine Benedict had come from Galway city. "You could tell she comes from money. But she gave it up. For God." At Christmastime, Sister had given Eileen a holy picture of her patron saint, Saint Catherine of Siena, and on the back had signed her name with a cross in front of it. Nora and Eileen would look at the picture; it seemed to them a sign of something that they valued but could not find or even name in the world that they inhabited; excellence, simplicity. One day, Eileen promised, she would bring Nora to the home so that she could meet Sister Catherine for herself. But it never happened, there was never time.

Because, really, Eileen hadn't lived with the Derencys very long, six months perhaps. Nora tried to remember how long it was; at twenty-three the seasons of an eleven-year-old seemed illusory: what could possibly have happened then to mark one month from another, or one year? Each day of her adulthood seemed like the dropping down of coins into a slot: a sound fixed, right, and comforting accompanied her aging, the sound of money in the bank. Childhood was no gift to a cripple, she'd often thought, with its emphasis on physical speed, with those interminable hours which required for their filling senseless, interminable games of jumping, running, catching, following, scaling, shinnying, those various and diffuse verbs that spelled her failure. Even now, in her well-cut suit, her perfumed handkerchief shaped like a fan tucked in her pocket, the gold compact she had bought herself with her first wages, even now she could think of those childhood games and bring back once again the fear, the anger, the thin high smell that was the anguish of exclusion. Even now, though her success at Mr. Riordan's law office was breath-taking, even now she could bring back the memory of her body's defeat.

Even now, at twenty-three, as she stood in the kitchen drinking black coffee while her mother cooked and her aunts lounged over their boiled eggs, even now Nora could feel the misery. She thought of Eileen and of the pleasure it had been to have her; one of her few physical pleasures as a child. She thought about Eileen's abundant flesh that seemed to have much more in common with a food than with an object of sexual desire:

the white flesh of an apple came to mind or milk, a peach in its first blush of ripeness, the swell of a firm, mild, delicious cheese. Nothing dark, secretive, or inexplicably responsive seemed to be a part of Eileen's body life. And Nora prized Eileen because it seemed to her that Eileen was as definitely cut off from coupling as she, although she could not quite say why. For it was Nora's body's brokenness that always would exclude her from the desiring eye of men, whereas with Eileen it was excessive wholeness that would turn men's eyes away: nothing could be broken into, broken up.

Six months it must have been, thought Nora, that she lived here. After that she moved into the convent. She felt embarrassed, she'd confessed to Nora, to be living with the family. She'd offered money for her board, but Kathleen had refused it. And she hated the remarks that Bridget made about her family. Family passion and its underside, the family shame, could make Eileen's high color mottle and her perfect skin appear sickish and damp. She knew what her family was, but after all, she said, they tried their best, their luck had been against them.

"You make your own luck," Bridget had said when Nora tried, just after Eileen had left them, to defend the Foleys. She'd mentioned their bad luck. "Every greenhorn in America came here through nothing but bad luck. If it was good luck that we had, we'd be back home in great fine houses."

"Still there's some like the Foleys that God's eye doesn't shine on," said Kathleen.

"God's eye, my eye, 'tis nothing wrong with them but laziness and drink, the same old song, and no new verses added," Bridget said.

"But what about the mother?" Nettie said. The two sisters looked sharply at her, warning her to silence.

"That was never proved," said Kathleen.

"What was never proved?" eleven-year-old Nora had asked.

"Time enough for you to be knowing that kind of story. Hanging about the way you do, you know far too much as it is," Bridget said.

I know more than you'll know when you're a hundred, Nora wanted to say to her aunt, whom she despised for her bad nature and yet feared. She felt that Bridget blamed her for her leg, as if, if she'd wanted it, she could be outside running with the other children. There was some truth in that, there always was in Bridget's black predictions and malevolent reports. It was the partial truths in what she said that made her dangerous.

It was only recently that they'd explained about Eileen's mother. Nora tried now to remember what the circumstances might have been that would have made the sisters talk about it. She could not. It wasn't that they'd seen Eileen, they hadn't, not since Nora's high school graduation, which was six years ago now. They had known the Foleys' house, so it was real to them, the news, when it came from her cousin Anna Fogarty, who had stayed on at home. Mrs. Foley, Eileen's mother, who everyone had thought was queer, had burned the house down and she herself and her youngest baby, a boy of six months, had both perished. Everyone believed that she had set the fire. Nora felt she saw it, the fixed face of the mother as her life burned up around her, the green skeleton of the boy baby, left to be gone over like the ruined clothes, the spoons, the pots and pans.

Eileen's father had married again, which just showed, Bridget said, the foolishness of some young girls. All the sisters thought of marriage as a sign of weakness: they made only partial exceptions for themselves. But the young girl who'd married Eileen's father seemed to prove the sisters' point. She'd left her family where she had considered herself unhappy, thinking she was moving out to something better. The parish had helped Jamesie Foley build a new house: that had turned the young girl's head. But what she got for her pains was a drunken husband and a brood of someone else's children whom she tormented until Eileen couldn't bear to see it and left to work in the orphanage in Limerick, where the nuns, knowing her wishes, got the place for her in their house in New York.

The sisters in both convents knew her dreams were for her brother Tom. Tom was twelve years younger than Eileen, the youngest living child. He was wonderfully intelligent, Eileen told Nora, and had an angel's nature. Every penny of her salary she could she put into the bank to bring him over; that was why she took the sisters' offer of her living in the convent instead of with the Derencys, she could save her carfare. That was what she said to the Derencys, but Nora knew there was more to it. Her pride, which couldn't tolerate Kathleen not taking any money. Nora could tell that Eileen worshipped Kathleen. And it troubled her that there was nothing she could do for Kathleen when Kathleen did so much for her.

As Kathleen's life had blurred, Nora's had been pressed into sharp focus. She had wanted to become a teacher, and her teachers encouraged her. Austere and yet maternal Protestants, romantic from the books they read, they treasured the pretty crippled girl with her devotion to the plays of

Shakespeare and to Caesar's *Gallic Wars*, to anything, in fact, that they suggested she should read. Nora had been accepted at the Upstate Normal School on the basis of her grades and of her teachers' letters. But none of them had mentioned Nora's deformity; she'd been born with one leg shorter than the other. She realized they hadn't known, the moment she arrived, nervous to the point of sickness, driven by her nervous mother. How shocked those men were, in the office of the dean, when they beheld her with her high shoe and her crutch. They blamed the teachers. "No one has informed us . . . You must see, of course, it's quite impossible . . . We must think first about the safety of potential children who might be in your charge. Imagine if there were a fire or a similar emergency . . ." They talked as if they were reading what they said from a book. They did not look at her. They said that it was most regrettable, but they were sure she understood, and understood that it was no reflection—not-a-tall—on her. They were just sorry she had had to make the trip.

She drove back with her mother in shamed silence, as if she'd been left at the altar and in all her wedding finery was making her way home. That was the way her father behaved, as if she had been jilted. He said he and some of his friends whose names he wouldn't mention would drive themselves up there and teach a lesson to those Yankee bastards. It was a free country, he said; you didn't get away with that kind of behavior here. He was very angry at his wife.

"Did you say nothing to them, Kathleen? Did you just walk out with your tail between your legs like some bog trotter thrown off the land by an English thief? Was that the way of it?"

Nora saw her mother's shame. She knew her father was just talk; he would have done no better. She herself had remained silent, and she bore her own shame in her heart. She would not let her mother feel the weight of it.

"I think, you know, Dad, it's a blessing in disguise. I'd make three times the money in an office. You were right, Dad, all along. I should have taken the commercial course."

"I was not right. You went where you belonged, there in the academic. You've twice the brains of any of them. Reading Latin like a priest. French too. I'm that proud of you."

She wanted to tell him that her education had been nothing, foolishness, Latin she was already forgetting, French she couldn't speak, history that meant not one thing to her, plays and poems about nothing to do with her life. She felt contempt, then, for her teachers and the things they stood for. She felt they'd conspired against her and made her look a fool. They could have fought for her against the men who sat behind the desks there in the office of the Normal School. But they did not fight for her, they kept their silence, as she had and as her mother had. And they had counted on that silence, those men in that office; it gave them the confidence to say the things they said, "regret" and "understanding" and "upon reflection." They had counted on the silence that surrounded people like Nora and her family, fell upon them like a cloak, swallowed them up and made them disappear so quickly that by the time Nora and her mother stopped in Westchester for a cup of tea they could forget that they had ever seen her.

She determined that she would be successful in the business world. She finished senior year with the high grades she had begun with: she owed her parents that. But her attention was on the girls she knew who worked in offices: the way they dressed and spoke and carried themselves. She would be one of them; she would be better than any one of them. She would take trains and manicure her nails. Every muscle in her body she would devote to an appearance of efficiency and competence, with its inevitable edges of contempt.

Her one regret was that she had to ask her father for the money for her business-school tuition. He was glad to give it to her, she could tell he felt that he was making something up to her, making it all right. She was first in her class in every subject. Easily, within a week of graduation, she was hired by the firm of MacIntosh and Riordan, where she thrived.

She almost became the thing she wanted. She grew impatient with home life, in love with the world that required of her what she so easily, so beautifully could give. The years of all the anger which her family had not acknowledged or allowed she put into a furious, commercial energy. Soon Mr. Riordan had only to give her a brief idea of the contents of a letter; she herself composed those sentences that shone like music to her: threatening or clarifying, setting straight. This new person she had become had no place in her life for Eileen Foley, or for her brother Tom, whom she had finally brought over after six hard years.

He was fifteen when he arrived in New York; two years younger than Nora, but he was a child, and she a woman of the world. Eileen brought

him to the Derencys to ask advice about his schooling; she was determined he be educated, although everyone advised against it, even Sister
Catherine Benedict. And certainly Bridget advised against it.

"Vanity, vanity, all is vanity," she said, and everyone grew silent. Any
kind of quote abashed them all.

"Well, what would you say, Nora, with your education?" Eileen asked.

It was a terrible word to Nora, education, all that she had had vio-
lently, cruelly to turn her back on, all that had betrayed her, caused her
shame. Yet even in her bitterness, she saw it need not be the same for
Tommy Foley. He would not want what she had wanted, Latin and the
poetry, the plays. He would want, and Eileen wanted for him, merely a
certificate. What he would learn would never touch him; therefore it
would never hurt him. He wanted, simply, a good job.

Nora felt her mother's eyes hard on her, wanting her to give encouragement to Eileen. She understood why. Eileen's desire for her brother's
prospering was so palpable, so dangerous almost, that it should not be
balked.

"Why not try?" said Nora in her new, sharp way. Her parents did not
know she'd begun smoking; if she'd dared, it would have been a perfect
time to light a cigarette.

Eileen was constantly afraid that her ambitions for her brother would be
ruined by the influences of the neighborhood. For her they were conta-
gious, like the plague; the greenhorn laziness, the fecklessness, the wish
for fun. Nora's success made Eileen worshipful; she grew in Nora's presence deferential, asking her advice on everything, ravenously listening to
every word she said, and urging Tom to listen, too.

Nora knew enough of the world not to overvalue the position that the
Foleys had invented for her. She knew her place; it was a good place, near
the top. And yet she knew that she would never be precisely at the top. She
saw in the hallway of the office building where she worked a hundred girls
like her. She was not the best of them; her bad leg meant she could not
make the picture whole. She could not stride off, her high heels making
that exciting sound of purpose on the wooden floors. She could not rise
purposefully from her typewriter and move to the file cabinet, closing the
drawers like a prime minister conferring an ambassadorship, as Flo
Ziegler or Celie Kane, the partners' secretaries, did. To really play the part
she coveted required speed and line, like a good sailboat. Nora knew that

her high shoe, her skirts cut full and long to hide it, detracted from her appearance of efficiency. Her work, the quickness of her mind, might earn the highest place for her, but she would always be encumbered and slowed down by what John Riordan, a kind man, called her "affliction." Even so, even though she would never be at the very top, she knew herself above Eileen and her brother; there was no place for them in her new life, except the place forced free by charity.

She tried to joke Eileen out of her subservience, reminding her of when they had shared Eileen's secret trove of almonds, nougat, crystallized ginger. But perhaps she didn't try wholeheartedly; her daily striving to achieve her dream of herself exhausted her; there was a kind of ease in lying back against the bolster of Eileen's adoration. Eileen had an idea of the game Nora was playing, even if she was mistaken about the nature of the stakes. Nora's parents and Aunt Nettie had no knowledge of the game. But Bridget did; she was contemptuous and mocking; when she saw Nora ironing, with passionate devotion, her blouses, handkerchiefs, or skirt; when she came upon Nora polishing her nails, she sniffed and walked by, loose and ill-defined in her practical nurse's uniform, trailing the scorn of her belief in the futility of every effort Nora made.

Eileen kept hinting that Nora should be on the lookout for a place in Mr. Riordan's office that Tommy could fill. She'd heard about boys who started in law offices as messengers and worked their way up till eventually they studied on their own, sat for the bar exam, and became lawyers.

"Well, I've heard of it. I've never seen a case myself," said Nora, smoking cynically. "You'd have to have an awful lot of push."

And this was what Tom Foley lacked completely: push. Pale, with hair that would never look manly and blue eyes that hid expression or else were supplicating, he was nearly silent except when he and Eileen talked about home. He could go then from silence to a frightening ebullience about some detail of their childhood: a cow with one horn only, a dog that barked when anybody sang, pears that fell from a tree once as they sat below it, soft, heavy as footballs, damaging themselves before they hit the ground. Then he would grow embarrassed at his outburst, would blush and look more childish than ever. It was quite impossible; she didn't understand why Eileen couldn't see it, he was not the office type and never would be. Right off the boat Eileen had put him with the Christian Brothers; he lived there while Eileen lived with the nuns. In the summer on her week's vacation they went to a boardinghouse three hours from the city in the mountains, a house run by an Irishwoman they had known from home. But Tom had never spoken to a soul outside his school except in Eileen's company, and Nora doubted that he could. She'd never mentioned him to Mr. Riordan, it would not work out and in the end would just make everyone look bad.

She suspected Eileen resented her for not doing anything for Tom. They stopped seeing one another; when the family got the news of Eileen they hadn't heard a word from her in longer than a year. She phoned to tell them Tommy had died. He'd got a job working for Western Union, as a messenger to start, but his bosses had said he'd shown great promise. He was delivering a wire and had walked by a saloon. There was a fight inside, and a wild gunshot had come through the window. The bullet landed in his heart.

Eileen said this in the kitchen drinking tea with Nora and her mother and her father and her aunts. As she spoke, her cup did not tremble. They had no way of knowing what she felt about the terrible thing that had happened; she would give no sign. She met no one's eye; her voice, which had been musical, was flat and tired. What they could see was that the life had gone out of her flesh. What had been her richness had turned itself to stone; her body life, which once had given her and all around her pleasure, had poured itself into a mold of dreadful bitter piety. She talked about the will of God and punishment for her ambitions. It was this country, she said, the breath of God had left it if it ever had been here. Money was God here, and success, and she had bent the knee. Her brother had died of it.

So she was going home, she said. She cursed the day she ever left, she cursed the day she'd listened to the lying tongues, the gold-in-the-street stories, the palaver about starting over, making good. It was the worst day of her life, she said, the day she'd come here. But she wanted them to know that she was grateful for the way they'd helped her when she first was over; she would not forget. She told them she was going back to her old job at the orphanage in Limerick. She said that she would write them, but they all knew she would not.

When she walked out the door, they felt one of the dead had left them, and they looked among themselves like murderers and could find no relief. When Bridget tried to blame Eileen or blame the Foleys, no one listened. They could hardly bear each other's company.

Nora went upstairs to her room and lay down on her bed, still in her work skirt. It would be terribly wrinkled; before the night was over she would have to press it. But not now. Now she lay back on her bed and knew what would be her life: to rise from it each morning and to make her way to work. Each morning she would join the others on the train, and in the evening, tired out but not exhausted, and with no real prospects that could lead to pleasure, with the others she would make her way back home.

Now I Am Married

I am the second wife, which means that, for the most part, I am spoken *to*. This is the first visit of my marriage, and I am introduced around, to everyone's slight embarrassment. There is an unspoken agreement among people not to mention *her*, except in some clear context where my advantage is obvious. It would be generous of me to say that I wish it were otherwise, but I appreciate the genteel silences, and, even more, the slurs upon her which I recognize to be just. I cannot attempt to be fair to her: justice is not the issue. I have married, and this is an act of irrational and unjust loyalty. I married for this: for the pleasure of one-sidedness, the thrill of the bias, the luxury of saying, "But he is my husband, you see," thereby putting to an end whatever discussion involves us.

My husband is English, and we are staying in the house of his family. We do not make love here as we do at my mother's. She thinks sex is wicked, which is, of course, highly aphrodisiac, but here it is considered merely in bad taste. And as I lie, looking at the slope of my husband's shoulder, I think perhaps they are right. They seem to need much less sleep than I do, to be able to move more quickly, to keep their commitments with less fuss. I wish I found the English more passionate; surely there is nothing so boring as the reenforcement of a stereotype. But it is helpful to be considered southern here: I am not afraid to go out on the street as I am in Paris or Rome, because all the beautiful women make me want to stay under the sharp linen of my hotel. No, here I feel somehow I have a great deal of color, which has, after all, to do with sex. I can see the young girls already turning into lumpish women in raincoats with cigarettes drooping from their lips. This, of course, makes it much easier. Even my sister-in-law's beauty is so different that it cannot really hurt me; it is the ease of centuries of her race's history that gave it to her, and to this I cannot hope to aspire.

Yesterday we went to a charity bazaar. One of the games entailed scooping up marbles with a plastic spoon and putting them through the hole of an overturned flower pot. My sister-in-law went first. Her technique was to take each marble, one at a time, and put it through the hole. Each one went neatly in. When it was my turn, I perceived the vanity of her discretion and my strategy was to take as many marbles as I could on the spoon and shovel them into the hole as quickly as possible. A great number of the marbles scattered on the lawn, but quite a few went into the hole, and, because I had lifted so many, my score was twelve; my sister-in-law's five. Both of us were pleased with our own performance and admiring of the rival technique.

I am very happy here. Yesterday in the market I found an eggplant, a rare and definite miracle for this part of the world. Today for dinner I made ratatouille. This morning I took my sister-in-law's basket and went out, married, to the market. I don't think that marriage has changed me, but for the first time, the salespeople appreciated, rather than resented, the time I took choosing only the most heartwarming tomatoes, the most earnest and forthright meat. I was no longer a fussy bachelorette who cooked only sometimes and at her whim. I was a young matron in stockings and high heels. My selections, to them, had something to do with the history they were used to. They were important; they were not for myself.

I had wanted to write this morning, but I had the responsibility of dinner, served at one. I do not say this in complaint. I was quite purely happy with my basket and my ring, basking in the approval of the shopkeepers and the pedestrians. I am never so happy writing. It is not that the housewife's tasks are in themselves repugnant: many of them involve good smells and colors, satisfying shapes, and the achievement of dexterity. They kill because they are not final. They must be redone although they have just been finished. And so I am shopping rather than polishing the beautiful Jacobean furniture with the sweet-smelling lavender wax. I am doing this because I am dying, so that I will not die.

I. MARJORIE

Bring her in for a cup of coffee, I said to him. I saw you on the street, and you were so happy-looking. Not me and my husband. Dead fifteen years, and a bloodier hypocrite never walked. I pretended I was sorry when he died, but believe me, I was delighted. He was a real pervert. All those public-school boys won't do anything for you till they're beaten; don't let them tell you anything about the French, my dear.

I was just in France. I was kind of like an au pair girl to this communist bloke, only he was a millionaire. Well, they had a great house with a river behind it, and every day I'd meet the mayor of the town there, both of us throwing our bottles from the night before into the river. They had men go round with nets to gather up the bottles and sell them. They know how to live there. The stores are all empty here. Not that I'm much of a cook. We start our sherry here as soon as we get up. Your coffee all right? Have a biscuit. I'll have one too. I shouldn't . . . look at me around the middle. I'm getting to look quite middle-aged, but there's some life in me yet, I think, don't you?

Look at your husband sitting there with his blue eyes just as handsome. Fancied him once myself, but he hadn't time for me. Keep an eye on him, dear, he's got young girls in front of him all day. Oh, I don't envy you that job. They must chase after him all the time, dear, don't they? Cheer up, a little jealousy puts spice in a marriage, don't you think?

Well, there's a real witch hunt out for me in this building. I've taken in all the boys around the town that've got nowhere to go. Just motherly. All of them on drugs, sleeping out every night. Well, my policy is not to chivvy and badger them. Tried marijuana myself once but I didn't get anything out of it because I didn't smoke it properly. But they all have a home here, and I do them heaps more good than some virginal social worker with a poker you know where. Of course the old ladies around here don't like it. Mrs. Peters won't forgive me since I was so drunk that night and I broke into her house and started dancing with her. A poor formless girl she's got for a daughter, afraid of her own shadow. Starts to shake if you as much as say good morning to her. Thirty-five, she is, if she's a day. Pious, that one. I've seen her chatting up the vicar every evening. You know what *she* needs. My husband was a parson. He was plagued with old maids. I'd 'uv been delighted if he'd rolled one down in my own bedroom just so's he'd leave me alone. Bloody great pervert, he was. And sanctimonious! My God! He looked like a stained-glass window to the outsiders. And all the old biddies in the town following him around calling him Father. Not me. I'd like to tell you what I called him.

Anyway, all the old bitches here think they can get me thrown out, but they're very much mistaken. This building happens to be owned by the Church of England, of which my husband happened to be a pillar. My pension comes from there, you know. Well, my dear, of course they can't throw one of the widows of the clergy out on her sanctified arse, so I'm really quite safe for the moment.

That's why I wouldn't get married again. I wouldn't give up that bloody pension for the life of me. I'll see they pay it to me till I die, the bloody hypocrites. "Yes, Mrs. Pierce, if you'd conduct your life in a manner suitable to a woman of your position." Bugger 'em, I say. They're all dust, same as me.

No, I'm quitting Charlie. I've been with him five years, but I must say the rigamarole is becoming trying. His wife sits home with their dachshunds, Wallace and Willoughby, their names are—did you ever hear anything so ridiculous—and occasionally she'll ring up and say, "Is Charlie Waring there?" and I'll say, "Who? You must have the wrong number." Five years. It's getting ridiculous.

I think I'll take myself down to the marriage bureau. Thirty quid it costs for a year, and they supply you with names till you're satisfied. Of course at my age what d'ye have left? And I'd want somebody respectable, you know, not just anybody. Of course, you meet men in pubs, but never the right sort, are they? My dear, you wouldn't believe what I come home with some nights, I'm that hard up.

Anyway, Lucinda's sixteen, and she's already on her second abortion. How she gets that way I don't know. She simply walked out of school. Told one of the teachers off when she ordered her to take off her makeup. She said to her, "My mother doesn't pay you to shout at me."

Dried-up old bitches those teachers were. Of course, in point of fact it's not me or her that's paying, it's the Church, but just the same, I see her point. You're only young once, so why not look your best. They'll never want her more than they want her now, right. Isn't it true, they won't let us near a man till we're practically too old to enjoy one. Well, I've got her a Dutch cap now, though I don't suppose she'll use it. I never did. That's why I've got five offspring. I'm sure I don't know what to do with them. Anyway, she's answering telephones for some lawyer three hours a day, and I'm sure he's got her flat on her back on his leather couch half the time. Smashing-looking Indian chap. But it's pocket money for her. And we don't get along badly, the way some do. I give her her own way, and if she gets into trouble we sort it out somehow. I suppose she'll get married in a year or so, only I hope it's not an ass or a hypocrite. Bloody little fool I was at her age. My dear, on my wedding night I didn't know what went where or why. Don't ask how I was so stupid. Of course my mother was a parson's wife, too, and I think she thought if she said the word "sex" the congregation would burn her house down. Dead right she was.

Well, you certainly are an improvement over the other one he was married to. My dear, she thought she could run everyone's life for them. Knew me a week, and she came over one morning and said, uninvited, "Marjorie, you should get up earlier. Why don't you watch the educational programs on the telly?" "Bugger off," I said, and she never came near me again.

Well, I have to go off and see one of my old ladies. This one keeps me in clothes, so I've got to be attentive. Let me tell you, if you could see how respectable I am in front of her, my dear, you wouldn't believe. Well, I take her cashmere sweaters and hope the constable won't see me on the way out. One visit keeps Lucinda and me in clothes for a year. I don't care, it cheers her up, the poor old bugger. Hope someone'll be as good to me when I'm that age. But I'll probably be a cross old drunk, and I bloody well won't have any spare Dior gowns in my closet, that's sure.

You don't mind if I give your husband a kiss goodbye. Lovely. Oh, perhaps I'll just take another one. Fancied him myself at one time. Well, you're the lucky one, aren't you? Come over again, perhaps you could come for a meal, though what I could cook nowadays I'm sure I don't know. I don't suppose that would set well with the family. Can't say that I blame them, they have to live here. Well, slip in some time on the Q.T. and

I'll dig you out some tea. Make it afternoon though, dear, I don't like mornings, though I'm ever so glad of your company.

2. DORIS

I don't go anywhere by myself now. Three weeks ago I got a car but I took it back. I was so lonely driving. That was the worst. I think I'm afraid of everybody and everything now. I'm always afraid there's men walking behind me. I won't even go to post a letter in the evening. I was always afraid of the dark. My mother knew I was afraid of the dark, so she made me sleep with the light off. She said if I kept on being afraid of the dark, God wouldn't love me.

Of course, it's all so different now George is gone. People are like things, d'ye know what I mean? They're very nice, of course, and they do care for me and call, but it's all, I don't know, shallow like. Of course I do prefer the company of men. Not that I run down my own sex, but men are gentler, somehow, don't you think? The first month after George was gone all I could think about was who could I marry now. But now I look back on it I shudder, d'ye know what I mean. George bein' so so sick and all that we didn't have a physical relationship for many years. And men like to be naughty. Sometimes, though, I do enjoy a man's companionship. After George lost his leg, he said, "I can't give you much in the way of the physical, Mother." But we were terribly close, really. Talked about everything. He *would* insist on having his chair here by the door so's he could see everybody coming in. I used to kid him a lot about it. Winter and summer, never come close to the fire. He'd sit right there by the door, winter and summer. And Gwen would sit on the settee at night and never go out. I used to say to her, "Gwen, you must go out. Go to the cinema." But she was afraid, like, to leave her father. Even though I was here. She was afraid if she went out he'd be gone when she got back.

Of course it was very hard on the children. It'll take them years to sort it out, I suppose. Perhaps they'll never sort it out. Gwen went down to eight stone. Bonny she looked, but I was worried. Then she got these knots like, in her back, and she stopped going to work altogether. Said she couldn't face the tubes anymore. She hated it; bein' smothered, like, she said, it was terrifying. But I think she wanted to be home with Daddy so we let her come home.

Colin has a lovely job now. Got a hundred blokes under him. But they're afraid he'll go back to university and quit so they don't pay him properly. He almost took a degree in logic, but he broke down after two years. You should see his papers. Lovely marks on 'em. His professors said if he sat right down, he'd come away with a first. But he got too involved, if you know what I mean. Forgot there was a world around him.

He's had a lot of lovely girls, and I guess he's had his fling, but I don't think he'll ever marry. After George died, he said, "I don't know how to put it, Mum, but I'm just not that interested in sex." Once a few years ago he came out to the breakfast table. He was white as a ghost; I was worried. He said, "Dad, may I have a word with you?" I said, "Do you want me to leave the room?" He said, "No, of course not, Mum." Then he told George he didn't sleep at all that night. He said he felt a kind of calling. He was terrified, he said; he was sure God was calling him to his service. Well, George held his tongue, and so did I. He asked Colin what it felt like, and Colin said, "Don't ask me to describe it, Dad." He had a lot of sleepless nights, and we called the vicar, and he took him to the place where the young men go for the priesthood, and Colin said that he liked it, but when the time came he never did go.

Him and his father were great pals. Colin, of course, was studying Western philosophy, and he was very keen on it and George just as keen on the Eastern. Oh, they would argue, and George would say, "Just read this chapter of the book I'm reading," and Colin would say, "I'm not interested, Dad." Then after George died he took all his books away with him to Bristol. I said, "I thought you weren't interested." He said, "I really always was, Mum."

Lynnie's going to be a mother in September. I'm not really keen on being a grandmother. I'm interested in my daughter; she's an adult. I'm not interested in babies. I've never seen anyone like her for being cheerful, though. That girl cannot be made miserable, not even for an hour. I'm sure it'll be a girl, the way she holds her back when she walks, straight, like. I suppose I'll be interested in it when it's born.

George had a kind of miraculous effect on people, though. One time our vicar asked him to address a group of young people. Four hundred of them there was, packed the house with chairs, they did. And up on the stage one big armchair for George. One night I made them all mugs of tea, there must have been fifteen of them here on the floor. Half of them admitted they were on drugs. Purple hearts, goofballs, whatever they call them nowadays. And when they left here they said they were all right off them now.

Of course he had this good friend, the bachelor vicar, Arthur. Like a father to him George was. A very intelligent man, but a terrible lot of problems. Spent all his time here, he did. He'd stay here till two o'clock on Sunday morning and then go home and write his sermons. Said George all but wrote his sermons for him. Once he told me he was jealous of George having me and me having George. Said it was the one thing he could never have. And him a wealthy man. His father has a big engineering firm in Dorset and a great house. Three degrees he has, too. But I think he's really like they say, neurotic. He *cannot* express his feelings. Me and George, we told each other everything. We kept no secrets. Not Arthur, though. He's taken me out to dinner twice since George died but I like plain food, d'ye know what I mean, and he took me out to this Japanese restaurant with geisha girls and God knows what. Well they gave me so much I sent half of it back, and they said was there something Madame didn't like, and I about died of shame. I think old Arthur's knocking, but I'm not at home to him. Of course he's a wonderful priest, the kids in the youth group love him. He cried during the whole funeral service. I was so mortified. And he will not mention George's name. He says he can't forgive God for taking George.

I used to feel that way but I don't anymore. When George was in so much pain, like, I'd go to the Communion rail and shake my fist at Christ on the cross and say, "What d'ye know about suffering? You only suffered one day? My George has suffered years." I don't feel that way now. I think there's a reason for it, all that pain, even. George died without one drug in his body, he had that much courage.

Well, I guess I'll be getting you a bath. It's good you've come. You'll never regret the man you've married. George thought the world of him. We've only water enough for one bath. So one can take it tonight and one tomorrow. George and I used to bathe in the same water, but I think we were different from most.

I feel like I've known you all my life. I knew you'd be like this from the letters. Old friends they were, my man and yours. You're not like the first wife. She was a hard one, that one. Ice in her veins.

Perhaps I'll come and visit you in America. I have a job now at the hospital and three weeks holiday in July. Perhaps I'll come out to visit you. But what would I do, the two of you out working. I hate to impose, you know. We used to have friends, widows they were, and we'd invite them over and they'd say, "Oh, no thanks, we'd be odd man out." I never knew what they meant, but now I know. Look at me talking. I can't even go to Epping by myself, and Lynnie made the trip when she was eight. Perhaps if you found out all the details for me. Wouldn't it be something!

It's good having someone in the house at night. I usually sleep with all the lights on, I'm that frightened on my own. I think I'm getting better with the job and all. But sometimes I'm very empty, like, and cold.

3. ELIZABETH

I like living here on my own. Dear lord, who else could I live with? Like old Miss Bates, she lived with another teacher, for, oh, twenty years it must have been. They bought a dear little house in the Cotswolds to live in for their retirement. Lived there a year and up pops some cousin who'd been wooing Miss Campbell for forty years, and off they go and get married. Well, Amelia Bates was furious, and she wouldn't speak to Miss Campbell, and they'd been like sisters for twenty years. Well poor Miss Campbell died six months later, and there's Amelia Bates on her own in that vast house full of regrets and sorrow.

Here's a picture of me in Algeria in 1923. Oh, I had a beautiful ride over on the ship, it took three days. Some people took the trip just to drink all the way, people are foolish. The first night I lay in my cabin and the ship was creaking so badly I was sure it was the end for me. I went up top, and the waves were crashing around the deck and they said, "You'd better go down below, Miss," and that's where I met Mr. Saunders.

Don't let the others in the family act so proud to you. When I found out that Ethel had cut you, ooh, I was so angry. I wrote her a very cross letter. Her mum and dad were separated for years and he was living with a half-caste woman in India and afraid to even write his wife a letter. Of course he should have left her and stayed with that other woman, but he didn't have that much courage. He's been miserable ever since. Poor old Lawrence, he's a decent old boy but terrified to death of Millie. You know she was just a governess for his family when he fell in love with her. She was good-looking though, the best-looking of all of us. Well, poor old Lawrence when he came to Mount Olympus (that was the name of my father's house, dear. It fulfilled the ambitions of a lifetime for him), well, when he came to Mount Olympus to meet the family he came down with malaria and was sick in bed for a month. Had to have his meals brought up to him and his sheets changed three times a day. Well, after that there was no getting out of it, he was quite bound. Not that he thought of getting out of it then. People simply didn't in those days, and that's why so many of them were so unhappy. I'm sure things are much better now, in some ways, but nobody seems much happier anyway, do they?

Here is a picture of the family I worked for in India. Now even I had my mild scandal, I suppose. It wasn't so mild to Father. Millie came home from India and told dear Father a great tale. Father wrote to Mr. Saunders and demanded that I be sent home. Then he wrote to me and said I must come back upon my honor as his daughter and an Englishwoman. We simply didn't answer the letters. Mr. Saunders hid them in a parcel in his desk drawer, and I simply threw mine in the fire. Then Mr. Saunders took the family back to England, and I went back to Mount Olympus. Father told me I must take a new name and tell everyone I was married, that I was the widow of an officer. I refused; I told him no one knew but him and Millie. Then we never spoke of it.

I started a kindergarten for the children in the town. Here is the picture of the first class, and here's one of your husband as a baby. Wasn't he golden? Then Mother got sick, and I had to give it up. Nobody took it on after that, it was a pity, really. I regretted that.

Here's a picture of Cousin Norman. Doesn't he look a bounder? Wrote bad checks and settled in Canada. He's a millionaire today.

I'm giving you these spoons as a wedding gift. They belonged to my grandmother's grandmother. I think it's nice to have a few old things. It makes you feel connected, somehow, don't you think?

I only hope my mind holds out on me. I love to read, and I wouldn't care if I were bedridden as long as my mind was all right. Mother was all right for some time, and then when she was in her seventies she just snapped. She didn't recognize anybody in the family, and one night she came at Father with a knife and said he was trying to kill her. We had to put her in hospital then. It was supposed to be the best one in England, but it was awful. There were twenty women in a room not this size, and in the evenings you could hear them all weeping and talking to themselves. It would have driven me quite mad, and I was sane. Then she said the nurses were all disguising themselves to confuse her, and they were trying to poison her. And then she said they wouldn't let her wash, and she was dirty and smelled ill. Well, we finally took her back home, and Father wouldn't let anyone see her. I gave up my position—I was working for that woman who writes those trashy novels that sell so well. And her daughter was an absolute hellcat—and came home. She'd call me every few minutes and say, "Elizabeth, what will we do if anyone comes? There isn't a pock of food in the house." And I would tell her no one would be coming. Then she'd say, "Elizabeth, what will we do if anyone comes, the house is so dirty." And it would go on like that. Sometimes she wouldn't eat for days, and sometimes she would stuff herself till she was quite ill. She died of a stomach obstruction in the end, but that was years later. Every night Father would go in to her and say good night and kiss her, and she would weep and say that she was wicked, that she was hurting us all. But sometimes she would just be her old self and joke with us after supper and play the piano and sing or read—she loved George Eliot—and we'd think she was getting better, perhaps. But the next morning she'd be looking out the window again, not talking to anyone.

I can't go near anyone who has any kind of mental trouble. When my friend Miss Edwards was so ill in that way she wrote and begged me to come, and the family wrote, and I simply couldn't. I get very frightened of those sorts of things. I suppose I shouldn't.

Here is a caricature my brother drew of the warden, and here is one of the bald curate and the fat parson who rode a bicycle. He was talented, our Dick, but of course he had a family to support, and that awful wife of his put everything on her back that he earned. And here is one of our father turning his nose up at some Indian chap who was trying to sell him a rug he didn't fancy.

Here I am in Malta, and here's one of me in Paris. Wasn't I gay then? When the Germans took over Paris, I wept and wept. I didn't want to go on. Have you been to Paris, dear? Beautiful city, isn't it? You feel anything could happen there. It wouldn't matter where you'd been or what you'd done, you could begin all over, no regrets or sorrows.

Here is a picture of your husband's mother, wasn't she beautiful? Turn your head like that, you look rather like her when you put your face that way. She would have loved you, dear, and she was a beautiful soul. She used to laugh and laugh, even during the war when we'd have to stay in the shelter overnight and we were terrified we wouldn't see the sunlight ever again. She'd tell us gay stories and make us laugh. She had a little bird, she used to call it Albert as a joke. She let him fly out all about the house on his own. And she taught the creature to say funny things; it was so amusing. She would be very happy for you, dear; she loved to see people happy.

I don't suppose I'll do any more traveling. I remember when I went to France last summer I said, "Elizabeth, this is your last voyage," and I felt so queer. But I have this house and my garden and Leonard's wife Rosemary and I go out every week and do meals-on-wheels—we take food around to the shut-ins, dear. I suppose they'll be doing that for me someday, but not for a while, I don't think. I like to be active and work in the garden. These awful pillow roses have taken over everything, and I haven't the heart to prune them. And then, when people come, it's so lovely, isn't it, I wish they could stay forever.

4. SUSAN

It's good to have company. Sometimes I feel as though I haven't had a day off in three years since Maria was born. Geoffrey doesn't seem to want to be weaned; he's seven months. I suppose he will when he's ready. It's the only thing that quiets him. I'm beginning to feel very tired. And now Maria wants everything from a bottle, she wants to be a baby too. I suppose they'll stop when they're ready.

My days are very ordered, though. I remember when I was single and I lived in London I'd think what will I do with myself now? And then I'd just go out and walk down the street and I'd look in the windows at the china and the materials and then I'd stop somewhere and have a cup of tea and go home and read something. It's so difficult, isn't it, to remember what that kind of loneliness was like when you're with people constantly. It's like hunger or cold. But now my time is all mapped out for me. I give everyone breakfast and then I do the washing-up and we go for a walk and it's time for lunch. It goes on like that. It's better now. When we lived in the high-rise building I felt terribly alone. There would be other pushchairs in front of other doors and occasionally I'd hear a baby crying in the hall but I wouldn't know whose it was and when I opened the door there was never anybody in the corridor, only that queer yellow light. And I hated the air in that building. It tasted so false in my mouth and we couldn't open up any of the windows. It was beautiful at night and I would hold the baby by the window and say "moon," and "star," and sometimes when they were both asleep Frederick and I would stand by the window and look out over the city at all the lights. The car horns were muted like voices at the ocean; it was very nice. I liked it then. But I did feel terribly lonely.

Sometimes I go up to the attic and I look at the piles of my research in egg cartons but I don't even take it out. I suppose I should want to someday. I suppose I should get back to my Russian. But it all hangs around me like a cloud and I feel Maria tugging at me, pulling at my dress like a wave and I think how much more real it all is now, feeding and clothing, and nurturing and warming, and I think of words like "research" and "report" and even "learning" and "understanding" next to those words and they seem so high, so far away, it's a struggle to remember what they mean.

I love marriage, though, the idea of it. I believe in it in a very traditional way. My friends from graduate school come over, and they say I'm worn-out and tired and I'm making a martyr of myself. I should make Frederick do some of the work. But it's the form of it I love and the repetition: certain tasks are his, some are mine. That's what these young people are all looking for, form, but it's a dirty word to them. I suppose I'm not that old, I'm thirty-two, that's young, I suppose, but I like feeling older. I wish I were fifty. I like not having a moment to myself, it's soothing, and my life is warm and sweet like porridge. Before Geoffrey was born sometimes I'd spend the whole day and Maria was the only one I would talk to. She was two then and Frederick would come home, and he was so terribly tired, and I was too. We scarcely said a word to each other except how's the baby today or your shirt got lost at the cleaner's. It was the happiest time in my life. She wanted to know everything, and sometimes we'd spend whole mornings doing things like taking the vacuum cleaner apart or boiling water or walking up and down stairs. Then Frederick would come home and he'd want to talk about Talleyrand or something and I couldn't possibly explain to him how perfectly happy I was all day, taking everything out of my sewing basket and showing it to Maria, he would have thought I was stark, staring mad.

But I love that: sleeping next to someone you haven't spoken to all day and then making love in the dark with our pajamas on and even then going to sleep not having spoken. It soothes me, like wet sand. We couldn't have that without marriage, I mean marriage in the old way, with the woman doing everything.

Here's something for your lunch. I cook such odd things now, sausages for the children, tins of soup, sandwiches. But I always make this stew for us. I just boil up a hambone with lentils and carrots. I suppose you're a very good cook. I used to be, but now I don't like that kind of thing.

The babies have broken nearly all the china, so we use everything plastic now. Do you think it's terribly ugly? I do miss that nice thin china and glassware, I miss it more than books and the cinema. And the furniture's terribly shabby now. We'll wait until they're grown to replace it.

Don't worry about what people say. When I married Frederick even his mum wouldn't come, and people would run down his first wife, thinking they were doing me a favor, and all the time they were making it worse because I'd think if she was so bloody awful why did he marry her, and then I thought if he loved her and she's so dreadful and he loves me I must be dreadful too. And I kept going around in circles and hating Frederick and myself and some poor woman whom I used to think of as a perfectly harmless, remote monster. I could scarcely get out of bed in the morning, and people thought they were being kind. You must simply shore up all your courage to be silent. That's what I have done and sometimes I am so silent I like myself a great deal, no, more than that, I admire myself and that's what I've always longed for.

You shouldn't listen to me either, I'm probably half-mad talking to babies all day. Only there's something sort of enormous and gray and cold about marriage. It's wonderful, isn't it, being a part of it? Or don't you feel that way?

5. GILLIAN

My mother had this thing about beauty, it was really very Edwardian the way she approached it. She had this absolutely tiny private income, and my father took off the absolute second I was born, and we hardly ever had any money, and my mother kept moving around saying these incredible things like "It'll be better in the next town" and "When our ship comes in" and things like that that you expect to read in some awful trashy novel.

But she was a beautiful woman and she taught me these oddly valuable things, about scent and clothes and makeup. I'm trying to be kinder to her now I'm forty. I suppose one gets some kind of perspective on things, but what I really remember is being terribly, terribly insecure all the time and frightened about money and resentful of other girls who wore smart clothes and went off to university when they weren't as smart as I was. My mother used to dress me in the most outlandish outfits as a child, velvet and lace and whatnot. I hated it in school. I was forever leaving schools and starting in new ones, and I was perpetually embarrassed.

Well, when I married for the first time, I was determined to marry someone terribly stable and serviceable. As soon as I could I bought these incredibly severe clothes, they just about had buttons on them, and I married Richard. I was eighteen. I suppose it is all too predictable to be really interesting—and we lived in this fanatically utilitarian apartment, everything was white and silver, and I couldn't imagine why I felt cold all the time. Suddenly I found myself using words like beauty and truth, et cetera, and I went out and got a job so we could buy a really super house. I spent all my time looking at wallpaper and going to auctions, and the house really was beautiful. Then I met Seymour, and he was so funny and lugubrious—I just adored it. Here was this Jewish man taking me to little cabarets. The first time we went out, he said to me, "You know, Gillian, girl singers are very important," and I hadn't the faintest idea what he was talking about. Here was this quite famous psychologist who bought a copy of *Variety*—that American show-people's paper—every day, but it was very odd, the first time I met him, I thought how marvelous he'd be to live with.

And then, of course, I did a terribly unstable thing, I suppose. Shades of my mother only more so, and I divorced Richard and married Seymour. He gave all his money to his wife, and I let Richard keep everything of mine, and we started out without a penny. We slept in the car in our clothes, but we were terribly happy. So I got a job and we got another lovely house, only this was a really cheerful one, a very motherly home. Then I went back to school. I suppose it's hard for you to understand how important it would be for me: doing something on my own with my mind and speaking up and having people listen. I'd had too much sitting on the sidelines pushing the silver pheasant down the damask cloth and cradling the saltcellar while the men spoke to each other. So I told Seymour I simply had to go back to college, and he agreed with me for a while in theory, but when the time came he said to me, "What about the house?" But I was very firm, and I told him, "The house will simply be a bit less beautiful for a while." Then he understood how important it was to me, and he stood right behind me. We didn't do much entertaining for a while, but I did very well, really, everyone was surprised. I guess everyone else was much less smart than I expected.

Then I took a job teaching secondary school, and it was a disaster, really. There were all these perfectly nice people who wanted to grow up and repair bicycles, and I was supposed to talk about Julius Caesar and the subjunctive. It was all too absurd, really. I simply cared about the books too much to do it. I suppose to be a really good teacher you have to not care about the books so. Well, one day I simply didn't go back. I suppose it was awful, but there were plenty of people who wanted the job. I didn't feel too badly about it. Going in like that every day was making me so ill.

Now I've gone back to writing. I don't know if I'm any good. I don't suppose it matters, really. It's a serious thing, and that's important. I see everyone off in the morning and I go up to my study—the window looks out on a locust tree—and I write the whole day. The hardest thing is closing the door on Seymour and the children—but I do. I close the door on being a wife. I close the door on my house and all the demands. I suppose art demands selfishness, and perhaps I'm not a great artist, so perhaps it's all ridiculous and pitiable, but in the end it isn't even important whether I'm great or not—I'm after something, myself, I suppose; isn't that terribly commonplace? Only the soul, whatever that is—whatever we call it now—gets so flung about one is always in danger of losing it, of letting it slip away unless one is really terribly careful and jealous. And so it is important really and the only answer is, whatever the outside connections, one must simply do it.

Who is right, and who is wrong? For years, I have waited for a sign, a sentence, periodic and complete. Now I begin to know there is loneliness even in this love. I begin to think of death, of solids. My friend, who is my age, is already a widow. She says that no one will talk to her about it. Everyone thinks she is tainted. They are frightened by her contact with dead flesh, as if it clung to her visibly. I should prepare for a staunch widowhood. I begin to wish for my own death, because I am happy now and vulnerable to contagion. A friend of mine who has three children tells a story about a colleague of his, a New England spinster. She noted that he had been out sick four times that winter; she had been healthy throughout. "But that is because I have a wife and three children," he said, "and I am open to contagion."

There is something satisfying about marriage at this time. It is the satisfaction of a dying civilization: one perfects the form, knowing it has the thrill of doom upon it. There is a craftsmanship here; I am conscious of a kind of labor. It is harder than art and more dangerous. Last night was very hot. I didn't want to wake my husband so I moved into the spare bedroom where I could thrash, guiltlessly. I fell asleep and then heard him wake, stir, and feel for me. I ran to the door of our bedroom. "You gave me a fright. I reached for you, and the bed was empty," he said. Now I know I am not invisible. Things matter. My feet impress a solid earth. I am full of power.

The most difficult thing is my tremendous pride. To admit that there are some things I do not know is like a degrading illness. My husband tries to teach me how to use a hoe, a machete. I do not learn easily. I throw the tools at his feet and in anger I weep and kick. He knows something I do not; can I forgive him? He is tearing down a wall; he is building a fireplace. I am upstairs in the bedroom, reading, dizzy with resentment. I come down and say, "I'm going away for a few days. Until you finish this." Then I cry and confess: I do not want to go away, but I hate it that he is demolishing and building and I am reading. It is not enough that I have made a custard and a beautiful parsley sauce for the fish. He hands me a hammer, a chisel, a saw. I am clumsy and ill with my own incapacity. When he tries to show me how to hold the saw correctly, I hit him, hard, between the shoulder blades. I have never hit another person like this; I am an only child. So he becomes the brother I was meant to hit. I make him angry. He says I should have married someone with no skills, no achievements. What I want, he says, is unlimited power. He is right. I love him because he is powerful, because he will let me have only my fair share. Stop, he says, for I ask too much of everything. Take more, there is more here for you, I tell him, for he is used to deprivation. We are learning to be kind to one another, like siblings.

Two people in a house, what else is it? I love his shoes, his shirts. I want to embrace his knees and tell him "You are the most splendid person I have ever known." Yet I miss my friends, the solitude of my own apartment with its plangent neuroses, the coffee cups where mold grew familiarly, the little grocery store on the corner with the charge account in my name only.

But I feel my muscles flex, grow harder, grow supple with intimacy. We are very close; I know every curve of his body; he can call to mind in a moment the pattern of my veins. He is my husband, I say slowly, swallowing a new, exotic food. Does this mean everything or nothing? I stand with him in an ancient relationship, in a ruined age, listening beyond my understanding to the warning voices, to the promise of my own substantial heart.

Acknowledgments

These stories originally appeared in the following publications: "Vision" in *Antaeus*; "The Deacon" in *The Atlantic Monthly*; "Rosecliff" in *The Columbia Review*; "My Podiatrist Tells Me a Story About a Boy and a Dog" in *Fiction*; "Conversations in Prosperity" in *Glimmer Train Stories*; "Bishop's House" in *Harper's Magazine*; "The Translator's Husband" in *Ms. Magazine*; "Sick in London" in *New Letters*; "City Life," "Eleanor's Music," and "Separation" in *Ploughshares*; "The Baby" and "Intertextuality" in *The Recorder*; "Death in Naples" in *Salmagundi*; "The Healing" in *St. Ann's Review*; "Storytelling" in *The Threepenny Review*.

"Agnes," "Billy," "The Dancing Party," "Delia," "Eileen," "The Imagination of Disaster," "The Magician's Wife," "Mrs. Cassidy's Last Year," "The Neighborhood," "Now I Am Married," "The Only Son of the Doctor," "The Other Woman," "Out of the Fray," "Safe," "Temporary Shelter," "The Thorn," "Violation," "Watching the Tango," and "A Writing Lesson" were originally published in *Temporary Shelter* by Mary Gordon (Random House Inc., New York, 1987).

CIRCLING MY MOTHER
A Memoir
Mary Gordon

**"An emotionally raw, wildly personal,
and beautifully crafted confession."** —*Elle*

In this triumphant return to nonfiction after two critically
acclaimed works of fiction and the 1996 memoir of
her father, *The Shadow Man*, Mary Gordon gives us a rich,
bittersweet memoir about her mother, their relationship, and
her role as a daughter.

Anna Gagliano Gordon, who died in 2002 at the age of
ninety-four, lived a life colored by large forces: immigration,
world war, the Great Depression, and physical affliction—she
contracted polio at the age of three and experienced the rav-
ages of both alcoholism and dementia. A hard-working single
mother—Gordon's father died when she was a young girl—
Anna was the personification of the culture of the mid-centu-
ry American Catholic working class. Yet even in the face of
setbacks she managed to hold down a job, to dress smartly, and
to raise her daughter on her own.

Bringing her exceptional talent for detail, character, and
scene to bear on the life of her mother, Gordon gives us a
deeply felt and powerfully moving book.

Praise for *Circling My Mother*

**"A daring and perceptive work of memory, catharsis,
and literary grace."** —*Los Angeles Times*

**"Inspiring. . . . The pleasure of Gordon's work is the coiled
pressure of her language and the severity of her observations. . . .
Accompanying the author while she comes to terms with
her mother is thrilling."** —*The New York Times Book Review*

ISBN-10: 0-375-42456-3 • ISBN-13: 978-0-375-42456-4
$24.00 (Can. $30.00)
 Pantheon Books • www.pantheonbooks.com

AVAILABLE WHEREVER BOOKS ARE SOLD

ALSO BY MARY GORDON

FINAL PAYMENTS

When Isabel Moore's father dies, she finds herself, at the age of thirty, suddenly freed from eleven years of uninterrupted care for a helpless man. With all the patterns of her life suddenly rendered meaningless, she turns to childhood friends for support, gets a job, and becomes involved with two very different men. But just as her future begins to emerge, her past throws up a daunting challenge.

Fiction/978-0-307-27678-0

PEARL

On Christmas night of 1998, Maria Meyers learns that her twenty-year-old daughter, Pearl, has chained herself outside the American embassy in Dublin, where she intends to starve herself to death. Although Maria was once a student radical and still proudly lives by her beliefs, gentle, book-loving Pearl has never been interested in politics—nor in the Catholicism her mother rejected years before. What, then, is driving her to martyr herself? Mary Gordon takes us deep into the labyrinths of maternal love, religious faith, and Ireland's tragic history.

Fiction/978-1-4000-7807-3

THE SHADOW MAN

A Daughter's Search for Her Father

Mary Gordon's father died when she was seven. For a long time she was content to remember David Gordon as the man who loved her "more than God" and then vanished. But thirty years later, Mary Gordon began to ask who her father really was. In *The Shadow Man*, one of our finest novelists sets out to retrieve her father from the mausoleum of mourning. What she discovers—in libraries, archives, and her own memory—tests her credulity and her forgiveness.

Memoir/978-0-679-74931-8

ANCHOR BOOKS
Available at your local bookstore, or visit
www.randomhouse.com